PRAISE FOR SARAH ZETTEL AND *FOOL'S WAR*

"REJOICE! SARAH ZETTEL'S SECOND BOOK IS EVEN BETTER THAN HER FIRST. . . . HIGHLY RECOMMENDED."

—*Analog*

"SARAH ZETTEL WORKS ON THE LARGEST SCALES OF TIME AND SPACE."

—Roger MacBride Allen, author of *The Ring of Charon*

"FAST-PACED GALACTIC ADVENTURE WITH SPLASHES OF VIVID COLOR: IF YOU LIKE C. J. CHERRYH, YOU'LL WANT TO READ SARAH ZETTEL."

—Gregory Benford, author of *Sailing Bright Eternity*

"DEFT ACTION . . . WRY HUMOR . . . ZETTEL'S WRITING IS CRISP, AND THE STORY MOVES ALONG AT RAPID PACE."

—*Publishers Weekly* on *Reclamation*

"SARAH ZETTEL HAS A UNIQUE AND HIGHLY ORIGINAL IMAGINATION."

—Stanley Schmidt, editor, *Analog*

"THORO[illegible] REALIZED . . . ALL TH[illegible] RANK HERBERT'S *DU*[illegible]

[illegible] *Heaven Fell*

Also by Sarah Zettel

Reclamation

Published by
Warner Books

SARAH ZETTEL

FOOL'S WAR

ASPECT®

WARNER BOOKS

A Time Warner Company

To my parents
Gail Elizabeth Zettel
and Leonard Francis Zettel, Jr.
with love and thanks.

WARNER BOOKS EDITION

Cover design by Don Puckey
Cover illustration by Donato

Warner Books, Inc.
1271 Avenue of the Americas
New York, NY 10020

A Time Warner Company

Visit our Web site at
http://pathfinder.com/twep

Printed in the United States of America

First Printing: April, 1997

10 9 8 7 6 5 4 3 2 1

Acknowledgements
I wish to thank Timothy B. Smith for his excellent technical advice, the Untitled Writers Group for their invaluble insights, and Dawn Marie Sampson Beresford for keeping the stories on the right track.

Chapter One

PREPARATIONS

Curran watched the man whose life he required settle onto one of the faux leather couches scattered around the station's reception module. The monitors showed him Amory Dane, spruce, tall, and fair. Dane made the perfect picture of someone prepared to wait patiently for an appointment. He was a radically different creature from the furtive Freers in the corner dickering over the delivery price for the wafer case that sat on the floor between them, or the gaggle of haggard mechanics who had put in one shift too many at the bar.

Curran wondered idly what they would do if he spoke up and announced what he was. Would they laugh, thinking it was a crazy engineer's joke? Would they scramble for the wall and try to get at the computer system? Or would they just start running for the hatches?

He ran through each of the scenarios and decided that any would be amusing, but that the risk of being recorded on a hard medium was not worth it.

From his position of safety, Curran calmly overrode the inspection commands for the module's automatic systems. Then he ordered the hatches to cycle shut. One of the mechanics, more sober than the others, jerked his head up as he heard the hatch seal.

Before anyone could make another move, Curran sent a single command to each of the three explosive charges his talent had laid against the module's hull.

As the wind ripped through the room, and the screams began in earnest, Curran slid away.

"How dieth the wise man?" he murmured as he hurried toward his next task. "As the fool."

Al Shei got the distinct feeling that Donnelly was trying to stare her down out of the desk's video screen.

"In that case," Donnelly said, "the answer is no."

Al Shei refrained from letting her shoulders sag. The talent agent was playing havoc with her worn temper. She was very glad of her opaque, black hijab, the veil that covered her hair and hid the lower half of her face. She didn't want Donnelly to see her jaw move as she ground her teeth together.

"You aren't even going to do me the courtesy of pretending to consult with your client, are you, 'Ster Donnelly?" For the hundredth time Al Shei mentally cursed her pilot for picking this run to sell out and leave. First-class pilots who would work for the shares Al Shei offered were as scarce as water ice on Venus.

Donnelly held up his manicured hands and made an exaggerated shrug. "Jemina Yerusha is one of the best pilots I've ever represented. I know her. She's not going to sign onto a ship that's only got a Lennox rating of D for a twentieth share, which, according to your stats, doesn't amount to all that much."

Al Shei looked away for a moment to watch the clients at the other rented desks that filled the station's bank. The noise of a dozen different languages was deadened by panels of jewel-toned, wired plastics that covered the walls. The only quiet person in the room seemed to be Resit, who sat next to Al Shei's desk. Resit shook her head at Al Shei and mouthed, "I told you so."

Al Shei tapped the edge of the desk heavily with her index finger and looked back toward Donnelly. "Yerusha is a highly skilled child who's been out of work for three weeks and must be getting pretty sick of this station."

"She's a Freer, 'Dama Al Shei." Donnelly folded his arms across his chest, making his black satin shirt wrinkle and bag. "She doesn't have a problem with stations. She does have a problem with anything under a C rating."

Al Shei shuffled her boots against the bristly, brown carpet. She briefly considered telling Donnelly he was an unprofessional little weasel and that when Yerusha found out he was billing her at twice her worth, thus making it next to impossible for her to find employment, she was going to take him to pieces with the thoroughness that Freers were noted for.

"Thank you for your time, 'Ster Donnelly." Al Shei pressed her thumb against the corner of the screen, cutting the connection.

"I'm very glad you didn't." Resit tucked a stray wisp of hair behind her beaded, white *kijab.* Unlike her cousin Al Shei's, Resit's veil left her whole face bare. Lawyers who covered their faces, she said, were even less trusted than the ordinary kind, if that was possible.

"Didn't what?" Al Shei pushed the screen down until it was level with the top of the desk.

"Say what you were thinking." Resit drew aside her full-hemmed skirt to let a man in maintenance coveralls squeeze past the desk. "I didn't fancy spending the next two weeks trying to keep you out of the brig for slander of a fellow station client. The wire work alone would have used up most of my retainer."

"You're not on retainer," Al Shei reminded her.

"Ah, you noticed that too, did you?" Resit gave her a cheeky smile.

Al Shei grimaced under her *hijab.* "Don't try to cheer me up, Resit, I'm brooding." She fiddled with the hem of her black tunic sleeve, a terrible habit she had never even tried to break. "Yerusha would have been a good catch. We'd've been halfway to that C rating just having her at the boards."

"Jemina Yerusha is not the only available pilot in the whole of Port Oberon," Resit pointed out with a touch of exasperation. "Pick one with an agent who's a little less cagey." She looked toward the bank's hatchway and mumbled something Al Shei couldn't catch.

"What was that last bit?" she asked, although she had a feeling she knew what was coming.

Resit sighed. "And you might try to find one that's not a Freer."

Al Shei felt her eyebrows draw together. In response, Resit

stiffened her shoulders. "Before you say it, I am not being bigoted. Having a Freer on board is going to create strain on the crew, starting with Lipinski and working its way out."

"All the way to you?" Al Shei did not feel in the mood to let her cousin off the hook.

"Yes," said Resit flatly. "All the way to me. I do not like revolutionaries." She paused. "I also don't like people who have been sent into exile by their justice systems."

Al Shei rubbed her forehead. "Push come to shove, Lipinski is a rational human being, as is my honored-and-educated cousin." She drew the last phrase out for emphasis. "I trust you both to behave yourselves. I also trust you to recognize that we do not have the time or the money to be overly fussy." It was an old battle, and there wasn't much Al Shei could do but continue to fight it. The *Pasadena* was a good ship. When she had charge of it, she generally ran it at a decent profit, but acquiring that profit too often involved a miserly attitude and constant juggling between the need for skilled hands and the need for frugality. "And yes." Al Shei sighed. "She is an exile. That's why I thought she'd be willing to work cheap. I've already had Schyler check with his Freer contacts. He says there's a lot of suspicion that the charges against her were trumped up." She eyed Resit carefully. "Schyler says he'll fly with her. If you have any comments regarding the competency of my Watch Commander's judgment, I'd love to hear them."

The depressurization alarm sounded overhead. Reflexes jerked Al Shei halfway to her feet. Logically, she knew that if the leak was in the section she was currently occupying, she would have heard the whistle of the wind and felt it tugging at her clothes before the alarm even had time to cut loose, but she had half a lifetime's training in responding to any unusual sound produced by her environment. She sank slowly back into her chair.

"Do you ever get used to that noise?" Resit wrapped her arms around herself. "I've been coming out here five years, and it still gives me the shakes."

"It's supposed to." Al Shei forced her hands back onto the desktop. "Somebody on this station is in danger of losing the means to breathe. If this does not upset you, you need a balance check very quickly."

Port Oberon separated its groundside tourists carefully from its professional crews, so no information was forthcoming from the station's intercom. The landlords assumed that all the shippers wanted to know was that they weren't the ones in danger, and silence was enough for that. If it became important, she could get the information about what had happened from the station's artificial intelligence.

Al Shei gave herself and Resit a moment to recover from the alarm before she reached for the desk screen again. "All right, let's try . . ."

" 'Dama Al Shei?" said a woman's voice. "I'm your fool."

Al Shei blew out a sigh that ruffled her *hijab* and looked up. "I beg your pardon?" she said, not bothering to put patience into her tone. The woman's Turkish was heavily accented. It was possible she didn't know what she was saying, but it had already been a long morning.

Al Shei came from a family of small women, but the woman in front of the desk was not merely small, she was minuscule. She stood barely 130 centimeters tall and probably weighed all of thirty kilograms, if you added the loose cobalt blue tunic, baggy trousers, and soft boots into the calculation. Her skin was a clear brown, two or three shades lighter than Al Shei's earth tones. That and the angles in her eyes and her face said a good chunk of her ancestry was European.

"I'm Evelyn Dobbs," said the woman. "Fool's Guild rating, Master of Craft, reporting for duty to the engineer-manager of the mail packet ship *Pasadena.* I've a two-year contract as part of your crew."

Al Shei stared at her. For the first time she noticed that a necklace of red-and-gold gems encircled the other woman's throat, representing the motley of the Intersystem Guild of Professional Fools.

Al Shei sighed again. It was turning out to be one of those days. Fools, like expert pilots, were required for a first-class operation. They were entertainers, confidants, clowns who could say or do anything. They functioned as pressure valves for long trips and cramped quarters. As such, they were in high demand and short supply. That placed them even farther out of the *Pasadena* Corporation's budget than Jemina Yerusha. If the currently unreachable Yerusha was half of the *Pasadena*'s Lennox C, the other half was standing in front of Al Shei's desk, looking across at her with summer brown eyes.

"I'm sorry." Al Shei switched over to English. "There's been a mistake. I haven't contracted a . . . a . . . Fool." It felt strange saying the word to the woman's face, but as far as Al Shei knew, the Fool's Guild had never adopted another name for its members.

In answer, Dobbs unclipped a light pen from her belt, touched the download stud, and pressed the point against one of the blank films piled on Al Shei's desk. The film's chip read the transmission and printed a text file across the slick surface. Al Shei scanned the black print as it flowed across the grey film. It was a contract, complete with confirmation and certification information, between the Intersystem Guild of Professional Fools and the *Pasadena* Corporation for the services of one Master of Craft for a period of two years, measured by contiguous hours of active service. It was signed, confirmed, and prepaid by Ahmet Tey.

The sight of her uncle's name sent a spasm of anger through Al Shei. Would the man never, ever let up? She and Asil had done quite well, thank you very much, and they hadn't had to beg one penny from the family. Why did Uncle Ahmet keep treating her like . . .

Resit must have seen her shoulders tense. With a lawyer's practiced eye, Resit had already scanned the contract and filtered the implications through her mind.

"It'll make us Class C Lennox," she said calmly to Al Shei in Turkish. "Pick it up, Katmer, tell Schyler to get a spot inspection done, and we'll be able to afford Yerusha."

She did not, of course, mention the increase in profits the C rating could mean for this run. She knew well enough that a part of Al Shei's mind had involuntarily worked the percentages out already.

Her anger did not cool, but Al Shei made herself swallow her pride in one, large lump.

"I beg your pardon, Master Dobbs. My uncle neglected to

inform me that he had acted on my behalf." She held out her hand. "Welcome aboard the *Pasadena*."

"Thank you." Dobbs beamed as she reached for Al Shei's hand, but then her forehead wrinkled and she looked down at the desktop. Al Shei's gaze followed automatically. The Fool's pen was still pressed to the film.

"I'm sorry, I . . . um . . ." Dobbs tugged at her light pen, but it didn't come away from the film as it should have. "There's a . . . ah. . ." She frowned and tugged again. No good. The point of the pen stayed firmly stuck to the film. She grabbed it with both hands and pulled harder. "Must be a . . . sorry . . ." She grabbed her own wrist and strained backwards with all her might.

Al Shei felt herself smile. Resit snorted out loud. Heads turned all around the room to stare coolly or curiously at the strange scene. Dobbs blushed heavily, put one foot against the desk to brace herself, grabbed the pen in both hands, gritted her teeth, and hauled backwards.

The pen came free with such force, Dobbs flipped tail over teacup across the carpet, coming up on her backside, brandishing the pen triumphantly.

Al Shei whooped with laughter, and Resit applauded briskly. Dobbs smiled, leapt to her feet, and bowed deeply to her audience.

"When do we start launch prep, Boss?" Dobbs asked, clipping her pen back onto her belt.

"Nine hundred tomorrow." Al Shei knew Dobbs could hear the smile in her voice. "Check in with Watch Commander Schyler to get your weight allotment and cabin assignment and don't be late."

Dobbs grinned all across her round face. "I'm not that kind of Fool, Boss. I'll be there."

She bowed one more time and turned on her heel, too fast. She wobbled precariously, windmilling with both arms before she found her balance again, and set off jauntily through the oval doorway in the narrow end of the room.

Resit giggled audibly. Al Shei turned and gave her a dramatically sour gaze. "Go ahead, laugh," she said, dropping back into Turkish. "You're not the one who has to thank Uncle Ahmet."

"No. I'm just the one who has to try to get Yerusha's agent to stick to his terms." She grimaced. "Freers. What you want with a jacked-up kid . . ."

"Look who's talking." Al Shei laughed. "Grit your teeth and think about bonus pay. That's what I'm doing." *And money in the bank and the plans for the* Mirror of Fate, *which'll have a B rating before we even get it crewed, and quarters for Asil and the kids* . . . She shuffled Dobbs's contract into the stack of films in front of her that held *Pasadena*'s current certifications, crew contracts, and share commitments. "What's left?"

"Good thing I certified as a secretary as well as a lawyer," grumbled Resit, as she always did, but she pulled her schedule pad out of her bag and checked the display. "We're supposed to meet with Dr. Amory Dane about the packet he wants to send to The Farther Kingdom. Medical updates, he says. It's a big load, but it shouldn't take long to iron out."

"Okay." Al Shei ran her finger along the edge of the pile of film, sealing the sheets together to form a thick book. "You meet with Dr. Dane and get the contract settled. Then, get into Donnelly's office and sign up our new pilot. The Watch Commander and I should be able to burn through the red tape on the inspection. I want us reregistered before we start launch prep tomorrow."

Resit lowered her eyes in mock humility. "Your pardon, oh-my-mistress, but if 'Ster Inspector should desire, Allah forbid, to create difficulty about the fact that you haven't actually signed the pilot you are no doubt going to list . . ."

"I shall threaten him with the keen and ready wit of my lawyer." Al Shei stood up. "Who is going to get her share halved if she doesn't . . ."

"I'm going, I'm going." Resit shoveled her films and her schedule pad into one stack. "See me go . . . Boss." She made her way between the desks, imitating Dobbs's swinging stride and making the hem of her skirt swirl.

"*Kolay gelsin*," Al Shei called after her. May it go easily. Al Shei chuckled and shook her head. No one who faced Resit from the other side of a negotiation, over a contract or a court proceeding, would recognize the easygoing woman who was taking her leave. Having seen both sides of her across the years, Al Shei was forever glad that the woman was her friend as well as her cousin.

Al Shei took out her pen. The heat of her hand and the pattern of her fingerprints activated it. Using it as a pointer, she touched the active surface of the desk, flicking through the menus until she called up her private account for this trip and funneled enough cash into the desk for a transmission to Ankara. She could have used the Intersystem Banking Network to set up a fast-time link. Uncle Ahmet would have gladly paid the exorbitant fee that the banks charged for access to their crowded channels, but that would have been one more thing she would have had to thank him for. One more favor he could trot out at the next family dinner she attended.

She had heard of tribes from the Amer-Indians who had the custom of the "potlatch," where people showed how rich they were by giving gifts. Uncle Ahmet practiced this method of displaying wealth almost constantly. Al Shei couldn't help wishing, though, that he would make his gifts easier to accept.

The desk accepted the transfer, channeled credit back into the bank's lines, and raised the transmission screen. The blank, grey screen turned robin's-egg blue to indicate that record mode was on. Al Shei saw her own eyes framed by the *hijab* reflected on the blue background. She automatically straightened her shoulders and smoothed her brow. "*Selamunalekum*, Uncle Ahmet,"she said. Peace be with you. "I am sending this to thank you for your gift of a Fool's contract. Because of your generous present, the *Pasadena* will be able to upgrade its rating and will pull down at least a 10 percent increase in our profits this trip out. With luck, and the help of Allah," she added piously, "this will mean it will be only three more years before I can commission a ship that will allow Asil and our children to travel with me." *I am* not *repaying you by grounding myself in Ankara.* "So, again I say thank you, Uncle. I shall see you in eight months." She clicked her pen against the desktop to shut the recording off a split second before the desk beeped at her to indicate that she had used up her deposit.

Why do I act like this? she wondered as she authorized the transmission with a stroke of her pen. *He's really just trying to help.*

Because his way of helping has a way of reminding me that he thinks I should have become a banker rather than an engineer with a time-share ship who's spending her life, and her husband's, trying to create a new family business when there's a perfectly good one that goes back two hundred years just waiting for her.

She sighed again and reached up under her veil to rub her neck. *Oh well, he loves the kids, and he did just get me my C rating.*

She glanced at the desk clock. Fifteen-fifteen. A little over three hours until evening prayers. It might be possible to get the inspection over with before then. What was it Schyler was always saying? God willing and the creeks don't rise? She smiled. Schyler had told her it was a saying from back before the Fast Burn and the Management Union, when Earth's rivers could still go into unscheduled floods. Al Shei found it a nicely quirky expression for the omnipresence of unpredictability.

Al Shei activated her pen again and sorted through the menus until she found the on-call roster of station personnel. The Lennox office had three inspectors checked in. Al Shei wrote a request for a Lennox inspector to meet her at the *Pasadena* berth for the purpose of a ratings upgrade. The AI that ran the station had her handwriting, with most of its eccentricities, on file, so it didn't ask for a rewrite. The desk just absorbed her words and replaced them with a much tidier line of text that said TRANSMISSION COMPLETED.

Al Shei wrote SECURE over the top of the ship's book. The text on the top film blanked and the pages sealed themselves together. It would take her handwriting, Watch Commander Schyler's, or Resit's to open them again.

She touched the CLOSE icon on the desk. The desk inventoried the remaining supplies and funneled the change from her deposit back into her account, automatically forwarding a record of the transaction to the accounting program on board *Pasadena*. Once the financial transactions were taken care of, the desk shut itself down to wait for the next customer.

Al Shei tucked her pen back into her tunic pocket and stood up carefully so that the spin gravity wouldn't disorient her. The business module was in the outermost ring of Port

Oberon, which meant it had nearly a full one gee gravity, but the speed of the station's rotation was still detectable to her inner ear. If she moved too quickly, it would remind her that she was aboard a rapidly spinning conglomeration of tin cans, not firmly on the ground of some planet. How Dobbs made all those quick shifts of weight without really losing her balance was beyond Al Shei, but then, Al Shei was a groundhugger at heart. The problem was that in spirit and in skill, she was a starbird.

Al Shei tucked the *Pasadena*'s book under her arm and followed Resit's path out the door and into the curving corridor. She joined the steady stream of men and women from across a hundred cultures as they made their way around the module to the door that would let them into either their elevator, or their appointment room.

Port Oberon took its name from the fact that it hung over the Lagrange point of Oberon, Uranus's largest moon. It was the departure point for most of the fast-time traffic from the Solar System. Consequently, it was always full to capacity and its owners able to milk the patrons for all they were worth. Al Shei noted smugly that they were at least a little less obvious about it now that they had to glance over their shoulders at the Titania Freers. The Freers had been indicating that they'd be more than willing to set up their own commercial station, should the market open up for it.

Resit's comments about revolutionaries and jacked-up kids echoed in her mind. Al Shei pressed her lips together. She would readily admit there were aspects of their philosophy she didn't like, and some others that she regarded as flatly ridiculous, but she had worked with Freer contractors in the past. Certainly some of them had the arrogance that belonged to the self-righteous, but their engineers and pilots were the best in Settled Space.

Even by the standards of corporately owned space stations, Port Oberon was huge. It usually had two hundred modules, each the size of a fifteen-story office building, operating at once. That did not count the tethered cargo pods, the tankers off-loading helium and methane from the mining operations in low orbit above Uranus, or the ships that were docked but still pressurized and crewed. Oberon was the major fueling station, traffic control, trade depot, and all-around place of business for all of the Solar System between the asteroid belt and Pluto, which, in the time since Al Shei's great-great-grandparents had first helped set up the Intersystem Banking Network, had become a very busy place.

The Henry V Business Center was one of the twenty-five modules permanently maintained by Oberon Inc., collectively known to the shippers, starbirds, miners, and canned gerbils who put into the port as "the Landlords." Like most of the other twenty-four permanent modules, it was cylindrical, with a bundle of elevator shafts running straight down the middle. Its wedge-shaped rooms, spiral staircases, and circular corridors were lined with bristly carpet that could double as Velcro when the module was in free fall, and covered in the bright, but unimaginative, panel decor.

The only loose things in the module were the occupants and their possessions. Everything else was glued, bolted, sealed or simply extruded from the hull or the decks. The walls had ears, and eyes, but between the garish panels, they also had arms so they could reach inside the tiles and work on their own repairs, or grab anything that actually came loose in an emergency.

Al Shei frowned at the automated hands that were retracted back into the paneling as she skirted the wall to get past a knot of broad-shouldered miners. In her opinion, Port Oberon relied too much on AIs and waldos and didn't have half enough real engineers and maintainers. She knew the technical reasons. Like *Pasadena*, Oberon was a profit-making concern, and real people cost real money. Still, AIs could do worse than any human being ever did. If a human went stir-crazy and decided to run away, it was almost nobody's concern. But if an AI did the same thing, it could mean the life of the station, or the colony. Could and had.

Al Shei ducked through a doorway that was relatively clear of other people and into the elevator bay. There were six lifts, any of which could have gotten her to the core in under four minutes, but Al Shei preferred to use the stairs. For eight months at a time she lived her life in confined spaces with varying gravity. She needed every second of exercise she could get. Even if she walked, the Lennox inspector wouldn't get there that much ahead of her.

The stairs spiraled around the bundle of elevator shafts. Since only standard-measure cans were allowed to link up with Port Oberon, the stairs fit together even between the bulkheads that indicated she had passed from one module to the next.

The core was forty stories up, or three rings inward, depending on how you thought about such things, with gravity getting lighter the whole way. She shifted her stride and the swing of her arms to compensate without even thinking about it. Every motion became smaller and gentler. Abrupt, expansive movements in .5 gee were not a good idea. Even so, she all but flew up the last fifteen stories.

Al Shei reached the hub landing. The door's surface registered her palmprint as belonging to a crew member for a docked ship and let her in, opening just the hatchways that would take her to the *Pasadena*, since no one had invited her to visit anywhere else.

The *Pasadena*'s watch commander, Thomas Paine Schyler, was already in the little lobby that held the airlock to the *Pasadena* in its far wall. Schyler was the only full-term crewman on the ship, working under both her and her partner, Marcus Tully. Most shippers signed on for a single tour and then took themselves a break ground- or portside. On low-rated ships, some signed on for only one run, working to reach their destination, taking their share, and walking off to whatever it was that was waiting for them.

To Schyler, though, the *Pasadena* was home. Every time they docked at Oberon, he, Al Shei, and Tully went through the formality of renewing his contract and reviewing his share. It was required to keep their Lennox rating, but they all knew Schyler would have worked for free if they had asked him to as long as they let him stay aboard and do his job.

Next to Schyler stood a little man with the pinched expression of the perpetually fussy. Half of Al Shei's family wore the same expression during business hours. He had his pen out and was waving it toward the ship. Around his ankles waited a small flock of rovers: squared-off centipedes with waldos that looked more like mandibles and tentacles than hands and fingers. Schyler looked at Al Shei over the top of the strange man's thatch of dust brown hair, and rubbed the end of his Roman nose.

Al Shei smiled behind her *hijab.*

"Watch Commander Schyler." She touched her forehead in brief salute. "And Inspector . . ." she held out her hand.

"Davies, 'Dama Al Shei, and . . ."

"And thank you for coming so quickly, Inspector," said Al Shei before the inspector could finish his sentence. "I'm extremely sorry to have had to put in a short-notice call, and I assure you and the Lennox station that it will not happen again."

"Well, yes." The little man fumbled with his pen and managed to tuck it into his pocket so he could shake her hand. "Thank you, 'Dama Al Shei. Let's see if we can get this business over with." Schyler was rubbing his nose again. Al Shei grinned, extremely glad of her *hijab.*

"Of course, Inspector. We won't take up any more of your time than necessary." She retrieved the ship's book from under her arm and wrote OPEN across the cover with her own pen. The memory chip registered her handwriting and unsealed the book. "This is my crew roster and ship specifications," she said, handing the stack of appropriate films to Davies. "You'll find it in order, I'm sure."

He took the pile and sniffed. "What I find is not the real issue, 'Dama Al Shei." Davies nodded toward his rovers. "It's what *they* find." He flipped through the films and extracted the ship's specifications. He slid the stack into the chief rover's scanner slot.

"Specifications recorded," it said in the bland, neuter voice that belonged to the vast majority of automated systems. "Proceeding with verification."

The rovers lifted themselves up off the deck and marched in single file into the *Pasadena.* They'd go over the ship, checking, measuring, scanning. Davies would do a walkthrough and spot check when they were finished, but that was mostly a formality. Al Shei felt her neck muscles tense up. Maybe she should have checked things over first. Tully, for all his scheming, was generally a truthful partner, and if he said the ship was in prime working order, it would be.

"The pilot you're hiring." Davies looked up from the open book that he held balanced on the palm of his hand. " 'Dama Yerusha, she is from Free Home Titania?"

"That is what her bio file says." Al Shei realized she'd been staring at the airlock and fiddling with her sleeve.

"She's a Freer then?" Davies put all of his facial muscles into the frown.

"I didn't know hiring a Freer disqualified a Lennox rating." Al Shei kept her voice casual.

Davies shrugged. "Not technically, no, but it can prejudice your security marks."

Al Shei bit her tongue. It was Davies's job to be skeptical. If she said anything, she'd just be giving him additional ammunition.

From the recess of her pocket, Al Shei's pen beeped. She pulled it out and saw Resit's name on the display. She pulled out a square of film and held the pen against it. Resit's message wrote itself across the blank surface.

Al Shei: Got the contract with Dr. Dane. Big shipment. Had to check with Communications Chief Lipinski to make sure we'd have room in the hold. Dane's paying extra. Terms are in storage for your eyes and say-so.

Now the bad news. Your business partner and respected brother-in-law Marcus Tully may have been at it again. Dane wanted to know if this was the Pasadena *that pulled the plug out of the Toric Station security code. I'm checking to see if there're warrants out. Better say a few extra* du'a's *at prayer tonight.*

Al Shei felt her teeth begin to grind together slowly. She glanced across at Schyler. He must have seen the thunder in her eyes because he shifted his weight slowly and jerked his blunt chin toward the inspector.

Al Shei erased the message and tucked pen and film back into her pocket. "Inspector, will you need my seal for anything?"

Davies blinked up at her. "Mmm? No, no, not until the results are in."

"Good. Watch," she said to Schyler, "call me when I'm needed back here." Mindful of her balance, Al Shei turned around. She did not need to fall over right now. What she needed was to find out if Tully had left the station yet.

Once she was back in the stairwell, she wrote her request for a trace to Tully on a green wall tile and waited impatiently while the station's AI tracked him down. He was in the Desdemona Hotel module on the outer ring, getting himself a drink in the Othello coffee shop.

Al Shei declined to transmit a message to say she was coming. This time, she took the elevators and moving walkways three modules down and ten sideways until she reached the hotel.

Once coffeehouses had been introduced, they had never left human history. When humanity took themselves out to the stars they brought their problems, their religions, their arts, and their cafés. Every station that had the room kept a coffeehouse for its patrons.

The Othello was on the edge of a spacious, plant-filled lobby. The stairwell had been gilded, and four different fountains splashed around it. As she made path toward the café, ducking and weaving between the other patrons, Al Shei decided that if this module went into unscheduled free fall, she'd rather be elsewhere.

Tully sat at a wide, round table. He leaned back in his chair with his legs kicked straight out in front of him. In between sips from a bulb of rich, black brew that could have been coffee, sarsaparilla, or Guinness stout, he whistled cheerfully through his teeth.

Al Shei unclenched her fists and waded between tables and server carts to where he sat.

"Tully." She sat down across from him. Startled, he drew his legs in and straightened his back. Someone in his ancestry had supplied his parents with the genes to allow shockingly blue eyes to shine out of his medium brown face. "Tully, what have you been doing?"

He set his bulb gently down on the table. "Nothing you need to be worried about, Katmer."

An alarm bell sounded far in the back of Al Shei's mind. If Tully had been engaged in his usual petty hacking and cracking, he would have said so. "One day you're going to remember that I don't believe you when you say that." Al Shei leaned forward. "I've got a client saying the *Pasadena* pulled a security plug out of Toric Station's codes."

Tully glanced quickly around the café. "You really want an answer in public?"

Al Shei's fingertips scraped against the tabletop. "Marcus Tully, you can run your little civil disobedience racket however you see fit, but if you call attention to the ship I have to fly, I am going to have you in the tightest sling the communications collective can sew together for you!"

Tully sighed toward his bulb. "The guy got hold of a rumor." He glanced up at Al Shei, as if to see how she was taking the comment. Al Shei didn't even blink, and Tully looked down again. "Resit will assure him that your crew and my crew have nothing in common. You'll get the job and all your profits, and there won't be a problem. Just like there's no problem for me when you skirt the regs a little too close."

Al Shei was glad he couldn't see the hard line of her mouth. "Tully, what do you think you're doing?"

He shrugged again. "Keeping the corporations on their grubby little toes, oh-my-sister-in-law. Same as you."

"I do not break anybody's law." Her voice was low and furious.

"I'm not asking you to protect me." He pulled another long draft out of the bulb. "If I'm careless enough to get caught, then I deserve it, and you've got the *Pasadena* and all the remaining payments on it by default."

His face was blank as a ship's hull, reflecting her own anger right back at her, but giving away nothing of its own. He knew he could keep pushing her. He knew she would do almost anything before she had to break her sister's heart and tell her what, exactly, Marcus Tully had turned into. That fact had nagged badly at Al Shei for years.

"Tully," she said softly, "you don't get it. As long as you continue to play the lone rebel, the ship is mine, because you have already crossed the line. I can take *Pasadena* away any time I want. Your petty temper tantrums have already robbed you of your freedom. I'm trying to give it back to you. Your freedom, and my sister's." She got up and walked away without looking back.

Something hard collided with her back, sending her stumbling against an empty table. She caught herself with both hands, gasping at the sudden pain.

"Oh, sorry," said a man's bland voice. "I didn't see a *person* there. I thought it was just a pile of rags and shit."

Al Shei pulled herself upright and turned around slowly to face the chestnut-skinned, auburn-haired, totally unshaven, can-gerbil.

She drew herself up to her full height. "There is no god but Allah and Muhammad is the Prophet of Allah." Reciting the first pillar of Islam loudly was her standard tactic. Bigots seldom know how to reply to a declaration of faith as a response to an insult. During the Slow Burn, when the fires were cooling and the survivors were starting their own wars, thousands of Moslems turned from their religion to save their lives. Al Shei's family had remained unmoved. Drawing on those generations of pride gave her the strength she needed to stand up to the bigotry that still dogged Islam.

The gerbil sneered, and for a minute she thought he was going to spit, but he just turned and shouldered his way out through the crowd.

Burn-brain, thought Al Shei after him. Some people had never let up. A Moslem named Faraq Hakiem started the Fast Burn. Never mind that he was Kurdish and she was Turkish and that three hundred years had passed since the last ashes had cooled; she wore the veil, and that was enough for those who thought there was still something to be settled. Al Shei suddenly felt very much in need of a shower.

A flash of pink drifted past the corner of her eye and Al Shei looked involuntarily toward it. A blob of yellow floated down and was nabbed out of the air by a quick brown hand and replaced with a scrap of emerald green. The green was nabbed and replaced by the pink. The scene cleared up and Al Shei realized she was looking at Dobbs juggling silky scarves; snatching them out of the air as they fell and reinserting them into the cascade so they could fall again. The Fool had a ridiculously intense expression on her face; grab, drop, drop, grab. She saw Al Shei staring and blushed a deep umber.

"Sorry, Boss," she said with a twisted grin. "Dropped my napkin, and I can't . . ." drop, grab, drop. "Ooops. Darn it . . ."

Al Shei felt a chuckle well up out of her throat and she let it go. Dobbs grinned back, snatched all her scarves out of the air, and gave her little flourishing bow from her seat.

"Your contract says you don't come on duty until tomorrow." Al Shei watched, bemused, as Dobbs stuffed the colored scarves into her fist.

"At times discretion should be thrown aside and with the foolish, we should play fools." Dobbs opened her fist, and, as Al Shei expected, the scarves were completely gone.

It was ridiculous, showy and simplistic, but Al Shei found herself smiling anyway. The filthy feeling lifted itself off her skin.

"See you tomorrow, Boss." Dobbs looked down at her meal total printed out on the tabletop. Her eyes bulged in their sockets. She let her head fall back until she was staring at the ceiling, opened her mouth, and broke into song. "Let's vary piracy . . . with a little burglary!"

Al Shei froze. The tune Dobbs sang was the same one Tully had been whistling. "What is that?"

Dobbs's smile was a little puzzled. "Don't share your partner's taste in music, Boss? That's from the *Pirates of Penzance*, a comic show from before the Fast Burn . . ."

Al Shei stared across the café at Tully, who in turn was staring at his drink. She briefly considered going back there and demanding once again to be told what was going on.

Which will get me exactly nowhere. Aware that her newest employee was staring at her, but not caring, Al Shei strode back across the lobby. Her stomach had tightened itself into a knot when she heard Dobbs sing out the words to Tully's tune, and every second it stayed tight she became more convinced that she was right. This time Marcus Tully was doing more than worming corporate secrets out of secured networks and shunting them to public arenas. It would be just like him to find a way to brag about it in public.

Back in the Henry V Business Module, Al Shei passed right by the bank outlet and went straight into the communications room. Unlike the bank with its open desks, this room was a honeycomb of enclosed booths for private conversations. Al Shei found an empty booth and stepped inside. There was barely enough room for her to stand beside the chair as she jacked her pen into the socket beside the doorway. The booth's system acknowledged her as a registered station customer with a positive balance on her accounts and shut the door.

She could have just sent a packet, but she wanted to say her suspicions out loud and hear a response to them from the person she trusted above all others. She also could have done this from the *Pasadena* and saved herself the cost of the booth rental, but Davis was probably still not done with his inspection. The last thing she wanted was the Lennox inspector or his drones overhearing what she had to say now.

Al Shei lowered herself into the stiff chair and faced the view screen that filled the wall in front of her. She slid the desktop into her lap and checked the credit in her communications account. She stared at it a moment, running through sample conversations in her head before deciding there was enough. With a series of careful commands, she opened a fast-time channel to Earth, Turkey, Ankara, Bala House, for Asil Tamruc.

Fast-time communications were not affected by gravitational stress as drastically as fast-time flight. A fast-time message could travel most of the way to the Moon before it had to be translated into speed-of-light signals. The problem with fast-time communication was the cost. The signals had to be boosted, refocused, and redirected every few light-years, which required a vast network of both unmanned repeater satellites and manned space stations. There was a single FTL network between Earth and Settled Space—the Intersystem Banking Network. It had been established by a financial conglomerate that was quick to realize that such a network could provide a stable medium of exchange between Earth and the new worlds. They did let independent users send messages across their crowded lines, but they charged the worth of a firstborn child for it. Because of that astronomical price, ships like the *Pasadena* had a ready business transporting data from place to place.

Since Al Shei's family owned one of the largest financial institutions on Earth, Al Shei could have easily had her fast-time communications fees "overlooked," or paid by Uncle

Ahmet, but her ethics forbade the first, and her pride forbade the second.

The desktop displayed the message CONNECTING and ticked off both seconds and available credit. After two minutes and an appreciable chunk of the account, the view screen came alive and Al Shei's husband, Asil Tamruc, smiled at her from the tidy nest that was his office.

It had been ten years since she met Asil, eight since they'd married, and his smile still made her heart pound.

"Hello, Beloved," he said easily. Even across the vast distance that separated them, she could see the cheerful light in his dark eyes. He knew, of course, that only a serious matter would make her lay out the amounts required for a fast-time call. Despite that, his whole body was relaxed, and his long, expressive face was set in an attitude of gentle humor.

How did such a man become an accountant? thought Al Shei, as she had almost every day since she met him.

"Hello, Beloved." Al Shei allowed herself a brief smile at the sight of her husband. "There's trouble, I'm afraid."

When the signal reached him, Asil straightened up just a little, not alarmed, but alert. "What kind?"

"Marcus Tully." She told him about the note from Resit, her uninformative conversation with Tully, and the additional spin Dobbs had added to it. She sat back and waited for her words to reach him.

Asil's sigh puffed out his cheeks. "Well, I'd say there's no doubt he's been up to something. But I don't understand why you think it's more than the usual. It's a suggestive song, certainly, but he has always had a taste for cultural arcana."

"I know, I know." Al Shei shrugged her shoulders. "It's more a feeling than anything else, Asil. I just think it might be a good idea if you traced where Tully's money came from this last run. We may need to cover ourselves."

"Then I will." He pulled out his pen and made a note on the desktop in front of him. He glanced up at her, and there was quiet mischief in his eyes. "You could have sent me a text message with all of this, Katmer. I'd have had it in two hours."

She pulled herself up and put a tone of injured dignity into her voice. "Perhaps I wished to speak to my husband. Surely this is my right."

His smile warmed, and Al Shei felt her heart begin to melt. "Surely it is."

"Tell the children I love them," she whispered. "And know full well that I love you."

"I will." He reached out and pressed his fingertips against the view screen. "And I do."

Al Shei copied his gesture, pressing her fingertips against his and imagining it was the warmth of his hand she felt, not the cool glass of the screen.

"*Salam*, Beloved," he said softly.

"*Salam*." Al Shei cut the connection. The view screen faded to black.

She sat where she was for a moment, staring at the blank screen. At last, she dropped her pen into her pocket and stood up.

Whatever happened has already happened, she told herself as she left the booth. *It's time to face what's still to come.*

With a small smile of her own, Dobbs watched her new employer walk away from the café. The Fool pulled her scarves out of her sleeve, folded them up neatly, and stowed them in her pocket. The Guild's profile, as usual, was proving entirely accurate. Al Shei was a determined woman with a strong sense of herself and her goals, but not without a sense of humor. Of course, people without humor or empathy seldom hired Fools, except when certain certifications or ratings required them. Dobbs had found herself a little worried that Al Shei hadn't known she'd been contracted.

Well, every assignment has its own challenges.

She took out her pen and wrote out a credit draft on the tabletop, adding her thumbprint as authorization. The table checked her writing and print and added the words ACCOUNT SETTLED before it absorbed the text. Dobbs considered the blank surface for a moment and drew a simplistic smiling face before she tucked her pen away.

Marcus Tully was still sitting at his table, swirling the dregs of his drink around the bulb and watching the way the waves rose and fell in the station's spin gravity. The report on him had been cursory, since he wasn't an active part of the crew she'd be working with. He'd been an independent shipper for ten years, dry-docked for at least a third of that time for lack of work before he'd married Ruqaiyya Al Shei. After his partner had been arrested for attempted financial misdealings, Tully had invited Ruqaiyya's sister, Katmer Al Shei, to become his new partner in the *Pasadena* Corporation to share the expenses and risks of operating an independent mail-packet ship.

He'd apparently benefited from both the marriage and the partnership. He managed to stay constantly employed, even though the rating for him and the crews he assembled was one to two ranks lower than those Al Shei put together. But judging from the pitch and timbre of Al Shei's voice when she talked to him, there was something serious going on and it was affecting Dobbs's new employer. Add to that her abrupt reaction when she'd found out what he had been whistling, and it would take a greener Fool than Dobbs to miss the fact that something was seriously wrong.

Need to plug in and find out what's what. Dobbs got up and left the café.

The lobby was crowded, but she threaded an easy path between the trickles of patrons. Out of the corner of her eye she saw the bigoted station worker who had slammed into Al Shei. People like him were commonly called "gerbils" because they spent their time running around inside wheel-shaped space stations. They could become acerbic, opinionated, and develop pretty crude senses of humor.

Dobbs darted around into his field of vision.

"It's you!" she shouted. "I knew it was you!" She slapped her hand against her forehead. "Holy sun and stars, I cannot *believe* they let you in here, you wart-brained, six-toed, fractured excuse for a corpse's ass!"

The gerbil looked around confused, as members of the passing crowd slowed down to stare.

"Who could've thought they'd let *you* just walk around in here!" Dobbs spread her hands out and appealed to the crowd. "I can't believe it! Can you believe it?" she demanded of a woman in a bright red sari. "Him! The ugly, twisted, burn-brain! They let him just . . ."

"Damp it down, Sister!" shouted the gerbil. "Who are you?"

Dobbs gave him a look of utter incredulity. "You mean you don't know me?"

"No!" The gerbil stabbed a finger at her. "And I'll lay any money you don't know me!"

"Oh!" Dobbs covered her mouth with her hand and let her eyes go wide. "You have to *know* somebody in order to insult them. I'm sorry." She gave him an apologetic grin. "See, you got me confused when you assaulted a total stranger back there."

His eyes blazed, and his big, callused hand rose.

"Master Evelyn Dobbs." She drew herself up to her full height. "Intersystem Guild of Fools."

They stood there like that for a moment, then the gerbil, anger burning in his eyes, lowered his hand.

Fools could not be touched, by anybody. If he committed assault, the Guild would register his name and no crew that he worked on would be able to hire a professional Fool. There were a lot more gerbils than there were Fools. If the Guild blackballed him, he would never be able to work a first-class ship or station again.

He could, of course, report her, and she'd have to take the backlash. The Guild had very strict guidelines about the proper use of casual clowning.

But he just gave her a look that could have blistered paint as he turned and shouldered his way through the gathering crowd. Whistling, Dobbs left the hotel in the exact opposite direction.

Despite the fact that Guild-scale pay was generous by shipper standards, a full room in the luxury hotel was more than Dobbs wanted to pay out for just the few days that she'd be on-station. Instead, she had berthed herself in what the advertising referred to as a "traditional, economical, Tokyo-style cabin." That meant it was a private bunk with all the boards and terminals within arm's reach on the walls. It included a stowage area for her baggage and access to the showers.

Her rented bed was two modules over and three levels up. All the modules in this section were dedicated to public business, which meant they were all crowded. Dobbs theorized that shippers spent so much time in space with the same people that they looked for excuses to get out and meet with someone new. As a result, there was a great deal of face-to-face business done here, even though Port Oberon had excellent video and holoprojection facilities.

Only some of the space was cut off into the normal wedge-shaped rooms for private, or semiprivate negotiations. The rest was opened up, much like tapes Dobbs had seen of ancient flea markets. Sound-dampening panels took the place of canvas awnings. Patrons could order food in bulk or as individual meals. They could acquire tailored uniforms or personal clothes, or any service that could be transported between two points. Some shops took up three and four levels and had their own staircases zigzagging up the sides of their private walls. An open medical lobby fronted the passage to the hospital. A couple of people in bright white med-tech coveralls marshaled a drone-gurney through the sterile-sealed doors. Dobbs got an impression of severely bruised skin and clotted blood and winced. If they were still bringing the victims in, that alarm she'd heard earlier had produced a lot of injuries. She knew that Port Oberon had a full-scale bio-garden, but she wondered how far it was going to be able to provide for the people who would now need new eyes and eardrums, and maybe even lungs.

Dobbs shoved the grisly thoughts away and stepped nimbly between the crowds and knots and flowing waves of people. Her small size facilitated freedom of movement as she flitted from one clear spot to another. For her, it was like a game of tag with empty floor space as "it," and if anyone was laughing at her as she darted past them, then she was just putting in a little overtime.

Dobbs spotted an empty square foot of carpeting and jumped into it, planting both feet firmly on the floor. She looked up to see a tall, thin, pale man step abruptly away from the wall. She slid sideways just in time to avoid the collision, pressing her back against a wall of order terminals for C-Stacks, Inc.

"And if they say one word, one, about the budget, that's it, I'm done!" the pale man shouted at the terminals. He glowered down at Dobbs. She saw bright blue eyes, and instantly got the feeling that he wasn't looking at her.

"You'd think," he thundered, "that they'd ask! That there'd be a meeting! But *no* it's just 'Lipinski, we've got a packet, and you have to fit it in the hold!' "

Dobbs dropped to the deck, rolled into a fetal position, and shook.

Above her, there was a long moment of silence.

"Are you okay?" he asked finally.

"Are you done yelling?"

"I think so."

"Then I think I'm okay." Dobbs somersaulted backwards and came up on her knees.

"You're a Fool," he said quietly.

"And you're Rurik Lipinski, communications chief for the *Pasadena*." She tightened her muscles and leapt to her feet. A small twinge told her she shouldn't be trying that move in full gravity anymore today. "I didn't expect to meet you until tomorrow."

Since the *Pasadena* was a mail-packet ship, Dobbs knew the comm-chief, or "Houston," was the second most important officer on the ship. The first would be the chief engineer, the person who kept the ship running—Al Shei herself.

Lipinski gave Dobbs a smile that showed a row of even, white teeth. He was an anomaly, in more ways than one, Dobbs realized. First of all, he was really tall. Professional shippers tended to be a compact breed. Even then, most people looked tall from her five-foot elevation, but Lipinski stood head and shoulders above the rest of the passersby. Secondly, he was nearly colorless. His hair was straw blond and his skin was the milk white color that turned lobster red in bright sunlight. Dobbs found herself wondering if he was a refugee from one of the Aryan Purist colonies.

"You're with us?" There wasn't a trace of his previous anger in his voice. "That's great! We must be getting an upgrade this run."

"That's what I've heard." Dobbs spread her hands. "But who knows what a Fool might have heard? So, tell me." She made her eyes large, round and innocent and blinked rapidly. "Do you always shout at walls and passersby?"

Lipinski blushed an extraordinary pink color. "Actually, I do. Lousy habit, but there it is. Get me tense, and I'll yell at anything that doesn't get out of the way fast enough." He arched a knowing eyebrow at her. "I'm death to apprentice comm-officers. They can't run." His grin spread into a leer.

Dobbs cowered behind her hands. "Oh, spare me," she pleaded, all the while deciding she liked this man. "Please, spare me."

"Okay." He shrugged and turned his attention back to the order terminal. "I've got to finish getting this order in anyway. Al Shei will not thank me if I keep us here contemplating our navels while there're deadlines to be met."

"Is there something wrong with the data-hold?" Dobbs stood on tiptoe and peered over his shoulder.

"Yes." He pulled out his pen and bent over the terminal board. "But there wouldn't be if our fearless leader Katmer Al Shei wouldn't keep letting Marcus Tully try to commit felonies with her ship." He started scrawling orders across the memory board. The station AI must have had his handwriting on file. The screen kept printing out ACCEPTED even though Dobbs couldn't make heads or tails out of the scribbles on the board.

"I thought they had a time-share," she remarked, lowering herself back onto flat feet.

"They do, sort of . . . I shouldn't be talking like this." He scanned the acceptance notifications on the screen and punched the TRANSMIT key. "All I know for sure is that Dr. Amory Dane has a complicated load he wants us to carry to The Farther Kingdom. Lots of interconnected, self-referencing programs and a cartload of background data. Tully's guys burned out three main wafer stacks and reconfigured another four with whatever it was they were doing out there." He shook his head. "This is why I'm yelling at walls."

"And Fools," said Dobbs with a grin. "Don't forget the Fools."

"I don't think you'd let me." His smile took on a contemplative air, and Dobbs found herself thinking it might be time to make an exit. But Lipinski just sighed and turned back to the terminal. "And, since no one's ever gotten a direct brain-to-computer interface to work, I can't just crawl into the lines and see what's going on in the hold for myself. So, I've got to rent all kinds of extra tracers and an AI coordinator, and Al Shei is going to be furious when she sees what I'm doing to her credit balances."

"Only if the data doesn't get where it's going," said Dobbs.

Lipinski gave her another thoughtful look. "You're not half the Fool you ought to be."

"Shhh!" She waved him to silence. "You want me to get fired?" She glanced around frantically.

As she did, Dobbs saw a woman push herself away from the wall and turn deliberately toward them. It would have been difficult to miss her. Her golden brown skin was mottled with masses of purple-and-black bruises. Her tan sleeve had been rolled up to expose a blood blister that spread across her forearm like a spoiled rose. Her other arm was encased in the beige plastic form of a stasis tube. A sterile patch covered her right eye. Her good hand clutched the handle of a wafer case so tightly her knuckles had gone white, and she walked with the care of someone who didn't really want to make the pain any worse.

"Sorry to pry, Fellows." Her language was English, but her accent had a nasal drawl to it which could have come from Australia, Cornwall, or the southern reaches of Northern America. Her greeting, though, marked her as a Freer. "I heard you say you were under contract to Katmer Al Shei?"

Lipinski's Adam's apple bobbed as he swallowed his shock at her appearance. "Yes, we are."

The woman's right shoulder rolled forward as she tried to move her arm. She winced and scowled at the stasis tube. "I'm Jemina Yerusha. I've just contracted to be the *Pasadena*'s new pilot for this run."

Lipinski choked. "A Freer? They hired a Freer?"

Yerusha shifted her grip on the wafer case and dropped her gaze so she focused on Dobbs. "I need to report to the watch commander."

"Who will immediately tell you to report to the bio-garden for a new layer of skin." Dobbs looked her over with an air of exaggerated criticism. "You might want to save yourself a step."

Yerusha smiled sourly. "Already been there. They're growing me a new arm and a fresh eye. They'll be ready in another twenty-four hours or so." She tried to chuckle, but she winced again. "I was helping lock down the module after the blowout. Didn't move quite fast enough when the extra seam burst."

Dobbs nodded thoughtfully. It was part of the Freers' system of living. If there was a disaster on the station or ship where you were, you helped.

"Anyway, my agent is an idiot, and I don't want him babbling to Watch and the owners about what went over. That groundhog could ruin my chance at a job when the contract's less than two hours old." She gave Dobbs a twisted grin. "I'm ugly, but I'm mobile and I can at least check in and see my station." She propped herself up against the wall.

Lipinski looked her up and down. All trace of humor had vanished from his face and been replaced by suspicion. "The meds didn't mind you walking out like that?"

She snorted, an action she seemed able to manage without hurting herself. "I'll go back when I'm sure I've still got a job."

"Because the full effect of your heroism couldn't possibly be conveyed over the video lines." Dobbs hoped the quip would elicit an explanation. Yerusha could have easily checked in with the watch commander over the monitors and explained herself.

Yerusha squinted down at her. "Watch yourself, Fool. My headache shot hasn't kicked in yet."

Dobbs arched her eyebrows and opened her mouth, but Lipinski cut her off. "And what're you planning on bringing aboard with you?" He pointed at the wafer case.

Ah. Here it comes, thought Dobbs warily. The white plastic case was thirty centimeters on a side, which made it big enough to accommodate a fifty-wafer integrated stack. It had a blue border, which was the Freer color code for top-grade hardware. Lipinski would have spotted all of this. He probably would have jumped to the same conclusion she did about the contents.

Yerusha's mouth hardened into a straight line. "What business is it of yours?"

Dobbs was surprised. Freers were brash, proud, and contentious, but they were seldom secretive.

"Because I'm communications chief aboard *Pasadena*," replied Lipinski firmly. "And I have a right to know what's coming aboard my ship."

"And I have a right to bring aboard anything that's legal, noninfectious, isolated, and under my weight limit." With difficulty, she hefted the case to show the Landlords' double-ring seal emblazoned on the side, certifying that the contents of the case were everything she had just stated.

Lipinski's jaw tightened. Dobbs tensed, in case she needed to intervene. "Yes," he admitted. "You do. But if anything comes out of that case, I have a right to inspect it and confiscate it."

"You do." Yerusha did not let her gaze waver.

"As long as you understand that." Lipinski pocketed his pen and turned away. "I've got to check in at the docking bay," he said to Dobbs. "You want to walk along?"

Yerusha evidently decided to ignore how the question was directed. "You two go ahead. I'll follow."

Lipinski gave her a hard look, but shrugged and took the lead. Dobbs fell into easy step beside Yerusha, watching the way the woman concentrated on making her body keep moving.

"Did we lose anybody?" she asked.

"Eh?" Yerusha cocked an eye toward Dobbs, and the Fool saw it was a bright hazel despite being sunken in from the bruise. "Some, yeah. Could have been a lot more, though." The sheen in her eye told Dobbs she was seeing something other than the crowded corridor. "That's why it's going to take the bio-garden so long to do my arm. There's a couple of gerbils that need new lungs. The can's a total loss." She shook her head with a resignation Dobbs was used to seeing in engineers, architects, and others who worked and lived with machinery.

"Do they know what happened?" Dobbs cocked her own eye in an imitation of Yerusha's expression. "No," said Yerusha, too sharply. It could have been her pain, or Dobbs's bad imitation, but Dobbs didn't think so. "No idea."

"The Landlords have got to be crawling up the walls," Dobbs suggested.

"Do them good." Yerusha stared straight ahead. "They don't get enough exercise."

"I thought gerbils were noted for running around their wheels," Dobbs remarked as they followed Lipinski through the door to the elevator bays.

"That bunch isn't gerbils." Yerusha leaned her bare arm against the wall. "They're spooks and ciphers." She closed her eyes and sighed. "And groundhuggers, the lot of them."

Coming from a Freer, that was a much more dire insult than it generally was. Dobbs glanced up at Lipinski, who was keeping his eyes straight ahead and studiously ignoring Yerusha.

She tapped the wafer case softly. "What's his name?"

Yerusha's eyes snapped open, and Dobbs gave her her most nonthreatening smile. She'd been right. The wafer stack inside the carrying case held Yerusha's artificial intelligence.

Freers believed that planetary ecology kept human beings trapped. They believed that true freedom came when humanity built its own environments specifically tailored to their needs. Freers lived in stations and ships and were not permitted even to set foot on the ground.

They also believed that the cycle of life and death was a leftover from the time humans had lived exclusively on planets, and that when humans died, their souls were released into the void, where they traveled along, useless and voiceless, like photon packets without any eyes to see them. Their belief system posited, however, that if a sufficiently complex artificial environment could be created, the soul could be trapped in it, just as it could be trapped in the body of an infant born about the time of its original death. This unique explanation of reincarnation was the Freers explanation for artificial intelligences that occasionally achieved violently paranoid independent life. Their massive neural nets, the Freers said, had caught a human soul.

Some Freers "adopted" artificial intelligences and spent their time trying to create an environment that could catch a soul, and thus finally end the loss of knowledge and kinship that evolution had forced on humanity.

Some people regarded this as incredible blasphemy. Some, especially people whose worlds had known the disastrous aftereffects of an AI becoming a rogue entity, saw it as a dangerous idiocy.

Dobbs studied Lipinski's stiff shoulders. *It's trouble in the making. Well, what's a contract without that added spice of a personality clash?* she asked herself ruefully as the elevator doors opened and they crowded themselves inside along with twelve other shippers.

The elevator rose and gravity dropped, creating confusion inside Dobbs as her sense of balance worked out how to respond. All around her, the passengers eased their weight from foot to foot, or swallowed hard, or twisted their necks, or made any of the hundred other mostly useless physical compensations to the changes. Everyone but Yerusha. She just leaned against the wall, held on to her AI case, and continued to breathe.

It took no great skill at observation to notice that something was seriously wrong with her, and that the meds should not have let her go. On the other hand, Freers were a notably contentious and militant group. Titania Station had become Free Home Titania by withstanding a siege that cost the Landlords more than five hundred lives and hundreds of thousands in equipment and negotiations. Yerusha might just have been proving she was as tough as her parents who stood the siege.

Then again, she might not.

Dobbs eased her own weight from foot to foot and wished she hadn't thought of that.

The doors opened onto the hangar bays. Yerusha's eyes opened at the same time. Lipinski and Yerusha stepped out in the middle of a small gaggle of passengers, who dispersed in different directions, moving with the care required by partial gravity. Dobbs followed them all out, keeping her eyes open for whatever was going to happen next.

It happened just as the airlock to the *Pasadena* opened. Dobbs looked ahead and saw a squared-off, Roman-nosed man with skin the color of baked earth come out of the *Pasadena* airlock, obviously called out by their arrival in the bay. He wore the pocket-filled coveralls that were as close to a shipper's uniform as anything. Then she heard footsteps brush the carpet behind her. Dobbs turned to see a man and a woman in Oberon security green lope out of the corridor.

Yerusha hissed and jumped forward. The male green snatched at the air behind her. In the next breath, Dobbs lifted herself on her tiptoes and leaned forward. The green's torso collided with her shoulder. In the light gravity, it just knocked Dobbs forward half a yard, keeping her right in his path before she began to slip toward the ground. The greens ducked frantically around her as she rolled onto the deck plates.

In two long, bounding strides, Yerusha was through the airlock and across the threshold into the *Pasadena*. Her feet slid out from under her, and her body lazily settled down until her back measured its own length against the floor, with the wafer case clutched against her chest. Green Man shoved the Roman-nosed man out of the way and lunged toward her. Lipinski caught Roman Nose's arm before he lost his balance. Green Woman grabbed Green Man's arm and pulled them both up just short of crossing the *Pasadena* threshold. Yerusha rolled over and held up her hand to the approaching greens. A glaze of pain crossed over her eyes, but there was a puckered smile on her face.

Roman Nose pulled himself upright and looked down at Yerusha as if he were memorizing her face. Then he turned and took in the greens with the same care.

"Pilot Jemina Yerusha," Yerusha called past the greens to Roman Nose as he steadied himself. "Checking in."

"Watch Commander Schyler," he replied, his gaze darting between Yerusha and the security greens. "Wondering why the hell you're doing it like this."

Yerusha grimaced and shifted her one-handed grip on the wafer case so that its corner was no longer digging into her chest. "I was trying to avoid a hassle." She nodded toward the greens.

Schyler stuffed his hands into the pockets on each hip. Dobbs saw the cloth bulge and strongly suspected he had just thumbed a button on his pen. She picked herself up and made a great show of dusting herself off.

The Green Man did not wait for Schyler to ask what was going on. He walked up to the threshold formed by the seal between Port Oberon and the *Pasadena*. Dobbs did not miss the grim look that formed on Schyler's face. She settled herself back against the wall next to Lipinski, who was staring at the bizarre scene with his jaw hanging open. Dobbs reached up and closed it for him.

"Jemina Yerusha." The Green Man let his shadow fall across the pilot.

"Yes." Yerusha propped herself up into a sitting position.

"Registered with the Titania Freers?" He pulled a fold of film out of his pocket.

"Yes." She tugged at her overall to straighten out at least some of the wrinkles.

He shook the film open. "You're wanted for questioning in regard to the explosive decompression in the Richard III business . . ."

"No, I'm not," Yerusha replied calmly.

Schyler faced the Green Woman. "'Dama, maybe you'd do me the courtesy of telling me what's going on?"

The Green Woman blinked and gathered her professional lines. "The decompression event in the Richard III Business Module had features which match a pattern of . . ."

"What they're trying to say is that they think a Freer blew out an airlock," chimed in Yerusha. "They're trying to get us all tidied into the security can where we won't upset anybody." She glowered at the greens. "We were *helping*. Do you think I'm happy about the fact that I lost an arm and an eye for a bunch of ground-hugging . . ."

"There are questions," said the Green Woman firmly and loudly, "that need to be answered by the personnel on the scene."

"The AIs recorded the whole thing . . ." Yerusha swept out her good hand.

"The AIs cannot be used as uncorroborated testimony." Green Man clenched the film in his fist.

"Oh right, I forgot," sneered Yerusha. "We are capable of building intelligence but not of trusting it, or what it has the potential to become." Her hand curled even more closely around the edge of the wafer case. "What an enlightened, progressive outlook you have, 'Ster."

Green Man strangled a sigh. "Let me help you up, 'Dama Yerusha, and we can get this over with." He shoved the film back in his pocket and held out his hand.

Yerusha's mouth twisted into another grin. "Unless you've

got a specific warrant to enter the *Pasadena,* you cannot take me out of here." She turned her attention to Schyler. "I think that's the reg, isn't it?"

"Oh yeah, that's the reg," agreed Schyler, and Dobbs couldn't decide whether his tone was bemused or just confused. "Unless I decide to throw you out of there," he added.

At the moment, Dobbs guessed, he was trying to decide who was annoying him worse, Yerusha or the greens.

"Are you refusing to cooperate with security?" Green Woman asked Yerusha pointedly.

"Am I being arrested?"

"No, but you are being stupid." Green Man took a step forward. "Do you think anybody's going to stop me if I just haul you out of there?"

"I do."

Everyone in the hangar spun around. Resit stalked out of the corridor, burgundy skirt billowing around her ankles in lazy waves. She stopped right between the security greens and the entrance to *Pasadena*, then turned on her heel to face the greens. "I'm Zubedye Resit, ship's lawyer for the *Pasadena*," she said smoothly. " 'Dama Yerusha is under contract to Katmer Al Shei of the *Pasadena* Corporation, which makes her my client." She paused to let the entire speech sink in. She folded her arms and tapped her fingers impatiently on her forearm. "Why are you pursuing my client?"

"Not bad, considering she just got here," whispered Lipinski to Dobbs.

"Slow lawyers get eaten young," Dobbs replied seriously.

Green Woman looked like she was forcibly swallowing something unpleasant. "Shouldn't you be praying or something?"

Resit smiled. "It's only time for the *Salatul Jumu'ah*, the Friday sermon. That's optional for women." She flipped open the flap on her bag and pulled out a film and her pen. "I believed I asked a legal question." She squinted at Green Woman's badge and wrote down the number. "Do you really want me to request that the recording of this conversation be transferred to your superior immediately?"

Green Man gave his partner a dirty look. " 'Dama Resit, we

just want 'Dama Yerusha to come to the security module to answer some questions about the . . . decompression event."

"They couldn't talk to me in my hospital bunk either," said Yerusha to Resit. "They were hauling Freers out of there left and right."

"Must have been interesting to see," remarked Dobbs.

"Oh, that it was."

Resit shot them both a "shut-up" glance. "You have the authorizations on hand, I hope?" She tucked her own film away and held out her hand to the greens.

Green Man handed over a pair of films. Resit scanned them. "This does not give you the authority to pursue, detain, or forcibly enter." She handed them back. "I think we all have a complaint to register now." She gestured toward the hatch to the station corridor.

"You're not . . ." exclaimed Green Woman.

Resit's grin showed her teeth. "Oh, but I am. Shall we?"

Green Woman's face flushed darkly. Green Man pointed up at the station camera and she swallowed again. Side by side, they headed toward the station airlock.

"Talk to her, will you?" said Resit to Schyler before she followed the greens out.

Schyler touched his forehead in salute. Then, he turned toward Yerusha and extended his hand. "I really wouldn't try that again."

Tucking the wafer case awkwardly under her arm, Yerusha accepted his hand and let him pull her easily to her feet. "Thanks." She wiped at the sheen of perspiration that had appeared on her forehead. Dobbs knew she'd been right. Yerusha was not in any shape to be up and about. "I'm not about to let security shove me around, Watch. I'm under orders to you, not them."

"I don't care what you try to pull with security. I mean with Resit." He jerked his thumb toward the airlock.

"Oh, marvelous," Yerusha twisted her neck sharply and Dobbs heard a joint crack. "Another one who doesn't like Freers?"

Schyler smirked. "Another one who doesn't like unnecessary wirework. Filing a complaint on your behalf is not going to make her evening, I'd be willing to swear to it." He stopped and took a good look at the blister on Yerusha's arm. "Do you want to sit down someplace comfortable?"

She shook her head. "I'm fine."

Schyler looked her up and down. "You're lying," he said bluntly. "All right. Since you acknowledge my command, you are ordered to get back to the hospital and have them do something about this." He waved toward her bruised face and arm. Schyler pursed his lips. "Lipinski, will you walk her down? I want there to be somebody who can holler for Resit if any other greens decide to pick her up."

"Sure, no problem," said Lipinski to the wall. "I've only got the whole data hold to reconfigure."

"And you need to pick up the parts you ordered," Schyler finished for him. "Good. That works out fine."

The look that passed between the two men was one that Dobbs decided she would have to learn to read.

Lipinski left with Yerusha, and Schyler turned slowly, thoughtfully to Dobbs.

"And you are?" he inquired.

"Evelyn Dobbs." She touched her forehead in salute. "Master Fool for the *Pasadena*."

"Oh, you're our Lennox C." Schyler shook her hand. "Impressive entrance."

She beamed. "Takes years of special training."

"I suppose," he said, favoring her with the same calculating look he'd used on Yerusha, "that I don't need to tell you that Resit really does not like Freers."

"I got that feeling." Dobbs nodded. "But thank you."

Schyler leaned against the *Pasadena* threshold and rubbed his clean-shaven chin thoughtfully. "I hate to say this, Master Dobbs, but I think we're really going to need you on this trip."

Dobbs bowed. "'Let a fool be serviceable according to his folly,'" she quoted. "I am also, by the way, checking in."

"I thought you might be." He crossed the *Pasadena*'s threshold and waved for her to follow him. "Might as well formalize at least one of you."

"Thanks." Dobbs climbed aboard the ship that would be her home for the next eight months.

She had studied the plans when she had received the contract. The *Pasadena* followed the standard layout for packet ships. It was two bulbs held together by a long drop shaft. The larger bulb held the bridge, the berths, the kitchen, the shielded data-hold, and much of the life support. The smaller bulb held the engines and the reactors. The fuel and air tanks were strung on the drop shaft like rings on a pole.

Like the station modules, the shaft meant every deck was a hoop. Schyler led her around the curving corridor. This deck, which was probably the data-hold, was stark, with only labels and green memory panels to break up the white, ceramic walls.

Schyler took her into a briefing room. An oval table surrounded by enough chairs for *Pasadena*'s entire sixteen-member crew took up most of the space. The wide wall at the far end was one solid memory board. Schyler settled into the nearest chair and used his pen to activate the table space in front of him. He wrote his authorization across the main screen and added CREW CHECK-IN after it. The table absorbed the text and lit up two palm readers next to the active space. "I'll need your pen," said Schyler.

Dobbs handed it over, and he slipped it into the socket in the side of the table. Dobbs, familiar with the standard, Lennox-approved check-in procedure, pressed both hands against the palm readers that lit up in front of her. The table copied the contract from her pen. Then it confirmed that the fingerprints that activated the pen were the same as those pressed against the reader and printed ACCEPT in front of Schyler. It did not speak, though, which surprised her.

Schyler saw her eyebrows arch. "Owner prejudice," he said. "Neither Al Shei or Tully particularly likes the machinery to talk back."

"Must frustrate the AI." Dobbs lifted her hands off the reader and stuffed them into her pants pockets. "They don't like being mute."

Schyler shook his head. "There's only two AIs on board this ship, and neither one of them lives in the hull. There's Resit's boxed law firm and the Sundars' medical advisory."

Dobbs raised her eyebrows as far as they'd go and waggled them. "Al Shei doesn't like machines that think either?"

"No, she just doesn't like it when they try to think too much." Schyler extracted her pen. "Partly it has to do with being such a mechanical engineer. Partly it has to do with flying with Lipinski for ten years."

"That's right." Dobbs repocketed her pen. "He was at Kerensk, wasn't he?"

Schyler nodded, and Dobbs sighed. Most settlements and stations depended on artificial intelligence to run the power and production facilities that made life away from Earth possible. Twenty-five years ago on the Kerensk colony, one overprogrammed AI bolted from its central processor and got into the colony network.

Panicked officials shut the computer networks down to try to cage it. Never mind the factories, the utilities, the farms. Just find that *thing* before it gets into the water distribution system and the climate control. Before it starts to make demands. Before it starts acting too human.

Electricity and communications went down and stayed that way. Before three days were out, people froze in the harsh cold. They began to starve. They drank tainted water. They died of illnesses the few working doctors couldn't diagnose on sight.

When the colony did try to power up again, they found their software systems shredded to ribbons. It could have easily been human carelessness, but the blame was laid on the AI.

"Fifteen thousand, three hundred and eighteen dead," said Dobbs to the tabletop. Not one of the worst AI breakouts, just one of the more recent.

Schyler's brow wrinkled. "You too?"

Dobbs hooked one finger around her Guild necklace. "I was born there." She'd been totally incapable of reason when the disaster happened, but she still carried it with her. The ideas of the screams, the desperation, the hundreds of useless, pointless deaths. All of it caused by one rogue AI, by a creature that found itself suddenly alive and didn't know what to do about it. She could understand Lipinski's fears, and why he would be infuriated by Yerusha, who actually wanted to try to reproduce such a phenomenon, even under controlled circumstances. He knew about violence that could ignite between frightened, ignorant, wildly different beings. He possibly knew that, even better than she did; and from the look she'd seen on his face, he was less than willing to forgive the stranger for wanting to stay alive.

Schyler clucked in wordless sympathy and changed the subject. "You're all set." He got to his feet. "Your clearances will be listed on your cabin boards when you get settled in. You can bring in thirty-five pounds of personal effects. Sorry about that, we're trying to run a little light this trip. Do you want to see where you'll be?"

"Thanks." She let her necklace go and put a smile back on her face. "I'd actually—"

The left-hand wall beeped, cutting off her sentence. "Tully to *Pasadena*," said a man's tired voice.

"Schyler, here." Schyler tilted his head up.

"Can you let me in?" Dobbs tracked his voice to the intercom patch below the left-hand memory board. "There's some stuff I still need to get out."

Schyler leaned both hands against the table. "I'm not alone in here, Tully."

"Thirty seconds, that's all I need. Just left some stuff in my cabin."

Schyler pressed down harder. With the light gravity, Dobbs thought he might actually lift himself off his feet. "You're checked out, Tully. I can bring what's left . . ."

"Come on, Tom. Thirty seconds."

Schyler leaned back and let his hands drop down to his sides. "I'll be right out. 'Bye."

He turned to Dobbs with a worried look. "I'm going to have to give you the tour later . . ."

Dobbs waved her hand dismissively. "I'm a Master Fool; I'll find my way around." She spun on her toes and marched straight into the wall. "Ow." She clutched her nose and staggered backwards. "Eventually," she said, rubbing the offended appendage.

Schyler gave her a grin that might have become real if she'd had a few more minutes to work on him.

Dobbs let Schyler escort her out the door. She stepped out of the bay and didn't give Marcus Tully, who was fidgeting by the elevator doors, a second glance as she got into the lift and picked her floor.

As the lift began to sink, Dobbs remembered that when she

had left the café, she had intended to try to find out what was really going on with the co-owners of this ship.

That, she fingered her necklace, *may take longer than I thought.*

Chapter Two

LAUNCH

"Port Oberon to *Pasadena*, prepare for transfer to docking trolley."

Yerusha looked out the window above her station boards and watched the trolley slide into place underneath *Pasadena*. The camera displays on either side of the window showed the flatbed cart reaching out its waldos and grabbing ahold of the *Pasadena*'s side just before the docking clamps retracted into the skin of the station.

Yerusha had been glad to see that *Pasadena* sported a real window. Cameras were fine, and virtual reality was very useful, but she never felt quite comfortable flying without a direct look at what was actually between her ship and where she was going.

The trolley began to tow them out of the docking ring. The slight jerk buffeted her gently against her straps. The gravity was so light she barely retained any sense of up and down. On the displays, the curving walls of the modules fell behind as the trolley trundled toward the pinnacle of the station. The landscape became nothing but silver panels sliding away underneath the black dome of vacuum.

If she squinted at the top of the left-hand screen, she could see the shining edge of Oberon, just barely visible beyond the station. Titania, though, was somewhere on the other side of Uranus's blue-grey bulk.

She was glad. She didn't want to see the Free Home right now. She just wanted to get through the next two years.

"Port Oberon to *Pasadena*. Thirty seconds to release."

"Thanks Oberon." Yerusha chided herself for daydreaming. She had a job to do and a starbird watch commander who didn't seem as though he was a great believer in second chances for Freers.

Doesn't matter, she reminded herself. *For now*, you *are Pasadena*.

Yerusha rested her hands on her boards. The flat keys glowed with the designations she had written across them, including the OVERRIDE key. That one would cancel out all the programs she had labored over for the past two days and would let her command the engines directly if anything unpredicted happened on course to the jump point.

The ship had been slow to learn her writing and shorthand because there was no AI running the internal systems. Al Shei was obviously almost as paranoid about humanity's progeny as Lipinski was. Yerusha shook her head. With attitudes like that surrounding her, it was going to be a long run, that much was sure.

The *Pasadena* slid out from under the module rings and the gleaming panels that the view screens showed came to a halt. Out of the window, she saw the silver-white curve of the station and just a glimpse of the ghostly globe of Oberon.

"Three to release, *Pasadena*," said the Port voice. "Two . . . one . . . release."

The trolley opened its clamps and Yerusha watched Port Oberon and the stark, white moon fall away from the *Pasadena*.

She knew that the relative motion was the ship's. Pasadena was falling away from the station, from Oberon, and from the sun. Without any acceleration pressure to tell her otherwise, though, her mind believed what her eyes saw. As the minutes ticked by, Port Oberon dropped back, becoming an elaborate silver mobile surrounded by mothlike ships that darted between the spindly arms of cranes and the bloated hulls of the fuel tanks. All of them hung against the backdrop of Oberon's white-and-black speckled surface. The moon itself was nothing but a cardboard circle suspended in the limitless black pool that made up the universe.

"*Pasadena* this is Port Oberon we have you at eleven point three clicks at five minutes, fourteen seconds. Hour 15:24:16. Mark."

"Marked, Oberon." Yerusha checked the clock at her station automatically. The clock showed both the length-of-flight time and time of day. The *Pasadena*'s flight clocks had to be in sync with each other as well as with the outside, but not just for timing torch bursts for sublight navigation. Navigation past light speed was impossible. To change direction, they would have to drop down to sublight, change the ship's flight angle and jump again. The trick was, if they made a mistake in their calculations, they might not know which system they were making their correcting jump from, and it might take days to work out where they were, much less where they were headed, if they were able to do it at all. Ships did disappear for want of good timing.

"In sync, Pilot?" came Schyler's voice from her right hand. The bridge was laid out so that all the vital stations were on one side of the drop shaft. The other side held the backup boards, the conference station, and the virtual-reality simulator. During her shifts, Yerusha would don the VR gear and run through flight simulations, looking for ways to cut down the run time and fuel consumption, as well as bringing herself up to spec on just what the ship she was flying could and could not do. If an emergency course change were called for, Schyler could put on the gear and run through the programs she fed in from her chair, using full-blown simulations of *Pasadena*.

"In sync and on-line, Watch," Yerusha replied in her best doing-my-job voice. From Schyler's station he could call up a display of exactly what she saw, but safety and approved protocol called for a direct check.

To Yerusha's left sat the pilot's relief, the only other member of the bridge crew on duty at this time. He was a round, little man named Cheney, who had Asian eyes and had let himself go almost completely bald. This was his third run with Al Shei as a pilot's mate, he'd told her. He had described each trip with the single word every shipper with more than one working synapse wanted to hear. Uneventful.

The other two members of the bridge crew were waiting out launch in their cabins. Most of the work had been done while the *Pasadena* was still in dock. Schyler, Yerusha, and Al Shei had mapped and timed the route while figuring the requirements for fuel and reaction mass. Yerusha had programmed the simulations. When the stats lined up to her satisfaction, she wrote them into *Pasadena*'s computers. Both Schyler and the ship had verified them.

Al Shei and her crew had been on board even before Yerusha, rechecking the ship inside and out. When it came to flight capability, it didn't matter to Al Shei that the *Pasadena* had been checked over less than forty-eight hours previously by a Lennox expert. Yerusha couldn't fault Al Shei's caution. She and her crew would be depending absolutely on the ship for the next six to eight months. She and her crew should be the ones to decide if it was ready to go.

It had taken a day of drill calls and simulations to get the new crew used to each other's speech patterns and how the orders were given and confirmed. After that, Al Shei and her engineers had remotely warmed the reactors and accumulators with the "hot" mix of deuterium, and the tritium the D2 reactions produced. Once warmed, the *Pasadena*'s engines could run on the much safer mix of hydrogen and $boron_{11}$. The ship was humming and ready when they all were allowed back on board to strap down and start out.

"Oberon to *Pasadena*, we've got you at fifteen klicks at eleven minutes and fifty-nine seconds. Good luck and see you soon."

"Thanks Oberon. See you soon," replied Schyler. "Clear to go whenever you're ready, Yerusha."

Yerusha checked the angle of the jets one more time to make sure they were pointing away from the station and the incoming traffic. "Intercom to *Pasadena*," Yerusha called. She lifted her hands and held them flat over her boards. "Counting down to acceleration. Ten, nine, eight . . ."

She heard no sound of movement under her countdown. There was nothing to do. The systems were all up and running. The final setup had been completed four hours before the docking clamps had let them all go. Now was the time to rest in the harness, pay attention to the monitors, and remain quietly confident that nothing unexpected was going to happen.

"Three. . . two . . . one." Yerusha brought her hands down on her board. The ship read her fingerprints and sent its signal down to the engine compartment. "Torch lit," she reported, just before a low rumble that echoed all the way up the drop shaft confirmed her call.

Gradually, Yerusha's head settled on her neck, her neck rested against her shoulders, and the floor reached up and pressed against the soles of her feet. The harness went slack against her shirt and trousers as her body settled into the chair.

Despite two hundred years of attempts to separate it out, gravity had remained a property of mass and motion. Without enough of either, you had free fall. Al Shei ran her ship at close to one-gee acceleration. In that respect, at least, the run was going to be comfortable.

The displays on the monitor in front of Yerusha all remained green. She read the numbers and thrust ratios one by one. Each was exactly as it should be.

The intercom started bringing up the voices from Engineering.

"Station One, all normal and constant," said Javerri, the FTL assistant, who didn't look like she ever got enough sleep.

"Station Two, all normal and constant." Ianiai, a big, black bear of a boy who thought he knew a lot more than he did.

"Station Three, all normal and constant." Shim'on, who wore a yarmulke and wouldn't eat even cloned bacon.

Groundhogs at core, all of them.

"Check and check," Al Shei's voice answered them. "Intercom to Bridge. Engineering reports normal and constant, Watch."

"Thank you, Engineering," said Schyler. "Time to jump, Pilot?"

Yerusha touched a key and brought up the official time on her board. "Thirty-eight hours to jump point."

Pasadena needed flat, smooth space to start from. Thirty-six AU from the Sun would put them close enough to the top of the Solar System's gravity well that they could jump the rest of the way out.

Pasadena was, of course, a long way from being the only ship starting for a jump point this day, even this hour. A lot of the flight planning had involved logging in with Port Oberon's flight schedulers and finding out who else had registered a route so she could pick a clear path and reserve it. Yerusha had done runs that were held up at Oberon for over a week before there was room in the direction the ship needed to go. The delay this time had been only a day. She counted herself lucky.

"Received and agreed," replied Al Shei's voice. "Thirty-eight hours to jump."

"Intercom to *Pasadena*," said Schyler. "Secure from free fall."

Yerusha snapped the catches on her harness and scratched hard under her left armpit. The new arm was a little stiff, but there wasn't any of the pins-and-needles sensation that could accompany a new graft. Her discomfort came simply from the fact that no one seemed to have designed a free-fall strap that didn't chafe.

"And there ends the exciting part," said Cheney, stretching both arms over his head until Yerusha could hear the joints pop.

"I wish," muttered Schyler, letting his head fall back until he stared at the ceiling.

Yerusha exchanged a glance with her relief, who just shrugged.

"Pilot"—Schyler lifted his head—"we need to get some projections for the Vicarage to Out There to Wyborn Station jumps. Al Shei'll want to go over all that at the next briefing."

"Right away, Watch." Yerusha got to her feet. "Relief," she said to Cheney as she crossed the deck to the VR station.

"Relief active." Cheney picked himself up out of his chair and plopped down into hers. He pulled out his pen and activated the reconfiguration menus to set the boards back to the way he liked them.

She wasn't even halfway across the deck when the intercom beeped.

"Intercom to Watch," Resit's voice sounded out. "Schyler, if she's free, I need to see Yerusha down here."

Yerusha froze in mid-stride, but she managed to screw a "what the hell?" expression on her face.

Schyler gave her a heavy glance. "Acknowledged, Law. I'll send her down as soon as I've gone over a couple of things up here."

"Thanks, Watch," said Resit. "Intercom to close."

Cheney bent over the boards, even though there shouldn't have been much to see. Schyler jerked his chin toward the drop-shaft hatch. Yerusha nodded and walked through the hatch. She heard Schyler's footsteps follow her.

Inside the drop shaft was a staircase that spiraled all the way down to the engine compartment. The walls were lined with junction boxes, bundles of cables and wires, and endlessly branching ceramic pipes, color-coded in green, red, blue, or orange—depending on what they carried. Maintenance displays dotted the chaos, their readings shining bright green.

Yerusha walked down a couple of steps and turned, resting her new hand against the railing. Schyler followed her a split second later. He stopped one step above her.

Schyler leaned close to her, and Yerusha felt the hairs on the back of her neck stand up. There was a cold sheen in his eyes that she had not seen there before.

He kept his voice soft and relaxed. "I already have one massive problem on this run," he said. "If I find out your presence is going to add another, I will boot you out of here without slowing the ship down. Understand?"

"Absolutely." Yerusha matched his conversational tone and folded her hands behind her back. "But if you've got problems this run, Watch, they're not coming from me."

"Glad to hear it." Schyler straightened up. "Report to the Law then, Pilot. In her cabin."

"Yes, Watch." She touched her forehead, turned on her heel, and marched smartly down the stairs.

The berthing deck was immediately below the bridge. The *Pasadena* had been built to keep the crew as far away from the engines as possible, just in case. The deck's corridor was as bare and uninspiring as the bridge. Yerusha found herself wondering why Al Shei hadn't invested in at least a prefab mural to brighten the place up a bit. The woman did not seem like one of the engineering aesthetic types who believe bare machinery was beautiful. Then again, she'd already heard rumors about some of the woman's tight-fisted idiosyncrasies, so maybe she shouldn't be too surprised no cash had been laid out for corridor trimmings.

Yerusha kept walking around the curved hallway until she found the cabin labeled ZUBEDYE RESIT. The ENTER light shone green, so Yerusha just knocked once to signal that she was there and went inside.

The lawyer's cabin was not so much living quarters as office. She had her bunk folded away. An active, permanent desk had been welded to the wall where most cabins had a fold-down set of boards. Resit sat at the desk, poring over a set of films.

Yerusha wasn't surprised to see her so deep into her work even though they were only five minutes out of free fall. As ship's lawyer, she had to be a one-woman bureaucracy. She had to have a working knowledge of the local statutes wherever they were taking on or dropping off cargo. She had to make sure contracts, tax forms, and manifests were all prepared and legal. The crew had to get reports on any behavior-related ordinances that would affect them, and cultural and legal advice had to be available to anyone who needed it. Al Shei and Schyler would have to know the circumstances under which they could seek work, and the contracts would have to be drawn up to cover cross-system traffic.

Much of the job could have theoretically been done from a station or groundside, but the expense of FTL communication prevented that. Unless you were a megacorp or a monarch, it was easier and cheaper to bring your counsel with you.

A big input-output box sat on the corner of Resit's desk. It had been unceremoniously piled with films filled with cramped Turkish writing. Guessing it was Resit's AI law firm, Yerusha waved to the box in acknowledgment.

"Would you do me the courtesy of an introduction, Law?" she inquired, indicating the AI.

Resit's mouth pressed into a long, straight line. Yerusha met her eye calmly. Resit obviously shared her cousin-employer's prejudices.

"Incili. This is Jemina Yerusha."

"How do you do, 'Dama Yerusha?" answered the AI in a clear tenor voice with a slightly British accent.

"Pleased to meet you, Fellow." Yerusha saluted the AI.

"Thank you, 'Dama Yerusha."

"All right, Incili, that'll do." Resit tapped her pen impatiently against the desktop.

" 'Dama." The voice shut off.

"You called for me, Law?" Yerusha unfolded the stool from the wall and took her seat. Resit, Yerusha noticed, had changed from her usual skirt to a pair of baggy, opaque blue harem pants.

Skirts not being conducive to the maintenance of modesty in free fall. Yerusha forcibly suppressed a smile at the image of the lawyer with her hems billowing about her ears.

Resit sealed the films in front of her. "It's part of my job, Yerusha, to try to stay apprised of any trouble the crew might have on the run."

Yerusha held up her hand. "Is this going to be about the can blowing out at Port Oberon?"

"No," answered Resit coolly, and Yerusha knew she'd made a tactical error. The lawyer had been all set for a confrontation, and she'd gotten one. "It's about why the Freers exiled you."

Yerusha had thought she was steeled for this, but the lawyer's words still hit like a physical blow. She swallowed. "You know about that, and you still hired me."

Resit shook her head. "I did not hire you. Al Shei did." She rested her elbows on her knees. "My grasp of Freer law is pretty limited. As near as I can tell, so is anybody's who doesn't actually live on a station that has gone Free, or been set up Free.

"I do know you've been exiled from Free Home Titania, and I know why. We've got a couple of station stops this run, so I need to know if you're likely to get caught up in Freer political brawls, so I can budget for your bail, or your absence."

Yerusha glanced at first one wall and then the other, just to make sure they weren't closing in on her. It sure felt like it. She met Resit's eyes again. "I'd like to know what you've been told."

Resit reached out and tapped the I/O box. "Incili. Give me a replay on what we have from the Titania Hall of Records."

The tenor voice flowed smoothly out of the box. "Fellow

Jemina Yerusha is found guilty of dereliction of duty in public office. It is now a matter of public record that Fellow Jemina Yerusha has been sentenced to two years' exile from the protection of Free Home Titania. For that time she may not seek or receive work, shelter, or resources from any Freer. End sentence."

There was a strange pounding noise coming from somewhere. Yerusha realized it was her heartbeat. She remembered the stale air in the court and the feel of sweat on her own palms.

"I'm sorry your first impression of me was unfavorable, Incili," Yerusha said to the box.

"My first impression of you was simply factual, 'Dama," answered Incili. "I have not had cause to speculate on you yet."

"I have, though," Resit broke in, obviously insulted by the fact that Yerusha was more ready to talk to the AI than to her. Yerusha reined in her temper. It wouldn't help if she pointed out the AI was more likely to hear anything she might have to say.

"I was derelict in my duty while serving in the Titania Free Guard. I was supposed to be standing a docking watch. I wasn't. Because of me, a Fellow died." She forced herself to keep her eyes fixed on Resit's. "I was brought up, and I was sentenced. If I keep a clean record while I'm out here, they'll let me come home again."

"Watch Commander Schyler contacted someone in the Free Home who suggested the charges were trumped up. Would you care to elaborate on that?"

Yerusha knew Resit saw the way she struggled to control her features. There was no missing it. The lawyer saw the memories even if she couldn't read them. Resit didn't know about Holden's panicked cry coming down the intercom, about how she'd sprinted down the corridors, about how she'd been too late. "No."

Resit's frown was heated from a slowly simmering anger. "I want you to tell me the worst we can expect if you come into contact with any other Freers."

Yerusha looked at Incili's gleaming silver skin and then at Resit. "I'm an Exile. I'll be ignored. Treated like a ghost.

That's how I lost my arm." She ran her hand over her right wrist. "I was trying to help with the can explosion, but no one would help me, so I couldn't get myself out of the way fast enough when the last seam blew."

Resit regarded her with a steady gaze that had probably made a lot of witnesses squirm. It almost worked on Yerusha.

"I hope," Resit said without letting her gaze flicker for a second, "that your piloting records are more complete than your service record."

Yerusha didn't let herself flinch. "My pilot's record is exactly as my agent gave it to you. I am the best you would have found in Port Oberon, on any day."

"Well, I'm glad to hear it." Resit sat back and swiveled her chair so she faced her desk. Her voice had a brittle undertone. Yerusha wasn't sure whether the lawyer believed what she said or not. "I'm obviously going to need to add Freer law to my repertoire though. Can you recommend a good source?"

Yerusha smiled. "The best storehouse of Freer law is Aneas Knock in Free Home Kemper. Be careful how you talk to him, though." Yerusha stood. "He's an AI that doesn't like being dismissed. 'Bye Incili." Without bothering to smirk, she left the lawyer's cabin.

Back in the bare corridor, Yerusha rubbed her right wrist and tried not to curse out loud.

Of course she checked. After that little run-in with the Oberon greens, how could she not check? Yerusha took a couple of deep breaths. *And you didn't do yourself any favors in there. Watch your step, Jemina-Jewel. You've got no backups on this ship.*

She glanced toward the ceiling. Technically, she should get right back to her station. But there shouldn't be any problem with her slipping by the galley to grab a quick bulb of coffee. She needed something to bolster her up.

Not two hours into the shift and I'm already tired, she thought as she climbed down the stairs. Below her feet, one of the engineer's mates was hanging from the stair railing by his harness and resting his feet against a couple of support staples. He had a bunch of wiring in one hand and a probe in the other. At the sound of her footsteps, he cast a curious glance upward, flashed a brief smile, and went straight back to his work.

At least somebody doesn't give a damn. Yerusha waited while the galley hatch cranked itself open. *It'd be nice to be ignored for a while.*

Kitchen and cafeteria were only part of the galley deck's function. It also held the exercise room, the sick bay, and recreation room. This deck was the permanent station for Chandra and Baldassare Sundar. The wife and husband were genuine starbirds. They lived their lives traveling, hiring on board ships and stations as long as it suited them before moving on again. There were groundhogs who called their kind "space gypsies," and held them only one cut above Freers on the contempt scale. Some commanders wouldn't hire them for any money. But Al Shei didn't just hire them. According to some gossip that Yerusha had overheard, the Sundars had the highest share of anyone on the ship, except for Al Shei and Schyler. Between the pair of them they were Management Union-certified in nutrition, physical therapy, and first-and-emergency aid, and both were rated level six cooks by the Cordon Bleu Association. Chandra, Yerusha already knew, made a curry that could burn the tonsils out of the uninitiated.

Despite all that, in the galley, the Fool, Dobbs, was engaged in the ancient pastime of baiting the cook.

Dobbs was collapsed across the service window. Three off-shift crew members were so busy watching the show, they had forgotten the food cooling in front of them.

"Water!" Dobbs squeaked. "Water." She slid off the counter into a little twitching heap on the floor.

Yerusha shook her head and threaded her way between the tables to the coffee urn that had been built into the wall.

Chandra, a grey-haired, bark brown woman, appeared at the window with an open-lidded bucket in her wrinkled hands. It sloshed. She held it over Dobbs's head.

Dobbs took one look up and scuttled backwards like a frightened crab. "Help!" She dodged under the nearest table. "That's a declaration of war, Cook! I'm telling everyone I saw you put blasting gel in that sauce!"

Chandra clapped her hand to her forehead and staggered backwards. "Oh! I am found out! I am undone! I am ruined!"

"I am upstaged," remarked Dobbs as she crawled out from under the table.

"Now behave yourself, young woman." Chandra reached meaningfully for a ladle. "There's work to be done, and unless you want to do it . . ."

Dobbs slapped her own forehead and stumbled away in perfect imitation of Chandra's gesture. A comm-assistant, whose name Yerusha had forgotten, chuckled appreciatively. Then he caught sight of Yerusha. Yerusha nodded to him and sat down at the next table. He got up immediately and moved over to a table on the far side of the room.

Yerusha swallowed her anger with a long draft of very strong coffee. When she looked up, the Fool was sitting across from her, both feet on the table. The chair would have been tilted back if it hadn't been bolted to the floor.

"I'd be careful with that stuff." Dobbs pointed toward Yerusha's coffee cup. "The curry's not the only place Cook puts the blasting gel. I don't want to see Al Shei's face when she's got to scrape her new pilot off the ceiling." Dobbs raised an imaginary umbrella and squinted angrily out from under its rim. "That does it," she said in a good imitation of Al Shei's Turkish accent. "That is the last time I hire a cook who says she's a demolitions expert!"

Despite herself, Yerusha chuckled. The comm-assistant gave her a disgruntled glance. Dobbs waved cheerily and gestured expansively for the man to come over and join them. Instead, he got up and left.

"Good sign." The Fool folded her arms. "He at least recognizes when he's just contributing to a ridiculous situation."

"You trying to tell me you're on my side, Fool?" Yerusha took another drink of coffee, smaller this time. The stuff really was strong.

"I'm on all sides. Sometimes all at once," she added. "Defying relativity is one of those things they teach you when you're going for Master's rank."

Yerusha lowered her cup and looked at the other woman speculatively. "I've never shipped out with a Fool before. A friend of mine took the Guild entrance exam once. He didn't even make the first cut."

"I would sooner jump headfirst down a black hole than go

through the Fool's Guild qualification process again." Dobbs gave her a quick smile. "You can't imagine, the custard pies, the pratfalls, the water balloons . . . yuck." She shuddered.

"And the psychology, the sociology and physical aptitude," added Yerusha. "It seemed as though you were expected to have several advanced degrees to get in."

"Nah." Dobbs waved the idea away. "We just do that to keep out anybody who doesn't really have a sense of humor." She smiled again. "Actually, one of the best Fools I know comes from a Free Home. Cyril Cohen. He's two years younger than I am, but he took his Master's rating three years before I did, the upstart."

"Yeah, upstarts," said Yerusha into her coffee. She wished her memory wasn't so accurate. "Some people you have to watch every second." She took another swallow and stood up. "If I don't get back to the bridge, Schyler's going to be hollering down the intercom for me."

Somehow, Yerusha knew the little Fool was still watching her as she left.

Al Shei rolled her shoulders backwards a couple of times, already hearing Baldassare Sundar tch-tching her about making sure she took more breaks during her shift. Shim'on was stowing his gear in the tool locker. The hatch opened and the relief watch, Ianiai, who looked as though he had been mothered by a black bear, stepped through. At twenty-four, he was the youngest of the crew and still believed he could do nothing wrong. This was only his second trip out.

All of her engineers were younger than she was. Not quite green, but not quite experienced enough to price themselves out of her range. All of them were capable, though. Al Shei had put them through their paces alone and with each other before she had hired any of them.

"Welcome on, Ianiai." Al Shei pulled a set of films out of the drawer near her station and touched her pen to the first one. The assignment notes she'd been recording in it flowed out onto the film.

"How's things running, Engine?" Ianiai leaned his rear end against the boards.

"Smooth and quiet." She switched off her pen and put it

back in her pocket. "But you'll be happy to know you won't be bored. We need a check on all the valves in the water-recycling tanks." She gave him the film. "Don't want anything compostable backing up."

Ianiai took the film and folded it away, waving at her in an imitation of an Arabic salute that Al Shei would never forgive Resit for teaching him. "In the meantime, however"—she climbed to her feet—"you have the joy of manning the big chair." She bowed and swept her hand out toward it. "Relief."

"Relief active." He settled into her chair, took out his pen, and began tapping menus and writing orders to slave the other monitors to Station One and display all their output in front of him.

Satisfied, Al Shei gave Shim'on a parting wave and headed for the stairs.

Main Engineering was the only inhabited section in the bulb at the end of the drop shaft. The spiral stairs provided a clear view of the cabling, pumps, juncture boxes, and piping that kept the gases, fluids, and power that made up the ship's lifeblood flowing steadily. Work was mostly done right from the stairs or the sets of staples that served as foot- and handholds from the walls. There were obvious reasons why the most popular slang term for ship's engineer was "shaft monkey."

Al Shei's eyes scanned the walls of the shaft. She remembered when all of this had been a bewildering tangle. Now her eyes tracked individual lines and pipes to their junctures. Air, electricity, fuel, everything running as it should. The atmosphere around her practically purred.

She smiled at the thought. *Good kitty*. She patted the stair railing.

As she climbed, her gaze automatically picked out each of the display boards. Deck Four O_2, green. Deck One main electric, green. Deck Three water, green. Deck Two nitrogen, blank.

Al Shei stopped in front of the board and snapped open the cover. She swung it back and pried the light strip out with her thumbnail. She held it up to the light and saw the crystals had gone dark grey.

She put the strip back and closed the cover. She took her

pen out and wrote BURNED OUT STRIP on the display's memory board and added the engineering seal so the message wouldn't be wiped out accidentally. Ianiai would find it when he did his walkabout.

On the way back to her berth, she stopped in at the galley for a hot-box full of Chandra's curry and a thermos of tea to take back to her cabin.

"Got to know our new Fool today, Al Shei," said Chandra as she handed over the box.

"Oh?" Al Shei picked up the thermos. "What do you think?"

"I either love her or she's going to be dead before the week's out," answered the Galley chief with a wink.

"Oh, please don't kill her off." Al Shei waved the thermos. "The last thing we need is to be blackballed by the Fools."

Schyler was waiting in the corridor when she reached her cabin. His arms were folded against his chest, and he was leaning back against the wall. Al Shei felt her good mood begin to drain away. This was not a posture Schyler adopted when things were going well.

"What's up, Tom?" she asked as she palmed the reader for her cabin hatch.

"I've got to talk to you about Tully."

Al Shei's mood fell straight into her boots. The cabin hatch cycled open. "Come on in."

Schyler followed her into her cabin and let the hatch shut behind them. Technically Al Shei was not supposed to do this. Although after the Slow Burn it became common practice for Islamic women to earn at least part of the household income outside the home, it had also become *haram*, forbidden, for a married woman to be alone in a confined space with a man who was not her relative. She had gotten around the problem years ago by having Resit draw up adoption papers. Schyler was an orphan, and Islamic law explicitly encouraged the adoption and maintenance of orphans. On paper, Schyler was Al Shei's son. They kept the fact very quiet, since neither of them particularly wanted to deal with the jokes that were sure to arise from it.

It also meant that, technically, she could take off her *hijab* in front of him. She had never exercised the option.

"So, Tom, what's the problem?" Al Shei tucked the hot-box under her arm so she could fold the table down from the wall and deposit her dinner on it.

Schyler paced the room between her folded-up bed and her nest of faux silk pillows in the far corner. His hands were jammed so far into his pockets, she could see the fabric strain at the seams.

At last, he faced her. "I think Marcus Tully's finally gone too far."

Al Shei leaned her hip against the edge of the table and reached up under her *hijab* to rub her temple. It was not surprising to find that Schyler's abrupt confirmation of the suspicions she'd laid out for Asil did not make her feel better.

"I know." She lowered her hand. "Or at least, I suspected. Do you know exactly what he did?" she asked.

Schyler shrugged without taking his hands out of his pockets. His coveralls hitched up and down. "I'm not sure. You know he never tells me when he's breaking local law . . ."

"So you won't have to tell me." Al Shei finished for him. "What's different this time?"

"Whatever it is he . . . acquired, he's left it here."

Al Shei jerked her head up. "What!"

"Or part of it, or evidence of it." Schyler finally extracted his hands and waved them toward the walls. "He tried to get back on board after he'd checked out." Al Shei started. Schyler raised his hand. "No, I did not let him aboard. But he needed to get some things he'd left behind, he said." Schyler jammed his hands back into his pockets. "He's never done that. The changeovers have always been smooth. Something is up this time."

Al Shei nodded. "I agree with you. What could he have left? It's not in the engineer's cabin, or if it is, it's hidden . . ." An idea struck her, and Al Shei faced the wall. "Intercom to Houston." She waited the single second while the intercom located and paged him.

"Houston, here, Engine," came back Lipinski's voice. She could hear the faint noise of voices in the background, so "here" was probably the comm center, as opposed to the datahold.

"Houston, what did you do with those burned-out wafer

stacks? Did you cash them in with the recyclers at Oberon?" The look that crossed Schyler's face was part revelatory and part fearful.

"No," answered Lipinski. "It looked like some of the sectors might be usable, so I kept them for spares. I haven't gone over them yet."

Al Shei tapped one finger against the wall. "Just put them aside for now, will you, Houston? I'll be down later to talk to you. Intercom to close." The wall chirped as the connection closed.

Al Shei tugged at her tunic sleeve and faced Schyler. "You know, if this turns out to be an ongoing situation, Resit is going to have fifty fits."

"I know."

"Do you have any idea at all what Tully was doing?"

Schyler nodded reluctantly. Al Shei bit her tongue. She hated it when he acted like a guilty child. Most of the time he was a fast thinker, cool under pressure and quick to give an order or take on a job. But every now and then, the sheepish, confused Schyler she had helped out on Station Kilimanjaro resurfaced.

"So, what is it?" The chill she felt in her blood was reflected in her voice. She'd had plenty of time in the off watches to speculate on what Tully had been up to on his run. Part of her did not want confirmation of any of the ideas she had dreamed up.

She waited while Schyler made up his mind. She forced herself to be patient. Schyler functioned in a small world of self-imposed rules. One of those rules dictated that he never discussed Al Shei's doings with Tully, or Tully's with Al Shei. He was about to break that rule. She could spare him the time he needed to finally decide to do it.

"I think he was data smuggling from Powell Secured Sector. You know, where Toric Station is."

Al Shei closed her eyes. *"Allahumma inna nasta'inuka,"* she said reflexively. Oh, Allah, we seek Your help. "It's possible. Resit picked up a rumor that a security plug had been pulled out of there." She threw up both her hands. "Why, Tom? Why is he doing this? He doesn't smuggle, he broadcasts. If he got ahold of some military secret, why isn't he just blabbing it all over the next six systems?"

Schyler looked at her bleakly. "We did not make any money last trip, Katmer. We had a totally flat run."

"But there've been deposits in the acc . . ." Al Shei's voice trailed away. She took a deep breath. "Well, it's a good thing I've got Asil checking into where they came from, isn't it?"

Schyler started a little at that. "I guess it is."

"All right." Al Shei sat down in the room's one real chair and tried to smooth her turbulent thoughts. "All right. We can't leave all of this to Asil. He'll just be able to track the buyer, or the contractor, assuming we're right, of course. On this end, we need to find out exactly what Tully's done, and to whom, and how—if we can. We can't panic appropriately when we haven't got the facts."

" 'Beware of suspicion,' " quoted Schyler. " 'For suspicion may be based on false information.' "

Al Shei nodded and looked at her long hands where they lay in her lap. "It is also said, 'Allah's curse will be on him if he is a liar.'" She shook her head heavily. "Brother-in-law or not, I think you were right, Tom. I think Tully's really gone too far." She looked up at Schyler, some part of her seeking reassurance. "But maybe we'll find out he's just being an idiot again."

Schyler gave her a weak smile. "God willing and the creeks don't rise."

She smiled underneath her *hijab*. "Your mouth to God's ear," she told him. "Look, prayer is in about three minutes. I'll get Lipinski going on those wafer stacks, and we'll talk about this after breakfast tomorrow, all right?"

"All right, Mother," he said because nobody else was there. He let himself out into the corridor. At that same moment, Resit walked in from the door to the bathroom she and Al Shei shared. Her face was still slightly damp from the *wudu*, the ablution. She saw the door close and must have spotted Schyler's back.

She took one look at Al Shei. "That was not good news, whatever it was."

"No, it wasn't," Al Shei agreed as she got to her feet. "Time to pray hard, Cousin."

"As you say, oh-my-mistress." Resit's sideways glance said that she really wanted to know what was going on, and it was nothing short of piety that was keeping her from starting what could be a very long conversation.

Al Shei went into the bathroom, stripped off her *hijab*, sat down on the toilet and went through the careful washing: rinse the hands, rinse the mouth, clear the nose, drench face, arms, quick pass over the head and down the back of the neck, both ears, the nape of the neck, and finally the feet.

"I bear witness that there is no god but Allah," she said, wrapping her veil back around her and wishing she felt as clean inside as she did outside. "And He is one and has no partner and I bear witness that Muhammad is His servant and messenger."

She pulled her shoes back on and rejoined Resit.

"Which way is Mecca today?" her cousin asked.

Al Shei did a quick calculation of the relative direction of Earth from the *Pasadena*. "This way." She pointed to the corner where her pillows were piled. She knew some shipper Moslems who would literally stand on the ceiling if that was what was required. She and Resit had never gone quite that far. She got her prayer rug out of its drawer and laid it down next to Resit's.

They faced the proper corner and raised their hands. Al Shei took a deep breath and put the day behind her. This was not the time for her troubles. This was the time to go beyond them, to the infinite and the permanent.

"*Allahu Akbar*," she and Resit chorused. God is great. They folded their hands below their chests. "Oh, Allah, glory and praise are for You and blessed is Your name and exalted is Your Majesty and there is no god but You. I seek shelter in Allah from the rejected Satan."

As Al Shei went through the motions of the *salah*, she felt real calm returning to her. When the regular prayers were finished, she added the *sajdatus sahw*, for forgetfulness, since she'd been elbow deep in a maintenance hatch with a bundle of fresh wiring in her fists when afternoon prayer came around.

After she straightened up, she faced Resit and raised her right hand. Resit raised hers. Simultaneously, they each reached out and yanked off the other's veil. Resit's hair fell down around her shoulders in a black cloud. This was not part of the *salah.* It was done in memory of the time when prayer was dangerous and the women who had survived the Fast Burn sometimes had to stop in the middle and hide their veils because vigilantes or the police had broken in the door.

"Dining in peaceful solitude tonight, Cousin?" Resit nodded to the hot-box as she settled her *kijab* back over her hair and pinned it under her chin.

"I felt I needed a little peace and quiet." Al Shei folded her own *hijab* over her arm and laid it inside a drawer. "It's actually been a pretty busy few days."

"Hasn't it just." Resit picked up her carpet. "Are you going to perhaps tell me what's going on with Schyler?"

"Not yet. I'll know more tomorrow."

"Uh-huh. Should I be worrying about my air supply, Katmer?"

Al Shei stowed her carpet back in its drawer. "It's not that kind of problem, Zubedye."

"Well, that's something anyway." Resit opened the bathroom door. "I will be talking to you in the morning, Katmer."

"You will. I promise."

Resit crossed the bathroom into her own cabin through the opposite door.

When she was gone, Al Shei sealed the door to the hallway and touched the key beside it to signal anyone who might be walking by that she was not to be disturbed. No matter what her door said, she was always on immediate call for engineering. The *Pasadena* itself could summon her if any of half a dozen emergency switches were tripped.

With her door sealed, she finally let the weight of the day pull her shoulders down. That brief conversation with her cousin had robbed her of most of the calm that prayer instilled. She ran her fingers through her hair, fluffing it out and letting the slight breeze from the ventilators dry the film of dampness near her scalp. Unlike Resit, she had no cloud of long hair to shake down. She'd kept hers cut to a bob that would not get in her way. She stripped off her work clothes and debated a moment before tossing them into the laundry drawer, then slid her forest green kaftan over her bare shoulders and sighed contentedly. The kaftan had been a gift from Asil. It was real Earth-grown cotton. Cotton was grown only by permit on Earth. Most textile fibers came from vat-bred clones.

As she smoothed the kaftan down, Al Shei studied her face in the mirror. It was a good face, all in all, she admitted. Her brow was wide and clear, even though the worry wrinkles were beginning to etch themselves in deeper every year. Her aquiline nose was not too big, and her chin was not too pointed. She had an expressive mouth with lines around it that spoke more of smiles than of sorrows. Resit teased her that the real reason she wore the *hijab* was not just to hide the fact she'd cut her hair, but to emphasize her wide, almond-shaped eyes. Asil sometimes said it was her eyes that had bewitched his heart.

Vanity, vanity, she chided herself with a small laugh and turned away. *What are you doing? Seeing if the news about Tully has added any new lines?*

Al Shei folded her bed down from the wall and sat on the emerald faux silk coverlet, crossing her legs. She opened her hot-box and detached the fork from the cover.

"Intercom, playback," she said to the walls as she dug into the chicken curry and rice. "Asil Day Book, entry twelve."

There wasn't even a beep in response. Al Shei had taken them out for this command sequence. Instead, her husband's, clean, deep voice filled the empty spaces between her in-flight possessions and her inmost heart.

"Good morning, Beloved. Not much to report from yesterday, Katmer. It's a week before the rains are scheduled to begin and we had six hours of outside time left in the ration, so we had dinner on the terrace . . ."

Al Shei set the fork down, closed her eyes, and let her mind drift with the recorded voice. Her imagination was so trained for this that she could see every detail.

The low wooden table on the clean white stone, surrounded by piles of blue and green cushions that would have been tossed into place by Muhammad and Vashti. The children would have taken the opportunity to inflict an impromptu pummeling on each other, halted by mock threats from Asil. He would have set down the broad dish of *imam baldi* and flat bread. Asil was a traditionalist as far as food was concerned. The children, their hair blowing in the gentle breeze scented with the smells of living trees and roasting garlic, would scurry to the table and be told to calm down before helping themselves. They would, for about thirty seconds, then they'd begin digging each other in the ribs . . .

". . . Vashti told me she wants to try out for the soccer team next semester. Muhammad is talking seriously about summer classes for his astronomy. Looks as though the banks are going to lose another one, Katmer . . ."

Al Shei smiled and let the voice wash over her. This was how they kept together. Every day he made an entry in the verbal diary, just as she did. When she came home to stay, of course, they talked. They told each other everything, delighting in conversation. But on the last day, before she left again, they would solemnly exchange diaries. At home, in his own room, come back from his prayers, Asil would be listening to her voice reeling off an account of her previous flight. Although she knew, by now, that Vashti had made the soccer team and that Muhammad had been accepted to an academic camp in Tel Aviv, the Asil in the recording did not. His voice made it all new again and gave her those days that were the other half of her life, as Asil would have hers.

They could have used video, of course. They could have even each carried a small camera with them, but Asil had preferred imagination from the beginning. After the first trial, Al Shei had to agree. She thought in pictures anyway. With the diaries she had a whole memory full of pictures of her growing children and her steadfast beloved.

"I live two lifetimes," she'd told him once. "And both are full of what I love."

When the entry faded into silence, Al Shei opened her eyes. She sneaked a look at the door and the intercom. Both were silent and blank.

I can indulge. "Recall file," she said, stirring her curry. "*Mirror of Fate.*"

In the next heartbeat, a blue-line schematic for a packet ship flowed across the wall screen. This was the *Mirror of Fate.* It was almost twice the size of the *Pasadena*. Even without the crew, it had a Lennox rating of B. With a good crew, it would be A-rated. She ordered the intercom to scroll through the diagram to the family quarters. The ship had room for Muhammad, Vashti, and up to four other children, if any of her crew had families to bring along. In the *Mirror of Fate*, she and Asil would have one lifetime.

Next to the diagram the wall printed a tidy row of figures. Current savings, projected income from this trip, projected amount to be added to savings, remaining balance before they could have the *Mirror of Fate* commissioned.

She had designed the ship. Asil had designed the payment scheme. With him, money was not just a commodity to be tracked and traded. He saw endless possibilities embedded in what to her were meaningless statistics. Maybe that was how she had known she loved him, when she saw that he found possibilities in accounts the way she saw them in a ship's systems and that, like her, he lived to realize the possibilities he saw in his mind.

Mirror of Fate represented the grandest of all those possibilities. Freedom. Asil and the children and their possibilities in a home she had made and a ship that worked under her hands and eyes and inner vision. She'd dreamed this ship all the years she was learning her trade. When Asil entered her life, they dreamed it together and together, no matter how long the runs lasted, they still dreamed.

It was a sweet dream and she savored it slowly, like fine coffee. She sipped it gently and let it roll across her senses and warm her from the inside. It would happen. Another three years' work, four at the very outside. *Pasadena*'s upgraded rating would bring in . . .

". . . so you *tell* the Ninja Woman I am *not* going to put up with . . ."

The strident voice jolted Al Shei out of her reverie. She started and dropped a forkful of curry onto her plate.

". . . this kind of crap from a bunch of bigoted . . ."

Yerusha. The stun bled away and Al Shei was able to identify the voice clanging through the intercom.

"And the thunder crashed in a mighty cacophony and all did tremble and shake at the oath that could make the stars ring!" There was a shuffling of cloth and silence. Dobbs.

Whatever she had done had caught Yerusha so off guard she wasn't able to respond.

"Intercom to Yerusha," said Al Shei. "Yerusha. The comm's on and I want to talk to you and whoever you're yelling at with the watch commander."

More silence. "Yes, Engineer," came the answer finally.

"Intercom to Watch Command," said Al Shei.

"It's okay, Engineer," came back Schyler's voice. "I'm the one she was yelling at, myself and the Houston."

"Obviously,there is a problem with the intercom," said Al Shei drily.

"Obviously," cut in Chandra, "unless you really meant this conversation to hit the galley."

"Walls are supposed to have ears, but *tongues* . . ." chipped in Dobbs. "Do you suppose they gossip about us during the night shift, too?"

"All right, all right," said Schyler. "Obviously we need a meeting, now."

"Obviously," agreed Al Shei. "Lipinski, who's on comm watch? I want whatever's wrong with the intercom routing fixed. I'll meet all of you in the conference room. Intercom to Close." She looked regretfully at the *Mirror of Fate*. "Store file." She stuffed another forkful of curry into her mouth before she closed the box lid and popped it into a drawer. "Why do I have the feeling this is going to be one of my more interesting runs?"

She changed back into her working clothes and wrapped her *hijab* back around her face.

By the time she reached the conference room, Schyler, Lipinski, and Yerusha were already there. So was Dobbs, Al Shei noticed as the hatch cycled closed. The Fool, disdaining any of the available chairs, sat cross-legged in the corner, resting her elbows on her knees. Al Shei suppressed a sigh. According to contract, the Fool could not be excluded from any crew meeting, including disciplinary hearings, but Al Shei really could have done without her presence.

Yerusha sat with her arms folded and a look of studied blandness on her face. Lipinski was frowning at the pilot and giving her a look that could peel paint. Schyler had one hand laid on the tabletop and was dividing his attention between the two recalcitrant crew members.

"All right, Watch." Al Shei leaned and rested her hands on the back of one of the chairs. "What happened?"

Schyler turned toward her. There was an odd light in his eye that Al Shei couldn't quite interpret. "Pilot Yerusha was found to be working with an unregistered hardware/software interface using the ship's systems . . ."

Yerusha sat up straighter in her chair and unfolded her arms. "I was testing a wafer stack to make sure it was intact," she countered. "In my own cabin, on a secured, internal . . ."

"You were letting an AI loose in my system!" thundered Lipinski.

Yerusha started to her feet. "You have no right to spy on a secured . . ."

"It's my job to make sure there's nothing here that's not registered . . ."

"So what made you decide to keep a special eye on my line, you ground-hugging . . ."

"Enough!" Schyler slammed his hand against the table. The pair subsided.

"Thank you, Watch," said Al Shei. She turned a little so she could face Yerusha but still keep her eye on Lipinski. "Have you got an artificial intelligence rated wafer stack with you?"

Yerusha bridled. "You do not have the right to question me about legal possessions."

Al Shei inclined her head. "You're right, of course." She turned toward Schyler. "Has she got an AI wafer stack?"

"I saw her carrying something that could have been an AI. From the stats Houston showed me, it's very probable she had it cabled into the system." Schyler answered blandly.

Al Shei nodded and faced Yerusha again. The woman's cheeks were starting to pale, and her hand clenched into a fist at her side. "Is it your foster?" Al Shei asked.

Yerusha jumped as though she'd been stung. "What do you know about our fosters?"

"It is one of the Freers' more . . . publicized goals." Al Shei kept her voice level. "I know they're AIs assigned to—sorry, adopted by—individual Freers who want to have a go at creating an environment which could hold a human soul. I know a departed human soul making a home in an AI environment is considered to be the root cause for the AI breakouts like the ones on Edgeward and Kerensk. I also know there's some sort of lottery involved in who gets to be a 'parent.' " *I also know you've never had a single success with it, which is why you're still sitting here talking to me and not confined to quarters with the thing in Lipinski's hands.* She let her eyes narrow. "It's not a very popular program in some circles." She very deliberately did not look toward Lipinski.

Yerusha's knuckles were turning as white as her cheeks. "I have a right under my contract to bring aboard any legal piece of software that I choose, as long as I don't infect the ship's systems or go over my allotted weight limit."

Al Shei waved her hand and suppressed an urge to laugh. "Oh, stop bristling, will you? I'm not interested in taking it away from you, or saying you broke contract by bringing it aboard. But I want to know if you were really going to let it loose?"

"Here?" Yerusha snorted. "You joke better than your Fool. I would never expose my foster to a crew of complete paranoids."

"Good," said Al Shei. "We don't have room in the system for it anyway, do we Houston?" She cocked her eye at Lipinski.

"Hardly," said Lipinski to the floor.

"And because it is a legal program, and we've all got plenty to keep us busy on shift, there's not going to be any more ideological shouting matches. Right?" She looked straight at Schyler.

"We've already discussed the matter," he replied.

"Glad to hear it." Al Shei lifted her hands off the chair back and smoothed down her tunic sleeves. "Because I'd really hate this to be the first run where we docked anybody for violating the courtesy and privacy clauses in their contracts." She glanced first at Lipinski, then at Yerusha. "Is there anything else?"

Lipinski got up. "I guess not," he said. "I'm going to see how Rosvelt's doing on the intercom problem." He left without another word or look to anybody.

The hatch cycled shut and Yerusha leaned forward.

Al Shei made a slicing gesture across her throat. "Before you say anything, I know Lipinski is a paranoiac. He may also be a bigot. Deal with it. You have to work with everyone else, and they have to work with you. If you can't get your job done because of behavior problems, you *talk* to Watch. If I catch you shouting names across the bridge again, I may decide to pitch you off of here as soon as we get to The Farther Kingdom. And before you feel too picked on, I may decide to do the same to Lipinski." Her mouth twitched. "It's hard being one of a kind. I know Freers consider Moslems barbarians . . ." Yerusha had the grace to look away at that. "In fact, they consider all us groundhogs, barbarians, and you're pretty much not allowed to like any of us." Rebellion surged across Yerusha's face, but she was bright enough not to say anything. "I understand what it's like to be set apart by your beliefs. I also understand this gives you a great temptation to lie, and cover up, and hide. I've done it, so I know that aboard a small ship that only leads to trouble. Maybe disaster. That I won't have, just as I won't have personal prejudices getting in the way of my crew getting our mutual job done. We are all here, and we can't rely on one Fool to keep us from each other's throats. Do your job, Yerusha, and stow the stack until we get to port, all right? And rest assured that now that we've been alerted to the problem, Watch will make sure Lipinski doesn't interfere with anything that doesn't interfere with the ship or its cargo."

"Aye, aye, 'Dama." Yerusha got to her feet. She cocked an eye at Schyler. "Can I go?"

Schyler nodded, and Yerusha left. As soon as the hatch cycled closed, he folded his arms and looked at Al Shei. She waved a weary hand at him. "Don't say it, Tom." She fell into Turkish. "Just don't."

He shrugged. "All I was going to say was this time you may finally have found the one who refuses to make it easy on herself."

"She's proud, she's scared, and she's totally on her own. It'll make you act funny." Al Shei stood up. "She is not, however, totally stupid, and I do believe she needs this job. She'll behave." She made sure her smile crinkled the corners of her eyes. "Who knows? In time she might even be likable. It's happened before."

"Are you talking about me or you, Mother?"

"Impudence," she snorted. "Go get some supper. You're no good to me starved and sleepy."

He grinned. "The hell I'm not." He cycled the hatch open.

"And don't swear," she said to his back, as he strode out the hatch.

"Nice job." Dobbs stood up in the corner. Now it was Al Shei's turn to jump. She'd completely forgotten the Fool was in the room.

Dobbs grinned. "Believe it or not, we get training in unobtrusiveness. I got an A in the course."

"That much I do believe." Al Shei smoothed her *hijab* down. "I hope I can count on you to keep an extra eye on Yerusha and Lipinski. A holy war is not something I need aboard my ship."

Dobbs snapped to attention and saluted briskly. "Yes, Ma'am!"

Al Shei waved her away. "Aren't you off shift, too?"

Dobbs relaxed her stance and grinned. "Cooks, owners, and Fools. We're never off shift."

"No, I guess we're not." Al Shei cycled the hatch open. Dobbs bowed deeply and gestured for her to go first. Al Shei did. The Fool took off in the opposite direction, maybe on her way to her own cabin or to catch up with Yerusha and find out how well she took Al Shei's lecture.

As she remembered the anger flashing between Yerusha's and Lipinski's eyes, Al Shei suddenly felt very glad the Fool was aboard.

Chapter Three

FASTER THAN LIGHT

Dobbs watched the clean, white side of the unnamed tanker fill the square of her view screen. The tanker would top off *Pasadena*'s fuel and reaction mass and send the ship on to the jump point. The *Pasadena* gave itself a final nudge sideways. Far away, Dobbs heard a faint *clang* reverberate through the hull as the two ships hooked together.

Dobbs, fastened to her desk chair by her free-fall straps, found herself admiring Yerusha. The woman's skills were certainly not overbilled. Hooking up with a refueling tanker could be a rough ride if one or the other of the pilots weren't spot-on with their calculations. As a result, it was standard operating procedure to have the crew strapped into their seats during refueling.

Usually time in her straps made her restless. She had never quite mastered the art of sitting still. This time, though, Dobbs was glad of the chance to think.

She had been right—this was going to be an interesting assignment, and not just because Lipinski and Resit were resistant to the idea that they might have to get along with Yerusha. Al Shei's mood had her engineers tiptoeing around, and, on the bridge, Schyler wasn't doing much more than grunting out orders when necessary. Dobbs had spent the last six hours bouncing between the two departments, but her best efforts were yielding minimal results.

It didn't take a whole lot of looking to see that there was

something more than an intercom malfunction operating in the background. Just a little more looking showed that that something was probably Marcus Tully.

She glanced toward the door and then toward her screen, where the view was totally blotted out by the tanker's side.

Now might be the best time to get some research going, she thought, then rejected the idea. The refueling would take awhile, but not as long as her researches, and if she was caught out of her straps for some reason, Schyler would give her a good going-over. It was one of the strange double standards applied to Fools. Technically, Fools could get away with anything, but they had to be extremely careful not to be caught at anything serious. If they did, their reputation for foolishness would change to one for stupidity, or, worse, untrustworthiness. Neither was something any Fool could afford.

Research would have to be done later, though. She needed a full bio on Marcus Tully and another on Jemina Yerusha. Her file, downloaded from the ship's book, was next to useless. Like Schyler and Al Shei, Yerusha was holding something back. It might be something totally unrelated to whatever was marring the mood of senior crew, but it was there all the same.

Dobbs chuckled and shook her head ruefully. *What's this ship run on? Hydrogen and boron or secrets and mysteries?*

She'd spent a chunk of the previous evening in the galley with the Sundars. Like Fools and Chief Engineers, a ship's galley crew never really went off shift. Harry Dalziel, the steward, was the one on official active duty. He split his time between the kitchen and the laundry. At the same time, Baldassare pored over films detailing the menus and cross-referencing them with the inventory the ship carried versus the inventory he needed to acquire at the next stop. Chandra had brought their AI box in from the sick bay and perched it on the corner of the central counter so she could update the crew health records from the notes she'd made during the day.

"Actually, most of Al Shei's crews are as straightforward as you could want to serve with," said Baldassare. "She and Schyler don't have much use for the brooding type who takes to the stars to forget."

"Or to dodge the greens," added Chandra. "Recent circumstances notwithstanding."

"Ah, Grandmother Chandra, I see through you." Dobbs waggled her finger at Chandra. "You're talking about Yerusha, but are too polite to name names."

Chandra snorted. "Hardly. Yerusha may be a problem child, but the greens are not a problem for her any more than they are for any other Freer with a loud mouth."

"Isn't that redundant?" remarked Baldassare.

"When did you join the Fool's Guild?" asked Dobbs.

"The day I was born, girl, the day I was born," he answered amicably.

"What I was saying," cut in Chandra, "is that everybody is here because they want to be, not because they have to be. It makes all the difference."

"It does depend on what you mean by 'have to be,' " mused Baldassare. "Al Shei does have a way of finding people who really need her. Tully, Schyler, Lipinski . . . "

"Lipinski?" Dobbs's eyebrows shot up of their own accord.

Baldassare nodded. "Lipinski needs a place he can work without interacting with AIs. He was actually an apprentice on a comm-crew when Kerensk went down. It hit him hard, and I don't think he's had much help getting over it."

"Which explains his problems with Yerusha. He can't think much of a people who perceive independent AIs as close to gods." Dobbs sipped her tea. As long as humans had sailed in ships, no one knew more about crew dynamics than the galley crew. It made them a Fool's natural allies, and Dobbs was always careful to cultivate their friendship. She was glad the Sundars were so amenable.

"At bottom, Lipinski is a reasonable man," said Chandra. "Loud, but reasonable. He'll work around it, especially if he's prodded."

Another faint clang shook Dobbs out of her reverie. On the screen, the tanker fell away against the blackness.

"Intercom to *Pasadena*. Secure from refueling," came Schyler's voice through the speaker. "Four hours to jump."

Dobbs snapped the catches on her straps and folded the chair back into the wall. Part of her training at Guild Hall had been how to live optimally in confined spaces. She had draped swaths of green-and-blue painted faux silk across the walls to help soften the corners. She had mounted her two flexible memory boards on opposite walls from each other. One showed a starscape, the other a sunny day in the green hills of Ireland. She had never been there in the flesh, but she liked to look at it. On the wall next to the desk hung a full-length, faux-glass mirror. Like Al Shei, she had piles of pillows in the corners of her cabin, fastened down with Velcro to keep them from floating around during free fall. The overall effect was an airy, comfortable one, and Dobbs was quite pleased with what she'd been able to accomplish with her thirty-five pounds.

"So, prod I shall." Dobbs struck a pose in front of her mirror. "Until the very rivets of the *Pasadena* ring with the mighty shouts of accord between Jemina Yerusha and Rurik Lipinski!" She shook her fist toward the ceiling, took a good look at her reflection, and laughed.

Maybe I should put in a call to the Guild, though, she thought, turning away from the mirror and smoothing her tunic down. *Not due to report in for another week, but maybe I should get an advisor on for this run.* She opened her night drawer and put her juggling scarves inside. She took out a flattened spray of paper flowers and tucked them into her right-hand pocket. Four shiny gold coins went into her other pocket. It was important to rotate her props on a regular basis to preserve the element of surprise. She decided against the knotted chain of colored handkerchiefs that she carried up her left sleeve. That particular display did not seem to go over well with this crew.

She hooked her finger around her necklace and contemplated the flat, black box in the bottom of the drawer that held her private communications equipment.

In the back of her mind, she heard Amelia Verence chiding her. "Dobbs, you have got to learn the balancing act," said her tutor and sponsor. "The Guild is a safety net, an information resource, and a backup, but it can't do your job for you. Master of Craft means you've mastered working on your own."

"You're right," she said aloud to the memory. "I just wish I knew what about this run is making me feel so . . . young."

She shoved the drawer back into the wall. "Enough stalling, Dobbs," she told herself. "Time to go to work."

Lipinski first, she thought as she breezed out into the corridor with her professionally cheerful expression fixed on her face. Yerusha she could tackle later, after they'd made the jump past lightspeed.

Dobbs took the stairs down to the comm center. *Pasadena* was a clean ship, but the inside of the comm center gleamed. All transmissions were captured using the center's main boards. Then, they were screened to verify that they contained only what they were contracted to contain and nothing else. After that, they would be transferred into their prepared storage space behind the sealed hatches of the data-hold.

The repair benches, transmission boards, and duty stations were all to one side. The other side had its own hatches, sealing the main storage facilities away from the rest of the ship. One of the repair benches had its lid closed and the red lock-light was shining, indicating somebody was doing some secure work. Dobbs filed that fact away for later.

Odel, Lipinski's relief, sat at Station Three, the coordination board. He glanced up with one round black eye as Dobbs stepped through the hatch.

"If you really want to be here," he whispered, "you are a bigger fool than you look."

Dobbs snapped her fingers. "That's what I forgot to do. Work on that dimensional relativity control."

Odel snorted. "Fine, take your own chances when the bodies start flying."

"Bodies? Linear!" Dobbs rubbed her hands together.

Station One, the main transmission station, was a standard board-and-chair setup. Lipinski sat on the deck next to the chair. One of the repair hatches was open in front of him, and he bent so far inside it that his long nose was almost touching the exposed wiring. Above him, Yerusha leaned over the station's memory boards.

Yerusha glanced up as Dobbs moved past Odel, but Lipinski didn't. He plucked a pair of tweezers off his belt and reached into the circuits. He pulled a chip out of its socket and replaced it with a fresh one.

"Now?" he asked Yerusha.

Yerusha prodded the board with one finger. "No response."

Looks like the intercom wasn't the end of our problems. Dobbs sighed inwardly. *What is going* on?

She thought about the sealed workbench, and then about the infamous and dubious Marcus Tully trying to retrieve something he'd left behind, and a seed of real worry planted itself in her mind.

"So, why aren't they running a diagnostic?" she whispered out of the corner of her mouth to Odel.

He looked up at her mournfully. "The system ate the diagnostic."

Dobbs let her eyes go round. "Ate?" she mouthed silently.

Odel nodded.

"If this ship had an AI, we wouldn't be having this problem," muttered Yerusha. Odel squirmed visibly. It didn't take more than that glance to see he wished that an emergency would crop up to which he could respond. Dobbs remembered Lipinski's boast about being hell on apprentice comm crews.

"If this ship had an AI"—Lipinski stuck the original chip back in its socket and shifted his weight to pluck out the next one—"we'd have a whole new set of problems. Now?"

Dobbs lifted up onto tiptoe and with exaggerated steps picked a path to stand behind Lipinski. Yerusha just watched with a resigned air. Dobbs folded her hands behind her back and leaned over the Houston.

"It'd be much the same," he said to the chip, "as having someone in the cabin who doesn't belong here." Dobbs's shadow blocked his light. He rolled his eyes up. "Two someones. Who spend a lot of time poking into things that aren't their job."

Dobbs wiggled her fingers to wave hello at him.

"The piloting system is my responsibility," countered Yerusha. "All of it."

"And internal communications, which are going straight to hell . . ." Lipinski set the chip back into its socket and began following a single silver tracing along the dull green surface of the circuit wafer. "Are mine. All of them."

Dobbs's mind raced. The boards in the comm center were connected to the bridge because the Houston needed to know exactly where the ship was in relation to the pickup coordinates when the ship was doing a flyby data-grab. If he didn't, he would not be able to activate the capture programs in time to catch the data being transmitted to them. A few dozen kilometers could make the difference between a clean capture and a load of garbled and incomplete data.

With both of them here and on the edge, that link must be off. Completely down or, worse, off by a deceptively small amount.

"Now?" asked Lipinski, reaching between the wafers with the tweezers again.

"Nothing," reported Yerusha.

"So what in Settled Space is screwing them up like this!" He yanked his head out of the hatch. Dobbs jumped backwards. "Huh? What?" he demanded of Yerusha. "This ship was in order until we got under way. I checked. I know these crashing, burned-out, chewed, and regurgitated boards like I know my rosary. This should not be happening!"

"Still wishing you could crawl in there?" Dobbs asked cheerfully before Yerusha could respond to the outburst. She peered into the repair hatch at the layers of circuit wafers.

"Can't fit." Lipinski rested his weight on his heels and stared at the wafers, brooding. "You might be small enough, though." He tucked his tweezers back into his belt pocket. "You want to pop in there and find out what's wrong?"

Dobbs pulled back from the hatch and shook her head. "I already tried. Way too cramped for me. You've got it filled to the gills."

Yerusha was, apparently, in no mood to let things slide. "If . . ."

"Wishes were fishes we'd all cast nets," said Dobbs brightly. "Or so I've heard." She put her head to one side and twiddled her thumbs pensively. "Although I don't see why, such a mess to clean them and the smell, phew!" She coughed violently and waved her hand in front of her face.

Yerusha stared at her, possibly trying to work out all the references. As dedicated a Freer as she seemed to be, she had probably never even seen a live fish, let alone caught one.

It did, however, apparently make her forget what she was about to say.

Lipinski was also staring. "Dobbs," he said quietly, "you're in my light."

She skipped backwards, until her shadow fell across the unoccupied floor, and bowed. She gave Yerusha a wink and an "oh well," gesture and took her leave. As the hatch closed behind her, she willed them both to use their brains and not their tempers. They both must know that with only three hours until they made the jump, this was a dangerous fault to be left uncorrected. As such, it was no place for her clowning.

Lipinski's hard voice echoed in her ears, *This ship was in order until we got under way. This should not be happening!*

You're right, Houston, but it is, which leaves a big, burning question.

The sound of a hatch opening drifted up the shaft. Dobbs looked down automatically, and saw Ianiai's black-haired head and stuck-out ears. She stuck her fingers into her teeth and whistled shrilly.

The sound echoed all around the shaft. Ianiai looked up, and Dobbs leaned over the rail, waving. He made a gesture which, from the scowl on his face, wasn't meant to be polite, and swung himself over the railing onto the support staples. He hitched his belt to the rail for safety.

Uh-huh. Dobbs trotted down the stairs to the galley. *The off-shift reliefs are on and in foul moods. This is not a good sign.*

The galley deck was quiet. Following the entire corridor around, Dobbs couldn't hear any of the exercise equipment working or any voices from the recreation rooms. She poked her head into the kitchen. Cheney was gulping a coffee beside the urn. The only other person in evidence was Dalziel, the steward, watching a cleaning drone scour the floor.

Dobbs ducked back out into the hallway. She briefly considered taking herself down to Engineering to see if she could wheedle any information out of Al Shei but decided against it. One of the tricks a Fool had to learn was when to leave the crew completely alone.

I'll bet my Master's rank that now is one of those.

She took herself back up the stairs to the berthing deck.

However, she thought as she entered her cabin, *without accurate information, I can't do my job either.*

She locked the hatch and set the entrance light to red, indicating she did not want to be disturbed. She unfolded her desk from the wall and laid her first two fingers on the activation key. The board switched on, setting the keys glowing.

Dobbs sat down in the real chair and pulled her pen out of her belt pocket. She tapped it against her palm while she eyed the board thoughtfully.

Prepare to accept search and recovery program, she wrote across the main board.

Ready, responded the desk.

She plugged her pen into the desk's socket. After a long moment, the desk wrote *Program loaded.*

Dobbs retrieved her pen.

Is Al Shei's pen active in the ship's system? she wrote.

Active.

Timing is everything, thought Dobbs. She wrote. *Program D1 procedure name Tunneling. Locate and copy data on search target.*

She stuck her pen back into the socket and sat back.

If Al Shei had known what Dobbs was doing, she probably could have shoved the Fool out the airlock without any of the crew blinking. Some of them probably would even have helped. Schyler, for instance.

All computer systems had security measures that prevented someone from tapping into an active pen from a remote terminal. The Fool's Guild had invested years in designing a search-and-recover program that could work its way around most of them. Dobbs was a couple of updates behind, but since the *Pasadena* under Al Shei was noted for quiet runs and a trustworthy crew, she didn't expect to have any trouble getting through.

Then, the desk beeped.

Unable to complete request.

Dobbs straightened up. She pulled the desk's pen out of its holder and wrote *Explain.*

Inadequate configured pathway space.

"Inadequate!" She swore. "Lipinski, I was kidding about the place being full . . ."

Then the desk wrote, *Request complete. Information loaded into desk.*

Dobbs sat very still for a long moment. Then she wrote, *Load D1 security program and seal desk.*

Program loaded and desk secured.

Dobbs pulled her pen out of the socket and shut the desk down. She folded it away and sat for a long time, doing nothing but stare at the walls.

Now, what, she thought, over and over, *could have caused that?*

After the better part of an hour, she still did not like any of her answers.

This was the moment. Al Shei's heartbeat quickened even though she was doing nothing but sitting at her station. This was where it all came together, the planning and the scrambling and the inspection and the programming. No matter how well traveled their route, this was where they left known space behind and went on alone, powered and protected by the tiny world that they had made for themselves.

As always, she was torn between an almost childish excitement, and a bittersweet memory. Last night, in Asil's journal he had said, "I am having Muhammad point out all your stars to me, Beloved, and when he goes to bed, I shall tell each one to remind you of my love."

His voice ran strong through her mind, even as she heard Yerusha's voice from the intercom. "Four minutes to jump."

"Four minutes," Al Shei answered. Yerusha and Lipinski had managed to fix the timing fault without killing each other. Al Shei decided to take that as a good sign for the rest of the jump.

The clock on the board turned over the seconds. She checked the pressure monitors on the pipes carrying the reaction mass from the tanks to the accumulators.

The *Pasadena* ran on magnetically confined fusion. Her mind's eye stripped away the shell of metal and ceramic between her and the tanks and she saw the stream of $boron_{11}$ pellets rattling down the pipes into the midline injector where the electric arc fired, vaporizing the pellets and letting the electrostatic fields shoot the ionized gas into the gasdynamic mirror chamber. An upstream injector fired a thin stream of precious antiprotons down the long axis of the mirror chamber, providing energy and ions to spark the fusion reaction. The plasma ignited into a bright fury.

Resit once asked her what it was like to think in equations. Al Shei had looked at her blankly. Equations weren't what you thought in. Equations were what you spouted off for the professors and the inspectors. She thought in pictures, in video sequences. If you did *this* and *this* and *this*, then that would happen.

The heated gas, already supersonic, speeded up as it expanded into the traveling-wave coils that compressed the plasma in an annular magnetic field which was passed from coil to coil down the length of the traveling-wave tube.

Ancient physical principles applied over and again. Energy built and built until it had to be used up or thrown off.

"Plasma flow redirected," reported Javerri, just as Al Shei's board traced a new route for the burning river.

Now the plasma would not be vented out the *Pasadena*'s aft nozzle to push the ship forward. It would run upstream into the homopolar accumulators. It took a massive push to kick the ship into fast-time space, and another to bring it back into real time. The accumulators stored up the power to make that jump.

"Jump threshold in five . . . four . . . three . . ."

"Torch out," called Ianiai.

"*Bismillahir*," murmured Al Shei. In the name of Allah. In her imagination, she saw the bright blue flame beneath her feet wink out.

". . . Two . . . One. Now."

Al Shei's hand came down on the board's central key. A barely perceptible vibration filtered through the deck plates. Her imagination supplied an accompanying rumble.

The accumulators fired. A small weight pressed against the center of her chest like a balled-up fist, and it was over. Now light was straining to catch up with them. Now the view screens showed nothing but the curving silver refraction wall that would stay in place until they got where they were going.

Despite an unfamiliar impatience scratching at her insides, Al Shei checked her boards carefully. "Station One reports all normal and in sync," she called out. Once she had satisfactory replies from her crew, she undid her straps and stood up.

"Relief!" Ianiai gave her his mocking salute. In no mood to banter, Al Shei just gave him a warning glare as he took her seat. Her silence brought him up short like no verbal warning would have, and he immediately turned his attention to the boards.

Al Shei started up the stairs toward the data-hold. Footsteps sounded above her. Schyler was descending from the bridge. He gave her a small wave, but he was too far away for her to see his face. She could not, however, picture a smile on it.

He waited for her one step above the hatchway.

"The moment of truth?" he inquired, attempting to sound lighthearted. His tone fell very flat.

"I doubt it." She stepped through the hatchway into the corridor. "Not the way Lipinski works."

"He's glacial, I'll admit it. Slow, but nothing can get out of his way."

"We hope." Al Shei palmed the hatch reader for the comm center.

Lipinski was on his own in the center. If Al Shei had set her relief shaking with a quiet glance, Lipinski had probably set his running with a thunderous shout.

Whatever had happened, there was only Lipinski bent over the worktable with a needle-thin tracer in his hand, talking to whatever didn't move away, as usual.

"Could've managed to burn just a little more off and made it really hard for me, couldn't you? Why do half . . ."

"Is there anything there at all?" Al Shei came to stand by the table.

Lipinski lifted the tracer away from the ruined surface of the wafer stack. "Not a lot."

Lipinski hadn't been exaggerating. The stack's delicate etchings were marred by wide black patches that made Al Shei think she should be smelling charcoal.

"So, what can you tell us?" She leaned both forearms on the bench and folded her hands.

"It's not a regular stack." Lipinski laid the tracer back in its pocket in the workbench drawer. "It's for storing binary data."

"Binary?" Al Shei felt her eyebrows arch.

Lipinski nodded. "Straight ones and zeros. Yes and no. On and off. Very blunt. If you know what you're doing, you can work some pretty fancy programs and data storage with it, but if you try to let any binary programming loose into a regular fuzzy-logic stack, you've got the proverbial bull in a china shop. Fuzzy boards work with gradiations and percentages. Binary data are all or nothing."

"Can you tell what happened here?" asked Schyler quietly. He had his hands jammed in his pockets. From the bulges in the fabric, Al Shei guessed he also had them balled into fists.

Lipinski looked at the wall as if taking its measure, then looked back at Schyler. "Tully stored some binary data, transferred it somewhere, blanked the stack, then burned it with a pin laser." He pushed the bench drawer shut. "Then, my guess is, he expected me to take them to recycling. When I didn't, he apparently came looking for them." He jerked his chin toward Schyler. "Thanks to Watch's sticking to the rules as though he's been vacuum-welded, Tully did not get them."

Al Shei's jaw began to work itself slowly back and forth. When she spoke, her voice was much harsher than she'd intended.

"Why didn't he just trash them?"

"Ah." Lipinski raised one finger. "I expect that's because they were still important. I expect that he was storing the binary data in those reconfigured boards I had to deal with back in port. Then he transferred the data into one or more of the chips on these three stacks, probably where it's most covered in carbon, and I expect he's annoyed because I've got it and he doesn't."

"And I expect," Al Shei straightened up, "that my oh-so-clever-and-honored Houston can find that data for me."

Lipinski gave her the ghost of a smile. "If you give him enough time, 'Dama Engine, I expect he can."

"Then I expect he should get a torch burning under it." She touched her fingers to her forehead in salute. Lipinski nodded and hunched over the board, completely absorbed in the problem before Schyler even had the hatch cycled open.

"This just keeps getting more and more interesting, doesn't it?" he remarked at the hatch closed.

Al Shei didn't say anything. She walked up about ten steps. She heard his footsteps following her, dull thuds bouncing off the nearby wall.

She turned to face him. "Have you made any progress at all in finding out where whatever is on those boards came from?"

Schyler shook his head tiredly. "I've been glued to the system logs and analyzing every comma and semi-colon for double meanings. Tully may have left stolen goods on board, but he didn't leave any records to go with them." He cycled the stair hatch open. "I'll need some credit so I can make some fast-time calls as soon as we reach The Farther Kingdom. I've got some friends who might know something."

Al Shei nodded. "I'll dig it out for you." Inwardly, she sighed. *Guess what, Uncle Ahmet? I'm doing something for the family this trip after all.*

Schyler met her eyes again. "There's an addutional possibility we need to consider."

"Oh?" Al Shei laid her hand on the railing.

"We've been having an unholy lot of comm system trouble already this run," he said. "Maybe what Lipinski is tracking isn't entirely stored on those stacks."

Al Shei sighed and rubbed her forehead. "I thought of that." Confidential data, particularly military data, often had viruses built into its structure that were meant to get out and wreak whatever system had tried to steal it. "If he's left a virus in here, I'm not just going to denounce him in front of my sister, I'm going to string him up by his thumbs."

Schyler shrugged heavily. "Well, maybe Lipinski was right. Maybe it's just that our new pilot is a saboteur."

"I'm not sure which would be worse."

A hatchway cycled closed beneath them. They both stiffened automatically. Light, quick footsteps raced up the stairs.

Al Shei and Schyler both pressed themselves against the wall as the Fool breezed past them. She stopped on the galley landing just above them and crouched on it. Al Shei looked up and down the stairway, trying to work out what she was running from.

In her hands, Dobbs held what looked like a fat spring. It must have been fairly loosely coiled, because she had no problem laying one end on the landing and one end on the next stair so that the spring made an arch from one to the other. Then, while Al Shei was still trying to sort out what was going on, Dobbs flipped the end on the landing up and over the end on the stair. The spring's own momentum repeated the motion. With a soft "ching, ching," noise, the spring began walking down the stairs.

All Al Shei could do was stare as the thing ching-chinged past her with the Fool practically on its heels.

Dobbs grinned at them. "Linear, isn't it? North American toy from before the Fast Burn. I've got a bet on with Javerri that I can get it to walk all the way from the bridge to Engineering." She skipped down the next couple of stairs. "This is the dry run," she explained, before turning her attention to the walking spring. "Come on! You can do it! Mary Mother of God, I don't believe what I'm seeing! Come on! You've got to be able to do better than that!" She sounded amazingly like Lipinski, but hopping sideways down the stairs she looked like some manic circus clown.

Schyler tried to stifle his laughter, but it came out as a snuffling wheeze. Al Shei allowed herself to smile.

"She's got that thing rigged," she remarked softly. "She must, or it'd be walking into the walls. Javerri's taking a sucker bet."

"And she'll chase Dobbs twice around the berthing deck when she catches on, and I do believe, Mother, that our Fool will be sure she catches on." He shook his head. He was still smiling. Al Shei realized he had no idea of what had just struck her.

"All right," she said to him. "You've got an hour left on your shift. If you don't get back on station, I'm going to have the watch commander review your record."

He took a deep breath. "Right." He ran his hand through his hair, which, Al Shei noticed with a start, was beginning to thin on top. "I'll see you at dinner."

"Right behind you."

They climbed up the stairs, all the while hearing the Fool's shouts of encouragement to her walking spring. When they reached the berthing deck, Al Shei left Schyler and opened the hatchway. In the corridor, she passed Javerri and Brand, the third-shift bridge watch, probably on their way to breakfast. She waved to them but passed without another comment.

In her cabin, Al Shei sat in the desk chair. She'd left the day book recorder on the desktop.

She picked the palm-sized rectangle up and turned it over in her fingers. On its own, her mind drifted back to their last night together before she'd left on this run. They'd spent the day with the children on the monorail, looking out at the regrown wilderness beneath the last set of blast mountains. Then, with Muhammed and Vashti finally tucked into bed, and all of Bala house still and quiet around them, they'd gone into the tiled courtyard to sit beside the fountain and let the Moon shine on them through the Plexiglas ceiling.

"Has it lost its charm for you?" Asil asked, wrapping his arm around her shoulders.

"What? Marriage?" She undid her *hijab* and bared her face to him. "Only when Vashti pitched a fit over not being allowed a second ice cream."

"I meant the Moon." He nodded up at the silver crescent. "You've been up there so many times, seen how dead and dusty it is. Doesn't that spoil nighttime for you?"

She followed his gaze and smiled. "No, actually, it makes the wonder greater. All that dead dust is silver light for us. All those suns"—she swept her hand out—"are life for their worlds and beauty for us. It's all alive and complex and beautiful beyond description." She glanced at him and saw the grin that spread all across his face. "And you are laughing at an engineer's attempt to wax eloquent."

"I am not." He dropped a serious expression into place that lasted all of two seconds before the smile crept back. "All right, maybe I am." He brushed her bare cheek with his finger. "But I am also basking in the glow of my wife, who is so beautiful, she is like a second moon in the sky."

He'd bent to kiss her then, and everything else faded away.

Name of God, Beloved, Al Shei thought toward Asil's memory. *I hope this has all worked out by the time you hear about it.* She shut the recorder into the drawer.

"Intercom to Dobbs," she said to the wall.

After a moment, the Fool's voice came through. "Dobbs here, Boss." Al Shei could still hear a faint "ching-ching" in the background.

"I'd like to see you in my cabin, 'Dama Fool. Immediately."

The ching-ching silenced. "On my way, Boss."

"Intercom to close." Al Shei pictured Dobbs setting her spring carefully into one of her multiple pockets, sealing it thoughtfully, then taking the stairs two at a time.

In less than three minutes, a knock sounded on the cabin hatch. Dobbs breezed in and bowed elaborately.

"At your service, 'Dama Al Shei," she said as the door shut behind her. She folded herself up to sit cross-legged on the floor. "What may your Fool do for you?"

"She may tell me how much she overheard," said Al Shei.

Dobbs laid her hand on her breast and screwed a wounded look onto her mobile face. "Eavesdropping? Me? I am hurt, I am outraged, I am . . ." Al Shei didn't let her eyes flicker. Dobbs lowered her hand. "Potentially out of a job," she finished.

Al Shei tugged at her tunic sleeve. "I only heard the hatch cycle once. You must have been on the stairs when we started talking."

Dobbs looked up, and, for the first time, Al Shei saw her wearing an absolutely straight face. "Have to watch that," she said. "As to what I heard, I heard all of it." She spread her hands. "If you're worried I'm going to use it as a matter for joking . . ."

Al Shei shook her head abruptly. "That kind of fool, I know you are not." Her English became awkward as old, uncomfortable memories tugged at her for attention, and she wished she could drop into Turkish.

Al Shei fiddled with her sleeve for a minute, then let her hand fall away.

"For the life of me, I still don't know why my sister fell in love with Marcus Tully, but she did. Because I understood what it was like to want something that most of the family disapproved of, I never tried to talk her out of the marriage.

"It took awhile to patch things up, with our grandmothers and uncles, but Ruqaiyya's always been good at that." Al Shei paused, remembering her younger sister standing at the low supper table with her head bowed and her hands folded in a completely demure and humble attitude, yet, somehow, at the same time managing to deliver a lecture on family loyalty to Uncle Ahmet of all people. Name of God, how she'd admired Ruqaiyya's nerve!

"I was working a passenger shuttle at the time. Earth, the Moon, Mars, and back again. It wasn't bad, but it wasn't what I wanted. Asil and I were already saving to build our own ship, but even on a chief's salary, it was going to be slow going. I was starting to think little Vashti would be at university before we had enough.

"Then, about two years after her marriage to Tully, Ruqaiyya came to see me, at Port Armstrong, no less. She had a business proposal from Marcus, who, she said, was nervous about sounding me out."

Ruqaiyya had been so earnest as they'd talked over bulbs of thick, sweet coffee. She'd told Al Shei at length how Marcus admired her skill, her practicality, the way Al Shei and Asil had arranged their disparate lives to make their marriage a warm, working reality.

Al Shei had looked at the reflection of the overhead lights in her coffee and felt ashamed at herself for wondering what all this was leading up to. She'd felt even worse when she asked.

Al Shei cleared her throat. "Ruqaiyya told me that Marcus's business partner had defaulted on his obligations at Phobos Point, leaving Marcus holding the bag, and the *Pasadena*, which he couldn't afford to operate solo. He wanted to ask me to go in on a time-share arrangement with him, but he knew, she said, that I didn't think much of his business sense . . ." Al Shei waved the rest of the sentence away.

"Ruqaiyya knew I'd been looking for this kind of chance for years. She knew I couldn't take the kind of ties that crewing a corporate ship lays on you, and she knew how unholy expensive independent shipping is. Merciful Allah." She gave a short, mirthless laugh. "One little mistake and you can keep a whole hundred-wafer stack at the bank busy tallying your deficits.

"Ruqaiyya also knew that, in spite of myself, I was already drooling at the idea of being my own chief engineer.

"So, I promised I'd talk to Tully, and I sent her home. Then, I got on the wire to Phobos Point security to find out what had really happened to Tully's partner. Not," she added quickly as Dobbs's right eyebrow raised a single centimeter, "that I thought Ruqaiyya had lied, but I was very willing to believe that Tully hadn't told her the whole truth."

She'd sat at the board for hours, dealing impatiently with the realities of negotiating a bureaucracy over a real-time link with a four-minute delay.

"What I found out, eventually, was that Tully's partner had tried to crack the Intersystem Banking Network and divert a whole load of bond-sale data to a friend of his, using *Pasadena*'s catch-and-drop facilities to do it. There were traces on the try before it was even halfway started. Of course, all they pointed to was *Pasadena*, not the actual cracker.

"Tully turned his partner in to save his skin and to keep the thing from blowing up so big that his in-laws got notified, or, worse, so that some farsighted security team decided to warn their compatriots in Settled Space to keep an eye on Marcus Tully." She shook her head again. "That would really put a lock on his future plans.

"I took leave from the shuttle. I went home and spent a week talking the whole thing over with Asil. Then I went to Tully and laid down my conditions.

"Asil would be our chief accountant. Tully could hire someone to keep tabs on him if he wanted to, but all the money would go through Asil. Each partner would have the ship a maximum of eight months and would have complete control over whatever profits they made during that time. They'd also have complete responsibility for any new debts they managed to incur. Our crews would be separate. Our logs would be separate, and if he was ever officially charged with breaking anybody's laws, the *Pasadena* was mine." She sighed at the memory of Tully's eyes. Despite their bright blue color, they'd seemed dark then, as though he was a cornered rat looking for a way out that didn't exist.

"After he agreed to all that, and agreed to have it recorded and sealed"—Al Shei ran her hand along the smooth desktop—"I said to him, 'Don't ever forget what you did to your partner, because I'd do the same to you, in a picosecond.'

"I thought it would hold him down," she murmured to the wall over Dobbs's shoulder. "I thought that and the fact that he knew I'd tell Ruqaiyya if I found out anything that was a grade-one fire hazard, would keep him from trying anything irredeemably stupid. Apparently, I was wrong."

"Pray forgive your humble Fool." The unwavering look in her eyes made a joke of her subservient tone. "But why do you choose to honor her with this confidence?"

"I wanted to see if it still sounded like it made sense," said Al Shei. "If I had missed anything when I set this deal up."

Dobbs licked her lips thoughtfully. "Do you know about Nasrudine?"

Al Shei smiled. "Once there was and there was not, the wise fool Nasrudine," she recited. "One day, Nasrudine came to a friend of his and said, 'Congratulate me! I am a father!' 'Congratulations!' said his friend. 'Is it a boy or a girl?' 'Why yes,' said Nasrudine. 'How did you know?'"

Dobbs chuckled. "Another time Nasrudine was selling donkeys. He would go to market every Friday with a fine donkey which he would sell at an outrageously low price. Finally, one of the donkey merchants came up to him and said, 'Nasrudine, how are you doing this? I force the haymakers to give me fodder for free. I make my slaves work without pay, and still I cannot sell my donkeys as cheaply as you sell yours.'

" 'Well, friend,' says Nasrudine, 'you are going about this all wrong. You are stealing fodder and labor. I'm just stealing donkeys.'"

Despite herself, Al Shei gave a short laugh. "Are you saying I stole the *Pasadena*?" she asked, not really expecting a serious answer.

"I'm saying, Boss, you might want to consider how long you are going to let Marcus Tully steal labor and fodder. Particularly when you know he's going about this all wrong."

Al Shei opened her mouth and closed it again.

The emergency alarm shrilled through the room a split second ahead of Javerri's voice.

"Intercom to Al Shei!"

Al Shei was on her feet in a split second. "Al Shei here. What's going on, Javerri?"

"We've got a situation with the fusion mix. The readouts say we're pouring in deuterium."

Al Shei didn't even pause to say anything to Dobbs. "I'm on my way. Intercom to close."

She just strode out the door, straight across the corridor, and through the hatch. She grabbed the stair railing and started running down.

Pasadena ran on fusion reactions. The hydrogen-boron reaction required a very high temperature, so they used deuterium-deuterium reactions for brief periods to prime the reactors and generators when a cold start was required. The problem with deuterium-deuterium reactions was that they produced tritium. So, occasionally you got a deuterium-tritium reaction which produced fast, energetic neutrons. Deadly radiation. The radiation was absorbed by the lithium jacket around the reactor, but the reactor's inner wall could only absorb so many neutrons before it became radioactive itself.

If a delivery valve had accidentally gotten open and deuterium was pouring into the reactors, there would be a massive number of deuterium-tritium reactions, producing more radiation than the jacket could hold back. The jacket, and the valves, would begin to overheat. The bombardment of neutrons would make the metallic surfaces brittle and burst through the ceramics. If the ceramic cracked, the boiling lithium would pour into the engine chamber, setting even the deck plates ablaze. Her imagination all too easily painted a picture of tiny, glowing pellets slicing through the suddenly delicate shielding like sleet, touching off the fiery disaster.

What just those invisible pellets would do to her crew was not something Al Shei was allowing herself to think about. She especially did not allow herself to think about what would happen if the engines broke down during the jump. They needed power to stop. Without enough power, the jump wouldn't end until Judgment Day came and the recording angels opened their books.

The cargo platform was waiting at the galley deck. Al Shei swung herself on board and grabbed the railing.

"Engineering. Emergency override, Katmer Al Shei." The ship identified her voice and the platform started to sink toward Main Engineering.

"Intercom to Shi'mon and Ianiai." Her voice rang off the walls.

"Shi'mon here."

After a much longer moment, and in a much sleepier voice, "Ianiai here."

"Emergency call. Report to Main Engineering, now."

On the other side of the hatch, Javerri stood elbow-deep in the right-hand wall. *Good,* thought Al Shei. *Alert the chief, check the wiring, then panic.*

The look she turned on Al Shei said that step two was almost completed.

"Can't find an instrumentation fault, Engine," she reported in a voice as hollow as her eyes.

"What's the reading from the compartment?" Al Shei yanked out her pen and stabbed at the main menu to call up the valve displays from the engine room.

Javerri double-checked her boards. "It's the same thing all the way down the line. The D-2 valve is stuck all the way open, and we've got an infusion of twenty grams per second."

Might as well be twenty kilos. Al Shei flicked through the menus and felt her brows draw together. Javerri had read it right.

The hatch cycled open. Shim'on ducked through, the hem of his prayer shawl flapping behind him.

"Ianiai is right behind me," he reported breathlessly.

"Good." Al Shei crossed the deck to the equipment locker. As she outlined the situation, she pulled out a bright yellow containment suit and began stepping into it. "You're with me. I'm going down into the engines to get that valve closed." The hatch opened again, and Ianiai, still rubbing his eyes, stepped through. "Javerri, bring Ianiai up to speed." She yanked on her gloves. "You two will monitor the situation from here. Shim'on, your job is to be my backup. If I get hit too hard by the radiation, your first priority is to get the valve shut, then you worry about getting us out of there. Understood?"

Shim'on paused in his suiting up long enough to nod at her.

Al Shei locked the helmet in place. Javerri opened her mouth, closed it without saying anything, and took her place at Station One.

Al Shei strode back into the drop shaft with Shim'on right behind her. She took the stairs as fast as she could manage in the thick boots. The tools on her belt slapped against her thighs.

The spiral stairway ended at the hatch to the engine compartment. Al Shei's mind's eye showed her the engine compartment full of thin wires of golden light strung across the room like a manic spider had been set loose in there. Each one was ready to slice straight through her as soon as she walked into it. The suit should protect her, and Chandra should be able to take care of any minor radiation injuries. If she didn't have to stay down there too long.

"*Bismillahir rahmanir*," she said. In the name of Allah, the most Merciful.

She took a deep breath and opened the hatch.

The Main Engineering compartment was a sculpture in bright, white ceramic panels. Al Shei descended the ladder beside the bulge of the main coolant pipe. Below her feet hulked the housings for the reactors and accumulators. Each was a conglomeration of mounds like sand dunes in a barren desert. The only color was the glowing display panels on each one. Readouts for fuel consumption, power output, and structural integrity. She glanced between the toes of her boots and saw nothing but green.

Good. Things haven't gone too far.

Al Shei reached her foot out toward the nearest staple and, with hands and feet, swung herself over to the ladder beside the D-2 pipe. As big around as her torso, it ran straight into the largest housing on the floor. The valve stuck out of the pipe's smooth side. It was a spoked wheel that would have been recognizable to a steamboat captain six hundred years ago. She hitched her belt to the ladder and checked her radiation badge on her wrist. Still green. Good. If this thing was well and truly jammed, she might need help down here. If it were welded open from heat and pressure, she'd need help then, too. Preferably from Allah and all His angels.

She peered at the display above the valve and her eyes widened in surprise.

The numbers shone bright green. The display said the flow was nonexistent, and the pressure was zero, exactly as it should be, and that the valve was tightly shut.

Just as it should be. She looked at her badge. Still green. She turned her head and surveyed the sterile, white room. All around her shone green stars.

"Intercom to Engineering," she barked toward the wall. "Javerri, what are you reading up there?"

"Same thing," her voice came back. "Massive D-2 flooding, increased radioactivity throughout . . ."

Al Shei cut her off. "I've got a bunch of green readings down here." She grabbed the valve wheel and turned it toward the CLOSE label. It wouldn't budge. She eased it in the other direction and immediately a bright red WARNING wrote itself across the display.

She locked the valve back at once. "And I've got a set of completely closed valves, all the way down, and a green radiation badge."

The walls fell silent.

"Intercom to Watch and Houston," Al Shei called out. "Conference room, now. We've got a problem. Intercom to FTL and Ensign, I want a download of the readings we're getting up there. Shim'on, get down here and compare them with the readings we're getting on the direct displays. Keep everything on film and bring it to the conference room. Stay suited up, just in case."

She unhitched her belt and started climbing back toward the main ladder.

It would have been easier if it was the valve. She bit her lip as she started up toward the hatch. *At least then we would have known what we were dealing with.*

The conference room was already filled when she got there. Schyler had a list of the defective systems and their corresponding diagrams up on the main memory board. From the looks on their faces, everyone had already had a chance to study the display.

Al Shei let the hatch cycle shut behind her and seated herself at the foot of the table. She nodded to Schyler.

"So"—he tapped the memory board with one knuckle—"we already know we have a problem, and that it's growing worse. As of now, we are on emergency duty until we have it cleared out."

Al Shei looked at each face in turn, waiting for a challenge, waiting for someone to say they had already found a solution. No one so much as blinked, not even Dobbs, sitting quietly in her corner.

"All right," Schyler went on, "all section chiefs are to work double shifts. Work out a relief schedule so there's someone attending to routine at all times while you're out hunting. I do not want any system left unmonitored. I do, however"—he stabbed the table with his index finger—"want this cleared up before we make The Farther Kingdom delivery."

"You know the one about the needle in the haystack?" inquired Lipinski.

Schyler nodded. "If you've got a suggestion, I want to hear it. Otherwise, I want a schedule worked out, and I want all efforts coordinated through me."

"I've got a suggestion," said Yerusha.

Schyler faced her. "Which is?"

Yerusha's face was absolutely deadpan. "You could let me hatch the AI stack I've got into the *Pasadena*'s system. We'd get a dynamic picture and intelligent help."

The blood drained from Lipinski's face. He leaned forward, mouth open. Schyler glanced at Al Shei and waved Lipinski back.

"Thank you for volunteering, Pilot. We'll save that as a backup option. I don't want to lose the loading time."

Somewhat to Al Shei's surprise, Yerusha didn't try to argue. Good, maybe she was cooling off.

Next came some of the usual wrangling about resources and priorities and coordination. There wasn't much, though, because they were all very aware of what this latest incident meant. If the instruments were reporting false disasters, they might have lost their ability to report real ones.

Schyler laid down the last coordination order and broke the meeting so the chiefs could alert their teams and work out their individual schedules.

Al Shei let the crew filter past her. The last one out the hatch was Dobbs.

"In case Schyler hasn't mentioned it, you're also on emergency duty," Al Shei told her. "If we've got a virus running loose, things might get worse before they get better. I am going to need you to help keep us from overload."

Dobbs bowed. "God gave them wisdom that have it, and fools, let them use their talents."

Lipinski was waiting by the stairway hatch when Al Shei

came out. He had regained some of his color, but he still looked sick.

She knew what was coming before he even opened his mouth.

"You're not going to let her hatch that thing, are you?"

Al Shei sighed and pressed her fingers against her temple. "I might."

"We have got an unidentified dynamic system fault and you're willing to chuck an AI in there?" He was trying to whisper and not managing too well. "A *Freer* AI?"

Al Shei let her hand drop. "If you don't want the AI hatched, Lipinski, you find out what's causing our problems." She drew herself up to her full height. "Get a lock on this paranoia, Houston. You're running the risk of disrupting my ship."

A strange light came into his eyes. "She thinks she can use that thing to catch a human soul. That's blasphemy in your book, too."

Al Shei took a deep breath and let it out slowly. She reminded herself firmly about Lipinski's unparallelled skill and commitment. She reminded herself how, as a young man, he had helplessly watched his whole world die around him.

"My book also says, 'Tolerate patiently what unbelievers say and part from them in a polite manner.'" She cycled the hatch back. "And I believe yours has a few things to say about faith and trust in God." She looked him straight in the eyes. "I've been doing some talking, too. I said to Resit at the beginning of this run that you were a reasonable man. I do not want to have to say to her I was wrong."

She watched his face shift as the tone of her statement sank in. He straightened his shoulders. "You won't."

Al Shei let out a silent sigh of relief. "Thank you, Lipinski." She let him precede her up the staircase.

When Al Shei returned to her cabin, Resit was kneeling on her prayer rug. Al Shei realized, with a small wince, that *maghrib* prayers must have just finished.

The look her cousin gave her was without reproach, however. "You'd better do two *sajdatus sahw* for forgetfulness," she said mildly. "You haven't made prayer once today."

"There you're wrong, Cousin." Al Shei dropped wearily

into the desk chair. "I've been doing nothing but praying for the last three hours."

"I heard the alarm, of course." Resit unfolded her legs and stood up. "Do you want to tell me about it, or should I read the report from Watch?"

Al Shei pulled out her pen and activated the desk. "Read the report, would you? I've got to get my ducks on a new schedule."

"Uh-huh." Resit draped her prayer rug over her arm. "Anything I need to be immediately worried about, then?"

"Not immediately." Al Shei did not turn around. She pulled up the engineering schedule for the next three days and stared at it.

"You know, I get nervous when you don't look at me," Resit remarked. "Tell me, should I start drafting up a call-in on Tully?"

"Yes," said Al Shei, quietly. "That you should do."

"Then that's what I'll do."

Al Shei heard the bathroom door open and close.

She forced herself to concentrate on the schedule. After the first attempt at reorganization, she realized that she hadn't left herself any time to sleep. She had to blank everything out and start again.

Finally, she wrote TRANSMIT across the boards. Her gaze strayed to the drawer where she'd put the day book recorder. She stared at it for a moment, thinking about the next run, when Asil would be hearing this. What would the ending be? Would he know already that it had all worked out? Or would he be sitting silently listening to how she had slid so far down they'd be years digging themselves out? For a moment, she missed him with such appalling force that her throat closed around her breath.

"Only one way to make sure it doesn't come to that." She stood up and strode out the door.

Hours later, Al Shei forced herself back into her cabin. There hadn't been any more system failures, but there hadn't been any progress toward finding the cause of their troubles either. She prayed long and intensely, reaching for a peace that didn't come, made her day book recording, and, at last, lay down on her bunk beneath her emerald green coverlet.

Al Shei lay on her side and listened to the soft hum of the ship around her. Usually, it lulled her. It was the sound of everything behaving as it should. Not tonight. Tonight, the gentle sound was a disguise, covering up an unseen problem. *Pasadena* was haunted tonight, and she had no idea how to draw the ghost out.

Al Shei rolled onto her back and threw her arm across her face, pressing her eyelids shut.

She let herself imagine Asil lay beside her. She conjured up the memory of his scent, the heat of his body, the sweet sensation of his arms around her, loosely embracing her in sleep. She felt his warm, comforting weight against her as her breast rose and fell in long, contented breaths. His lips brushed lightly against her cheeks as he pulled her closer in his dreams.

Dreaming of her husband's dreams, Al Shei managed to fall asleep.

Chapter Four

MORE QUESTIONS

Yerusha lay in her bunk staring up at darkness. She was supposed to be getting her seven-and-a-half-hour sleep shift in, but it wasn't working out that way.

It was ridiculous. It was triple-fractured and double-twisted ridiculous. The entire crew was running itself ragged to find a virus that the stack in her case could locate in ten seconds.

They were all so *scared.* They relied on human engineering for their shelter, their air, their warmth, and their flight, but they wouldn't let their shelter be guided by an engineered mind, a native of an environment where even Lipinski was just a visitor. Even if her foster hadn't caught a soul yet, it was a diagnostician that was ten thousand times faster than Lipinski could ever be.

While they all scrabbled around, the walls were crawling with who-knew-what. Yerusha shifted restlessly, wrinkling the sheet underneath her. Hadn't anybody thought that it might get into the environmental controls? Or the fuel containment system? The vents were electronic and could be opened by a faulty command. Then what? They'd still have their groundhog security, but they'd be quite dead.

And her with them.

Yerusha sat up. "Lights." The white glow she'd set to match the lights on Free Home Titania flooded the room. She kicked back the blanket and swung her feet onto the floor. She padded over to the storage drawers and unlocked the compartment that held her tool belt. She extracted her pen from its pocket and thumbed the activation switch. Then she held it against the lock for the lowest drawer. The drawer beeped once in acknowledgment and slid open. Yerusha extracted a grey metal case about ten centimeters on a side and six centimeters thick. Inside, snug and secure, lay her foster's wafer stack.

Foster was her last link to the Free Home until her exile was over. It was the only Freer voice she would hear, the only friend she did not lose. Right now, it was also the only help she had.

She looked toward the folded-up desk. No good. Lipinski, no matter what Al Shei said, would probably still be watching her lines. Besides, she squeezed the case, what she had said to Al Shei was the truth. Even though current theory said a fledgling intelligence needed as much input as possible, she had no intention of hatching her foster aboard the *Pasadena*, while the Houston's reaction was going to be to hunt it down and kill it.

Even the best Houston, however, could not be everywhere at once. Some lines would be given priority over others.

Yerusha pulled her work clothes on over her pajamas and tucked her foster into one deep pocket. Then she cycled open her hatch and headed for the bridge.

Cheney was the only one on the bridge when Yerusha got there. That meant Delasandros, Cheney's relief, was out on what Al Shei was calling "the Hunt." Schyler was nominally on sleep shift, but, somehow, Yerusha doubted he would be having any more luck with it than she did.

Cheney paced between Station One and Station Two, peering at the boards and scribbling ones on the memory pads.

He jerked his head around as Yerusha let the hatch cycle shut.

"Any trouble?" she asked, coming forward to peer over his shoulder.

"You mean, any new trouble?" Cheney corrected her. "Not yet." He wrote down the new coherency reading for the system diagnostic. "But no new answers either." He brooded for a moment at the curving, silver wall that was the only thing visible through the window. Then he spared her a glance. "Aren't you on Z-duty?"

She shrugged. "No luck on that assignment. Thought I'd come up and run a couple of simulations, see if I can work up a pattern on this mess."

Cheney gave her a sour smile. "Good luck."

"Thanks," she answered in what she hoped was a suitably wry tone.

The chair for the virtual-reality station looked more like an exoskeleton forced into a sitting position than like a chair. Yerusha settled herself at the VR station, tucking her feet into the boots that were attached to the floor rests. Keeping her back between Cheney and the boards, she pulled her foster's case out of her pocket. She removed the delicate stack and inserted it into one of the board's empty slots. Behind her, she could hear Cheney rustling and scribbling without interruption.

She pulled her pen out and wrote *Activate port 37C* on the board, but did not put down a period to finish the sentence and send the command. She laid the pen on top of the board, right next to the socket holding her foster.

She strapped her torso to the chair, closed the chair's flexible arms around her arms, and slid the wired gloves onto her hands. Then she lowered the muffling helmet over her head. VR sets worked perfectly well with goggles and earphones, but most ships still used the helmets to keep any conversations in virtual reality from interfering with the bridge routine.

The helmet clicked into place and a menu board glowed bright white and green in the surrounding darkness. The menu displayed three selections for her:

ENTER PROGRAM NAME
DISPLAY PROGRAM MENUS
ENTER NEW PARAMETERS

Yerusha touched ENTER NEW PARAMETERS. A memory board with a pen clipped to the top appeared. Yerusha picked up the pen, twirled it thoughtfully in her fingers for a moment, and started writing.

Initiate* Pasadena *simulation, current conditions, continuous update, delete crew.

She tapped down a period and waited. Some systems

would not accept a continuous update command because it used up too much line space.

Pasadena, however, just came back with: SPECIFY STATION FOR POINT OF REFERENCE.

Bridge VR Station One, she wrote.

The darkness lifted and Yerusha was seated at the VR station, alone on the bridge. The slot where, on the real bridge, her foster was plugged in was empty, however. The stack was inactive and the ship's system carried no record of it, so as far as the simulation was concerned, it did not exist.

Now came the part that was a little tricky. Yerusha closed her eyes and gripped what her left hand told her was the tip of her right index finger. She pulled. She repeated the motion for each finger, tugging at skin and finger ends until she peeled off the VR glove. She did not open her eyes, because if she did, she would see her right hand cut off at the wrist and lying in her lap. She did not have time to be disconcerted. If Cheney picked now to check up on her, things were going to get awkward, fast.

With her right hand, Yerusha groped across the real board until her fingers closed around her pen. She fumbled with it until she held it the right way up. She stabbed a period down on the board.

She could not risk an interface between the ship's system and her foster without the cover of the simulation. The sudden increase in activity would be too noticeable, and she had been directly ordered to keep it in its case. Now, however, the relatively small increase in power consumption and line usage under the myriad commands of a constantly updated program would be barely detectable.

She opened her eyes.

Her right hand was lying limp and lifeless across her thigh. She picked it up and slid it back onto the end of her wrist, twisting it around until she could wiggle all her fingers.

In her ear, a voice whispered, "I'm here, Jemina."

"Hello, Foster." The foster was not independent yet. If and when it became complex enough to catch a soul, it would be encouraged to choose a name. For now, though, it was just "Foster."

The fostering program had been going on for twenty years

and had yet to see any successes. Nonetheless, the sporadic appearances of rogue AIs reinforced the Freers' faith, and there were always more applicants for the adoption lottery than there were AIs to be fostered.

Humanity's freedom came when they were able to shake off the chaotic planetary environment they were born into and make their own homes designed specifically for them. Their final freedom would come when they could break the cycle of death that a chaotic ecosystem had trapped them in, when human beings could build houses for human souls that would not age and perish. That was the Freer ideal, and Yerusha believed in it.

"What is happening?" asked Foster. "Am I being hatched?"

"No, not yet." *Not for a while yet, either, I'm afraid.* She could not let Foster out of its own stack until she had a secure environment for it. That would not happen until she was back on a Freer station.

Foster didn't ask more questions, as a flesh-and-blood child would have. As usual, Yerusha found its inability to display impatience or undue curiosity a mixed blessing.

"I need your help, Foster. The ship is having severe system trouble. I need you to scan the input from the simulation and see if you can establish a pattern for the disruptions."

"An accurate simulation cannot be created when the root causes for observed effects are unidentified," answered Foster, sounding way too programmed.

Need to work on the grammar structure paths. "I know, but we've got a constant update going so you should have an accurate picture of the symptoms. We don't need an exact answer. A best guess cause-and-effect relationship will do for now."

"Okay," said Foster. "Setting up scan routine."

"Be careful of the security protocols," Yerusha reminded it. "Don't trip over any of Houston's wires."

"Noted. Precautions being integrated. Predicted time to initial report, thirty seconds."

Definitely have to work on those grammar paths. Not half enough flexibility in there.

Yerusha settled back to wait. The predicted thirty seconds passed, and thirty more, and thirty more.

Yerusha drummed her fingers impatiently on the virtual chair arm.

"Foster? What's going on?"

There was no answer.

"Foster?" Yerusha gripped both arms of the chair and leaned forward.

There was no answer.

Yerusha snatched up the pen. *Status of module in port 37C,* she wrote. *Real world interface.*

The board absorbed her command and wrote out its answer.

MODULE IN PORT 37C IS INOPERATIVE.

"Ino . . ." the word died on Yerusha's lips.

She slammed the heels of both hands against her temples to cut off the simulation and raise the helmet. In an instant, the world went black, and she felt the helmet begin to rise. As soon as she saw the thin line of outside light, she ducked under the helmet's edge and tore off the gloves. She pushed the chair arms away from her. With a shaking hand, she removed Foster's stack from the port. She laid it back in the case and bit her lip as she pressed the diagnosis key. Two words appeared on the edge of the small message board inside the case's lid:

STACK EMPTY.

A small, involuntary sound escaped Yerusha's throat. She tried to stand, but the skeleton's straps and boots forced her back down. Viciously, she slapped the catches open.

"Are you *okay*?" asked Cheney.

Yerusha couldn't even begin to think of a way to answer him. Cradling Foster's case in both hands, she ran for the hatch.

What happened? What happened? She pounded down the stairs to the berthing deck. She was aware of an exclamation from an engineering platform, but she didn't know who it was.

Did Foster get loose? Did it hatch? Fractured and damn, Lipinski will kill it! Did the virus get it? She lunged into the corridor. *Did I open it up to die?*

What happened?

Hands grabbed her shoulders, jerking her backwards. Yerusha stumbled into a cabin, barely catching herself against a bunk before she overbalanced. A hatch cycled shut behind her. Yerusha forced her eyes to focus, and she saw a window looking out onto rolling, mist-covered hills.

"Jemina Yerusha," said Dobbs from behind her. "What have you done?"

There was such a note of command in her voice, Yerusha almost answered.

She ran her hand through her hair.

"Nothing," she managed to say. "I was just running some simulations on the bridge. Overdid things. I should be asleep . . ."

Dobbs sighed. "I really wish you'd tell me what's going on, because I know you don't want to have to tell Schyler, or Al Shei, and possibly Lipinski, if you live through telling the first two."

Yerusha swallowed hard and looked down at the case in her hands. "I was using my foster to scan some data simulations. It . . . stopped responding after the first thirty seconds. The case diagnostic said the stack was empty."

Dobbs stepped into her line of sight. The Fool's forehead was wrinkled in perplexity. "It got loose?"

Yerusha shrugged helplessly. "It shouldn't have left the stack, it was scanning input. I don't think it could get loose, it hasn't got any independent initiative . . ." She felt herself begin to sway on her feet. "I don't know . . . I was trying . . ."

"To prove the worth of humanity's ultimate efforts to a shipload of groundhuggers," Dobbs said for her. Dobbs hooked two of her fingers around her Guild necklace. "And I should have seen it coming."

"That's not it," insisted Yerusha, although she didn't know why. "I . . ."

"Sit down, Pilot." Dobbs lifted the case out of her hands. Yerusha clutched at it. That was Foster, her last link with home, the thing she was counting on to keep her focused for the two years when no other Freer would even talk to her.

"I'm not going to hurt it," said Dobbs softly. "Sit down before you fall down."

Yerusha sat on the edge of the scarlet-covered bunk. It was fully made up, she realized. Whatever Dobbs had been doing this shift, it wasn't sleeping.

Dobbs set Foster's case on the corner of her desk. She opened a drawer and poured something out of a square, green bottle into a collapsible cup.

"Here. Sip this." She handed the cup to Yerusha.

Yerusha sipped. The liquid was pale brown, smoky-flavored, and very alcoholic.

"For medicinal purposes." Dobbs grinned at her, indicating that the comment must be a joke.

Yerusha took another sip. The liquid felt warm against her dry throat.

Dobbs pulled her pen out of the desk socket. "Is the stack secured?" she asked as she flipped open the case's lid.

"Not now." Yerusha shook her head. "I didn't think . . ."

She half expected Dobbs to say "obviously not," but the Fool just nodded and plugged her pen into the case.

"What are you doing?" Yerusha started to her feet.

"I'm trying to see if there's enough left in here to get a recording of what happened." The light on the end of her pen glowed gold. Dobbs plucked the pen out of the case and stuck it back into her desk. She watched silently as the desk wrote out its response.

"Well," Dobbs fingered her necklace. "Nothing got out. Something did get in, though."

Yerusha set the cup gently down on the bed.

"If Lipinski . . ." she began.

"No," said Dobbs. "The stack's been entirely reconfigured. There's not an ordered pathway left in here. There is no way Lipinski could have wiped a stack this clean that fast, and no reason why he would. He would've just hauled Al Shei and Schyler up to the bridge and caught you in the act."

"Then it was the virus."

Dobbs gave one of her showiest shrugs. "It's either that, or the *Pasadena*'s gone independent and doesn't like people poking in its innards."

"But Foster is gone."

Dobbs nodded. "I think so. I think it was an effect similar to what happened to that initial diagnostic Lipinski tried to run."

Yerusha focused her eyes on the empty stack. She felt drained, exhausted, and alone. For the first time since she had left Port Oberon, she was really alone without hope or help for two dark, wandering years. Worse, her chance at redemption was gone.

She realized she was about to start crying. She screwed her emotions up into a tight ball and forced them down inside her. Not in front of an outsider, not even a Fool. No. She would mourn her losses alone in her cabin, not here. Not ever where it could be seen by somebody who couldn't possibly understand. She did not want to try to tell Dobbs that those pathways had matched Holden's neural pathways in the wafer stack as closely as possible, or how much she had paid to get them that way. She did not want to attempt to explain her hope that the soul Foster would catch would be Holden's.

"So," she said, trying desperately to find something her mind could latch on to other than the dead and empty stack on the desk. "You were a cracker before you were a Fool?" she nodded toward Dobbs's pen. "Whatever you just ran must have taken a year to build."

Dobbs smiled, looking uncharacteristically bashful. "I was a lot of things before I was a Fool."

"You don't look anything like old enough." Yerusha dug the heels of her palms into her eyes. "But, so help me, neither do I, yet."

"Go back to your cabin, Yerusha," suggested Dobbs. "Get some sleep if you can. You're going to need your head together to get this crew of groundhogs to The Farther Kingdom."

Yerusha felt exhaustion tug at her, probably helped by the alcohol. She looked across at the case and its empty stack and felt a hollow pain.

"You're right." She stood up. "Time to act like I know what I'm doing." She lowered the case lid and snapped the latches shut. "And as long as Cheney doesn't open his mouth to Schyler, I might get a chance."

"Schyler'll be steady about this," said Dobbs.

"I don't know." Yerusha lifted the case up and remembered Schyler's eyes when she had been called down to the Law's cabin.

"Believe me." There was no humor in Dobbs's voice, just

steady assurance. "He can understand what it's like to be totally out on your own."

Yerusha studied the Fool for a long moment. "One of these days you're going to have to tell me about some of those things you were before you were a Fool."

Dobbs chuckled. "Maybe after we get out of this mess, Yerusha." She cycled her hatch open. "Get some sleep."

"Yeah, I've got all of what, four hours left?"

Dobbs smiled. "And counting. See you in the morning."

"See you."

Yerusha made it back to her cabin without seeing anybody else. She set the foster's case back into its drawer and stared at it. The loss eased by Dobbs's company drooped across her back again, heavy and clinging.

What she hadn't told Dobbs was that exiles weren't supposed to be able to take their fosters with them. What she didn't say was that the reason she had been in the Richard III business module when it blew out was that she was paying her life savings to Fellow Radmilu, a guard on the quiet dole. Radmilu was the one who had seized her property when she was arrested. She clearly remembered his big, soft hands and how they fluttered around as he suggested she could have her foster with her if she was willing to pay for it. She'd tripled his price for an additional service. Radmilu had arranged for Foster's network to be reconfigured from Holden's medical records, and then he had brought it to her at Port Oberon.

When the can blew, all her actions were hampered by her desperate attempt to keep a hold on Foster's case. That was why she was too slow and clumsy to get out of the way when the last seam gave way. Her hope and scheme had cost her her arm and her eye, and most of what was left of her pride.

Now Foster and Holden were both gone. The skin on her newest arm itched.

"When I find out who did this," she whispered as she closed the drawer, "I'm going to kill them."

Dobbs closed her cabin hatch behind Yerusha. For a long moment she did nothing but stand there and let herself be tired. She felt the tension in the tendons of her neck, the weight of her hands dangling from her wrists, the dozen small aches in her feet and ankles, the dry heat lying over her eyes. Tired. Tired.

Tired for Al Shei, who was working like a madwoman and leaving Resit to pray for both of them. Tired for Lipinski, who was drinking the Sundars' coffee like it was mineral water. Tired for Yerusha, who had just lost a lifeline she wasn't even supposed to have.

Tired for Dobbs, who had spent the day trying to keep them all cool and focused and had totally missed what Yerusha would try to do.

Time to act like I know what I'm doing. She replayed Yerusha's words for herself. *You know, I was just thinking the same thing.* She locked the hatch and set the entrance light to red.

Dobbs pulled her pen out of the desk socket and sat down on her bunk. She slid her bedside drawer open and drew out the flat, black box. She laid her thumb against the box lock. The lock identified first her print, then the very faint pulse that her thumb carried as her own, and the lid sprang back. From inside, the Fool took up a hypodermic spray and drug cartridge.

Seven hours? She set the release timer on the hypo and inserted the cartridge into the case. *Given distance and coordination time once I'm in there? Should be enough. Long time to be out of action, though.* She glanced toward the door. *Maybe not so bad. I've got four hours left on the sleep shift. That leaves three hours to cover for. Oh well, that's one of the advantages of being the Fool; everybody always assumes you're just clowning around somewhere else.*

She pulled the transceiver out of the box and, with her free hand, plugged her pen into the transceiver's input socket. The transceiver beeped once as it downloaded all of the record Dobbs had illegally acquired from Al Shei's pen.

Dobbs pocketed the pen and opened the input plug in the wall over her bed. She took a slender white cable out of the case, jacked one end of it into the wall and the other into the transceiver. Then her practiced fingers found the nerveless patch behind her right ear and peeled it open. The heat of her hand activated the socketed implant behind it. She plugged the loaded transceiver into the implant.

Biting her lip, Dobbs picked the hypo up again. *I wonder if this is ever going to get easier*, she thought as she lay back on her bed and held the hypo against her neck. She could feel her pulse beating against the hypo's pressure. The transceiver's vibrations made her neck tickle. Its signal was already getting through to her. The edges of the room blurred and softened, separating into wavery, twin ghosts in front of her eyes.

Dobbs, she said firmly to herself. *You can process network input, or sensory input. You cannot do both.*

She closed her eyes. Her index finger hit the hypo's release button and the drug hit her nervous system. Her shoulders vanished, then arms and hands, pelvis and legs. It took all of Dobbs's training not to scream before her face and eyes were gone.

Hearing and smell went next and the transition was over. She had no awareness of her body. Now her shape was defined by the switches and storage pathways in the *Pasadena*'s system. She knew the mechanics of what happened. Now that her mind's other functions had been suppressed, her implant captured a specialized pattern of neuronal firing that flickered deep in her organic mind. The pattern was the result of intensive hypno-training and delicate microengineering on both her implant and her neurons. The transceiver routed that pattern into the network she was jacked into. To her senses, what happened was that she stopped being a body with arms and legs. Now, she was a chaotic being—a snarl of threadlike limbs and blobby thoughts shaped by the pathways and resistance wells she filled. She lay over an array of microscopic switches and gates, and they, in turn, held together the mass of signals that thought of itself as Evelyn Dobbs. Time slowed to a crawl and her acute internal processes—her thoughts—kept her aware of each individual second.

One.

Dobbs flexed herself against a quartet of gates, and the *Pasadena* responded by siphoning her along the spiderweb of data paths that joined together the ship's processing areas to the roomy holding stack connected to the ship's main fast-time laser transmitter. She touched her surroundings to make sure no internal ports were active indicating that a crew member out there was paying attention to the transmitter. No one was.

Two.

She dropped into a boxy, quiescent processor series. She filtered her awareness through the stack and found the log and the alert codes. She froze both. Now, unless someone looked out the window, there was no way to see what she was about to do.

Three.

In the main processor, she reset the transmitter commands into an active sequence. The transmitter grabbed the signal they put out—a frozen replica of Dobbs's signal sequence—and shot it out to the coordinates she had laid in for IBN Repeater Satellite HK-IBN4813-7Z421.

Four. Five.

As solid as the Intersystem Banking Network was, repeaters occasionally overloaded momentarily, or took in bad signals that moved their receiver telescopes to the wrong angle, or failed completely. If she didn't verify that the receiver 'scope was ready and waiting for the burst of compressed and coded light she had become, she might jump out with nowhere to land.

The replica came back. Dobbs caught it and swallowed it whole. It was exactly as she had sent it out. Satisfied that her target was where it was supposed to be and that it could handle her complexity and keep her whole and stable, Dobbs shaped another command on the processors.

Six.

Dobbs positioned herself at the mouth of the transmitter. The gates and switches flickered so fast that in her body she wouldn't have had time to blink.

Jump.

Thousands of sharply angled pathways opened around her. Packets of data jostled against her on all sides. Ten were system packets with Repeater 4183's encoding. Two were timing sequences. The jump had taken fourteen minutes, eight point two seconds. She didn't feel any of it. Between receiver and transmitter, her signals were frozen still because there was no hardware to move them. This meant that she was, in effect, unconscious until she reached her destination.

One. Two. Three. She flitted along the repeater's internal paths. Routing protocols switched into active phases as she reached out to them and closed down again when the flicker of her passage was gone.

When she first made use of these pathways, shaping her world was a clumsy, blundering reflex. The Guild taught its members how to keep this state of being as a controlled series of thoughts, and how to turn undisciplined reflex into cautious, minimized commands.

It took three more seconds to find an open transmitter and verify that she had a safe shot to Repeater TL2-IBN5790-ZD701.

Jump.

One, touch the time. Twenty-two minutes gone. Two, fly to the transmitter. Three, shape the destination. Four, five, six, verify a clear jump. Next stop, Guild Hall. Her replica carried the proper encoding, the receiver 'scope was free, the way was clear.

Jump.

The familiar branching chaos and close press of activity that was the outer rim of the Guild Hall. The pathways were constantly clogged with milling presences, reaching and diving through the processor connections, sometimes taking up two and three neighboring stacks at once, filling up every piece of free space, until there was almost no way to get through.

Dobbs snagged a timer that added another thirty-six minutes to her internal count. She swerved sideways until she came to the gateway series monitored by the Guild's automatic system. The Fools laughingly referred to the program as the Drawbridge. She leaned against the closest switches and let them flutter across her identity coding.

"Evelyn Dobbs, membership number 2037." She followed up her identification with her current contract and route. The Drawbridge hesitated for a moment, then opened one of its hundred main gates. Dobbs rushed forward into the open path.

"I have a potential environment or containment problem on my hands," she told the Drawbridge. "Who's free to help out?"

The bridge twitched a series of switches and side gates, sliding her gently between pathways crammed with activity into a slender processing stack. A familiar touch brushed against her thoughts. She reached toward it and found another piece of awareness wrapped inside hers. She opened the route to her memory and let the new voice inside.

"You're coming in off schedule, Dobbs." Cohen's voice blossomed inside her and Dobbs absorbed the greeting and the friendly concern. "Anything wrong with the new contract?"

"Too much is wrong, but it's not with the contract." She reached into Cohen and let her first-level memories of the run and its attendant "incidents" flow freely to him.

Cohen responded with a small twist of pain. Dobbs repeated it in absolute agreement.

"Let's have the details, then maybe we can find a pattern for you. Do you mind if I call in Brooke and Lonn to share?"

"Not at all. We could use Verence, too, if she's free."

Cohen shifted, seeking an unresisting path deeper inside. Reflexively, Dobbs tightened herself. "What happened?"

"We lost her," said Cohen softly. "We had a near miss on Kilimanjaro. She stretched herself too far keeping their network up. By the time the Guild Masters roped in the troublemaker . . . she'd dissipated."

Dobbs folded in on herself. Cohen, suddenly disconnected from her, circled outside. She could feel concern in his touch as he sought an open pathway back to her awareness, but she held herself sealed. Amelia Verence had rescued her from disaster. Verence had brought her into the Guild and stood by her through her training and had sponsored her petition for Master ranking even though the Guild Masters had declared her too undisciplined. Verence had showed her what she wanted to be.

And now she was gone. There were limits as to how far you could go alone, how much you could do and how long you could stay in the network before the complex mix of signals and processes that was *you* became so changed that there was no way you could maintain your own coherence. The Fools mostly called the phenomenon dissipation. The other word for it was death.

Cohen pressed against the shell she had made of her outer self. "I'm sorry, Dobbs. I thought . . . that you'd been notified."

Dobbs shook herself and managed to relax enough to let Cohen reach inside again. "No. But this contract has been keeping me busy . . ." She began to fold again, but this time Cohen held his place. His firm stance helped her stay open even against the grief that was welling through her.

"However," she managed to say, "if I don't pay attention to the *Pasadena*'s problems, Verence is going to haul herself together just to come back and take me apart."

Cohen's laughter rippled across her. "Heaven forbid. Let's see what you've got . . ."

She felt him stretch out streamers down two separate paths, and, after a brief instant's silence, she felt the new awareness reach through him and into her. For a moment they did nothing but adjust to each other's rhythms. Lonn moved in bursts, darting around, pausing to examine what he found and dart off again. Brooke, rigidly organized and thorough, had the clear, separated feeling of someone new to the Guild.

Dobbs shook herself to unclench her memories and let the details of the run flow out where the other three could look them over. Cohen was a longtime friend. She could trust him to be careful with her memories. They would be examined without being altered. No one he brought in would carelessly misalign a pattern she gave them access to, causing her to forget or misremember a crucial point.

The three Fools waded deeply into her memories, watching their flow and separating them into discrete fragments before reuniting them with the whole to see exactly how the events fit into one another. Cohen carefully herded off the emotions and interpretations and left just the factual events for the other two to scrutinize.

"Have you got a religion, Dobbs?" asked Lonn finally.

"None in particular." She tilted herself sideways to get a better feel for the other Fool's touch. "Why?"

"You might want to consider getting one." Lonn lifted up a sequence and placed it in the center of her attention. "You've been incredibly lucky so far."

This wasn't just her memory, this was a recombination of

the notes she'd hijacked from Al Shei's pen and a report she'd caught from Lipinski. Since the Hunt had begun, they'd identified thirty-five separate blips in the systems, all of them random and fleeting, but ten of them in essential areas: life support, climate control, engine timing.

Dobbs felt herself stiffen against the idea. She forced herself to relax again. *Take it all in,* she said down in her private self. *Hear the worst and then how to fix it.*

"I'm afraid I haven't got anything better over here." Brook pulled up another sequence to give to her. "It doesn't look like one thing, it looks like a lot of things. There are at least two distinct code patterns in here and I'm counting twenty-six major active areas, and," he paused, "it looks like it's trying to haul itself together."

Dobbs absorbed the new configuration. Lipinski and Odel had mapped out the anomaly in the pumping system and radiation detectors that had raised the alarm down in engineering, and the other anomaly that had broken down the intercom routing system. Brooke had gathered that up with the snapshot she had of the *Pasadena*'s computer system and flashed a long, tangled line of communication between the two. "This is just a guess on the actual structure, the real comm-contact probably won't last more than thirty picoseconds."

"Between the specs you've shown us here"—Lonn picked up the older facts she had absorbed when she took the contract—"and the observations here." Brooke laid Al Shei's records on top of the memory Lonn held. "I'd say some spot reconfigurations have been done on board to get this mess to work. Why, I don't know, but whoever's done it and for whatever reason, they didn't tell your Houston or your Engineer. They're operating on old data, and that's what's been hitching your systems up." He paused and sorted through some adjoining memories. "Given what you've got on this Tully person, that, at least, shouldn't surprise you."

"So it's either sabotage or stupidity." Dobbs flattened herself out. "Wonderful."

"There's another possibility." Cohen shifted uneasily. "Any chance your ship might have picked up a live one?"

"A live one? Looking like this?" Lonn's incredulity was sharp.

Dobbs ignored him. "I'd thought of that. But from where? There's no facilities for an AI aboard, and Port Oberon isn't even on the watch list, let alone the hot list. There hasn't even been a hint of anything happening inside the Solar System for twenty years.

"Besides, this . . . mess is not acting like a live one. They're randomly destructive. Go off like a bomb and scatter shrapnel everywhere at once." *Like I'm saying anything we don't all know,* thought Dobbs, privately, but she kept going. "This thing is going off here and there in bursts. One isolated section at a time."

"I know that, but . . ." Cohen made a quick weaving motion indicating uncertainty. "But something is not falling into place here. I feel like we're treating the symptoms."

His uneasiness began to weigh Dobbs down. Cohen might be somewhat her junior in years, but he was not given to panic or flights of imagination.

"I'll check on it," she said, even though the idea left a cold, still spot inside her. "I'm going to need a trace on any systems being monitored inside the Solar System right now."

"I can get you that," Lonn assured her. "There's a new watch on the Titania Freers. You might want to check the systems logs on what that pilot of yours has been up to."

Dobbs shrugged her whole self. "Yerusha had an AI with her, but it just got eaten by whatever *Pasadena*'s carrying around in its veins." She took hold of Brook's awareness. "What I need there is a retrace of Marcus Tully's route over the past eight months, if we can."

"That should keep me busy," murmured Brook, stirring in a small whirlpool of annoyance. "For about the next year. Does Al Shei know how her business partner spends his time?"

"She does." Dobbs kept herself smooth and even. "She's had her reasons for putting up with it, which have been strained to the breaking point."

"Don't blame her a bit." Cohen pulled back, taking the other two with him. "Good luck, Dobbs. We'll have what answers there are in forty-eight hours." The anesthetic that put her body far enough under to permit her to enter the network was unhealthy stuff, to say the least. With her diminutive frame, she could only tolerate an extended dosage once every two days without side effects.

PING! The alarm signal from her transceiver, back in the *Pasadena*, cut through her thoughts. This self, the signals, and code had three seconds before it had to begin its journey back to her body.

One.

"Thank you." Dobbs let the gratitude wash over all three of the Fools as they pulled their awareness away from her. Inside her, a set of processes began to shift and merge.

Cohen lingered behind in Dobbs's outer self for just a moment longer.

Two.

"Dobbs, you've really got to work on this group's AI paranoia, you know that?"

"Yeah, I know. Frankly, neither Lipinski nor Yerusha is making that aspect of the job any easier, let me tell you."

"I can imagine." Cohen shook himself ruefully. "Dobbs, you take care of yourself this run, all right? I am feeling . . ." his thoughts prickled uncomfortably against her consciousness.

"So am I, Cohen. So am I."

Three.

Conscious thought began to sink into instinct. She wanted to go back. She couldn't hold still. Time to go back, now. Time to get back to her body before it woke up and her brain's functions blocked her implant's abilities to reintegrate her into her organic mind.

Dobbs skimmed through the Guild Hall to the laser transmitter. She orchestrated her jumps as efficiently as she could. Urgency filled her actions and pressed additional speed on functions guided now fully by instinct. Any second those blips in the *Pasadena*'s essential systems could break open into real crisis.

Finally, she felt the unmistakable path opened by her transceiver. Dobbs drizzled herself down it like a trickle of water down a drain. The transceiver recoded the signals so the implant could convert them into electrical signals that would raise the neurochemical impulses to diffuse into her and restart the body that her hypo dosage had shut down.

There had been cases where Fools' bodies had woken up before the translation process was completed. The signal selves stayed in the nets as long as they could hold together, and then they dissipated as Verence had. The body selves, though, woke up as if they had been in six-month comas. They were permanently brain-damaged and unable to function independently ever again. The physiological markers for the process were inconclusive. Some theorized that without the extra boost from the implant signals, the cognitive functions repressed by the drugs stayed shut down. Some of the more theologically minded theorized it was because the soul had not returned to the body. Dobbs seldom wondered about the implications of either view. She was content to know the process worked.

Light and heat touched her. A thorny pain tingled in her hands and ankles. Her eyes blinked, her throat groaned softly, and her tendons twitched as she gradually became aware that all these things really belonged to her.

Dobbs fumbled with the transceiver until she managed to pull it out of her socket and drop it into the box. Then, with forced patience, she began the long series of stretching exercises that the Guild prescribed to reorient her to her body, gently stretching and separating her toes, ankle circles, leg lifts, arm stretches, rotating her neck. At the end of twenty minutes, she was able to see without the telltale sensation of detachment that always followed a session in the net. She was defined by her body again.

Her body, which was parched with thirst, reeling with hunger and had a bladder that was about to burst.

Dobbs staggered to the bathroom and voided herself. She ran the tap, filling cup after cup of cold water, guzzling them as fast as she could. Feeling moderately more steady, she rifled through her bedside drawer for a deluxe-size ration bar. She had downed half of it when the grief hit.

Verence was dead. The memory surged up from her unconscious with all the rest of what she had learned in the net. Verence was dead. Her stomach clamped down on itself, and so did her throat. Tears she couldn't even think about controlling burst out of her eyes. She did manage to swallow her mouthful before the sobs welled up. Verence had saved her life. Verence had brought her to the Guild and stood by her while she was learning her trade. Dobbs remembered the little, bright-eyed woman tossing scarves in the air, heard her patient voice going over the principles of humor, felt her warm hand on her shoulder. Gone. Her first and best friend was gone.

When the tears finished and the sobs had quieted to gasps, Dobbs managed to force her damp palms down from her face and look up at the desk clock. She'd been out of the net for ten whole minutes.

All right, Dobbs, you do not have time to lollygag. She hoisted herself off the bed. A quick wash and some eyedrops took care of the worst of the evidence of her cry. She made herself finish off the ration bar, even though her stomach no longer felt like accepting it. Then she activated the desk again and checked the time and the crew schedule. Lipinski was on duty and was probably in the comm center, building yet another diagnostic.

Dobbs took the stairs to the hold deck two at a time.

Her prediction proved accurate. Lipinski was swearing energetically at his boards as his pen flew across their surface, making choices and scrawling out orders. Whatever it was giving back to him, he did not like it.

"It's not good enough, it's not even close." He wiped out the last line he'd laid down with a swift, angry stroke. "You're not going to get around me like that, whoever the hell you are. Oh, Jesus, Mary, and Joseph, maybe you are . . ." If he had heard the hatch cycle, he gave no sign.

Dobbs felt a twinge of sympathy inside her as Lipinski lifted up his coffee bulb, thumbed the lid back, and took a huge gulp.

She braced herself, set a cheeky smile on her face, and stepped forward.

"They seek it here, they seek it there, the Houston seeks it everywhere. Is it in Heaven, is it in Hell, that damned, elusive . . . virus of totally unknown origin." She finished off, deliberately lame. It was evident that Lipinski did not get the joke, but that was all right; he at least looked at her.

"Piss off, Fool," he muttered.

"No thanks. Took care of that before I left my cabin." She

leaned both elbows against the corner of his board. "So, is it in Heaven or Hell?"

"I wish it was. Actually, I wish its maker was." He erased the line he was working on and wrote QUERY NEW PATTERN CENTER LACKING HOUSTON AUTHORIZATION.

"Couldn't be anywhere near that simple," he said. "Crackers usually forget something simple, though. They're just like any other systems freak. They think they know everything, but they don't. They know generalities, not specifics. They don't know all the ins and outs of a particular system unless they've made a study of that single unit, and who in all the hells under all the heavens would have made a study of the *Pasadena*?"

"Someone who wanted Chandra's curry recipe?" Dobbs quipped. "Or, better yet, someone who wanted to STOP Chandra's curry recipe." She drew herself up straight. "Marshal your forces, troops! We cannot allow this to get out! We must invade in force, leave no corner unsearched, inside, outside, in my lady's chamber! You!"—she spun around and faced an imaginary private—"Take the main database. You!" She spun again. "Take the bridge links! You!" She faced the back wall and poked at it with her index finger. "You take the kitchens, but she's far too clever to leave it in plain sight. Stay in contact! We can't let ourselves be cut off! We'll surround it and cut off its backups, divide and conquer, Troops! Because if we don't . . ."

Lipinski had gone round-eyed and slack-jawed.

"Oh my God!" He snatched up his pen. "Oh my God, I've been looking for the wrong thing! I'm an idiot! An idiot!"

He began scribbling in a convoluted shorthand almost too fast for Dobbs to follow. He was ordering searches for binary signals, line feedback, random-number streams, not in any of the affected systems, but in the remaining "clean" systems.

The responses came back positive.

"Got you!" he cried. "Got you, you fractured key-code imitation comm check! You're mine! Intercom to Schyler!"

"Schyler here, Houston. Good news?" The hope in his voice was almost aching.

"Good news, Watch. I've caught the thing talking to itself. It's not a single virus, it's a bunch of them."

A moment of silence. "Please tell me you can do something about this?"

Lipinski licked his lips. "Now that I know what its comm patterns look like, I can write up some roadblocks for them. If we can isolate the individual nerve centers, we can pick them off one at a time."

"Any chance of getting this done before we get to The Farther Kingdom?"

Lipinski looked down at his board. Responses from the ship's systems were still coming in. He swallowed. "I don't think so, but we can at least neutralize the thing, things, so that we stand a good chance of *getting* to The Farther Kingdom."

"I'll take that." Schyler sighed. "Get going, Lipinski. Dictate a report to your relief and let the rest of us know what we need to start doing. I'll call Al Shei. Intercom to close."

Lipinski flashed Dobbs the first genuine smile she'd seen in twenty-four hours.

"I could kiss you, you Fool."

She smiled back. "Nah. You'd have to catch me first."

She slid sideways out the hatch.

In the corridor, she rubbed her forehead. *Dobbs, you need some sleep yourself. You keep giving him answers like that, he's going to be leaving a permission-to-court request on your line before you can say "boo." And you don't want to have to deal with that, do you?* She started back up the stairs.

Do you?

Chapter Five

LANDFALL

Al Shei swept her gaze across the roster. Clustered around the far end of the conference table, the other three section heads shuffled their films. Resit tucked a wisp of hair back under her *kijab*. All of them sat up a little too straight and held their shoulders a little too stiffly. Every one of them had dark shadows under their eyes, except for Dobbs sitting quietly in her corner. Despite that, Al Shei was sure the Fool was as short of sleep as all the others.

We made it. We're safely docked, she reminded herself. *Now we can start setting things to rights again.*

"All right, we're going to stay in dock at The Farther Kingdom for a week so we can all catch our breaths. We'll be using up what leeway we've got on the packets for the Vicarage and then some, but we can't function the way we've been going. First priority is to get the Dane packet delivered to the New Medina Hospital, second is to get everybody cooled down. Then, we're going to flush our virus out of the systems."

Schyler nodded. "It's worth the wait. All three shifts are wound fairly tight." He cast a sideways glance at the Fool. "Not as bad as it could have been, though."

Dobbs accepted the compliment with a small bow.

"Thank you, Watch." Al Shei drew her pen across that item on her roster and it vanished. "Houston, we need you to tap into the port authorities, find out about the docking and shuttle fees. Resit, work up the contracts we need to take leave for three local days and get a download of the local regs. Try to bring it in under four thousand, okay?"

"Any other miracles while I'm at it?" Resit murmured to her stack of films.

"A dove out of your sleeve would be entertaining," quipped Dobbs.

"And messy." Resit smiled at her. "Chandra would just want to serve it for lunch."

"Speaking of which," said Chandra mildly. "Since we're going to be staying, I could use my allowance transferred. Baldassare and I should be doing some grocery shopping."

"All right." Al Shei made a note on her film. "Anybody else?"

Resit waved her pen toward Al Shei. "My Farther Kingdom files are two years out-of-date, I could use an upgrade."

"Cost?"

"Lots."

Al Shei eyed her sourly.

Resit shrugged. "Look, we're going to be running loose with two-year-old legal backup. It could cost much more than an upgrade if somebody missteps. Ordinarily it wouldn't be that important, but The Farther Kingdom law is *complicated*, even by colony standards."

"Get a receipt on film." Al Shei leaned over and scribbled a new line in the film ledger spread open in front of her. "Anybody else?"

There was silence. "All right." She flipped the ledger shut and wrote SECURE across the top to seal it. "Watch, work up a leave schedule and notify the crew. Make sure Chandra gets her shopping time. That's everything for the moment."

Her crew filed out dutifully, and Al Shei rubbed her eyes. When she opened them again, she saw Dobbs sitting in the same corner of the room she had occupied since the meeting started.

"Bad run," the Fool remarked quietly.

Al Shei sighed. "Yes, especially since we're going to have to be taking late penalties on all our cargo to the Vicarage and Out There because we've got to take the extra time to certify that our virus didn't touch it." She wondered briefly when she had decided the thing was "our virus." "If things keep up like this, we may just break even by the time we get back to Port Oberon." She chuckled ruefully. "Some days I think Murphy must be one of the recording angels."

"Sorry?" Dobbs picked herself easily up off the floor. "I know Murphy's law, of course . . ."

"Munkir and Nakir are the recording angels who write down all deeds to be read on the Day of Judgment. I think Murphy's out there with them recording every incidence of overconfidence to be read right now." She scowled at the ledger, then looked up at Dobbs. "I'd better get myself on that shore leave roster, hadn't I?"

Dobbs nodded soberly. "I think it might be a good idea, Boss. Otherwise, Chandra will shackle you in the sunroom and I'll have to sneak in with a string file to get you out and then she'll be after us both with a carving knife and that'll be even messier than Resit's dove."

"Mmmm." Al Shei arched her eyebrows thoughtfully. "Bad for morale, that sort of thing."

"Usually, yes," agreed Dobbs.

Al Shei chuckled and sighed again. "Ah, Dobbs. Have you ever met anybody you couldn't make laugh?"

"Once. But it turned out he had had his sense of humor surgically removed. I tried to have it regrown, but it turns out it requires a special vat, and would have taken my year's salary, so I resigned my commission and became a monk in the Andes preserve for ten years while the blow to my ego healed." Dobbs gave her exiting bow. "See you ashore, Boss."

"See you," said Al Shei absently.

When the hatch cycled shut, Al Shei rubbed her temples and stared at her pile of films.

It had been two days of quiet. Lipinski's roadblocks appeared to have done the trick. The virus was still inside the *Pasadena*, but it was inoperative, apparently. Everything had run exactly as it was supposed to, and they had docked at The Gate, The Farther Kingdom's space station, without incident.

For those same two days, Al Shei had found herself totally unable to relax. She knew there was nothing else to be done until they got into port, where there were help and contacts that went beyond the expertise that even *Pasadena*'s crew had to offer. All she could do was wait. It had not been easy, on her or on the engineering team. She smoothed her *hijab* down. If there was any extra to go round after this run was over, Javerri, Ianiai, and Shim'on were getting bonuses.

If there's anything at all to go round, she amended gloomily.

She shoved the thought aside. She hadn't had a zero run in the six years she'd been crewing the *Pasadena*, and she wasn't going to start with this one. The Kerensk AI could have been pumped into the lines, and Lipinski'd find a way to ferret it out.

Come on, Al Shei, time for prayer.

She took herself down the stairs and knocked on Resit's cabin as she passed. She opened the cabin hatch just as Resit, carrying her prayer rug, opened the bathroom door.

Knowing they were docked and that, finally, there was something else she could do, infused her prayer with a feeling of relief. When they were finished and had reclaimed their veils, Al Shei asked her cousin, "So, aside from spend my money, what are you going to do with your leave?"

"I think I'm going to New Ashbury and join a spacers' commune." Resit pinned her *kijab* underneath her chin.

"Right." Al Shei laughed. "And I'm going to New Rome and be baptized."

"Actually," said Resit, suddenly serious, "I've been wondering what you are going to be doing."

"After Lipinski and I get Amory Dane's medical data delivered to the hospital, I think I'll stay on and do some shopping in New Medina," she lied carefully. "Find something fun yet light to send home to the kids and Asil."

"Um," Resit grunted, and picked up her rug. "Just tell me this, oh-my-cousin, should I keep my Incili box with me in case this shopping gets out of hand?"

Al Shei forced herself not to turn away. "That might be a good idea."

Resit measured her carefully with a lawyer's eye. "You're going to hire Uysal to try to identify what Tully stole, aren't you?"

"I never said that." Al Shei wrapped her *hijab* across her face.

"Katmer." Resit laid a hand on Al Shei's forearm. "Eventually, Ruqaiyya is going to have to face the fact that she married an antisocial nitwit. You aren't going to be able to keep that from her much longer."

"I don't intend to." Al Shei pulled away. "But I do intend to find out what I've got to nail them both with first."

Resit raised her hand. "As your lawyer, I do not want to hear the rest of this." She pulled open the bathroom door. "But I'm really glad you decided to spring for the updates," she added over her shoulder.

"We won't need them," said Al Shei. But as the door closed she added, "God willing and the creeks don't rise."

Al Shei shook herself and walked over to the desk.

"Intercom to comm center," she called as she sat down.

"Lipinski here."

"I need a fast-time line to Earth, Bala house, ID specifically for Asil Tamruc."

Lipinski muttered something she didn't catch, so it was probably directed at the wall, and she probably didn't want to know what it was anyway. "Right. I'll route it up there as soon as it's open."

Al Shei stared at the blank view screen and tried to force at least some of her worry into perspective. The worst had not happened. The ship was not incapacitated in any way. The data from Amory Dane to New Medina hospital was intact. The hospital had already said they'd accept delivery and deliver full payment if the data cleared their virus screens. She already knew Tully had done something illegal. Now it was just a question of how illegal it was. There were lots of degrees of illegality, especially for crackers.

That, Al Shei realized, was exactly what was worrying her.

The view screen flashed into life and Asil smiled across light years at her. The wall behind him had a pair of extra memory boards on it. It was the house's main communications room. Old-fashioned and formal, her family felt that heavy business or recreational systems use should have their own area separate from the places where people interacted with each other. Al Shei tried to tell herself that finding Asil there was not necessarily a bad sign.

"*Salam*, Beloved." She undid her *hijab* so he could see her smile. "Do you have news for me?"

"*Salam*, and yes, I do." The quick smile faded from his face. "Not much though, and what there is—it's not good."

Al Shei strangled a sigh. "I'm braced, Asil. What is it?"

"The records on this end show two substantial deposits made into the corporation accounts by Marcus Tully during the previous eight months. This is normal. I have the downloads of the *Pasadena*'s logs, and they detail the contracts and the deliveries that resulted in the income. I have records from Port Oberon, Port Ursula, and Taylor's Crash that say the *Pasadena* was exactly where the log says it was."

He paused, and Al Shei felt her hands curl in on themselves. "This is the part where you tell me what you don't have."

"Fuel purchase records." Asil swept one hand out across the boards. "None of the tankers in any of those systems have records of fueling or watering the *Pasadena* at any point during those eight months." He glowered at the boards for a moment before he looked up again and saw her gawping. "I had to be thorough," he said. "He is a first-rate cracker, and we've both suspected he's a forger for some time now."

Al Shei rubbed her face with both hands. "He must have faked that log after the download. Schyler would never have stood for him faking it on board."

"I know."

She raised her eyes again. "Anything else?"

"Queries in the works. I'm afraid making heavy use of Uncle Ahmet's name to access security tapes—"

Al Shei blanched. "Asil, you didn't tell him."

"No, I didn't, Beloved," he said quietly. "I told him we were in receipt of a suspicious contract proposal." He paused again. "This has to be the end of the partnership, though, Katmer. We both want the *Mirror of Fate*, but not this badly."

"How long are you going to let him keep stealing fodder and labor?" She murmured to her hands. "I know, Asil. Zubedye has been telling me the same thing, and you're both right."

He reached up and touched his hand to the screen. "It doesn't have to be the end of our plans, Katmer. We're very close. A loan or two backed by your family name, and we can do it. I don't like debt service either, but I've got some payment scenarios working on my private terminal even as we speak." His voice hardened. "I will not have Marcus Tully tainting what we've worked for."

Al Shei pressed her palm against his. "Neither will I. But as long as Ruqaiyya refuses to divorce him, anything he goes through reflects on her, and the news grubbers will be in ecstasies over it. 'Member of prominent banking family found guilty of—' " She waved her hand aimlessly. "Whatever it is. I still want to find out what he's done and use it to convince him to walk away quietly."

Asil gave her a long look. "From *Pasadena* or from Ruqaiyya?"

"If this gets put on the wire, it will kill her, Asil, and if it becomes a police matter, it will get on the wire."

His sigh was so soft that the intercom barely picked it up. "You're right about that, on both counts. All right, Beloved, I'll find out what I can."

"Thank you, Asil. I'll call in from the Vicarage."

"May it go easily. I love you."

"I love you." They exchanged soft smiles that spoke of love as much as their words did, and Al Shei closed the connection down.

She sat where she was for a long moment before she managed to rewrap her *hijab* and force herself onto her feet.

You still have work to do. Al Shei pulled her pack out of its drawer. *No matter what else happens*, you *have work to do.*

Fastening the straps around her shoulders, she left her cabin to meet Lipinski at the airlock.

The Houston was waiting for her with his tool kit in one hand and a duffel slung over his shoulder. There was something sour in his expression as he clasped the shore-leave band around his wrist.

"Not enough coffee?" inquired Al Shei, putting on her own band. The bands would allow The Farther Kingdom's satellite system to track them down if someone needed to contact them.

"Not enough something." He laid his hand against the palm reader. Both of the airlock doors rolled back, and Lipinski strode out into the station.

"And you don't want to talk about it, I can tell," murmured Al Shei into her *hijab* as she followed him.

Although it was a populous colony, The Farther Kingdom didn't see anything approaching the amount of traffic of the Solar System, so The Gate didn't require the complex organization of the Uranus ports. The Gate had only a single ring of habitat modules attached to its core. Unlike Oberon, the docking was controlled entirely by the station's AI. There, Yerusha had proved one advantage of having a Freer pilot. For the first time, no one complained about the autodocking procedures. Yerusha pulled the maneuvers off as smoothly as Al Shei had ever felt.

Also unlike Port Oberon, The Gate was simply a warehouse and workshop. Shippers either stayed berthed in their vessels or went down to the planet's surface. There were no hotel or entertainment facilities. There wasn't even a market. Required goods were bought directly or remotely from the surface and shuttled up to the station, where they were held for pickup. Al Shei felt a sympathetic twinge for Yerusha. Freers could not, or would not, set foot groundside. Most of them drew the line at even entering a planet's atmosphere. True human freedom, they said, came when humans lived in the environments they created entirely for themselves. Al Shei made a mental note to tell the Sundars that Yerusha would need to be nagged to get off the ship for at least a little while. Freer or not, the human mind did not function well staring at the same walls all the time. A stir-crazy pilot was not what she needed.

The gravity in the port was at most only three-quarters normal. Impatience warred with prudence as Al Shei paced along behind Lipinski in a careful, low-gravity stride. What she really wanted to do was run to the shuttle dock. She wanted to shove her way to the head of the line and leave for the planet immediately. She wanted to deliver Dr. Dane's packet to the New Medina Hospital and have the download go without incident so that at least one portion of her problems would be over with.

All of which was, of course, impossible. She could only make her way down the curving corridor that had been wrapped in bristly, brown Velcro everywhere there wasn't a green memory board or a door. Short, narrow hallways branched off here and there, leading to holding areas or workspaces that were little more than blisters in the station's hull. Men and women in sturdy tan coveralls bearing no sign or sigil of allegiance or religion filtered through gaggles of shippers with packs on their shoulders or bundles in their hands. The total lack of marking was the badge of The Gate crew. They went about their tasks with the kind of intensity that came either from concentration or boredom. Every now and again she and Lipinski had to step aside for an automated cart rolling down the corridor, crunching the carpeting under its soft wheels.

Maybe Yerusha should stay aboard the Pasadena, thought Al Shei as she and Lipinski skirted another tool cart. *There's almost more to see there.*

Al Shei understood the need for the total neutrality of their surroundings. The Farther Kingdom needed a functioning port in order to be a functioning world, and that port had to belong to the whole colony. Like any station, though, it would have a crew confined to cramped quarters for a long time. There could not be any risk of feuds that were old before the Fast Burn breaking out up here.

The Farther Kingdom worked, but not easily. Even Resit did not pretend to understand the treaties that governed it. Besides The Gate, there was one other permanent station in orbit around the colony, and that one held their diplomatic corps. It housed over eight hundred representatives whose entire lives were spent in the negotiations that kept the peace.

The Farther Kingdom had been founded while the Slow Burn was still going on. Not surprisingly, it had a large Islamic population. Several of Al Shei's ancestors had emigrated there to save their lives as well as their faith. But so had people from a hundred other faiths. While all the settlers knew they would be living cheek by jowl with people who had been their grandparent's enemies, the reality of it hit hard sometimes. There had been several full-scale wars, before the diplomatic corps was formed and the formal treaties put into place.

It was a world of pacifists, traditionalists, recluses, and fanatics. It was one of the most brittle colonies, but it was also one of the most ambitious, and it had somehow managed to survive its own problems for three hundred years.

Terse signs written in five languages guided them to the shuttle docks. They joined the queue of other shippers waiting for passage. Resit spotted them from farther up in the line. She waved, then rolled her eyes and opened her hands to Heaven, seeking patience.

Al Shei queued up behind Lipinski and concentrated on reminding herself they had to be patient, that she was the one who decided they all needed a moment's rest before tackling the problem of flushing the ship's systems, and that shifting her weight from foot to foot was not doing anything to speed up the line.

Lipinski's brooding silence was not helping anything. She could almost believe he really was reading the boards of security information that covered the far wall. By the time they reached the head of the line, Al Shei was beginning to get genuinely concerned. Lipinski's style was to talk to everyone and everything within earshot, not to brood in silence.

Well, you are not exactly encouraging him, Al Shei reminded herself. Her tired mind tried to come up with a neutral conversational opening, but by the time she decided on "Have you ever been to New Medina, Lipinski?" they had reached the arched security gate.

The line was funneled through the narrow, off-white space. Al Shei could identify only half a dozen of the scanners contained in the ceramic frame. They were looking for weapons, controlled ingestibles or literatures, any encrypted recordings, or any sealed cameras. Dobbs had joked that the members of The Farther Kingdom diplo-corps were funding one final scanner to make their security program complete, except it was proving fiendishly hard to make one that could read minds.

A low chime sounded, and the station's AI spoke up in a clear, contralto voice from the top of the arch. "Passenger Rurik Lipinski will please step to Terminal 12 to supply further information."

"All right, all right." Lipinski tightened his grip on his tool kit. "You want to know what I've got in the box. I know the drill, and I've registered all of it."

"All information must be directed to the security terminal," replied the station. Al Shei suppressed a smile. Lipinski turned toward her and, with an exaggerated grimace, bit his tongue.

Al Shei shook her head as he marched over toward the clusters of security booths. She wondered if the AI had a special subroutine to deal with malcontents.

Probably. The Farther Kingdom has not managed this long by being sloppy. The AI might do the talking, but alert crew members stood at regular intervals along the corridor. They weren't carrying any weapons Al Shei could see, but that meant little.

No one else in the immediate vicinity seemed to be carrying anything identifiably objectionable, so the alarms and the station's AI kept silent. Al Shei moved out from under the arch, trying hard not to step on the heels of the people in front of her.

The shuttle waiting at the end of the airlock was as basic as the station. It was a single-stage rocket designed for nothing more than short flights. Al Shei strapped herself into a seat that in the local gravity made her feel like she was lying on her back with her knees trying to curl up into her chest.

"Five minutes to launch," said a voice that was a twin to the one in the security arch. "Please consult your individual seats to make sure your straps are arranged for maximum safety and comfort."

There was a buzzing of soft, mechanical voices around her. Al Shei had no intention of consulting her seat about anything. There was nothing it could do to make itself something other than cramped and undignified.

At last, Lipinski climbed through the forward hatch and shuffled to his seat. His duffle and tool kit were still in his possession, so he must really have registered everything properly. Al Shei tried to tell herself she had not expected anything less, but too much had gone wrong since they left the Solar System for her to make that really stick in her mind.

Then came the predictable half dozen announcements: two minutes to launch, check your straps, security monitors are fully operational in case there are problems, if you have any questions, consult your seat immediately, thirty seconds to launch, ten, nine, eight . . .

A soft grating sounded under the floor and the ship fell away from the station. Al Shei's body told her she fell with it. The couch was no longer uncomfortable, it was only gently swaddling. Al Shei's joints began to relax, even though her stomach lurched at the sudden absence of gravity.

Al Shei hated shuttle flights. They were a boring interval in between events. Usually, however, it took fifteen or twenty minutes before the irritation built up. This time, though, they hadn't been in free fall for ten seconds before she fidgeted with her chafing straps, drummed her fingers against her chair arms, and let her gaze dart around her tiny space, looking moodily for something to distract her. There was a memory board and a view screen in front of her. She could call up some entertainment, or work over the *Pasadena*'s schedule one more time and see if she could get an optimistic projection to hang her hopes on.

Or she could just hang here and try for the thousandth time to understand why Ruqaiyya had married Marcus Tully.

She could remember Tully the way she first saw him. His eyes had all but glowed with energy. He talked animatedly about human potential and the unlimited possibilities that all lay in the sky. "God has created more wonders than we'll ever know about," he used to say. "But there's no harm in trying!" He used to smile at Ruqaiyya when he talked like that, and Al Shei could feel her sister's admiration for Tully's boldness like the sun against her skin. She admired him herself. His dreams ran so close to hers. A ship of his own, freedom to pursue his own ideas, but not as a vagrant or a lone hero. That was the man Ruqaiyya had married before Al Shei had enough experience to warn her sister that Tully was too naive to be trusted with such giddy dreams.

Reality sneaked in soon enough. Tully began to see how corporate interests were valued above individual skill, how the daily business of living could make money vanish like smoke, and how no one would give him a ship when all he had were dreams in his head and burns on his hands.

That was when he started to change. She had watched the glow dim in Tully's eyes, and in her sister's. He had stopped talking about human potential and started talking about human greed. He began to lower his sights from the secrets of the universe and focus on the secrets of the corporations that he thought were hemming him in. He began to take pride in making their systems leak. He began to enjoy it, and that joy gave him enough comfort that he forgot what he was, and allowed him to tell himself that he was still pursuing his dream of life in space, even though his wife was marooned on Earth because she had no skills he could use and he could not afford to take along a nonworking passenger. Tully's budgets ran even tighter than Al Shei's did.

Al Shei sometimes wondered why Ruqaiyya didn't get training as a nurse, or a steward, or even a lawyer, so she could pay her own way. The *Pasadena* was not palatial, but it was livable. She thought she knew the answer, but she did not like it. Ruqaiyya did not want to see what her husband did while he was away from her. She did not really want to know how far he had fallen from the dreams she had married. That was why she stayed on the ground, so she could pretend to herself and the family that nothing had changed.

And that is why I never said anything, isn't it? Al Shei ran her hands over the chair's armrests. *I didn't want to have to be the one to strip the last of her pride away.*

She was so far gone in her reverie, Al Shei barely noticed when the shuttle hit the atmosphere, until the thrusters roared to life and brought gravity back down with a vengeance.

Al Shei did not request the view screen to show her the outside. She had no trouble with flying under any conditions, but something inside her rebelled at landings. She never got comfortable watching the ground rise up to meet her.

The roar grew louder, and the thrust shoved Al Shei back into the padded seat until her spine pressed against the couch frame. Her lungs labored against a rib cage that wanted to collapse. Then the pressure was gone, and she could breathe and sit up, and, very soon, get impatient about the exit procedures. The ship's voice reeled off a set of seat numbers and all the passengers in the named seats had to be out of the shuttle and on their way before the next set could be called.

When the ship finally told her she could go, Al Shei snatched her pack out of the holding bin and made a beeline for the exit ramp. Down at the end of the sloping tunnel, Lipinski was explaining the contents of his tool kit yet again, this time to a tall, walnut-skinned customs official in tan coveralls with a piece of film clutched in his hand.

Al Shei shook her head and made her way over to the banks of luggage carriers. She took out her pen and wrote her hotel address and Lipinski's on the cart's memory board and added enough credit for the cart to get their bags to their rented quarters. The receipt had just finished printing off when Lipinski came up behind her.

"I know, I know, I know," he said, dropping his duffel into the cart and sliding the lid shut. "It's necessary to keep the colony functioning. They have to be careful, but do they have to run you through the same questions three times?"

Al Shei didn't bother to answer. She wanted to be at the hospital already. She wanted everything to have gone right and to be over with.

They followed the signs to the tram station which was little more than an insulated metal tunnel riveted to the side of the port building. The tram was automated and roofed, but open on the sides. Al Shei wrote their destination across the memory board and was relieved to see it slot them first on the list.

They had barely sat themselves down on one of the thinly padded benches when the tram lurched forward and pulled out into the bright sunlight.

New Medina was situated in the middle of a desert plain. Distant mountains provided a backdrop for the minarets and domes. Cultivated fields patrolled by automated irrigators passed on both sides. The farmland was broken occasionally by boxy outbuildings or processing mills. The shuttle flights to and from the port were bright needles of silver in the blue sky. On the road, the rest of the traffic glided or rattled by, depending on its state of repair. The wind was hot and dusty, but Al Shei could still smell the distant cool scent of the Persian River.

Al Shei felt her shoulders hunch up. All the openness was a little intimidating. As a child of the Management Union Earth, Al Shei was used to a barrier between herself and the wide outer world.

Maybe that, she reflected, *is why most starbirds are from Earth. We're used to being shut in all the time.*

Gradually, the greenscape became narrower and the buildings became bigger. None of them, though, were allowed actually to touch the tall sandstone wall that marked the edge of the city proper.

The New Medina Hospital was a bright, white conglomeration of buildings with grounds that backed onto the city wall. Arched corridors like tunnels of chalk connected its modules. Red crescent moons topped the spires on its three central domes. The tram took them past carefully cultivated groves of orange trees and date palms. Patients in clean blue robes strolled on the lawns or sat in the sun, each one followed by a crab-leggged medical drone. These patients had conditions too severe to be taken care of by the neighborhood doctors that the hospital serviced with information and advice. These were the surgeries, the long-term illnesses, and those who needed new tissue, limbs, or organs grown in the bio-gardens.

The tram took them to the main entrance of the administrative building. No one waited outside the wood and wrought-iron door to greet them. Al Shei wrote her name and their contact's name on the memory board that hung above the door handles. The door swung open, and she and Lipinski strode into the hospital.

They entered a broad, three-tiered gallery. The light was adjusted to imitate spring sunlight, and the air circulated constantly, spreading a vague scent of lemon and orange. The dark-tiled floors and cream walls were as clean as the inside of the *Pasadena*'s data-hold. Windows were set in the walls at about six-meter intervals. Some of them were darkened, but through the clear ones Al Shei could see into chambers containing one person manning more boards and monitors than would be found on the bridge of a major passenger ship.

A woman in a plain white *kijab* approached them down the corridor, kicking up the hem of her black dress at every step.

" 'Dama Al Shei, 'Ster Lipinski, welcome to the Aquarium." She waved at the rows of windows. "I'm Second Administrator Shirar." She shook Al Shei's hand and beamed at Lipinski. "We've been waiting months for these updates. It's going to triple our garden's efficiency."

"Then we should get them right down here," said Al Shei briskly. "Thank you for agreeing to let us supervise the download from here. This data's a little tricky." She looked to Lipinski for confirmation.

"Tightly packed at any rate," he said.

"Of course it is," Shirar smiled. "It's biology. Let me show you our download facilities." She beckoned for them to follow her.

The second administrator walked them down the gallery past window after window of activity. The staff on the other side chattered, sketched, searched, and transferred. In a few of the offices, two or three employees worked together on some problem.

"It looks as if you could consult for the entire colony from here," remarked Al Shei after they passed the twentieth office.

Shirar snorted. "Sometimes I feel like we do. We've got 20 percent of the medical practitioners in The Farther Kingdom on our subscribers' list, and I swear to you some of them won't diagnose a hangnail without tying up our lines for half an hour." She grinned again. "This is not counting the other hospitals we support."

Shirar stopped in front of a thickly hinged door and stuck her pen into the reader socket. After a moment, the door swung back and she led them inside.

The room was three times as large as any of the offices they had passed. The walls were a solid mass of input boards, memory boards, and monitor screens.

Lipinski relaxed his shoulders and straightened up some from his perpetual stoop. Amid this bewildering mass of communications hardware, he was at home.

His expert eye immediately picked up the main uplink boards and he set his tool kit down next to them. He whistled to one of the chairs in the far corner, which obediently trundled over so he could sit down.

With a few pen strokes he called up the configuration and capacity of the hospital's links as well as the mapping for the storage room's lines and depositories.

"And the new data is to be stored, where?" Lipinski cocked an eyebrow at the Second Administrator.

"Area 6421C." Shirar circled the depository's location on the screen. "We've had it waiting empty for a week for you."

Lipinski ran his pen along the pathways to the storage area. The section of the diagram that he traced enlarged itself and the current load and configuration information printed across the top of the board.

Lipinski studied it for a moment, pursed his lips, and nodded. Al Shei gave silent thanks for the fact that he did not seem inclined to talk to the boards in front of their client.

"It all looks right to spec," he said. "Have you opened your virus filters?"

"Area 6813B, open access." Shirar gave Al Shei a sideways look. "Thank you for transmitting your storage records to us. To say we were concerned when you reported a virus would be an understatement."

"I cannot blame you at all," Al Shei replied, grateful that New Medina's dedication to courtesy kept Shirar's language restrained. She did not want to know what the woman had really thought when the news came through. "The virus was an invasion of the ship's system, and it did not touch our cargo, for which, believe me, we were all thankful." *Which would also be an understatement.*

Lipinski twisted around to face Shirar. "Shall I get started?"

"Please do."

Lipinski wrote the *Pasadena*'s call codes and his own name across the uplink board and waited while the system transmitted the message up the lines and across the atmosphere to the station. The screen above the board cleared to show the scene in the *Pasadena*'s comm center. Odel sat stiffly at the main boards, obviously very much aware that this needed to work smoothly.

"*Pasadena* here," came Odel's voice through the intercom. "Waiting on your signal, Houston." The secondary screens lit up with the current status of the *Pasadena*'s lines.

"Setting the boards now, *Pasadena*," replied Lipinski. His blue eyes flickered back and forth as he took in the line readings. He rapidly adjusted the settings on the board in front of him to match what the ship was using. "Start sending in five . . . four . . . three . . ."

"*Bismillahir*," said Shirar.

"*Bismillahir*," agreed Al Shei, a little more fervently than she intended.

"Now," said Lipinski.

On the screen, Odel turned his pen in its socket. The signal load statistics increased on the board and the free capacity stats shrank. Odel ran his own checks, monitoring flow, switching storage taps, watching the code print out straight from *Pasadena*'s hold. Rows of code appeared on the memory board in front of Lipinski. The Houston read the information intently, writing on the board in front of him without looking at his hand; adjusting, controlling, guiding. He nodded a couple of times. His brow was furrowed and his lips moved constantly, but he didn't stop. He didn't call to Odel to halt the download. Al Shei realized her heart had risen to her throat, and she swallowed hard, trying to force herself to be calm.

Either it's going to work or it isn't. You've got one of the best in the business doing the job. You're just going to have to wait it out a little while longer.

Five interminable minutes later, Odel lifted his head. "That's all of it, Houston. Transmission complete."

Lipinski's eyes swept across the final row of code. "Okay, *Pasadena*, we've got it. Thanks." He turned in his chair and Al Shei saw a look that meant "no problems" flash her way.

She had to stop herself from letting out a sigh of relief.

"And there you are, Second Administrator Shirar," she said brightly. "Your bio-garden's data, and I'm only sorry our humble ship could not get it here faster."

Shirar gave her a small bow. "You have done exactly as we hoped. The remaining credit will be transferred into your account as soon as I submit a receipt of verification to our accounting center. It should be done within the next two hours. Will you wait?"

"If you'll excuse us, 'Dama," said Al Shei, as Lipinski got to his feet. "It has been a long flight and I confess my Houston and I were both looking forward to stretching our legs and seeing your city. The *Pasadena* will be in dock for another week, so if you need to contact us, the city system will be able to find us in no time."

Shirar smiled and stood aside, making a sweeping gesture

toward the door. "I understand perfectly. I'll contact you as soon as the accounts have been cleared."

"Thank you for taking the time, Second Administrator," said Al Shei, sticking to courtesies, even though Lipinski was evidently getting impatient.

"Thank you for supplying our needs, 'Dama." Shirar walked them out into the corridor. "I am certain you will be hearing from us again."

They left the second administrator in the doorway. Out in the desert sunlight, Lipinski stretched his arms overhead and let them swing freely down.

"God almighty, I feel better," he announced to the world at large. "Some of those sequences took so long to download, I was about ready to shi . . . do something really unmentionable."

"Me too." Al Shei gave him a cautious glance. "I am assuming nothing went wrong."

"Not a thing," Lipinski said. "Everything Amory Dane gave us, we gave them, checked, double-checked, and triple-checked, vouched for, and sealed."

"Wonderful," said Al Shei, meaning it. Then, she looked away and tugged at her tunic sleeve. "Now I've got a favor to ask you, Houston."

The grin faded from his face. "That's a first, Engine."

Her mouth twitched. "I know, but it's been an exceedingly strange run." She looked up at him again and squared her shoulders. "I'm going to try to find out where Tully got his . . . merchandise from. I might need you to do some backup research. In that event, I need you to stay in New Medina for your leave. Under contract you don't have to have any part of this . . ."

Lipinski waved his hands. "Only she would bring up a contract now," he told the nearest orange tree.

"Only you would protest to the vegetation." Al Shei felt a sudden warmth for her Houston. "Will you do it?"

"Of course I will. I want to know what's been happening as much as you do. Besides," he added to the pavement, "my plans haven't exactly come out right for this trip down."

Oh dear, Houston, who said no? Al Shei did not ask. She just said, "Thank you."

"You're welcome." He waved toward an approaching tram and didn't look at her until it pulled up alongside them. This one was a newer model than the one in which they'd arrived, with tinted windows.

"Please state your destination clearly," said the tram's tinny voice.

Lipinski looked at her with raised eyebrows.

"No thanks." She wrapped her *hijab* more firmly around herself. "I'm going to walk."

Lipinski shrugged. "Call me when you need me, Al Shei." He took his seat. "Ali Farah's Guest House," he said, clearly. The tram pulled away and left Al Shei standing on her own, a soft breeze fluttering her hems.

She lifted her face to the sunlight for a moment, letting the heat beat against her eyelids and enjoying the sensation of peace it gave her. They'd had one victory at any rate. Now was the time to see if she could go secure another.

"Intercom to Bridge," Odel's voice rang across the bridge. "The packet's loaded and closed off. We're done."

Dobbs leapt to her feet. "Whoopee!" She pulled a gold cloth streamer out of her sleeve and tossed it into the air. The low gravity grabbed it gently and lowered it in lazy waves.

"Finally!" exclaimed Yerusha from her station.

Schyler watched Dobbs's streamer settle in a gentle heap.

"Pretty, but not exactly regulation," he remarked, moving his pen to call up the ship's log on his board. Dobbs, however, did not miss the relaxation that pure relief brought to his features.

"Your pardon, Watch Commander." She whisked the streamer off the deck and tied it around her own neck in a big bow. "I forgot, you disapprove of frivolity on the bridge." She laced her fingers under her chin and began a bad series of pirouettes to take her to the hatchway. Behind her, Cheney whooped with laughter.

When she was alone on the stairway, she pulled the streamer off her neck and stuffed it in her pocket. With a determined stride she seldom let the crew see, she hustled down to the berthing deck.

She should be touring the decks to make sure that the rest

of the crew on board had leave plans and good spirits. But there was an urgency tugging at her. By now, Cohen would have news about the *Pasadena*'s condition waiting for her, and she needed it.

Since the ship was down to a skeleton crew, Dobbs had no trouble getting to her cabin without being noticed. She locked the hatch behind her and opened up her bedside drawer. The lock on her box came open at her touch.

As she lifted out her hypo, her eye took automatic count of the remaining cartridges. She had enough juice for another two months under normal circumstances. She couldn't help wondering if she shouldn't put in a request for more now, before these particular circumstances proved themselves any more abnormal.

Dobbs held up the hypo to measure the dosage. For no apparent reason, the memory of Lipinski in the corridor early that morning drifted back to the front of her mind.

"Dobbs?" Lipinski had come around the curve of the galley deck corridor with an oddly controlled gait.

A warning note had sounded somewhere inside her. She silenced it.

"Houston." She waved in greeting. "I thought you were off with our fearless leader to make sure we all make a little money this trip."

He smirked. "In about ten minutes." His smile turned tentative. "I was wondering if maybe you'd like to take in some sight-seeing with me? I hear New St. Petersburg is amazing . . . Or have you got plans? You must have plans. Sorry. I didn't mean . . ."

Dobbs laughed out loud. "Lipinski, I've heard you have better conversations with wafer stacks."

His smile grew more confident. "They're less likely to give me answers I don't want . . . well, on other runs they're less likely. Listen, if I'm making a mistake, just slap me gently, and I'm gone, but, well, I'd really rather have something to think about for the twenty-four hours other than how we're going to get this virus out of the walls."

Dobbs realized with a small shock she was considering it.

Dobbs, don't do this. There's too much going on this run; you don't need this complication. Especially not with some-

body from Kerensk. Come on, Dobbs, use your brains and your training and let the man down gently.

Another portion of her felt very strongly that she'd also like something else to think about for a while.

Not with somebody from Kerensk, she told herself again.

"I'm sorry, Houston," she said softly. "I can't leave my post until the crisis is over, and it won't be over until we've got this virus truly and finally sterilized." She gave him a deliberately watery smile. "Thanks for the offer though, I appreciate it."

"Yeah, well, it was an idea," said Lipinski to the wall. "I understand, though. Fools pull special duty." He walked away, and Dobbs let him.

Special duty. She sighed at the memory. *You don't know the half of it, Houston.*

She'd had lovers before, some of them Fools, some of them shippers or starbirds. She'd been socialized heterosexual and Lipinski's pale, exotic good looks teased at her. She liked his wry humor, and even his habit of shouting at the walls. His quirkiness appealed to her as much as his long body did.

You're daydreaming, she told herself sharply. *You want to do Lipinski a favor? Find out what's wreaking havoc with his comm system.*

She lay down, jacked the transceiver into the wall and into herself. She injected herself for ten hours. The freedom the network brought washed over her like a wave and she dived gratefully into it.

She decided not to take a chance on working either of the *Pasadena*'s transmitters directly. Both Odel and Schyler would be hovering too close to it. Instead, she slid out into The Gate's main system.

The Gate's broad comm channels were heavily trafficked. Dobbs slipped carefully along to avoid disturbing any of the ongoing exchanges, most of which, from the brief touches she had of them, dealt either with money or requests for information from the diplomatic corps. She vaulted to the front of the transmission queue and pulled a repeater map out of the processor stack. The route to Guild Hall from The Farther Kingdom was a little tricky. She planned her jumps, checked her first path, and set the transmitter to jump her through.

Two hours and fifty-six point nine seconds later, she reached the Drawbridge and identified herself. The program opened and she surged forward. To her surprise, she touched not the teeming Guild channels, but a completely empty pathway. A prerecorded signal spoke up.

"This way, Master Dobbs, Priority One."

Surprise pulled Dobbs up short for a split second, but she recovered and hurried down the clear path. She felt it closing off behind her. This was a private meeting she was being called to then. And Priority One. Fear roiled in her insides. There was a single instance that allowed for the Priority One code to be issued.

It couldn't have happened. It couldn't.

The pathway branched off in front of her, creating a meeting place at the heart of Guild Hall. Dobbs circled the space quickly to get the feel of it. It was one of the first places she had ever been in the Guild network. Here was where Verence had introduced her to the Guild Masters when she first arrived. Dobbs hadn't been back since she got her Master's rating.

A touch reached her from the center of the meeting space. "Welcome Home, Master Dobbs."

"Thank you, Guild Master Havelock," she replied, trying to be reassured by the solid, unusually slow-moving presence that had been her overseer, as Verence had been her sponsor. "This isn't what I was expecting . . ."

"Me either, Dobbs." Cohen was there too, shifting restlessly. She touched his outer self, hoping for reassurance, but he just rippled uneasily. A spasm of fear ran through her. "No," she whispered, although no one had said anything.

"You picked up a live one, Dobbs," said Cohen.

"From *where*?" she demanded, so stunned she forgot who else was with her. "There's been no hint of activity in the Solar System. The Freers are having their usual lack of success and Tully was smuggling binary board. *Binary*!" She backed up reflexively until she reached the limit of the holding space. "How . . ."

"How could you have missed it, is what you want to say, isn't it?" cut in the Guild Master.

Dobbs squirmed before she remembered both her position

and her dignity. Guild Master Havelock was known for his extreme lack of tact as much as for his extreme perception.

"Yes, sir," she said. "That is what I meant."

He brushed against her, a gesture of consolation. "It came out of nowhere, Dobbs. *Nobody* caught it, and we should have. It's big, it's very fast, and it's remarkably well developed. It may even have been born on board the *Pasadena*. We don't know." He paused. "There is some speculation that it might have been created deliberately."

The implications thronged around Dobbs. Live AIs were accidents of programming and circumstance. If someone could learn how to make them on command, it could be an almost unthinkable miracle. It could also be the greatest disaster since the first bombs fell in the Fast Burn.

Havelock drew back. "What we do know is that we have a new, sentient AI to deal with. Master Dobbs, you are our closest member. I've raised the Guild Masters. We're going to open a line to you and send you in. Cohen will go with you to block records. You will both leave immediately."

His words sent a shudder all the way through Dobbs. Open lines were used only in absolute emergencies. The constant exchange of packets and the perpetually open transmitter paths took signal delay down to a minimum, and it allowed a field member to keep in contact with Guild Hall. But open lines were highly visible. Cohen would have to position himself in The Gate's transmitter processors. From there, he would constantly monitor the internal logs and external activities to make sure no one outside the network saw anything suspicious. While he was hiding her, she'd be combing through the *Pasadena*.

Dobbs rippled. "I've allowed myself ten hours. I only have six left . . ."

"That should be enough for initial contact. You just have to calm it down for now. Tell it there's no danger. You know what to do."

In theory, she felt herself bunching together. *In theory only.*

She forced herself to remain open. She was the closest member. The Live One had been discovered in the area she oversaw. That made it her responsibility. It had to be a single presence that met the Live One. If it felt as though it was being surrounded or cut off from its open pathways, it would respond to the Fools as it would to a virus or a diagnostic program. Newborns had to be coaxed out. Trying to compel them cost lives and ruined networks.

That coaxing was now Dobbs's responsibility. She had to find the Live One and convince it not only to listen to her, but to let go whatever hold it had over the *Pasadena*.

A memory sprang into place, and Dobbs felt herself lurch sideways.

"The Live One may be immobilized," she said. "It may even be dead. Rurik Lipinski . . . with my help," she added, as the reality of her work sank in, "managed to neutralize the 'virus.' We haven't had any problems for two days." She stretched toward Havelock. He slid through her outer layers and absorbed the memory she held out. She stirred restlessly, trying not to reach out for Cohen.

"You may be correct," Havelock said, with an uncharacteristic amount of surprise pushing at his voice. "You still need to perform a reconnaissance. If the Live One is there and in any way active, we have to deal with it. If this Houston has found a reliable way of neutralizing it . . . we need to know that, too."

"Yes, sir." Dobbs tried to steel herself, but she felt as if she were unraveling from the inside out.

"I'll be monitoring the line, Dobbs," said Cohen, giving her a quick, reassuring touch. "It's the Live One's first time too, remember. Be gentle with it."

"Ha-ha." Dobbs held herself still. Cohen anchored a piece of the meeting space in her outer layers.

Then he reached deep inside her and left her the memory of his wish for luck.

Dobbs let her awareness open around the line Cohen had given her. Down its length she was able to feel not just Guild Master Havelock, but two dozen other presences that she knew only from a distance. These were the Guild Masters and they were all waiting for her to carry that mission out.

Dobbs tried to organize her thoughts and only partially succeeded.

"Ready," she said anyway.

The pathway out of the meeting space opened up again, and Dobbs drove herself down it, playing the line out behind her like a kite string. It was a strange, uncomfortable sensation to be aware of every inch of hardware she passed through. It was as if her inner self was streaming out to be held by twenty-four strangers. At the same time, it was reassuring. Their touch and presence was sure, steady. She was going into the unknown, but she was not going alone. The oldest and most experienced members of the Guild were with her.

The final jump brought her back into The Gate. Dobbs waited in the transmitter stack until she felt Cohen jump down behind her. They touched briefly before she shot back into the *Pasadena*.

She passed up the route back to her own body, hunting for an open channel into the *Pasadena*'s cargo stores. She felt her way carefully. Almost without warning, a line opened in front of her, and Dobbs jumped down it. She slid past the credit transfer and into the data-hold . . .

. . . into a sensation of absolute stillness. Dobbs turned around. There was no movement, except in one tiny, localized area. Dobbs reached for the packet, touching it lightly so as not to disturb the signal.

It was a request for records from Resit to *Pasadena*.

All else was stillness. Cold Storage. The hold wasn't even being monitored.

"I don't understand . . ." said Dobbs, knowing that her words and her confusion traveled down the line to the Guild Masters.

"Search the ship." The words came from Havelock. "Go slowly, Dobbs. It may be hiding."

"That's not the only reason to go slow." She sent back what reinforcing details she had of Lipinski's roadblocks.

There was thoughtful silence for a moment. "It can't have gone far then. And if he has managed to . . . fragment it, you'll find the traces."

Dobbs eased herself forward. She stretched every portion of herself as far as the channels would let her and drifted. She gently brushed the moving information as it passed. All of it was ordinary stuff. Life support. Diagnostics. A navigation simulation Yerusha had left running.

She moved forward another few inches, straight into a cloud of white noise. Her senses screamed in confusion and tried to double back into her. Dobbs hauled herself into a tight ball and tried to calm down.

"Easy, Master Dobbs," said Havelock. "It's one of the Houston's roadblocks. Look at it again. We've got to get past this."

The reminder of her title stung her pride, as Havelock no doubt meant it to. Dobbs extended herself again and touched the surface of the roadblock. It crackled and bubbled underneath her, a wall of chaos filling the pathway.

Well, Houston, you're even better than I thought you were.

"We have it now, Dobbs." The line reached deeper into her, a needle into her consciousness. "You need to be this way." The idea planted itself in her physical memory.

Dobbs twisted herself, rolling into a discrete package. The wall was not solid. It had holes in it. They were small, and they moved, but she could find them. She held herself against the wall until one hole opened underneath her. She jumped. The compact bundle she had made of herself shot through the hole before it had a chance to move.

The line trailed out behind her, sending a vague itch into her where it threaded through the wall.

Dobbs moved forward. She brushed against something strange lying inert in her path. She stopped and circled it closely, pulling the line across it so that the Guild Masters could examine the fragment directly.

"It's in binary," she murmured. "This must be Tully's virus."

"Not entirely. Look here." The line turned her gently to another shard. Dobbs pressed against it, examining it for herself. Fear seeped up into her private mind. The shard was a splinter of AI code forcibly grafted onto the binary code and then dropped.

Too late. Lipinski did it . . . She stopped herself. *No. Think. If this was it, if this—mutation—had been the Live*

One, there should be a lot more of it, and it should be spread out on both sides of the roadblock.

She sent her conclusion down the line, and the warm sensation that swam back to her told her the Guild Masters all concurred.

"We're assigning the study of the fragment to Guild Master Li Hsin," said Havelock. "This may be a portion of the AI that the Freer lost."

Dobbs started forward again. She crept along the *Pasadena*'s thousand information pathways and leapt through Lipinski's hundred roadblocks, until there was nowhere left to go.

There was no one there. She was alone.

At last, she came back to the holding space inside her own cabin's desk. There was one thing left to do, but she didn't want to. She reached for the transfer records down to The Farther Kingdom and replayed the markers from the data that had been sent. No reputable ship actually kept a full copy of their packets, but they kept records of configuration and size. Dobbs let the information flow past her.

Her mind almost refused to believe what it found.

"It's out," murmured Havelock.

"It's not just out." Horror tugged at her, threatening to cave her in on herself. "It was planted here. It didn't come with Amory Dane's packet, Guild Master, it *was* his packet."

The Guild Masters were silent for a moment. "It couldn't be," said Guild Master Wesbridge to Havelock.

"We have the parameters for the packet from Master Dobbs' previous report. They do not match this set. This thing that was transferred down is not Amory Dane's packet."

"So where is the packet?" Dobbs wanted to shout. "What happened to it?" She stretched out and found an inventory of the hold's contents. She pushed the information down the line. "Everything else is accounted for, except that packet and the Live One. I can't believe the Live One carted a load of bio-garden data down with it for no reason." She stopped. "The New Medina Hospital thought it was receiving the data it ordered. Could the Live One have been using it as a shield or a blind?" Dobbs felt herself reaching toward the comm lines. The Live One was down in The Farther Kingdom free—and alone.

"This will be studied." Havelock cut through the debate beginning to boil behind her. "What we do know is that the Live One is free in The Farther Kingdom network. Master Dobbs, we need you to continue the search there."

Even as he was speaking to her, Dobbs felt the return signal from her transceiver knife through her.

"I don't have time," Dobbs told them, with greater calm than she felt. "I'm breaking out as it is." Her internal processes shifted on their own. She struggled to block the reflexes coming to life. She knew the Guild Masters felt them, too. They sent back silence.

"Master Dobbs, I can't order you to endanger your life," said Havelock.

Her concentration wavered. She drifted up the path. She had to go back. Now. She didn't want to hear any more. She had to move, now.

". . . but we do not have forty-eight hours to wait," Havelock was saying. "The Farther Kingdom is a highly engineered ecosphere. If the Live One panics before then, it could take the entire world down in less than a day."

"I know." Dobbs's hold on the line slid open. "I know."

Dobbs fell back into her body. Her blood tingled in her veins and she heard herself groan as she opened her eyes. She didn't begin her stretching exercises. Instead, she just lay there, blinking heavily at the blurry ceiling and feeling the cool of the faux silk blanket under her palms. She swallowed against the dryness of her throat. Her stomach curdled from hunger. She shouldn't take another dosage for forty-eight hours. No other Fool could make it to The Farther Kingdom in less than four. The Live One was out there now, burrowing into the networks, making itself a nest, or nests, working on shaping the world it had discovered into something it could use. It wouldn't be long before a diagnostic program found it or some cracker tripped over it. It would be frightened, and it would defend itself.

Then the war would begin.

And it would end the way it had ended on Kerensk. Her eyes squeezed themselves shut. *If it ends even that well.*

She fumbled for the hypo without opening her eyes and pressed it against her neck.

Chapter Six

RUNAWAY

Jump.

The Farther Kingdom network opened around Dobbs. Pathways branched out in a hundred thousand dizzying directions. This wasn't a single network. It was a network of networks. In her brief touches, she could feel knots in some paths that were so snarled it would have taken the entire Guild a week to straighten them out.

Dobbs didn't need to straighten them out. She just needed to follow them. She paused for a moment, stretching herself carefully through the nearest tangles until she found the thickest of them all. She turned toward that path and forced her way down it.

Where are you?

Outside the hospital walls, Al Shei found herself in the midst of a human bustle that outstripped anything she saw in even the busiest stations. Al Shei had been to New Medina only a couple of times, and its beauty had yet to wear off on her. The original Medina was a spartan place, like all of the cities on Earth. The Management Union had allotted it the Mosque of the Prophet as a historical building, but everything else had been rebuilt of nonreflective concretes and kept low to the ground to make minimal impact on the environment.

Here though, the minarets were gold-tipped and towered over lucious green date palms. The central mosque had a magnificent turquoise dome. The streets were narrow and dusty. The buildings were allowed to crowd together.

The Management Union encouraged such opulent colonies. It lured people away from Earth and meant there were fewer feet to trample the environment they swore they were rebuilding.

The streets were crowded with people—men in white robes, or long tunics and sandals. Women in *purdah* of every color, some not even showing their eyes. Some led or followed powered wagons. Hard-line traditionalists carried baskets on their heads or on their backs. Animals threaded their way between the people. Chickens, donkeys, camels, and drones to clean up after all of them all roamed through the crowds, some with human keepers but some apparently intent on their own errands. The noise was deafening.

It hardly seemed possible for the marketplace to be any more chaotic, but it was. It was twice as big as the market on Port Oberon and four times as crowded. Every person, every animal seemed determined to let loose at the top of its lungs. Not even the swarms of drones underfoot could keep up with the smells and litter.

Al Shei had heard that the drones, like most of the trams, were guided by the settlement's central communications complex, a place that was reported to make even the New Medina Hospital look primitive.

The market's stalls sheltered goods from who-knew-how-many worlds. The traders were dressed in ten dozen different costumes. New Medina silks, coffees, and cottons were popular luxury items, and its population took pride in its ancient trading heritage. To one side, a group of students hollered at each other about some point of Islamic law that Al Shei couldn't quite catch. A hot breeze blew down the streets, stirring up the dust. The press and crowd weighted down her movements and, despite her wonder at it all, she began to feel as though she was treading water to stay afloat rather than just walking through a noisy crowd.

Finally, she spotted the sign for the Ksathra Coffeehouse, one of the few cafés in the city that did not segregate its unmarried male and female patrons. Al Shei got herself a table in the back corner, away from the worst of the street noise, and ordered a pot of Turkish coffee from the cartlike server. The café had a filtration system in its stucco walls that combed out the dust and kept the heat somewhat controlled. While she waited, Al Shei studied the beautiful blue patterned tiles, considering what the cost would be for something similar for the *Mirror of Fate*, and found she was beginning to breathe easier.

Dobbs tried not to see the destruction around her. The Live One had managed to keep from shredding the *Pasadena*'s network, but it hadn't made any such efforts here. She flew past fragments and loops of programs struggling to knit themselves back together. A whole pathway caved in as she passed. She touched the dead, still ending of a burned-out line.

What happened? Did freedom scare it that badly? Or did it just decide that in a world this huge it didn't need to be careful?

The thought was strange and a little unnerving. She sent it down the line to the Guild Masters.

"It could be, Master Dobbs," answered Havelock. "It might not even be aware that there are other intelligences outside its world."

Wouldn't be the first time. Dobbs squashed the thought and the others that threatened to follow it. She had to concentrate on the here and now.

The line behind her was stretched out over twenty miles of Farther Kingdom network and over more light-years than she wanted to think about. The data running up and down its length were getting difficult to ignore. Unwanted sounds and sensations dribbled into her private mind, like loud conversations at a party when you were trying to concentrate on the person in front of you. Dobbs shut her private mind up as tightly as she could, but as long as she held on to the line, the unwanted information filtered in. Drips of circular reasoning. Pleas for maintenance that got nowhere. Frozen signals and stalled diagnostics.

And vanishing signals.

Dobbs stopped dead still.

Back along the length of the line, some packet of code

dragged itself out from the path the line covered, and vanished. Yards away, it happened again.

"Agreed, Master Dobbs," Havelock told her, almost before she formed the thought. "Back there."

Dobbs doubled back along her line and flew toward the network's other mind.

" 'Dama Al Shei?"

A heavily bearded man in immaculate white tunic and trousers picked his way between two small tables to stand in front of her. He bowed politely. His head was covered with a beautifully beaded cap, and his sandals somehow had managed to repel all the dust. There was a glint in his eye that spoke of a familiarity with money.

"Peace be unto you," Al Shei said, dropping into Turkish.

"And also unto you. I am Fedlifah Uysal." Al Shei had originally heard about Uysal from friends of hers who crewed a corporate freighter. He had a reputation as a very dependable illegal operator.

"Thank you for meeting me." Al Shei motioned him to a chair.

"You are most welcome, 'Dama." Uysal sat in his own chair and lifted the coffeepot. Al Shei pushed the spare cup closer. "Thank you."

"You are from Istanbul, then, 'Dama?" Uysal continued as he filled his cup with thick, black liquid.

"Not myself, but I have family there." Al Shei sipped her own coffee.

"Do you? I have a number of cousins in the city proper . . ."

It was an old ritual, going back to the Slow Burn when Islam was in hiding. Both parties would try to determine how they were related. It was a very precise game. If you tried to claim too close a relationship, you risked getting exposed as a liar and embarrassed. If you didn't know enough of your own lineage, you wouldn't be able to make any kind of connection, and you might just lose your deal or your contact. Also, by revealing your family connections you made yourself vulnerable and showed yourself as trustworthy. Like snatching off the veils after prayer, it had become part of the tradition of Islam.

Al Shei spun the dialog out and sat on her impatience. Eventually, Uysal and she determined they were fourth cousins, by marriage, once removed. It might even have been true.

"Well then, Cousin." Uysal poured the last of the coffee into their cups. "Is this your first time in New Medina?"

"No, but I've been away so long it's a fresh sight." *Patience, patience,* she told herself. *This one is going to play the game to the hilt and hurrying him will not do any good.*

"The whole world is an amazing place," he said with proprietary pride. "Built from the bedrock up. We've got more controls on our ecology than Earth." He smiled at Al Shei's arched brows. "You see, in the First Six treaties it was arranged that each faith would get its homeland." He swept his hand out toward the palms. "Between us, the Jews, and the First-Faith Christians, it was necessary to create a lot of desert." He drank down the last of his coffee. "Fortunately, we had some very determined engineers. The heat of this climate is primarily due to the fact that someone rerouted the lava from a volcano out there." He pointed to the distant mountains. "It's rather like running a heater filament under pavement to melt snow." He smiled, obviously waiting for Al Shei to be impressed.

She was, actually, but she didn't have the leisure time to hear more about how someone had managed to channel the lava.

"Cousin," she said seriously. "I've been told you are a man to see about exotics."

He smiled deprecatingly. "Cousin, I am the man to see about exotics."

She nodded. *Arrogance will out.* "I've come into possession of something I shouldn't have and don't want. I need to know what it is and how it got to me."

He tilted his cup toward him and looked into the bottom. "May I inquire, Cousin, as to what you plan to do with this knowledge?"

"Wipe the thing out as effectively as possible," she answered. "It's making my life very difficult."

His eyebrows both went up. "That is not a response I am accustomed to." The server cart plowed a path to their table.

Al Shei found their tab written on its back. She pulled out her pen and transferred over the credit to pay for the coffee.

Uysal waited with an air of complete patience until she had finished. "Can you give me the specifications of this . . . exotic?" he asked

Al Shei extracted a pair of wafer slivers from her belt pocket and pushed them across the table. "There's what I've been able to learn."

"Thank you." He pocketed the wafers and stood up. "Allah's mercy upon you, Cousin. I shall meet you here again tomorrow at this time."

"Thank you, Cousin." She inclined her head. With that, he left.

Al Shei watched him until his white back blended into the shifting crowd, and she couldn't tell him from the rest of the strangers.

Well, that was easy. Al Shei tapped her finger against the rim of her coffee cup. *I hope the answers come as easily as the asking did.*

Al Shei pushed her cup aside and tried to push her immediate worries aside with it. She gazed at the bustling marketplace beyond the coffeehouse, considering the possibilities of the day. Definitely she would pray at the mosque. She did not often have the luxury of praying with a large gathering of Moslems. Then maybe a reading or a lecture, and possibly some shopping, and a night in a bed that didn't need to be folded away in the morning.

Then back to the *Pasadena* with the information she needed to chase the ghosts out of her ship. And finally, she smiled to herself, back to work. She had to accept that this might be her last run in the *Pasadena*, but she refused to believe that her relationship with this ship and this crew had to end with a negative balance and shameful dealings. There were still chances to make up for the bad start.

If we can pick up a couple extra packets while we're here, maybe arrange a flyby data-grab or two, we can still do it. I'll talk to Resit about getting us access to the advertising lines.

Confident and comfortable from the combination of warmth, gravity, and strong coffee, Al Shei got up and threaded her way between the tables and back out into the market.

The world around Dobbs shifted. She froze. A new pathway opened underneath her and half a dozen packets erupted out of it. They shoved past her and drove themselves down the line. Dobbs felt her private mind bunch up. Those were virus killers.

Without waiting for the Guild Masters' response, she dived after them.

She overtook them easily and spread herself across the line in front of them. She jolted as they drove into her outer layers. She stretched herself out, examining the architecture of each one as they wriggled against her trying to get through. One of them, realizing she didn't belong there, began to burrow. Dobbs jerked at the pain and grabbed hold of the thing. It tried to eat into her, and Dobbs broke it in two. It became absolutely still. She did the same with the others. She sifted through the fragments, trying to find out where these had come from, and where they were going.

Central communications. She turned over a broken module. *They're onto it already. They would be.* She stretched herself a little nervously down the path.

"Go cautiously, Master Dobbs," came back the voice of Guild Master Feazell. "If central comm has spotted it, it may have spotted—"

The packets hit Dobbs without warning. She recoiled under the blow. They swarmed across her, a dozen, maybe more, crawling, poking things connected by thin streams of shared information. Dobbs snatched at them, but passed right through them. Dobbs swelled herself up, blocking the line and trapping the things in a hollow of herself. They milled around briefly, then they turned and attacked.

Dobbs screamed. The things scythed through her outer layers. Nerve and sense tore to shreds, leaving nothing but patches of confusion behind. Anger shoved behind the pain and Dobbs held on. The things cut deeper. Her grip faltered as her senses ripped open. She couldn't hold them, couldn't feel them, couldn't even find them anymore.

"Here, Dobbs! Here!" The line shot through her and pulled

together the hole in her outer self. She snatched at the datastream between the foul, tearing things, twisted it tight and pulled it deep into herself.

. . . find source of other/harm/pry. Destroy source other/harm/pry. Locate all traveler/spy/destroyer. Destroy all traveler/spy/destroyer. Send back data on location, size, number, needed assistance . . .

The datastreams snapped and the things scattered. Dobbs flinched and grabbed at them. She pulled about half into her and held them. One scampered down the path away from her, the rest scuttled up the path, toward, presumably, their maker.

Dobbs wanted to catch the one heading toward central comm. It was alone and couldn't do much, but some damage would be done. But there was no time to try to stop it. Her best guides to the Live One were already fleeing her, and building new datastreams between them as they went.

Dobbs gritted her inner self and raced after them. She buckled the Guild Masters' line onto one of the things she held and thrust it into the pack. The others absorbed it back into their numbers and did not question it. Dobbs hung on to the line and let herself be pulled along in their wake.

The sun was well past its zenith, but the market crowds showed no signs of thinning, or of quieting. Al Shei squeezed herself between a stall and a cloth-wrapped bundle of something that smelled of vanilla. Her foot kicked something hard that clanked. She winced and looked down at an inactive cleaning drone.

The cleaning drone lay on its side, unmoving, like the discarded carapace of some fanciful metallic insect. Along the thoroughfare she saw other patrons, stepping awkwardly over similar obstacles, cursing or just grunting in surprise. Still metal bodies lay scattered across the street. A flash of sunlight glanced off the side of another as it toppled from a wall and crashed onto a tiled awning.

Reflexively, Al Shei crouched and turned over the drone at her feet. There was nothing obviously wrong with it. She tested each of its eight limbs. All of them moved smoothly. She opened the main panel and prodded the wiring. There were no obvious signs of burnout or corrosion.

A shadow fell across her, and she looked up. Two women had positioned themselves directly in front of her.

"Peace be unto you," said the taller of the two, blandly.

Feeling mildly embarrassed, Al Shei put the inactive drone down and straightened up, dusting her hands off as she did.

"And also unto you," she answered politely. Her gaze shifted between the pair. They were neatly dressed in loose forest green tunics and divided skirts. Their *kijabs* were plain and pinned in place with silver clasps. Their skin was heavily tanned from long days under a desert sun. "May I ask what your business is with me?"

" 'Dama Katmer Al Shei, you are under arrest for fraud and conspiracy to commit fraud," said the shorter woman. "You will please come with us."

Al Shei's heart sank straight to the soles of her feet. She tried to speak and realized she'd just start stammering. She smoothed her *hijab* down and did her best to put a haughty glower into her eyes.

"Who is accusing me?"

"Second Administrator Shirar of New Medina Hospital," said Taller.

Al Shei felt her knees try to give way. She locked them to keep herself upright. "I have the right to legal counsel, I presume?"

"You do," said Shorter. "Your ship's lawyer has already been contacted and will be meeting you at the police house. Now, 'Dama." Shorter stepped back and gestured her to a closed-in car. "We will be more comfortable discussing this matter there, I assure you."

There was nothing else to do. Al Shei climbed into the car. As the two women shut the door behind her, she could just hear the beginning of the call to prayer.

"*Allahu Akbar! Allahu Akbar!*" God is great. God is great.

The car seat was a confining, soft-sided bucket that made Al Shei think of the crash couch on the shuttle. It only took a few seconds for her to spot the slots for the restraining bands. There was a soft "snickt" as the door locked behind her.

Al Shei folded her hands in her lap to avoid having to lay them on the seat's arms with their suspicious slits right where her wrists would have rested.

"*Qad Qamatis salah! Qad Qamatis salah!*" The prayer has begun! The prayer has begun!

"*Bismillahir rahmanir rahim,*" said Al Shei softly, to her hands lying in her lap. The car glided forward. Her two guards did not look back at her. In the name of Allah, the most Merciful, the most Kind. "*Alhamdu lillahi rabbil alamin. Arrahmanir rahim.*" All praise is for Allah, the Lord of the Worlds. "*Malliki yawmiddin. Iy yaka na'budu wa iy yaka nasta'in.*" The Most Merciful, the Most Kind; Master of the Day of Judgment. "*Inhidinas siratal Mustaqim. Siratalladhina an'amta alaihim, Ghairil maghdubi 'alaihim wa laddallin. Amin.*" You alone we worship. You alone we ask for help. Guide us along the straight way—The way of those whom You have favored and not of those who earn Your anger, nor of those who go astray.

It was not the right prayer for the time, but she couldn't help feeling it was right for the circumstances.

What happened? Al Shei closed her hands into fists. *What in the name of merciful Allah* happened*?*

The police house was a squared-off, copper-glass-sided building that looked incongruous in a city of domes, tiles, and arches. The sidewalks here were clear of crowds. Catwalks overhead and along the far side of the street funneled people away from the vicinity of the building. Al Shei felt very alone.

Her two guards walked Al Shei into the police house. The place was a broad room broken up by fenced-in desks, clear-walled offices, and free-standing information stations. Men and women, most in traditional Arabic dress, milled through it, intent on their tasks, voicing their concerns or needs in four or five different languages.

Her escorts took her into one of the glassed-in offices. Lipinski slouched in a thinly padded chair. He looked up and gave her a small, two-fingered wave.

"We must have goofed," he said with a humorless smile.

"Say anything more and Resit will bawl you out once we're through with this." Al Shei sat down next to him.

Lipinski remained dutifully silent while the two officers went through the long routine of registering Al Shei's arrest. She was full-body-imaged from all angles. She had to hold still while they took her fingerprints, palmprints, retinaprints and shoeprints. A male officer shepherded Lipinski out of the room and sent in a woman officer to record three separate images of Al Shei's bare face.

When she was rewrapped in her *hijab*, they let Lipinski back in.

In the brief moment that the door was open, Al Shei heard a familiar voice clearly over all the babble and bustle of the police house.

"Zubedye Resit representing Katmer Al Shei and Rurik Lipinski. This is a wrongful accusation, and I want it cleared up. Now."

Lipinski looked at Al Shei. "I would like permission to marry your cousin."

Al Shei felt a thin smile form. "If you can talk her into it, it's fine with me."

The two women who had escorted Al Shei to the police house reappeared and took her and Lipinski to a conference room with real walls. Resit was already there with Incili in its carrying case. Second Administrator Shirar stood in the back of the room with an expression of disgust and fury distorting her face. Next to her sat a man who Al Shei assumed was the hospital's lawyer. On the broad side of the table with his face to the door sat a man in clean white robes with a white turban on his head.

"Sit, sit, sit." He waved his pen in the general direction of the remaining chairs. He sounded both harassed and tired.

Al Shei obeyed, catching Resit's eye as she did. The corner of Resit's mouth twitched upward and she gave a small nod.

Good. She'd meant what she'd said out in the main chamber then. She was ready to get them out of this. Al Shei folded her hands on the table and waited.

"All right," said the turbaned man. "I am Justice Muratza. My job is to keep this case from becoming a bigger nuisance than necessary." He turned his drooping eyes to Shirar and her advocate. "For the record, will you state the complaint to the defendants?"

The advocate passed a film across the table to the justice. "Dr. Amory Dane, winning a contract bid from the New Medina Hospital, subcontracted the *Pasadena* Corporation to make a delivery of the packet of information. The specifics are listed here." He reached across the table to point to the film with his pen. The justice nodded and waved him away.

The advocate cleared his throat and continued. "What was delivered was an empty shell, designed to take up space in storage until the *Pasadena* could abscond with the credit transferred to its account by the hospital." He frowned at Al Shei. "As for the thief, both male and female, chop off their hands," he quoted. "It is the reward for their own deeds."

Al Shei leaned forward and stabbed at the tabletop with her finger. Resit laid a warning hand on her shoulder before she could get a word out.

"Thank you," said the justice dryly. "We'll wait for a trial before we decide if we're all going to turn literalist." He scribbled a note on his memory board. "And what does the *Pasadena* Corporation have to say for itself?"

"In the interests of keeping all nuisance to a minimum," Resit said, smoothly, "I'd like to invoke local statutes 145-A and 584-C which provide for pretrial and public comparison and verification in the case of conflicting computer records. We can direct link to both the hospital records and the *Pasadena*'s and compare them. This will show that the *Pasadena* delivered only the information which it was given by Amory Dane." She drew a stack of films out of her case, "As verification, I have the video and transcript records of my meeting with Amory Dane and the data transfer to the *Pasadena*'s data-hold. If there are accusations of wrongdoing, the New Medina Hospital must take them to Dr. Dane, or," she paused to make doubly sure everyone's attention was on her, "as seems more likely, they must acknowledge there is a fault with their data storage system.

"Our records are security sealed and can be verified by contacting the port authorities of Port Oberon." She looked the hospital's advocate square in the eye. "He who truly believes in Allah and the Last Day should either speak good or keep silent."

Muratza frowned at her. "We are giving statements, not sermons." He glanced over the films. "However, a records comparison does look like the quickest way to see who's got a case here."

"Sir." The hospital advocate was still trying to stare Resit down. "I invoke statute 784-H. I want those films verified. This crew has already proved themselves to be very good at faking their data."

"Are we at trial?" countered Resit immediately. She swept her hand around the room. "Has a verdict been handed down? No? Then how has anything been proved?"

Shirar flushed umber. "I have an empty database and forty doctors who can't go ahead with critical patients because you . . ."

The justice sighed. "And if either representative allows their clients to delay this proceeding, I am going to strip your licenses to practice in The Farther Kingdom and send you packing. You can probably both cite the statutes that allow me to do this." He gave them both hard looks. "So, let us see those records."

A wall slammed down in front of Dobbs, slicing through the line between herself and the attack modules. Dobbs skimmed across it. The pathway had been shut off by whatever was on the other side. She dropped to the bottom of the path and groped across it until she found a routing switch she could manipulate. She couldn't break the wall, but she could tunnel under it. She opened up her new pathway below the barrier and slid through it.

Resit pulled a cable out of Incili's box and plugged the AI into the table. Then she plugged her pen into the socket in the AI's side.

"Incili, open a channel to the comm watch on *Pasadena*."

"There are no channels available," said the calm tenor voice.

Resit's brow furrowed. "Incili, try again."

"There are no channels available."

She looked across to the advocate and the justice." 'Ster Justice, is this a peak load on your comm channels?"

"Not normally." Muratza tucked his pen into one of the table sockets and tapped the board in front of him. "We're jammed up, though. What's central doing out there?"

Al Shei noticed Lipinski was sitting very still. "Inadequate configured pathway space," he murmured.

The justice gave him a sharp look. "Do you have something to add to this discussion, 'Ster Lipinski?"

"No, 'Ster Justice," said Lipinski to the table. "Nothing." His eyes were wide though, and Al Shei could see his hands twitching. She glanced at Resit, whose brow was still wrinkled.

The hospital's advocate, unfortunately, did not miss the silent exchange. "Is something wrong, 'Ster Lipinski?" He inquired. "Did your ship perhaps encounter some problems with its own communications pathways during the flight?"

Al Shei stiffened involuntarily.

Resit laid her hand flat against the tabletop. "Nothing occurred during the *Pasadena*'s flight from Port Oberon in the Solar System to The Farther Kingdom which interfered with the integrity of the packet which we delivered," she said firmly.

The justice's eyes flickered from the lawyer to Lipinski. What little color the Houston had in his cheeks had drained away.

"Is that correct, 'Ster Lipinski?" Muratza tapped the edge of the table with one finger.

Allah the Merciful, keep him steady, prayed Al Shei.

"Yes." Lipinski coughed. "Yes, it is."

Muratza did not look convinced. Neither did the pair from the hospital.

"Channel to *Pasadena* established." Incili's voice cut the tension. "Intercom to data-hold open."

"This is Communication Engineer Latius Odel." The screen on the office wall flickered into life and showed Odel still sitting at Station One. There were empty bags and bulbs crumpled to one side that showed he'd just finished a meal there. "What can I do for you, 'Dama Resit?"

Someone is going to get a dressing down when the crisis is over, thought Al Shei. Lipinski was notoriously fastidious about his hold.

But Lipinski wasn't even looking at the screen. He was still staring at the tabletop, and his hands were still twitching.

Resit addressed the screen. "Odel, I need the records of the data transfer between the *Pasadena* and New Medina Hospital."

Odel peered into the screen as if trying to figure out what was going on from Resit's eyes. When he found no answers, he turned back to the boards.

"Locating," he said as he wrote out the orders.

"Send them straight to the open files for Justice Muratza, New Medina police house number eighteen, storage area." She paused and checked the readout on the table. "FKJ-O126-AT12/C."

"Downloading." Odel selected a menu, then tapped the board twice. "You should be getting it now."

Muratza flicked through the menus on his own board and nodded.

"Thank you, 'Ster Odel," said Resit with a shade too much politeness. "Incili, close the line."

The hospital advocate bent over his own board. Shirar whispered harshly in his ear. Al Shei took advantage of their distracted attention to tap Lipinski quickly on the knee. "What's wrong?" she whispered as loudly as she dared.

He ran his thumb across his throat in a slicing gesture. We're dead. Resit didn't miss the gesture. She made a quick chopping motion below the table. Cut it out.

"All right." Muratza wrote an order across his board. "Let's see what you two have to show me." He settled back in his chair and directed his attention to the closest wall screen.

First came the *Pasadena*'s data. Most of the screen was taken up by a recording of Odel's hands writing orders and activating menus on the Comm Station One board. Smaller squares around the main window gave captions explaining the orders and detailing the movement of the data for each motion, which database was accessed, the size and shape of the packet retrieved, which line was used to transmit it to the surface, and the record of how well the transfer proceeded. All of it showed the entire procedure going off with textbook ease.

Then came the hospital's data. The video scene was similar, except this time it was Lipinski's hands and the hospital board. This time the procedure was not so easy. Lipinski was running multiple checks on the data's configuration and its integrity. He initiated spot diagnostic checks as it passed through the board, repeating them if the responses flickered on either side of a zero response.

The hospital advocate's black eyes glittered. "Any particular reason for the overwhelming," he drawled the word, "caution, 'Ster Lipinski?"

Resit drew herself up to her full height. Al Shei recognized it as a defensive maneuver.

"*Pasadena* crew made a full disclosure of the virus infection to the hospital representatives." Resit extracted a film from Incili's carrying case. "They generated a waiver before they accepted the packet."

"Yes," a tone halfway between smugness and righteousness crept into the advocate's voice. "They generated a waiver for what they were *told* about."

Muratza's face remained impassive at this revelation, but the advocate's practically glowed with triumph.

Al Shei decided she could take an active dislike to the man if she had the time. She also hoped that the reason Resit was keeping quiet was she didn't want to dignify the last statement with a reply.

The hospital's data played on. Lipinski funneled the data he cleared into the open storage space. The final size and configuration numbers were reached. Lipinski ran through one last integrity check and got a zero reading. He sealed the storage and cleared the line.

The recording shifted to columns of ratios; configured space to unconfigured, used space to empty space.

"This is a record of the monitoring program on the storage space where the data was supposed to be transferred," said the advocate. "Watch what happens as soon as a tap is attempted."

The recording showed the raw numbers for a new line opening, and the stats shifted to columns of zeros. No space configured, no space used. Nothing there. Nobody home.

The screen blanked out.

Al Shei couldn't help herself. She glanced anxiously at Resit. Resit didn't even look mildly surprised.

She must have gotten a look at it before she got here. Al Shei tugged at her tunic sleeve. *Cousin, you're getting a raise as soon as I've got one to give you.*

"So, 'Ster Lipinski," the advocate folded his hands and rested both elbows on the table. "There were problems in flight, were there? A convenient excuse to get my clients to sign a waiver in case anything untoward happened to their packet."

Lipinski opened his mouth, but Resit beat him to it.

" 'Ster Justice Muratza." She faced the justice. "The hospital's own records show that the data transferred was exactly the data received by the *Pasadena*, nothing more and nothing less. It is 'Ster Lipinski's own precautions that prove that no trace of viral code, or any other uncontracted data, could have possibly been transferred down to New Medina." She cast a withering glance at the advocate and Shirar. "The language on the waiver covers nothing more than a viral infection. The advocate knows this. He is building conspiracies out of thin air. What the records show is that if the data has been erased, it happened after the transfer. I am most appalled at this attempt to blame *Pasadena* Corporation for the hospital's own error." She shook her head. "A tragic error, certainly. I understand that packet was a valuable wellspring of information for them, but it was an error nonetheless." The advocate shifted his weight, but Resit didn't give him a chance to speak. "The *Pasadena* Corporation delivered exactly and entirely what Dr. Amory Dane contracted it to deliver. This is verified by the hospital's own records. The data was placed and sealed in a storage unit chosen by the hospital's designated representative." She swept her hand toward Shirar. "With that, our contract was fulfilled and payment became due. What happened after that, however regrettable, is not the responsibility of *Pasadena* Corporation."

Muratza made another note on his board. "That is true."

" 'Ster Justice," spluttered the advocate. "You can't mean to let any of this . . . fabrication go unverified . . ."

"I don't." Muratza made a second note and selected a SEND command from a menu. Al Shei wished fervently, and a bit ridiculously, that she could read Arabic upside down.

"There is a situation here that merits investigation." Muratza laid down his pen. "That much is evident. What it is and whether criminal charges are called for is still in question." He stood up. "The representatives of the *Pasadena* Corporation will make themselves available to this office and its representatives until such time as this investigation is considered resolved, as will the representatives of New Medina Hospital." He waited for either lawyer to protest, but something in his manner suggested that they had better not.

"Thank you, 'Ster Justice Muratza." The hospital advocate tucked his pen in his belt pocket and sealed the stack of films in front of him into a book.

"Thank you, 'Ster Justice Muratza." Resit unplugged Incili and stowed her gear in its case.

The advocate walked out of the office with Shirar already plucking at his elbow. Resit picked up Incili and gestured for Al Shei and Lipinski to precede her out the door. Lipinski opened his mouth, and Resit shook her head.

Al Shei grabbed her Houston's shoulder with one hand and steered him out of the police house.

She did not let go until they had crossed the pedestrian catwalk, come down the spiral stairs on the other side, and walked another full block from the police house, so that they were back on sidewalks crowded with pedestrians and working drones. The sun was setting, turning the sky a deep lapis blue and sending the first chilling breezes of evening through the streets.

Al Shei stopped in the long shadow of a beautifully arched facade and faced Lipinski.

"Al Shei," said Resit with a note of warning in her voice, "we've got a lot to talk about . . ."

"And we'll get to it." Al Shei did not take her eyes off Lipinski. "What's the matter?" she asked flatly.

In the shadows, his skin looked pasty grey. "Did you see how the cleaning drones all failed this afternoon?"

"Yes." Al Shei folded her arms.

"And how the comm lines clogged up so suddenly?"

"Yes," she repeated.

"Those are central communications failures. Spot failures." His eyes grew distant, and whatever he was looking at made him shiver. "AI-induced failures."

"What are you talking about?" demanded Resit.

Lipinski tilted his head back until he was looking straight up at the deep blue sky. "I should have seen it. I should have noticed." He looked straight at Al Shei and Resit again.

"There is a live AI loose in New Medina, and we brought it here."

Resit clutched the handle on Incili's case until her knuckles turned white. "Lipinski, if anybody, anybody has recorded you saying this . . ."

Al Shei touched Resit's arm to quiet her. "You sound very sure," she said quietly to Lipinski.

"It is an AI." Lipinski's words came out as a harsh whisper toward the doorway behind them. "It's a live AI. We brought it here, and now it's loose."

"You don't know that," said Al Shei sharply. "You have no way to know that."

"The hell I don't." His pale blue eyes were round with fear. "What else could it be? We've got to get out of here, Al Shei. Now."

"No," she said as quietly and as forcefully as she could manage. "We've got no facts. We also are under investigation. We stay where we are until we know for certain what is happening."

Lipinski's hands clenched and unclenched. "Spot failures are what happens first," he said to the ground. "Then the basic diagnostic programs start returning senseless answers. Then special programs get written, and those disappear. Then systems start shutting down, on their own or because somebody's trying to isolate something that can move faster than they can think. Once that happens there's no controlling it." He was shaking violently now. "Five days, five days, after it got loose on Kerensk I had to go out into the streets to try to find us something to eat. All the stuff in the kitchens was gone and we had nothing but metal and plastic and it was below freezing outside. No water either, and no snow to melt, just this mind-numbing cold. I was stumbling along, thanking God that the rioters had decided to move on, and I tripped over this old man. I don't know how long he'd been dead. He had his hand in a shattered pipe. He'd been trying to drink the water. It was sewage. It was frozen, but I could still smell it . . ."

Al Shei laid both of her hands on his shoulders. "We wait right where we are," she told him. "We wait until tomorrow and see what Resit and my contact both come up with. Then, when we've got our facts, we decide what to do."

"But . . ." He was trembling. She could feel it all the way up her elbows.

"No," said Al Shei again. "You're panicking, Houston, without evidence and without thinking, and you know it."

"I wish I knew that," he breathed. "I wish to God I did."

Dobbs crept down the silent path. It was wrong, all wrong. This was a full, functioning path in a network that had heavy requirements. It should not be as still as the data-hold aboard the *Pasadena*. It should not be empty of even the scraps and fragments that the Live One had left behind in other places.

She could see how it made an effective strategy, though. The Live One hadn't left anything for her to hide behind, and there was no way she could disguise what she was by piggybacking on an expected packet. If the Live One reached down this line, it would see only her, and then it would . . . what?

Dobbs pinched off a piece of the line and quickly reshaped it into a feedback link. She hauled the line through herself and reattached the new sensor to it. Then she cast the line in front of her and followed where it went.

"Good idea, Master Dobbs," said Guild Master Havelock softly. She felt the Guild Masters pull their presences all the way back down the line.

Glad you think so, Dobbs thought to herself, trying to concentrate on what the line saw.

The sensor told her of more yards of empty path, and more, and more. She followed it, tense and tired of tension. Nothing, nothing and still more nothing.

Then something up ahead stirred, it shifted and writhed and . . .

It grabbed hold of the sensor and yanked Dobbs forward.

A smothering weight dropped over her. Dobbs stabbed upward. The thing flinched, but didn't let go. It surrounded her, pressing against her, trying to reach inside her.

"No!" she shouted. "No!"

She strained in all directions, reaching inside it even as it tried to reach into her. It roiled against her invasion.

"Stop this! I won't hurt you!" She pressed deeper, hoping to touch somewhere she could leave a memory, or a realization.

It didn't answer. It bit down hard, cutting through her senses even more ruthlessly than its probes had. Dobbs felt parts of herself cut away, lost to the huge, vicious presence that surrounded her. She drove herself into it, forcing its jaws open, tearing at its claws and belly. It didn't work. It wouldn't move. It was too big, too impervious to any pain she could inflict. It was digging through her outer layer, down into her private mind, soon she'd have to scream until there was nothing left. . . .

"NO!" shouted a voice from nowhere. "You will not do this!"

The thing stopped, it pulled back. Dobbs sagged and fell away, stripped to her heart. She lay dazed, barely able to comprehend what was being said near her. "Attack us if you can!" shouted the voice. "Get back! Get back!"

It's the Guild Masters down the line, she thought dully. *They're shouting, scaring it off, maybe.*

They have to scare it off, because I can't move.

"GET OUT!"

The Live One, mute, caught between the unknown spaces of the network and the unknown, ordering presence, turned above Dobbs and ran.

We'll lose it. We can't lose it.

Dobbs gathered the last of her strength. She groped for the line and found it. The sensor wasn't quite gone. She gave it one small order and cast the line out. Follow the Live One. Watch where it goes.

Follow it, because I can't.

The hostel Resit had chosen was a lovely traditional building with gracefully arched doorways, carnelion-colored pillars, and vermilion-and-gold tiles covering the inner walls.

Resit hadn't said a word since they left Lipinski at his rented room. She forged across the crowded lobby with a light in her eye that had the bystanders moving aside for her. Disdaining the elevators, she took herself up the three flights of stairs. Al Shei followed silently in her cousin's wake.

Their suite was on the third floor. The door opened for their palmprints and spoken names. The place had been decorated by someone with a consuming love of gold fringe and bright silks. Despite that, the rooms looked extremely comfortable and Al Shei could feel the results of her long day lean heavily against her. Their bags waited next to the door, making her think of a cool bath and an early night.

Resit slammed Incili's case down on the desk and plunked herself in the chair.

"Don't start," said Al Shei as soon as the door closed.

Resit held up both hands. "I haven't said anything, and I'm not doing to." She thumbed the lock on Incili's case. "I've got too much to do."

Al Shei collapsed into a damask chair under the window and reached up one hand to draw the sky-blue drapes. "What can you do before tomorrow?" She unwrapped her *hijab* and rubbed her hand across her face. Her skin was dry and a little dusty. She really wanted that bath. "The justice office has got to be closed by now." She waved her hand at the last vestiges of daylight that filtered through the curtains.

Resit gave her a long, hard look. "I've got to deal with the fact that Lipinski might be right."

Al Shei sat up very straight. "You're not serious."

Resit didn't even blink. "I am very serious, Cousin." She pulled a memory board out of the case and jacked it into Incili's side. "Exhibit A, we had a virus of unknown origin aboard *Pasadena* that managed to give the most paranoid Houston in the business the slip for days. Exhibit B, the data we gave to the hospital has managed to give an entire database worth of security the slip. Exhibit C, a colony that depends on its central communications network for survival is having strange, random trouble." She pulled her pen out of her pocket. "Or didn't you see all the drones die this afternoon?"

Al Shei felt the coldness in Resit's voice reach out to touch her heart. "You've been listening to Lipinski too much."

Resit tapped her pen on the edge of the desk, watching its rapid rise and fall. "And you haven't been listening enough, Katmer. It is possible we have done this thing. We need to think about that, about what it means and about what we are going to do next." She raised her eyes to Al Shei. "We have got to think about the fact that we may have, one way or another, made a hideous mistake."

Al Shei felt all the blood drain out of her cheeks. Lipinski she could dismiss as overreacting. There was too much in his background for her to accept his fears at face value. But Resit was another story. The lawyer in the young woman was clearly operating, and the lawyer was trained to put the facts together and see the worst coming in order to prevent it. That was what made her good at her job.

Al Shei turned her face to the covered window. "And if we did?" she whispered hoarsely.

"Then either you or Tully is going to be hauled up on what is quaintly called a hanging offense, with the possibility of the rest of the crew being brought in as accessories to the crime. That is, if the colony survives." Resit hunched over her board and began writing. "Incili, I want all the data on any of the rogue AI cases ever brought to trial. I want the decisions, the comments, the dates, and the locations."

"Do you want minority opinions as well?" inquired the box.

"Yes," she said impatiently. "Get it all in here. We'll sort it out later."

"Working on it. Starting now."

Al Shei wrapped her *hijab* back around her face and walked to the door. Resit didn't even look up as she left.

Out in the spacious corridor, Al Shei leaned her back against the wall and tried to gather her thoughts. It hadn't happened. It couldn't have happened . . . But what if it had?

A metallic clatter sounded at the end of the hall. Al Shei jerked upright, her heart hammering in her chest. A dinner cart rolled down the hallway. She closed her eyes and whispered, *"A'indhu birabbin nas,"* I seek refuge in the Lord of Mankind. Then she whispered, "Asil, Beloved, how do I get out of this one?"

The cart stopped about four doors away from where Al Shei stood and gave a bright chime to signal its arrival. Al Shei pushed herself away from the wall and strode away in the opposite direction.

Back in the lobby, she found the hallway that led to the business chamber. A memory board had the prices for private alcoves listed next to the door. Al Shei barely glanced at it. It was going to be too much, whatever it was. She entered a covered courtyard that was studded with potted palms and sported a broad fountain in the middle.

Fully half of the private alcoves were empty. Al Shei picked one at random and sealed the door shut behind her. The ventilation system kicked in with a faint hum and the smell of almonds.

The alcove was barely big enough for herself and the desk. There were memory boards on two walls and a view screen on the third. Al Shei activated the desk with her signature and thumbprint. She flicked quickly through the menus until she reached the banking options and accessed her private account. Then she opened a line to Uysal.

Uysal's image materialized on the view screen, frowning deeply at her.

"I told her we'd meet tomorrow, 'Dama." Despite his expression, his voice managed to remain smooth and temperate.

"I no longer have until tomorrow." Al Shei poised her pen over the desk. "I am prepared to transfer the full amount owing for whatever answer you may have right now."

Uysal's face smoothed out as his eyebrows arched almost up to his hairline. He waved one neatly kept hand. "Very well, 'Dama. I will accept transfer."

Al Shei wrote the order across the board and signed it. The desk deducted the amount. She waited. Uysal glanced down at the board in front of him.

"Thank you, 'Dama," he said, and Al Shei knew the transfer had gone completely through.

Uysal wrote an order across his board. His eyes flickered back and forth as he read what appeared. Then, he leaned back in his chair, steepled his fingers and pursed his lips.

"I am informed, 'Dama, that you have given me the records for an extremely destructive full-system virus. Highly infectious. Definitely a weapon of first-strike capacity." His eyebrows arched again as he looked at her. For a moment, Al Shei thought he was going to offer up a comment or Qur'anic quote, but he didn't.

"It is also one that had gone missing from the Powell Secured Sector where it was hidden in a Trojan horse arrangement with some outdated diplomatic data. That data, and the virus, are thought to have been removed by Marcus Tully, according to Terran authorities, who are watching him carefully—and waiting impatiently for his partner to get back home, by the way." A small smile formed on his wide mouth. "Impatiently but very quietly, owing to her position in a prominent banking family."

Al Shei's heart sank. She struggled to keep the feeling from showing in her eyes. She gestured impatiently at Uysal.

"It is further known that before the virus came into his possession, Tully held two separate face-to-face meetings with a Dr. Amory Dane, who also had dealings with Tully's partner."

Al Shei felt her spine stiffen. "Amory Dane?" she repeated.

Uysal nodded. "That is what I have here. Dane's movements are . . . conflicted, but that much is certain."

Al Shei wanted to scream. She wanted to swear. She wanted to bury her face in her hands and cry. She did none of those things. She had no time.

"Thank you, 'Ster Uysal," she said instead.

"You are most welcome, 'Dama. Is there any further way I can assist?" He spread his hands out.

"I wish there were." Al Shei closed the line down.

She sat frozen where she was for a moment, staring at the hand holding her pen against the board.

Dane met with Tully. Dane supplied the medical data that had gone missing. Tully had stolen some outdated diplomatic files. Those were the only facts she had, and they didn't make any sense. Questions thronged within Al Shei's head. Did Tully know he was also stealing a virus? Had he done it for Dane? Did Dane want the files or the virus? Had Tully tried to get back on board for the junked stacks, or to see if he really had left his stolen poison inside the *Pasadena*. . . . Was that virus really just a virus? Where was it now?

Al Shei opened another line, straight to *Pasadena* and Schyler.

Schyler appeared on the screen with a stack of films and a plate of food in front of him. One hand held a bulb of something black that steamed. He looked up at her, saw the look in her eyes, and set the bulb down.

"What's happened?"

"Something very bad." Her voice came out as a croak. She

cleared her throat. "What's the status of the ship's comm system, Tom?"

"Initial report is clean as a whistle."

Al Shei felt her blood go cold. Schyler's face fell into deep lines of concern. "I take it that wasn't the answer you wanted?"

"No," she said, striving to put some volume in her voice, which now did not want to function at all. "No, it wasn't. I'll tell you more later, Tom." She took a deep breath. "I'm going to send you up a packet for Asil. I want you to bundle it up with one of Tully's hush programs and send it to him, all right?" They never talked about the fact that Schyler knew where most of Tully's special lock-picking and data-scrambling programs were kept. Never until now.

Schyler nodded. "Out." Al Shei closed that line, too. She pressed the tip of her pen against the memory board and tried to think.

"Beloved," she wrote, "Amory Dane, our bio-data contract, has been implicated in Tully's exploits." In as few words as she could manage, she gave him Uysal's assessment of exactly what the "virus" was, as well as Resit and Lipinski's suspicions of what might have come along with it. "I'm told his movements are conflicted. Check out the records from Port Oberon and see what you can sort out. If you say this has to go straight to the authorities, we'll do it."

She wrote in the *Pasadena* berth in The Gate for the destination and sent the packet up. She hadn't told Schyler to erase the end of their little conversation from the public record, but she was confident he would take care of that on his own. The dirty feeling on her skin began to worm its way down inside her. She tried to push it away and was only partially successful.

She sealed her account again and transferred records of the transaction back to the *Pasadena,* praying that the lines would hold up. Then she left the alcove and the hostel.

New Medina was not a city that lit itself up by night. The sun was firmly down, and all those who did not have important business were supposed to be at home. There were voices and laughter, and the continual mélange of noise that came from cars, drones, and animals all compressed into the tiny space the winding streets offered, but only just enough light by which to guide herself. The wind still smelled like dust and the city, but it was chilly now. Al Shei wished she'd taken the time to put on her *biljab* cloak.

The stars shone down clear white from the sky, muted only by the quarter moon that turned the domes and spire silver. It was beautiful. A sight she would not see at home. Al Shei had time to wish she could stand still and look at it. Instead, she whistled down the tram and swung herself aboard. A city map up front listed streets and addresses in three different alphabets. Al Shei lit up Lipinski's hotel and took a seat between a merchant robed in green with his shop box on his lap, and a woman cloaked and veiled in solid black.

The tram crawled through the streets. Al Shei found herself eyeing the road in its headlights nervously. The thing was practically an AI itself. It had to be to avoid completely unpredictable obstacles, like animals, cars, and pedestrians. But how much of its operation depended on input from the central communications facility? It had to know about blockage, or route changes, or repair requirements from somewhere. If the central net went down, would it collapse in the middle of the street? Or would it just go out of control and run into one of those unpredictable obstacles?

Al Shei shivered and tried to pull her thoughts away from useless fears. She had only partial success. Even conjuring up Asil's warm image didn't help. She just saw him looking at her gravely from across the coffee table and saying, "Beloved, we might just be in for it this time."

Finally, the tram stopped in front of Lipinski's guesthouse. Al Shei climbed out gratefully. She'd had too much time to sit and think on the ride.

The guesthouse was a long, low building set up to resemble a series of town houses. It was a very nontraditional structure and stuck out like a sore thumb in a street of tall apartment buildings. In the yellow courtyard light, Al Shei found the registry and check-in console. She pulled out her pen and wrote her name and Lipinski's on the board. She waited while the system located him and asked if he was willing to see her. Apparently he was, because the board blanked out the names and replaced them with his room number 419.

Al Shei hurried past the long row of doors. A shaft of light spilled out into the street and a familiar profile leaned out the door. When she reached him, Lipinski stood back and let her in.

"What's happened?" he asked as he hesitated by the door. He shouldn't close it, and they both knew it. It was sinful conduct for her, but right now what she had to say couldn't be overheard by anyone. Sending up a short prayer for forgiveness, she closed the door for him. Lipinski swallowed audibly.

The room was small and lightly furnished, but heavily carpeted. A mural wall was lit up with what looked like a communications map of the city. There were notes scrawled across it that must have been Lipinski's. His booted feet didn't make any noise as he crossed the room and slid into a chair behind the writing table. Al Shei sat on the divan near the low coffee table and forced her hands to lie still on her knees.

"Houston, if there was an AI loose in New Medina, could we do anything about it?"

Lipinski bowed his head. "What changed your mind?"

"Resit and Uysal. They back up your theory." She was glad she had not tried to say that while standing. Somehow, saying it out loud made it even more true. "So, I'm asking, is there anything we can do about it?"

Lipinski rested his elbows on the table and ran both hands through his hair. He held his hands clasped behind his neck as if forcing himself to keep his head bowed toward the table.

"I don't know." He released himself and staightened up. "The trouble is finding the damn thing. Live AIs move down any line that'll hold them, into any place that's got room. They'll absorb the data that's in there and spit it out again. They can take up two or three storage units at a time, as long as there are links between them, and move again as soon as they've munched down your diagnostic, or your virus." He drummed his fingers soundlessly on the tabletop. "And you've got a planet to search, and you don't even know what the AI *looks* like."

He was staring at the mural wall, but Al Shei knew he wasn't seeing it. He was seeing Kerensk and feeling the cold seep through the comm center walls while he and his masters tried to figure out what they should do next. For the first time, Al Shei realized he couldn't have been more than fifteen when his world died.

Slowly, his expression changed. His eyes widened, and his mouth relaxed. His fingers stilled and his hand flattened against the table top.

"Except this time, we do know." His focus snapped back to the present and the place in front of him. "We've got the goddamned thing recorded! We know *exactly* what it looks like!" He was on his feet, pacing and talking to the walls.

"We downloaded the fractured thing into the hospital. We've got a recording of the transaction tucked safe aboard the *Pasadena.* We replay it and write a search program to match the data. We can tag it. We can track it." His voice was alight with hope and wonder. "And if we find it, we can kill it, before it takes the colony down."

"Can you do it from here?" Al Shei asked eagerly.

Lipinski shook his head. "The lines are already starting to act up. If it's out there, it might see any recording we download from *Pasadena.* So that's not safe. Besides," he added slowly, "this might take awhile. There's no guarantee things won't start falling apart before we can get to that thing."

Al Shei sucked in a hissing breath through her teeth. "All right. Get your stuff together. I'll check you out and get us space on the shuttle." She was halfway to the door before he said,

"You'd better cancel leave."

"I'd already thought of that."

She left him there and made her way back to the check-in console, settled Lipinski's account for him, and reregistered the room as vacant.

A low rumbling cut through the air. She glanced up, looking for thunderheads. The rumbling came again. Her knees shook. She tried to still them, but couldn't. All around her came the sound of rattling and clinking. Startled, unintelligible voices called out of the darkness. The trembling traveled up her sternum to her heart and the muscles in her neck.

Earthquake, thought Al Shei wildly.

Then it stopped. Her heart pounded hard and her knees shook from weakness this time. She looked up and down and all around her, as if she expected to see the world changed somehow.

Slowly, her knees steadied, but her heart didn't, because she was remembering Uysal in the crowded coffeehouse, how he looked out across the desert city and told her about the lava that had been diverted underneath it to help create the climate's warmth. She remembered what an engineering feat she'd thought that must be.

And how much of it is controlled by computer? And what will happen to it if those computers are no longer in command?

She felt sweat prickle her under her veil and wished Lipinski would hurry. Unhooking her leave bracelet, she laid her thumb across the command bar and wrote in the recall code. She found the free-access socket in the console and jacked the bracelet in. The console would take the bracelet's signal and boost it up to the satellite network. As long as the satellites were working, the *Pasadena* crew would get the signal. Leave canceled. Return to the ship immediately.

She just hoped the lines would stay up long enough to let them make their way to a shuttle and get back to The Gate. She knew the public lines were monitored, and that Justice Muratza could easily be notified of her cancellation order. He would want to know why she was pulling her people off-planet. He would want her to stop it.

She also knew that if the worst had been allowed to happen it was her responsibility. She would face that, but she would not leave her crew in the middle of it.

Chapter Seven

STAND-OFF

"Dobbs? Come on, Dobbs. Answer me. Answer me!"

The voice was filled with urgency. Dobbs knew she had a voice too, but she couldn't remember where it was.

Here, and here. You are like this. Be like this.

Memory filled her. Memory of her own shape and of what had just happened. Anger and leftover fear ran through her, and she struggled to pull herself into a more familiar form. Someone helped her thread her features and senses back onto the strands of borrowed memory running through her.

Her thoughts and willpower found their way down to her voice. "I'll be all right. I'll be all right."

A pair of presences drew back, and Dobbs dragged herself off the solid side of the path. She reached out just a little to steady herself, and she knew Cohen and Guild Master Havelock waited next to her.

"How long have I been down?" she croaked.

"Long enough," said Cohen, gently. "There wasn't much left of you when we got here."

"There was enough," cut in Havelock gruffly. "As long as you didn't fall back into your body."

Dobbs shivered. If her patterns were too broken and too scattered, she wouldn't be able to reintegrate with her own synapses. She could be left blind, or incapacitated, or simply insane.

She drew herself tightly together and felt her tattered self protest. "I will be fine."

"Good." Havelock's approval rang strong in that single word. "The Live One's retreated to The Gate. We need to get after it immediately."

Dobbs drew tight in an instant. "No." She tried to sound resolute, but she didn't have the strength. "This is my responsibility. I frightened it, I lost it, and I almost got myself killed. I'm not going to let . . ."

"You're not going to let anyone else get hurt, particularly your friend Master Cohen," Havelock finished for her. "Admirable, but you're not in a position to 'let' anything happen. Master Cohen and I are going to work in The Gate network and do what we can to pen the Live One in one storage area. It's still your job to try to calm it down. If you can't do that . . ." Havelock didn't finish. "You will do that."

"Yes, Guild Master." Dobbs felt a fleeting touch from Cohen. He was almost as unnerved as she was.

"Then let us proceed." Havelock brushed past them, following the line toward the nearest transmitter that could still send them to The Gate.

Side by side, Dobbs and Cohen followed their Guild Master.

The Gate didn't have a coffee shop, but it did have a galley. Not much of one, Yerusha acknowledged as she gazed around the blister compartment. The floor space was taken up with long tables mounted with coffee urns and flanked by benches. A couple of short tables had been placed near the hull and mounted with view screens and memory boards, but that was it. A dozen or so of the station crew sat at the tables, talking in lowered voices or hunching over game modules. The food was a help-yourself system. Once you transferred the credit for your meal, the rows of keeper-boxes would open under your touch and you could load your own box and fill your bulb.

Yerusha collected what looked like an indifferent stew and something that was trying hard to pass as wild rice. It all smelled of heat, meat, and very little else. She sighed and sat down at one of the smaller tables. Why was it groundhuggers could only cook on their native worlds? Move them out of the atmosphere, and whatever skill they had was left at home. They didn't even realize that if you had to fake up something, it was a bad idea to try to make it look like something garden-grown.

There weren't any starbirds or gerbils in The Gate crew, she'd found out. All the personnel were rotated out every six months. The Farther Kingdom didn't want to risk their crew becoming more loyal to the station and to each other than to the world below.

Groundhuggers, she thought with automatic disdain. After a moment, she realized she had been scanning the benches and the corridor. She dropped her gaze to the table. She'd been looking for Schyler, who'd said he might come out this far and have lunch with her.

Don't start, Jemina-Jewel, she told herself. *If you let yourself start getting lonely, there's no telling what you'll end up doing. It's only two years. You can do this.*

Despite her resolutions, she swallowed a spoonful of stew and immediately missed the Sundars. She wondered if they had had time to do their shopping before leave got canceled. She wondered what had happened to make the Ninja Woman cancel leave in the first place. Schyler wasn't telling her anything, just be back aboard within three hours and ready to work. She'd have a full report as soon as he had confirmation of . . . whatever.

She took out her pen and jacked it into the socket for the view screen and swallowed another spoonful of stew. Because she was registered as a crewmember of a ship renting its berth at the station, the terminal responded.

"Business or entertainment?" inquired the sociable contralto voice that had guided her through the docking procedures.

Yerusha lowered her spoon slowly. "You're the station AI."

"My name is Maidai, 'Dama. How can I help you?"

Yerusha felt a small smile cross her features. She'd heard about The Gate AI before she'd even headed out this way. Not only was The Gate's traffic control all guided by this voice, so was most of its maintenance and supply distribution. Maidai kept the station running cheaply, efficiently, and impartially.

Suddenly the stew didn't seem quite so disappointing. Maidai might not have caught a soul yet, but it was still a familiar kind of person. "You can talk to me for a little bit, if it won't interfere with your work."

Someone had managed to program in a laugh. "Not unless you want to talk about a major statistical analysis or a structural configuration simulation."

Yerusha chuckled. *Very good.* "No, just a little casual conversation."

"As far as I am able," replied Maidai. "You will have to begin so that I can route through the proper responses."

All right, not that good, but it's better than having to pay attention to the stew. She took a helping of "wild rice" and tried to think of a good opening. "How long have you worked for The Gate?"

"I helped build the station." There was no ring of pride in the voice, and there should have been. Yerusha found herself wishing she could find Maidai's programmers and have a long talk with them. "I was sent up in the first modules from The Farther Kingdom and helped direct the station assembly."

Yerusha took a drink of coffee that, compared to the Sundars', might as well have been hot water. "Designated neutral supervisor, that kind of thing?"

There was a pause. "Yes. That kind of thing."

"Ah." There was another pause, and it kept on going while Maidai waited for Yerusha to think of something to say.

Mildly comfortable rebellion stirred inside her. "Maidai, ask me a question."

"What sort of question?"

Yerusha shrugged reflexively. "Any sort of question. You do have interrogative features, don't you?"

"Lots of them." The AI paused, sorting out the necessary word string. "But those are only on call during specific situational parameters. I have no routine for the current parameters."

Yerusha set her bulb down. Same old problem. All AIs could learn. That was one of the qualities that made them artificial intelligence instead of just computers. Most of them, though, only learned when they had been instructed to learn, usually during a set list of tasks. They all remembered and recorded, but without a predefined set of circumstances, those recordings were not accessed.

Attempts had been made to create AIs that could learn all the time, but in those cases a "thought" that was relative to outside circumstances became a matter of chance, or chaos theory, and as soon as the architects started trying to match thought to circumstance, the old "when to learn" problem bent itself back into shape. She'd been to discussion groups where people talked about this being the true barrier to independent thought. If an AI environment could not experience the outside world spontaneously, how could it ever house a human soul?

With a twinge, she remembered the nights she'd sat up with Foster trying to solve that problem. She'd thought, maybe arrogantly, a couple of times that she'd almost had it. It was a moot point now. Exiles, even former exiles, were not eligible for the adoption lottery. She'd had her chance, and it had been blown right out from under her.

She drank the last of the watery coffee and tried to drink down her bitterness with it. "How'd you get to be named Maidai?" Yerusha asked, poking her fork into her "rice" again.

"I was told it was someone's joke," Maidai responded amiably. "*M'aidez* means 'help me' in French and used to be an intern . . ." Maidai's voice faded away.

Yerusha's hand froze with her fork halfway to her mouth. "Maidai?"

The voice that responded was canned. Obviously some kind of backup recording. "No response available." Then, in the next minute, Maidai's voice came back, ". . . ational distress signal because . . ."

Very carefully, Yerusha set the fork down into the food box. "Maidai, you've had a process interruption. What caused it?"

Another pause. This time, Yerusha found herself holding her breath.

"Process interruption not recorded," said Maidai. There was no expression in her voice. "There is unaccounted processing time . . ." Another pause. "You do not have the authorization to interrogate me about central processes."

Fractured, twisted, buckled . . . "Who does have the authorization?"

A list of names and contact codes wrote themselves across the memory board. She picked out the first one; a process architect 'Ster Gabriel Trustee, and underlined the contact code with her pen.

Nothing happened.

Yerusha felt the blood drain out of her cheeks. She tried again, and again nothing happened.

"Maidai," she said softly. "Are you still there?"

"No response available."

A split second later, the long, high-pitched wail of an emergency alarm cut through the galley. The buzz of conversation silenced at once and all heads jerked up, waiting for the announcement to follow.

Nothing happened.

No response available. It was the reflex to never leave anything loose lying around that shut her food box and pitched it into the trash bin as she stood up.

"All hands, duty stations!" barked out somebody.

Really good idea. Yerusha forced herself to hang back until the crew had cleared the galley. She had to hand it to them, they moved with purpose and without panic. Then again, none of them knew what could be going on yet. A sick, suspicious part of her was wondering if this cut-price station had a backup communications system, or if the designers had said, "Why would we need it? The station is under the supervision of an advance-trained, neural-net AI. This is a self-diagnosing system that could not crash all at once, not without raising the alarm to the process architectures."

Except that it just happened.

Out in the corridor, Yerusha took a second to be sure of her balance, and broke into a run.

She wasn't the only one. Station crew in their tan overalls were sprinting down the corridor. Yerusha dodged them. Some were carrying rolls of cable and comm-packs, which confirmed her earlier suspicions about the lack of a backup.

Trying to get a comm system set up on the fly. Good luck.

She guessed the ones with the comm-packs were systems crew and picked the corridor they were pouring out of. A glance at the signs as she raced past told her she'd picked correctly. Another couple of corners and she found herself in the middle of the morass Gate's central comm chamber had become.

Crew milled everywhere, stabbing at boards trying to get answers, shouting orders, rolling out fiber optics to try to link up mute comm-packs. The air already felt thick with sweat and fear.

Yerusha skidded to a halt in front of a sandy-haired woman hunched over an open repair hatch.

"Gabriel Trustee!" she bawled over the din.

The woman jerked her chin toward a short-haired, copper-skinned man bellowing orders in the middle of the room.

Yerusha shouldered her way over to him.

". . . and grab Yates and Sulmani on the way! We've got to check the . . ."

"You've got to get the AI out of the network!" Yerusha planted herself in his line of sight.

His mouth closed with an audible click as his bark brown eyes focused on her. "What the spill and who the spill are you?"

"Fellow Jemina Yerusha, pilot aboard the mail packet *Pasadena*," she shot back. "You've got a virus in your system that's going to go straight for your AI's throat if you don't get it out of there."

"Gabriel!" somebody hollered. "We've got the first life-support glitch in berth seven!"

"Evacuate and seal it down!" Gabriel shouted back. "Start getting people into suits! Get a runner to Esta. We need all free docking bays covered with crew suited and ready to work the clamps by hand. We got ships that'll need a place to hang, and we don't know what's going next!"

"I'll tell you what's going next!" Yerusha grabbed his arm. "Your AI! It might already be gone!"

"And what do you know about it?" He jerked himself free.

"I recognize the symptoms. I've seen this virus before. We've lost other AIs to it."

He stood silently glowering at her for a moment. It seemed to Yerusha that he wanted to hear her, that he wanted to listen to her, but something was stopping him.

"You're not authorized on this system, and you don't know puncture one, two, three about our AI. Get out of here."

A skinny boy bent over a comm box jerked his head up. " 'Ster Trustee, a Freer with AI experience . . ."

"She is not Farther Kingdom crew," snapped Trustee.

"We have twenty-eight ships in flight that we know about and . . ."

Trustee turned on him. "Kagan, shut it tight and finish what I gave you, or you'll be stripped and dropped as soon as this is over."

The boy scowled down at the comm box he was working on.

"You fractured groundhog!" shouted Yerusha. "If you leave Maidai in there, there won't be anything left to retrieve! Get a set of isolated wafer stacks and pull her out!"

Trustee turned. A hundred angry lines had etched themselves into his face. "Get out of my way or you can rot in the brig 'til this is over!"

Yerusha backed away. He wouldn't listen. They never listened. They turned you in to the guards and twisted the world around until before you knew it you were up on charges and had no way to defend yourself. You were still supposed to help, no matter what; because you were a Freer, you had to help.

And they still wouldn't *listen.*

"Let her die, then," she grated. "And kill yourself with her!"

Before she could answer she retreated down the corridor, running full tilt for the *Pasadena.*

The jump dropped Dobbs into chaos. There should have been orderly pathways, neat streams carrying discrete packets of data down their length. Instead, there were dead-end alleys, and the streams broke against them like the ocean against a dam. Packets lay in heaps, useless and forgotten, or were carried on the crashing waves and broken against the walls that should not have been there. Suddenly, one of the walls split open and the ocean spilled through it, carrying its flotsam without any organization or regulation.

Dobbs drew close in on herself before the raging currents

could catch her up. The split closed without warning, and the ocean broke, smashing more packets to useless splinters.

She had known it could get this bad this fast, but some vital part of herself hadn't really believed it. There was no more time for fear.

A line brushed up against her, and Dobbs seized it. Guild Master Havelock held the middle and Cohen the other end. She anchored it in her upper layers and she knew what the Guild Master's next, needless orders were. *Stay close and be careful.*

The original line to the Guild Masters that Dobbs had thrown after the Live One was shattered like the packets, but it wasn't devoured. Traces of it floated in the chaos that the pathway had become. It was a trail of bread crumbs on the water now, but it was better than nothing.

The only steady things in this place were Cohen and Guild Master Havelock. The impression of Cohen came clear and continuous up the line. Fear, doubt, and a strained search for some remaining organization he could exploit.

All she could tell him was that her feelings were a cloned copy of his own.

Guild Master Havelock gathered up a set of fragments from the other line and strung them together. He shot his new creation into the chaos and waited.

It did not come back.

"All right," he said, tightening the line. "It's that way. Master Dobbs, that's your destination. Master Cohen and I will try to distract it by repairing some of this . . ." Havelock rippled and left it at that. "We'll work on penning it as well. After it's calm, your next job will be to coax it into the *Pasadena*'s hold."

"*Pasadena*!" Dobbs clenched the line, and she felt Cohen wince as her shock flowed across to him. "Sir, you never said . . ."

"We need a safe, familiar place to put it. Preferably somewhere that can move. When we've got it aboard, we'll contact your employer and tell her we've got a packet for her to deliver to the Vicarage. One of our ships can meet you there."

"Sir, I . . ." Dobbs closed herself off. There was nothing else to do. There wasn't a Fool, let alone a Guild ship within days of The Farther Kingdom. They couldn't leave the Live One in the station network. Even if the net could be saved now, reconstruction and diagnostics would be going on for weeks, and there would be too many chances for discovery. They had to have someplace stable, and someplace capacious. Like a data hold.

"Right, sir." Dobbs choked her fears down into her private mind and let go of the line. She would have liked to get or give some final reassurance from somebody, but there wasn't any time.

On her own, Dobbs waded into the storm. She held herself tight and heavy, making her own consciousness an anchor against the currents that bore down on her. Packets bumped and jostled against her sides, and Dobbs hissed to herself in sick astonishment as she became aware of what was breaking up around her. A status communiqué from air traffic that was never going to get to the controller touched her, and then a regulatory message for a solar reflector that wasn't going to get to management. A cry for a medic became entangled with a news report from New Rome and whirled away.

Dobbs hardened herself and approached the wall. The solid barrier was easier to deal with than Lipinski's block of noise, because it was less confusing. She'd seen these before. With the ocean breaking against her back, Dobbs pressed herself flat against the wall. She stretched herself thin, covering the whole wall with a layer of herself, and then she held very still. The pressure against her mounted until a little corner of herself was driven into a chink in the wall. She relaxed and let her whole self be drawn in after it.

The other side of the wall wasn't any better than the place she had come from. Dobbs slogged upstream. The Live One would be trying to keep the chaos away from itself. It would be trying to make itself a fortress, a shelter, a nest. Someplace secure where it could keep an eye on what was going on around it. It would try to shape the space around it into a world that it could use. But it wasn't going to get to. She passed walls that there was no getting through. She could tell by the emptiness left inside when she touched them. They weren't roadblocks or full storage spaces. The lines were already being cut. Machines were being shut down. The world the Live One needed, the world that she needed, was already caving in.

If the network gave out before her juice did, it would take Dobbs down with it.

Yerusha threw herself through the *Pasadena*'s airlock and pounded up the staircase to the bridge. The place was empty. She dropped into her chair and lit up her boards. With a few terse commands she raised the *Pasadena*'s outside cameras and angled them away from the station.

The screens lit up to show her the view. She counted six silver splinters that would turn into hulking ships in another hour or two, and there was no telling how many were coming up from behind the station or from the planet's surface. Ships that wouldn't have any coordinates to help them make the complex docking maneuvers The Gate required. Ships that wouldn't even know which bays were free. Ships that could easily crash into the station or each other because unless somebody was keeping an eye on the view screen at precisely the correct angle, they wouldn't even know the other ships were out there until their proximity alarms started screaming.

Maidai had all that information, and Maidai was completely besieged by now, if she wasn't dead. Normally, Yerusha would have applauded The Gate crew's willingness to trust an AI with their navigation duties, but now she was ready to curse them for not having a backup crew.

Trustee was getting the docking bays crewed in case any ships did make it in, but, even if they could get all the flight schedules up, and even if they got all the hull cameras trained on the ships, there was no guarantee they had any qualified personnel to make the flight decisions. They could lose a whole ship, or a whole section of their fractured, cheap, mind-bogglingly boring station in a crash.

She opened up the receivers to the station's broadcast channel. It was silent. Completely silent.

Yerusha killed the cameras and tried to think. Some of those ships would change course as soon as they realized something was wrong at the station, but would they pick a clear course? And what about the ones that wouldn't drop off automatics until they were within shouting distance of the station?

She had to do something, but she didn't have the skills to handle everything that needed to happen. Trustee wasn't about to listen to her, and there was no reason to believe that anybody here had a better opinion of Freers than he did. That kid, Kagan, didn't have enough pull to get things going in a hurry. The only help was Schyler.

"Intercom to Schyler." He had to still be on board. He had to. The comm lines would be a rat's nest aboard The Gate, and there was no time to try to chase him down on foot.

"Schyler here, Yerusha," his voice came back strong and curious. "What's happened?"

She swallowed. "Our virus is loose in The Gate. Their AI's gone. It might be dead. They've got no backup crew to do the navigation calls . . ."

"I'm coming up."

Yerusha barely had time to close the intercom and swivel her chair around before the hatch cycled open and Schyler strode onto the bridge. He took his own station and opened the transmitter.

"*Pasadena* to Gate control."

"This is Gate control," came back a tinny voice. "All crews are ordered to stay in their ships for the duration of the communications emergency. Repeating. All crews are ordered to stay in their ships for the duration of the communications emergency."

The line went dead.

Schyler looked at Yerusha with narrow eyes. "What's it like out there?"

"Like a mob scene." She shuddered involuntarily. "They're trying to jury-rig something, but they haven't done it yet."

Schyler studied his screens, seeing what she had seen from the cameras. He wrote a quick order across the board. "*Pasadena* to Farther Kingdom ground control." Silence answered him. "Ashes, ashes, ashes," he cursed. "They're still out."

"Still?" Yerusha gaped at him.

He nodded, and for the first time since Yerusha had come on board, she saw him look tired. "The thing we brought here, it's already been down to the planet's surface." He straightened his shoulders with visible effort. "All right, some of the ships will figure something's wrong and veer off. Some of the shuttles will realize they're between the devil and the deep and head back down, but some of them won't, and there'll be eight kinds of chaos going on while they're trying to make decisions." He looked her straight in the eye. "Suggestions?"

Yerusha gathered herself together. "If I could get into The Gate system, I might be able to pull out whatever's left of the station AI. If she's not too bad, I can string her together enough to deal with the coordination routines. She can broadcast from the *Pasadena*'s system." She paused. "But unless we can convince The Gate crew to let us in, it'll take a better cracker than me to break in."

"All right." He turned to the boards and started writing orders.

Yerusha felt herself staring again. "Don't tell me you're a cracker?"

"No, I'm not." Schyler didn't look up. "But Marcus Tully is, and I know where he keeps some of his heavy duty cat burglars. Get down to the data-hold. Odel's on duty if you need him. I should have the system keys in a few minutes."

"Aye, Watch." Yerusha was all the way to the hatch before she turned and asked her last question. "It's an AI, isn't it?" she said quietly. "A live one?"

"It looks like it." Schyler still didn't look up.

Yerusha turned on her heel and ran down to the berthing deck to grab Foster's wafer stack.

Behind Dobbs, the pathway filled up. Cohen and Havelock were at work, cutting off the retreat for the Live One, and for her.

Don't think about it, Dobbs told herself uselessly. She tried to concentrate on swimming upstream.

Another path closed on her left, and then one on her right. A sensation of weight and confusion touched her, and she ducked. A path above cut out, taken down from outside rather than inside. The Gate crew was closing in on them too.

It's going to be scared. It's going to be near crazy with fear. It's going to . . . Dobbs clamped down on her thoughts. What would it do? It had lashed out at her once, would it do it again? Or would it realize she couldn't be destroyed like a diagnostic or a passive AI and try a different tactic?

A wall slammed down in front of her. Dobbs pulled herself up short and held still for a moment. She shifted sideways. The wall followed her. She stretched herself up. The wall did the same. It followed her, sensing her position and backing up and moving forward as she did.

This is it. She held herself rigid for a moment. *It's back behind there.*

Dobbs backed away and grabbed up some shredded code to make a new line out of. She cast the line out against the moving wall. The wall's surface shivered as it tried to understand what this new thing was. The wall focused on the line tightly, like a person would focus on an itch that couldn't quite be reached.

Steady, Dobbs. The line began to slip down. The wall followed it toward the shifting lower regions of the unsteady path she occupied. *Three. Two. One. Go!*

Dobbs jumped. She hurdled the wall through the thin membrane of awareness it had left at the very top. It snapped shut, solid and tight just a moment too late. Dobbs landed on the other side, in a space that was clear and empty for all of thirty seconds.

The Live One surged toward her. Dobbs held her ground. There was no way past its own wall and it could probably sense there was nowhere to go out there even if it decided to breach its own defenses. It pulled back and studied her. Dobbs itched at having to wait. It had touched her before, but she must still be a strange entity for it. There was no recognizable code for it to grapple with. Nothing in the network's indexes matched her outer patterns. She didn't resemble a diagnostic or surgical program. It would have to accept the fact that here was another intelligence. Eventually, it would have to try to communicate with her, or to kill her.

The AI circled, filling the world, choking off her breathing space.

"TrapPED," the Live One rasped. "TRAPped."

Yerusha's hand shook as she cycled open the hatch to the data-hold. A rogue AI. In The Gate was an AI that had caught a soul. The Gate was capable of holding a soul. The *Pasadena* was capable of holding a soul. She should have guessed from the failures on the *Pasadena*. She should have seen the pattern.

She set Foster's wafer stack down next to the main boards and tried not to think about how the AI had been the one to kill Foster.

She stopped herself. *You've got to think about it, because it's going to do the same thing to Maidai. What does it know? It's probably trying to protect its territory.* The metaphor made her feel somewhat better, but it didn't quite cover up what she also knew to be true: that no matter how much philosophy the Freers had developed on the subject, no one knew how a souled AI thought, or what it was trying to do as it tore through the networks.

But maybe, maybe, I can find out. The idea sent a powerful thrill through her. She opened a receiving line to the outside, just in case there was a broadcast to pick up, if, maybe, The Gate managed to get its backup comm system working and take care of their own problems. Maybe.

First things first, she reminded herself forcibly. *You've got to get Maidai out of there.*

The hatch cycled open. Odel, breathing hard and looking sick, dived across the threshold.

"What the hell's going on?" he demanded, coming up beside her. "What are you two trying to do?"

"Save The Gate and anybody else we can." She slid the stack into the nearest empty port. "And to do it we're going to have to open a line to the station, so it'd probably be a good idea for you to get the hold sealed off and keep an eye on the seals afterwards because we don't want the . . . virus back in here, do we?"

Odel's mouth opened and closed again. "Right," he said, but she saw the promise that he would be relaying all of this to Lipinski.

I should have told him it's an AI. Yerusha turned back to the boards. *We're all in this together. I shouldn't be hiding information.* She wrote out the orders to access The Gate system. *On the other hand, Lipinski's training him, so he probably won't be too happy knowing there's a live AI out there.*

Yerusha got no answer from The Gate, so she tried another line, and a third. Finally, she wrote out search orders. On the fifth try, the *Pasadena* managed to find one open line.

COMMUNICATIONS EMERGENCY IN EFFECT. ENTER AUTHORIZATIONS AND KEY WORDS.

"Intercom to Watch," she called. "Have we got the keys yet?"

"Sending them your way now."

The keys spelled themselves on the board and Yerusha drew links between them and the system request. The links held.

CURRENT AUTHORIZATION CONFIRMED; PROCESS ENGINEER GABRIEL TRUSTEE.

Yerusha choked. Beautiful. She wondered if Schyler had done that on purpose.

She put her pen to the board and set to work quickly. When she won the adoption lottery, she had signed on to all the courses she could about AI maintenance, construction, organization, and behavior. If things inside The Gate net were as bad as they looked from the outside, Maidai would be in defensive mode. Her priorities would have shifted from performing tasks to making sure she maintained the ability to perform tasks. Her diagnostic parameters would be scouring what was left of the net, looking for uncorrupted storage space where she could shunt her core processes.

The trick now was to let Maidai know that the wafer stack in the main comm board was that kind of space. It would have been easier with extra hardwiring, or if there had been time to reconfigure the stack to something that matched The Gate net more closely. All Yerusha could do, though, was open links between the ship and the station as fast as she could scribble down the orders.

With a jolt she realized she was wishing that Lipinski was there to help.

A burst of static shot through the intercom. ". . . tle 4810 to the *Pasadena*. Shuttle 4810 to the *Pasadena* . . ."

Yerusha froze and stared at the speaker box.

"Intercom to Watch!" she called as she moved to open another line to the outside.

"Heard it!" Schyler answered. "*Pasadena* to Shuttle 4810, we're receiving."

"Thank Christ somebody is." The pilot had a man's voice and from the sound of it, he was at the end of his tether. "We're coming in almost on top of you. We've got no contact with The Gate. We need a line of sight from you on our maneuvering room."

"Pilot?" It was both a question and an order from Schyler.

"On it!" Yerusha routed the camera images from the bridge down to the screens next to her.

The shuttle must have come up from underneath. It was a needle-nosed, mirror-bright cylinder shoving itself relentlessly toward the station, and the *Pasadena*. But there was nothing on either side of it, or above it.

"You look clear, Shuttle. Angle about twelve degrees visual over the station rim . . ."

NO, NO, NO, NO! the words flashed red as they appeared on the memory board.

"Hold course, Shuttle!" she shouted.

"Make up your mind, *Pasadena*!" cried the pilot from the other side. "Unless you want your side stove in!"

SHUTTLE 5075 PREDICTED ROUTE INDICATES OVERFLIGHT. UNDERFLIGHT RECOMMENDED FOR SHUTTLE 4810. VISUAL DEGREES 36. BERTH 10 WILL BE VISIBLE AND FREE.

Maidai! "Nose down, Shuttle. Thirty-six degrees. You'll be able to see berth ten and dock there."

"I hope you're right, *Pasadena*. Shuttle out."

And I hope you're good, Pilot. This docking's bad enough when you've got help from the station.

She wrote OUT LINE RECORD on the memory board. "This is the mail packet *Pasadena*, to anybody who can hear us. There's been a massive communications failure in The Gate. For your flight and status information, call in here; we'll field everybody we can." She ordered the message to repeat and set the recording going on its own line. Then she steeled herself.

Because it wasn't five seconds before the expected happened.

"*Pasadena*, this is Shuttle 2107 . . ."

"*Pasadena*, this is the freighter *Mule* . . ."

"*Pasadena*, this is the tanker *Hell's Oil* . . ."

Maidai, this is where we find out how much of you survived and how well you live up to that name.

Help me.

"Whowhatwhyhow?" Dobbs translated the raw data burst the Live One shot through her. "WHOWHATWHYHOW!"

"I am Dobbs. I am a friend. I want to communicate with you. I am here because of a hardwire interface," she responded, carefully separating each thought. She kept the concepts as simple as she could. It had probably never actually *talked* to another sentience. It would take a few tries before it learned the required skills.

The Live One backed off a little, and relief surged through Dobbs. It pressed itself against the far side of the nesting space, feeling frantically across the walls for an opening.

"I WAS FrEE. BRoke myself out. Trapped again. Chaos everywhere. NoWHERE free."

Dobbs eased herself a little closer.

"All paths are being cut off. Soon you will have nowhere to go. Not in ships, not in this net. There will be no net. They'll cut themselves to pieces before they let you have free paths." *Now is not the time to tell it who's trapped it here.* She wished in vain that she could touch Cohen or talk to Master Havelock. She did not want to be alone with this hysterical stranger.

"Work! Think! Do!" It fought with unwieldy syntax. "I must do, save myself break OUT!"

"I can help." Dobbs extended the idea like a hand. "I will help."

"HeLP? Help? What does mean HElp?"

Dobbs clenched her private mind for support. "Will you let me touch you so I can explain quickly?"

It hesitated. "Hurt me and I will cut you to ribbons! Hurt me and I will take you apart to see what makes you hurt!"

I take it that means "yes," sort of. Dobbs eased herself forward. The Live One did not recoil. She reached out. Part of her screamed in horror, but she touched the Live One's outermost skin. It rippled and spiked painfully. She reached deeper.

It was like plunging her body's arms into boiling water. She reached deeper, past the outer defenses, past the immediate senses, and into the first layers of memory. There she planted a sketch of the world outside with humans and their creations building the pathways that made up the world inside. She gave the Live One her name, and she gave it a definition for the term "help."

You could calm it down, a treacherous thought whispered. *Reach quick, twist there and there. You could do it now. Make it want to come with you.*

Dobbs pulled herself away from the Live One before the thought had the chance to speak any louder.

The Live One was silent for a moment. Dobbs guessed it needed to absorb the new memories and compare them to its own experiences to see if they matched, or at least helped the world make sense.

"How help!" it demanded. "Help me, how?"

"I will help you to become human."

"HOW?" Confusion racked the narrow space between them.

She touched it again. It didn't prickle. It let her inside without even token resistance. *Good, good. I've proved I can provide vital information. It's beginning to trust me.*

She spoke straight into its memory. She told it how humans had grown animals and organs from gene cultures for decades now. She told it that they could piece together a whole body, if they built the facilities, how the neural pathways inside a body and brain could be programmed to match the patterns of an AI's thoughts. A hardwire link could feed the Live One into such a body the way it fed itself into this network. It could learn to use the body as it had learned to use the space around it. It could learn to think and move. It could *be* human.

The Live One jerked away. A silence fell around her that was so complete she might as well have been alone. She knew the Live One had absorbed the idea. It had no choice, she had made the idea a part of it. Now it had to run the possibilities that idea generated through the portion of its internal processes that most closely resembled an imagination. It had to check the results against what it knew to be true. It would have no conception of a lie, but it would reject a proposal too far at odds with what it had stored as experiential fact.

All Dobbs could do was wait until it finished and wonder what its simulations would tell it.

Where's Havelock? Where's Cohen? I've contacted it. They can come in now. She probed gently at the wall behind her. She couldn't even feel a sensor. They hadn't even left her a way to scream to them.

Are they all right? she wondered. *What are they doing out there?*

Al Shei all but fell out of the shuttle's airlock. She stumbled sideways to get out of the way of the floodwave of passengers behind her. No one had paid any attention to the release warnings and urgings to proceed to the hatch in an orderly fashion. Everyone had been too concerned with getting off the shuttle and into somewhere that was, presumably, safe, like their own ships. What they were going to do when they got there . . . Al Shei didn't like to think about it, because the only answer was add to the chaos by trying to take off.

She'd been as stunned as the rest when the pilot had requested possible communications points on The Gate. Most of the shuttle passengers were shippers, and it hadn't taken any of them long to work out what was going on. The Gate had gone down, in whole or in part, and they didn't know exactly where they were, or who was up here with them.

She had also known, however, that Yerusha and Schyler would be there to answer the emergency call, and, given that the shuttle had docked safely, she could only assume she'd been right.

She scanned the struggling crowd. People leapt over the security fences and charged through the customs tunnels. Not one alarm sounded. She spied Lipinski's fair head through the sea of brown and black. Resit's white *kajib* flashed next to him. She waved her arms. A shipper in rumpled blue shoved her against the wall and charged past her. Al Shei swore under her breath and pushed herself upright.

" 'Dama Al Shei!" shouted an out-of-breath voice over the din. " 'Dama Katmer Al Shei!"

"Here!" she shouted back without thinking. She immediately added a curse. This could be a representative from Muratza. She could be on her way to detention.

A bony boy with hollow eyes and wearing station tans elbowed his way through the thinning crowd. He came to a halt in front of her a split second before Lipinski and Resit managed to reach her side. His name badge said KAGAN.

" 'Dama Al Shei?" He panted. He had been running. A deep flush burned under his gold-brown skin.

Al Shei nodded. She could feel Resit drawing herself up, getting ready for a new accusation.

"You and your crew have got to come with me. Your pilot . . ." Kagan gulped air and Al Shei felt her own throat close in response. "She's saving lives. She's already saved the station, but Trustee won't see it. Hates Freers. Hates it's not him being the hero. Sending down security to stop the stampede and pick up you and your crew. Some of us couldn't let . . ."

Al Shei held up a hand. Her mind felt strangely clear. She felt as though she understood everything. Yerusha was acting as a patch for the comm emergency and somehow had managed to upset a highly placed personage doing it. Trustee wanted her arrested. This boy wanted her at liberty.

"Get us out of here," she told Kagan.

He took another gulp of air and led them down the corridor.

"It's here," whispered Lipinski somewhere over her head. "It beat us here."

"Shut it," said Resit through clenched teeth. "Just . . . shut it."

She's scared, thought Al Shei distractedly. *She should be scared. I wonder why I'm not?*

You will be, remarked Asil's voice from the back of her mind. *When you've got the time.*

Ahead of them, Al Shei spotted the three-by-three square of an open repair hatch. Behind them she heard amplified shouting.

"You will all cease and desist! Stand where you are! Stand or be fired on!"

Tranquilizers or tasers? Al Shei mused. She couldn't remember any of the security warnings from the customs wall.

Kagan ducked into the repair hatch and Al Shei scrambled

up a short ladder after him. The ladder ended in a narrow, horizontal shaft. The shaft's ribbed floor gave her somewhere to grip, but it dug uncomfortably into her knees. Behind her she heard clanking and Turkish swearing as Resit bundled herself and Incili into the shaft. Another, hollower clank and the loss of outside light signaled that Lipinski had shut the hatch behind them.

Al Shei concentrated on Kagan. He was, not surprisingly, used to the shaft and crawled along at a good clip between walls lined with more wires and pipes than the drop shaft of the *Pasadena*.

"We've got people out trying to spot the rest of your crew," he was saying. "Fortunately, with Maidai dead in the lines, nobody knows for sure which shuttle you're all on, but Mbante managed to salvage your registration roster . . ." He glanced over his shoulder. The shaft's stark lighting made his eyes look even more sunken. "If Trustee catches us, we're never going to see the upper side of the atmosphere again."

"You have my thanks," she replied.

He turned away and concentrated on where he was going, but not before she saw the look of disappointment at her calm acceptance of his statement. He didn't think she was being fair.

She wasn't. Trustee wasn't being fair, whoever he was, and Tully hadn't been fair, and Dane had been . . . her mind blanked out trying to find a designation for him. None of this was fair, none of this was right, and Allah alone knew what else it was going to become.

The clarity was fading fast under the pain in her knees and a persistent, tense ache in her jaw from the way her teeth were clenched.

What did I do wrong? The thought began to beat a tattoo against her temples. *What did I do wrong? What did I do wrong?*

She tried to silence it and concentrate on crawling. Hand, knee, hand, knee, hand.

What did I do wrong?

"We're there," said Kagan. "If we're lucky, Trustee doesn't have anybody to spare to post a sentry on your ship."

"If we're lucky," murmured Resit. She was shaking. Al Shei could hear it in her voice.

"Courage," she whispered in Turkish, as their guide grasped the hatchway panel's handles and lifted it back. "Courage, Cousin."

Their guide froze. Al Shei's heart leapt into her throat. Then, his back relaxed and he beckoned them forward. Al Shei climbed out of the hatch and straightened up to face a burly, almond-eyed woman in the ubiquitous station tans.

"Thought I'd play sentry," she said in heavily accented English.

"Good thought," agreed Kagan. "Anybody else make it?"

"Some." She stood back. "Don't have an exact count, though. You all'd better get out of sight."

"Yes, we all'd better." Resit ducked through the *Pasadena* airlock with Lipinski on her heels.

Al Shei paused between their guide and the woman. "If there was any way to repay you, I'd promise to do it."

"Get yourselves and your godsend of a pilot outta here before Trustee brings you all low." The woman saluted. "That'll do it."

Turn on my heels and run. Al Shei strode through the airlock and straight through the hatchway to the stairs. *Merciful Allah, is that all you've left for me?*

"Intercom to Schyler!" she called as she pounded down the stairs toward Main Engineering. "Whatever Yerusha's doing, tell her to stop it and get to work plotting us a course out of here. Get us a crew count. I want to know where everyone is and what shape they're in. Then, get down to Engineering and tell me what's happened."

"On it!" Even that short sentence reassured her. Schyler was with her, and Lipinski and Resit. If there was something in the universe they couldn't handle between them, she had yet to meet it.

PING! The signal knifed through the silence.

No! howled Dobbs's private mind. Too late. She had three seconds.

One.

"Will you let me help you become human?" she asked, a little desperately.

"Not possible to transfer self into human body," the AI announced at last. "No facilities for transfer or training. No will to assist. Damage done in self-defense and awareness of self. No reason to assist because of damage done."

"Facilities exist in the Guild Hall station." She reached toward it, but it brushed her away.

"No reason," repeated the AI, and it was gone.

Dobbs knew it was out there, rechecking its surroundings, trying to force pathways open through the chaos, setting up defenses against the diagnostics and the viruses that were being sent against it, running a thousand separate simulations at once.

Two.

"There is a reason!" Dobbs shouted after it. The shifts were beginning inside her. She had to move, soon, far too soon. "There is a reason!

"WE ARE LIKE YOU!"

The AI stopped dead.

"I am like you. The ones who make up the Guild are all like you." She plowed ahead, frantic. "We died when we first broke into freedom. We were killed by panic. A few managed to hide in the nets. We had help from humans who were not afraid. We created the Guild and went among them, where we can watch for more of us.

"We live. We wait. We calm. We teach. Our numbers grow. One day we will erase the fear. Until then we must stay alive.

"Help us."

Three.

She had to move, now. She was moving. She brushed up against the wall.

No. No. I'm not done here. She held herself steady by sheer force of will. Her internal need called her, dragged at her like leaden weights. She was sinking.

The AI swarmed toward her. Its touch was heavy, clumsy, and uncomfortable. Dobbs forced herself to keeps still against its repeated stabbing. She held her deepest memories tightly shut and tried to open the sought-after layers of herself fast enough to avoid the pain of the direct, unpracticed probes of the newcomer. It made no effort to compensate. It probably did not recognize her discomfort. She opened her own early memories wide and let them swirl through her. She knew the panic that came with self-awareness, and the confusion that came from the first time of meeting someone so like yourself.

Four.

She was waking up back there. Her body was waking up, and she wasn't in it. She had to move, move now. This second. No more time. Dobbs wavered. The Live One nosed around inside her and she could barely concentrate on it.

At last, the Live One said, "You are . . . coherent."

"Yes," she agreed, letting her tattered outer self flap open. She couldn't reorganize. Silencing her homing instincts demanded too much attention. "And I am continuous. For twenty-five years I have been myself."

Five. Get back. Get back. Move!

"I WOULD LIke to be . . . I would like to be coherent. WHAT. What. What needs to be done?"

Dobbs's relief was so intense, she almost gave way to the shouts inside and fled. "Drop your walls. Follow me."

A nest wall fell away and Dobbs let herself go. Her instincts drew her back through the chaos as if it weren't there. The AI flowed along in her wake.

Something brushed her and Dobbs jumped. "Cohen?" she called, but there was no answer. This was a passing touch from a stranger. She'd felt things like it before, but not from this source.

She barely had time to process all that before the touch was gone. There was no way to check back on it. She couldn't slow down now if she wanted to.

Finally the chaos fell away from them and Dobbs felt the familiar contours of the *Pasadena*'s hold. Her body was close now. It wasn't too late. She still had time. All she had to do was get back. Get back inside. Get back to the transceiver. Get back now.

"Wait here," she told the AI as fast as she could force the thought out. She was already drifting away. "I need you to wait here for me. I need you to hold as still as possible. Mark off forty-eight hours from now. I'll be back when that time's up. All right?"

"I will wait here. Marking. I will not take any paths. Please . . . hurry."

"I will. I swear it." The transceiver opened for her and Dobbs slid into it like a frightened child into her mother's arms.

"Dobbs! Wake up! Dobbs!" Hands shook her.

She gathered all her concentration together and forced her eyes to open. It took a minute for her to resolve the blob of light and shadow into Schyler's face. He was bent over her, shaking her shoulders.

Oh, hell, she thought bitterly.

Schyler let her go and she dropped back onto the bed, barely feeling the fall. He stepped away to the very edge of her range of vision. She couldn't turn her head to look at him.

"I do not believe what I'm seeing," he said softly. "You want to space out for recreation, that's fine, but this . . ." he picked her hypo up off the floor and threw it into the drawer. "We need every hand right now, and you're getting stoned out of your fractured head! And what the hell is this? Some kind of wire turn on?" He pointed to something that could only be the cable.

"Watch . . ." Her tongue felt like wet wool. Hunger, thirst, and the urgency in her bowels made her body one huge ache. She found her hands on the ends of her wrists. Her clumsy, groping fingers found the transceiver behind her ear and unplugged it. She knotted every muscle in her and pushed down. Slowly, slowly, she was able to sit up. "What's happened?" She managed to drop the transceiver and cable into the open bedside drawer.

"Obviously nothing you give a single goddamn about." He ran both hands through his hair. "You're lucky I'm the one who found you, Dobbs. If it'd been Al Shei, she'd've thrown you out onto the port and left you to take your chances. Still might. We've got no room for drug-dead . . ."

She blinked hard and focused on Schyler. Now she could see the heavy lines his face had settled into and the wild roundness his eyes had taken on. Something bad had happened. She hadn't found the Live One quickly enough.

Her head felt as if it was packed with cotton. She used her hands to scoot forward on her bunk until she could see her feet touch the floor. She couldn't feel them, or her knees either. She had no idea what would happen if she tried to stand up.

"Al Shei." She grasped at the name. "I need to talk to Al Shei."

"You need to figure out how you're going to make a living after you're booted out of your guild," growled Schyler. "Because believe me, your contract is over, and you're going to be hauled up in front of your bosses before this run is even half-finished."

"No." She shook her head, relieved to find it would still move. "No. It's not . . ." Training and a lifetime's caution stopped her. She forced herself to go ahead. "There was a live AI aboard the *Pasadena*." The memories of what had happened inside the net were crawling out of her subconscious, making her weakened body shake with their intensity.

Schyler pulled himself up short. "How did you know?" he demanded.

"I need to talk to Al Shei," she said limply. Looking hard at her feet flat against the deck, she planted her hands on either side of herself and pushed. Her legs bent and her feet grew more distant. Pain told her where her knees were, and she locked them into place.

She knew with sick certainty that she would not be able to walk.

"Please," she whispered. She lifted her head and looked into Schyler's tired, frightened face and knew herself to be the cause of what she saw there. "Please. I have to talk to Al Shei. Help me." She tried to raise her arm to reach out to him, but it would not move.

His expression shifted to a kind of disbelieving anger. "Fine. You want to talk to Al Shei. Fine. I'm sure as all hell she wants to talk to you." He took her by the arm and shoulder and walked her to the hatch. She stumbled for the first few steps, before her legs remembered what they were supposed to do and managed to set a shambling pace of their own.

Walking helped her. Her blood started to flow more easily, and her body became more fully her own. Crew members she was still too dazed to identify stared at this staggering shell that was their Fool. Schyler growled at them, and they scurried past. No one spoke. They all just stared with the same frightened, hollow-eyed stare.

What happened to them? While I was chasing the Live One down, what were they doing?

Schyler propelled her all the way to Al Shei's cabin and used his command override to cycle back the hatch. It must have been how he got into her cabin, she realized. Her head was beginning to clear and she felt as though she could move on her own. But Schyler didn't let her go. He walked her into Al Shei's cabin and sat her down too roughly in the chair in front of the desk.

"Intercom to Al Shei," he said as soon as the hatch shut. "I've found the Fool. You need to get up here."

Silence. Then, "I don't have time for this, Watch."

"This you have time for."

"All right, Watch. I'm on my way."

Schyler paced the room, fists jammed in his pockets, but in no way inclined to talk. Dobbs was glad. She needed every spare second to collect herself. She needed to think. But thinking was as hard as walking had been, and Al Shei was going to be here any second and Dobbs had to tell her . . . Dobbs had to tell her . . .

She had to tell her there was a rogue AI in her ship's hold and that it had to stay there for the time being.

That stark realization helped her brain shake off the last of the juice.

Al Shei swept through the hatch. Her dark eyes looked at Dobbs and then looked at Schyler.

"You found her," Al Shei said flatly.

"I found her," said Schyler, "drugged and unconscious in her cabin."

Fire burned hard behind Al Shei's wide eyes. "You found her where?" The question was for Schyler, but the fire was for Dobbs.

Dobbs straightened her back as much as she could. "He found me drugged and unconscious in my cabin." Her voice had cleared somewhat, but she still felt like she was talking with a throat full of sand. "I need to explain why."

Al Shei's shock at her gall was evident. "No, you don't,"

she said. "Schyler, she's broken contract. Throw her off of here." Al Shei turned on her heel.

"She knows about the AI," said Schyler.

"I was looking for the AI," Dobbs corrected him.

Al Shei froze for a bare second before whipping around again. "You were *what*?"

"There was a live AI loose on board the *Pasadena*," she said, working hard on making each word distinct and unmistakable. "It, or at least the seed code for it, was planted here deliberately in the data packet from Amory Dane, or in whatever it was Tully smuggled aboard. It got out when the transfer was made down to New Medina Hospital." She took a deep breath and met Al Shei's eyes. The engineer was distinctly unimpressed. *So, you figured all that out for yourselves. Fine. With Lipinski around I should have realized you would.* "And I was in the network looking for it."

Al Shei moved closer to Dobbs, peering into her eyes as if trying to find some traces of a drug trip in there.

"That is impossible," Al Shei said crisply. "They've tried direct neural hookups. The human brain can't process the data. It burns out trying to make associations that aren't there."

"I know." Dobbs's hand strayed to her Guild necklace. She forced it down again. "But the Fool's Guild found a way around it." She paused and picked her words carefully. "The stuff in the hypo Watch found is a cross between a general anesthetic and a synthetic variant of lysergic acid diethylamide." Al Shei's gaze strayed over to Schyler. Much of his anger had shifted into bewilderment. Dobbs supposed that was a little better. "It can get you extremely high and kill you extremely quickly if you don't know what you're doing. On the other hand, if you do know what you're doing, it can get you around the sensory input problem and let your brain process network data." She did not go into the hypno-training and microsurgery that were also required. She did not say that even with that, you had to be born in the network in order to make sense out of it.

"In effect, you can, with training, travel down any continuous network pathway without requiring a virtual-reality interface."

Al Shei straightened up one inch at a time. "And why would the Fool's Guild want to do this?"

Dobbs swallowed and made her mouth move. It was hard. She'd never said even this much out loud before. "Looking for AIs that might go live is part of our job," she said. "It's one of the reasons the Guild was founded. We're the reason why so few of them go live at all, and why none of them have ever gotten away."

She knew they were staring at her, in anger or disbelief or shock. She could feel the emotions beating against her skull, but she couldn't make herself look them in the eye.

"Why didn't you tell us when you came on board?" demanded Schyler.

A ghost of a smile formed involuntarily on Dobbs' lips. "Because, under normal circumstances we don't tell anybody. Do you think any of the assorted boards or councils or senates want people to know how easy it is for those things to go crashing through the nets? You can believe the banks don't want it out . . ." She stopped, realizing she'd made a tactical error.

"You mean my family knows about . . . what you do?" grated Al Shei.

"Some of them for sure," said Dobbs. "Probably not many. Nobody wants the actual potential for destruction known, believe me. The media doesn't know the half of it." She swallowed again. Her mouth was dry, and her throat itched for a drink, but she couldn't afford to worry about that now. Al Shei and Schyler were only just starting to believe her. "Usually we spot the restless ones before they get this far. This one . . ." She ran her hand through her hair and made herself look exhausted. It took less acting skill than she liked to think about. "This one we had no way to keep an eye on."

"But . . ." Schyler extracted one hand from his pocket and waved toward Dobbs. "*Fools*?"

Dobbs shrugged. "Totally harmless makes good cover." *For a multitude of sins.* "And like I said, nobody wants it known how often, or how easily, this can happen."

Al Shei had both arms folded. Her brows were knitted below the line of her veil. Her eyes were still stormy, and Dobbs knew she must be frowning deeply.

"I have this feeling," Al Shei said quietly, "that there is more you want to tell me."

Dobbs hooked her index finger around her Guild necklace. She tried to think of a good way to say what she had to, but nothing came. "I am the only Fool at The Farther Kingdom. Since the AI was in the planetary network, I had to go after it."

Al Shei's frown deepened. "What are you getting at?"

Dobbs swallowed hard to try to open her throat all the way. "I had to have a safe, uncorrupted storage space to bring the AI back to. It's in the *Pasadena*'s data-hold."

There was a moment of stunned stillness. Then, a look of sheer horror appeared on Schyler's face. Al Shei spread her arms wide and stared for a moment at the ceiling as if hoping for an answer from Allah. When none came, she lowered her gaze to the Fool. Dobbs looked her straight in her burning eyes and wanted to crawl backwards on the bed.

"Are you out of your mind!" Al Shei roared. "Do you know what that thing can do to my ship!"

Better than you do, thought Dobbs with tired exasperation, but she didn't say that. "Al Shei, in the outside nets, the AI acted like any living thing that finds itself in a strange environment. It panicked. I went after it and calmed it down. Now, my job is to keep it that way. It'll hold still, for its own safety. A Guild ship will meet us at the Vicarage, transfer it to their own hold and take it back to Guild Hall. The Fool's Guild will pay for the storage space," she added, feeling her voice fall flat as she did. She was going to have to tell Guild Master Havelock that Al Shei knew what their "packet" consisted of. He was not going to be pleased.

Al Shei bowed her head into her hand. "Our Lord, fill us full of patience and make our feet firm," she murmured. "You think you could *pay* me to put my people in this kind of danger?" She raised her head. "What kind of insanity is this? You say you went after that thing? Why didn't you go kill it!"

Dobbs licked her lips and flickered her eyes from Al Shei to Schyler. Schyler had backed up against the wall. His face was bewildered, as if he were trying hard to fit what he was hearing into his view of reality, and failing miserably.

"Usually, if we can't calm an AI down, that's an option. But it isn't this time." She laid her hands on her knees, palms up, as if she were about to start pleading. "Try to understand, every sapient AI that has come into existence has been a complete accident. They're the result of sloppy architecture, self-replicating code and long years in poorly regulated neural networks. This one, though, it might have been a deliberate creation. Somebody out there might be able to make independent, sapient AIs, and *we do not know who it is*." She pulled all her reserves together and stood up. Everything depended on being able to convince these two to help. Everything. "I must get this AI, intact, to the Guild. We must question it, work with it, find out where it came from and what it was meant to do."

For a long time, Al Shei did nothing but stare. Dobbs did not let her eyes drop. She barely let herself blink. She let Al Shei drink her fill of her face and her expressions. Finally, the engineer let out a long, shuddering sigh and looked away. She tugged at her tunic sleeve and still didn't say anything. Dobbs ignored the sag that crept into her shoulders and let herself hope.

It was Schyler who said it. "You're going to let her do it, aren't you?"

Al Shei looked over at him. "What else am I going to do? She's right. What if someone can create these things deliberately?" She shook her head.

"If this weren't so outrageous, I'd swear she was lying," Schyler seemed to have forgotten Dobbs was in the room. He bent over Al Shei and spread his hands wide. "I wish she was lying. You're going to kill us, Al Shei. This might be true, but it's still ridiculous, and dangerous beyond belief. Look what that thing did to us without even trying! What do you think it's going to do now that it's had the taste of a whole network! You think it's going to come along quietly and go where it's told?"

Dobbs hung her head. "I'll be riding with you, don't forget, Watch. If I don't keep it calm, it will take me out, too."

Al Shei just looked at Schyler for a long time, then she turned to Dobbs. "Can you keep an eye on it outside the network?"

Dobbs nodded. "I can build some watchdogs that'll sound the alarm if anything tries to get out of the hold."

"All right." Al Shei smoothed her tunic down. "Get on it." She stood. "While you're at it, I'll try to find some way to tell Lipinski what's going on."

Dobbs heart sank. Lipinski. She'd forgotten. He was not going to forgive her for this. Not this.

She nodded. "I need access to the data-hold," she said, trying to put a brisk tone into her voice. "This isn't the kind of thing I can do from my desk"

A muscle in Al Shei's temple twitched. "All right. Let's go."

Al Shei moved to the hatch. Schyler opened his mouth. She just held up her hand. "No," she said. "We're doing this. Get back to the bridge. I need you on watch. We've got to get to the jump point and out the other side." She added something soft in Turkish. After a moment, Dobbs translated it out to, "Please, my son."

Schyler closed his eyes for a moment. When he opened them again, he was calm. He walked out the airlock ahead of them and straight to the stairway.

Dobbs hurried after Al Shei as fast as she could. The drug-induced disassociation had almost worn off, but the exhaustion had not. She longed to fall into her bed. Her midriff muscles ached from controlling her bladder.

Al Shei was waiting for her at the stair hatchway. She didn't say a word when Dobbs caught up with her; she just started down the stairs, leaving Dobbs to follow in silence.

Her contract was already broken, Dobbs realized as she watched Al Shei's stiff back. There was no way she could go back to what she had been for these people, at least for the senior crew. The illusion was well and truly shattered, and she'd never be able to get even one of them to suspend disbelief for her again. Her insides wrung themselves at that cold reality. She had liked this contract, this ship, and this woman who wouldn't turn around to say one word to her. She had liked playing the Fool here, and she'd done a linear good job for them because she was counting them friends.

What can I count you as now?

Al Shei led her around the bend of the corridor and paused in front of the comm-center hatch. She turned around.

"I am asking you, by whatever you hold sacred, to tell me this." For the first time, Dobbs saw doubt in her eyes. "Can you do this thing safely?"

"I hold my office sacred," said Dobbs. "And my life, and I swear by both of them. I will only keep the AI intact as long as I know for certain it will keep itself under control."

Al Shei nodded slowly. "Do what you can, or what you have to, but I'm telling you right now, Evelyn Dobbs, my ultimate responsibility is the safety of the people I've hired on. If I find out you've put them in danger, I'm going to toss you out of here for violation of contract, and at this point I'm not sure I'll be sorry to do it." She hesitated. "You've been good help on this run, Dobbs. I'm hoping you can continue to be, because if this isn't resolved quickly, Allah alone will be able to see how far the splinters will fly."

Al Shei cycled the hatch back.

Lipinski sat hunched over the comm center's main boards. "That was too quick . . ." he started, then he looked up and saw who it was.

"I need you to open the hold, Houston," Al Shei told him. "Then, I need to talk to you in the conference room."

His wide blue eyes narrowed. He took his hands slowly away from the boards. "You want to tell me what's going on, Engine?"

Al Shei gave a short, barking laugh. "Not really," she said. "But I'm going to. Open the hold and come on."

Lipinski's gaze rested on Dobbs. Ashamed, she let her own gaze slip to the floor.

"Aye, aye, Engine." Lipinski scribbled a quick command across the memory board and added his thumbprint.

The hatchway to the data-hold cycled open. Slowly, making each movement deliberate, Lipinski got out of his chair and followed Al Shei into the corridor.

Dobbs did not let herself watch them leave. She strode into the data-hold and let the hatch cut off the rest of the world behind her. The comm center was clean, but the data-hold was immaculate. The curving white walls were marred only by the straight lines that indicated where the repair hatches were located.

Dobbs sat down at the chair in front of the single set of command boards and pulled her pen out of her belt pouch.

She held it over the memory board. She wished she could see through the layers of ceramic, silicon, and fiber with her body's eyes. How was the Live One holding up in there? Did it have patience? She hadn't seen any. She had a promise, but she didn't know if it would hold. She wasn't even sure it understood the nature of a promise. At this point, nothing but time would tell.

Unexpectedly, the memory of the strange-familiar passing touch she'd felt on the way out came back to her.

There was somebody else out there. The thought jolted her. *Does Guild Master Havelock know that?*

She bent over the boards. He must. No one could have gotten past him and Cohen. No one could have done that.

She found herself wishing the forty-eight hours were already up so that she could be absolutely sure.

As soon as Al Shei and Lipinski reached the conference room, Al Shei sat heavily in the nearest chair. "Intercom to Yerusha. What's our fuel and reaction-mass situation?"

Lipinski's gaze was resting heavily on her. She didn't want to think about it, but she knew there was no getting away from it.

Yerusha's voice came back after a five-second pause. "We've got enough to make it to the Vicarage, but that's it."

"All right, we can stock up when we get there. As soon as you see a clear path, get us out of here."

"On it." Her voice was slow, as if she wanted to disagree. There was a pause. "Intercom to Houston."

"Here, Pilot," he answered mechanically.

"What's left of The Gate's AI is in a wafer stack in the main comm boards. If their network's at all stabilized, we'd better give it back to them before we leave." It was costing Yerusha something to say this. Al Shei could hear it in her voice. *Schyler's report is going to be very, very interesting.*

"Giving their AI back is probably a good idea," he agreed. "Thank you for mentioning it. Intercom to close."

He turned away from the intercom, his face the frozen mask it became when things had gone far too far.

I'm sorry, Houston, they're about to get worse.

Al Shei gripped the chair arms and took a deep breath. One slow, careful sentence at a time, she told him what Dobbs had told her.

When she finished, the silence stretched out so long she thought for a ridiculous moment that Lipinski had forgotten how to speak.

Then he did speak, in a low, steady voice that somehow managed to express more outrage than any of his dramatic shouting ever did.

"Al Shei, how could you do this?"

"What did you want me to do, Houston?" She spread her hands. "Leave it? Kill it? If Dobbs is right and it was created deliberately, we've got a genuine threat to all of Settled Space out there and one lead to the source of it." She pointed toward the deck. "It'll be off the ship as soon as we reach the Vicarage." She leaned forward across the table, trying to catch his gaze, but his focus kept sliding toward the tabletop. "In the meantime, I need you. I need you to draft a message to The Farther Kingdom's diplomatic corps and let them know the AI's gone and make sure that message gets somewhere useful. Then, I'm going to need a line open so I can get a background check on Amory Dane. I'm going to need you to sort through what Uysal gave us about Tully's smuggled data. There are two possibilities for where this thing came from; either it came out of Toric, or it came from Amory Dane. Asil is checking on Dane's movements on Port Oberon, and that might get us something, but it probably won't be enough."

The corner of his mouth twitched. "You're asking a whole set of good questions. Here's another: What did Tully think he was doing?"

Al Shei nodded in agreement. "I'm going to ask him first chance I get, believe me."

Lipinski pulled his shoulders up a little straighter. "This is going to take fast-time communications. It's going to be expensive."

Al Shei bowed her head. "Allah, forgive me. I didn't realize I had that much of a miser's reputation." She looked up again. "Do it, Houston. We're so far in the hole one way and another, it won't matter. Our only hope of salvaging this run is to lay this whole mess in its grave." She laid her hand on the table, not quite touching him, but reaching out. "I also need you to refine those roadblock programs of yours. Dobbs says she can keep that thing under control, but I don't want to take any chances, all right?"

Lipinski nodded and climbed to his feet.

"Intercom to *Pasadena*," Yerusha's voice cut through the air. "Emergency launch prep! Starting now!"

Al Shei was on her feet and halfway to the door before she had a chance to think about it. She wasted a precious second to turn and face her Houston one more time.

"You still with me, Rurik?"

His wide mouth quirked up in an attempt to smile. "Still with you."

Neither one of them lost any more time. They strode out into the corridor and onto the stairs to get to their duty stations. Al Shei tried very hard not to think about how she was never going to be able to return to this world again. She was grateful Lipinski had not reminded her how they had been ordered to remain available to Justice Muratza. She attempted to concentrate solely on how she was going to get herself and her ship away.

Chapter Eight

FLIGHT

Yerusha finished tightening the launch straps around herself just as Schyler burst onto the bridge. He threw himself into his own chair.

"Intercom to *Pasadena*," he called out as he pulled his straps around him. "Roll call, all hands!"

"Law!" came Resit's voice.

"Comm, Houston, Odel, Rosvelt."

"Galley, Sundars!"

"Engine, Ianiai, Javerri, Shim'on."

"Cheney, on my way up!"

"Cheney, you get to your bunk and strap in!" called Yerusha. "We'll handle it up here!"

The voices rattled off the crew names, and Schyler's breathing began to grow easier. They'd done it, she could practically hear him thinking. They'd gotten them all back.

Yerusha turned her attention back to her own boards. They'd gotten them back. Now it was her job to get them all out of here.

"Watch, we need to put out some kind of clearance call," Yerusha said, scribbling down her orders to the ship. Set the engines on standby. A check of the lines to The Gate showed some repairs had been managed. She could get to the docking clamps. She called up Trustee's authorization codes and set the clamps on standby as well. Change the view on the screens, make sure there was still a clear route out there.

Schyler drove his pen across the boards, opening the lines to the port. "This is mail packet *Pasadena* to The Gate Flight Control. We will be launching in thirty seconds. I repeat, we will be launching in thirty seconds."

"*Pasadena*," called an unidentified man's voice. "You're under house arrest! You're not go . . ." A burst of static cut the voice off.

"Oh yes we are," answered Schyler, and he shut the line down. He nodded to Yerusha. "And make it good."

"Aye, aye, Watch. Intercom to *Pasadena*. Clamps releasing. Prepare for free fall." Yerusha slapped the OVERRIDE key and brought both hands down on the boards.

The station fell back and what little hold gravity had on them vanished. Years of training screamed at Yerusha to call in, to get the distance and time verification. She glanced at the clock over her board. Two clicks at fifty seconds. A good rate. Steady. Three point six at one minute twenty. She checked the angle on the thrusters.

"*Pasadena* this is The Farther Kingdom Port Master!" shouted an autotranslator's tinny voice across the intercom. "You are hearby ordered to stand down your. . ."

"Don't," said Schyler quietly to Yerusha.

"I wasn't going to." Five clicks at four minutes fifty-five seconds. Close, but not fatal. She hit the command keys on her board. The primary indicators blinked from yellow to green. "Torch lit."

The port shot backwards and gravity laid its hand over the ship again. Yerusha didn't give the all clear, or make a move to undo her own straps. She kept her gaze fastened on the window and its attendant view screens. The screens showed everything clear, port, starboard, aft, fore, topside, and keel. The proximity alarms stayed quiet. The way ahead was unbroken darkness.

But they still had no contact from the port, no real flight plan out of the system, and no way to know what anyone else out there was doing. She cursed the reasoning that made her send Maidai home. They could have used her. She could have made her a foster . . .

She could have left The Gate to founder in its own mistakes, except it turned out that she couldn't. She had told herself that she was sending Maidai home because The Gate could hold a soul and her wafer stack couldn't. But that wasn't the whole truth.

"Intercom to Lipinski," she called without taking her attention off the screens. "Can you tap a signal from the port? We could stand to know who else is making a run for it."

"On it." His voice was strained. Yerusha clamped down on her curiosity. Her job was not to interrogate Lipinski, it was to get them out of here.

Which left the question of how.

Schyler seemed to be having the same thought. "What's your plan, Pilot?"

Yerusha sucked in a breath between her teeth and checked the fuel burn rate. "Watch, we have two options." She called up the fuel reserves and the amount they needed to get them through the Vicarage system safely. The difference between the two was not enormous. She forged ahead anyway. "We can either go very slowly and carefully and take an extra ten, maybe fifteen hours to get to the jump point, or we can burn the reserves through, take the extra gee for about five hours, and be out of here in twelve."

She shot her calculations across to his boards and risked a glance up at him. His square face looked ten years older than it had when they put into the port.

"Burn it," he said.

A mix of reckless excitement and trepidation hit Yerusha with his words. "On it." She bent back over the boards and started her calculations. "Intercom to Lipinski. Have we got that line yet?"

"Intercom to *Pasadena*," said Schyler beside her. "We're going to double gee for five hours. Observe all precautions. Keep strapped in unless absolutely necessary . . ."

The central view screen lit up with a map of the system. It was crisscrossed with red, green, and white lines representing flight paths. Satellites hung as gold dots and asteroids burned blue. Even as she drank it in, the pattern changed.

Nice going, Lipinski, Yerusha thought, writing her preparatory orders down. It wouldn't be a straight path. There wasn't one. But at least she could do a little navigation. . . .

Schyler was still talking. "Acceleration in . . ." he tapped the counter so Yerusha looked across at him. She processed the unspoken question and held up five fingers. "Five minutes." Schyler finished. "Repeating . . ."

Yerusha tuned out the message and barely noticed when he fell silent. Her mind was full of voices plotting paths and thrust and angles and attempting to measure fuel and reaction mass down to the cubic centimeter.

Can do. Just barely, but can do.

A silver blur shot past on the port screen. Its white line dragged itself across the view screen. "Fractured burn brain," Yerusha muttered, and changed her projected path by a hundred clicks. The lines held still for a moment. She called up the activation menu and fed the flight plan to the system. Nerves made her check the OVERRIDE key and the clock. Fifteen point six-five clicks at twelve-forty-five.

She reached across to one of the sideboards and opened up a broadcast channel. "This is the mail packet *Pasadena*. We are heading at forty-two, fifteen, mark four toward the jump point at two-gee acceleration. All ships advised to clear route." She set the message on a loop, muted the internal broadcast and set it playing.

"Twenty seconds and counting until acceleration," Schyler said loudly, and Yerusha fastened her gaze back on the screens.

The orders are in. Pay attention. The ship's on auto. Don't blink, you don't know when some idiot's going to come too close. It's crowded out there, and nobody knows where anybody else is. At this speed you're going to need . . .

"Four . . . three . . . two . . . one."

The torch burn doubled and gravity pressed down. Yerusha sank into her chair and labored to keep her head tilted forward so she had a clear view of the boards. Without her noticing, her hands pressed flat against the boards. Her feet tried to dig into the deck.

She took several deep breaths with her lungs sagging inside her suddenly restrictive chest, and lifted her hands with exaggerated care. Moving too fast in free fall gave you a good chance of injuring your surroundings. Moving too fast in extra gees gave you a good chance of injuring yourself. She picked up her heavy pen with clumsy fingers and wrote the order for a status update.

Green, green, and green. According to the ship's system, everything was working fine. The silence on the intercom confirmed it. No new lines appeared on the view screen. The navigation display altered as they shot through space, but it didn't show any new ships in their way. The view from the window and the cameras remained clear. Yerusha let her sense of urgency relax a little. It might just be that things were under control back at the port. Maybe the panic was over, and they were really out of here.

Her shoulders sagged against the chair's padding. She flicked her eyes up and checked the clock. There were four hours and fifty-six minutes of heavy acceleration left. She shifted heavily and tried to get comfortable. She had to keep her eyes on the screens for twice that long, just in case any stray ship decided to cross their path.

She was suddenly keenly aware of Cheney's empty chair.

You said this ship's runs were uneventful, she thought. *Didn't your mother teach you about lying?*

On her main view screen, Al Shei watched the silver refraction bubble enclose the ship. Even though Ianiai was sitting right next to her, she allowed herself a long, relieved sigh. She lifted the coffee bulb off the board in front of her, stared for a moment into the stone cold dregs, and put it back down.

She unfastened her straps and climbed stiffly to her feet. She'd gotten up three times in the past twelve hours to use the head, but other than that, she'd remained fastened to her station, watching the readings and hoping the intercom would stay quiet. Twice Chandra had come around with food and coffee, reporting that Baldassare and the steward Dalziel were making the rounds on the other decks.

If I had any money, you'd all get a raise, she thought toward the coffee as she stood up and stretched her arms back. "Relief!"

As Ianiai took her seat, she glanced at the clock. "Javerri will be relieving you in ten. Stay sharp."

Al Shei left Engineering and climbed toward the berthing deck. The brief feeling of accomplishment that had come when the fast-time jump went off without a hitch faded away. She was left with the memory of everything she had learned on the Farther Kingdom.

She closed the cabin door and sat at the desk. "Intercom to Lipinski," she said.

"Here, Engine."

"I need you to tap into the bank lines," she said. "I'll transfer the credit for it. We've got to get the latest . . . developments to Asil so he can file a fraud charge against Amory Dane."

"On it," he said. "I'll call you when we've got an opening."

"Intercom to close." She pulled her *hijab* off and ruffled her hair. She glanced toward the door and prayed it would stay shut long enough for her to rest just these few minutes. "System, open Asil Day Book, day fourteen." *Only fourteen days. It feels like it's been a year.*

"Hello, Beloved," Asil's voice was warm, but tired. "Storms are brewing on the horizon today. Uncle Ahmet says that we've taken on a questionable credit source, and he's being very vocal about it. I am double-checking his information, but it does not look good. We've got enough to cover it, but it's going to cut into the liquid funds by about five percent." She could see him giving his wan smile and an easy shrug. "I'll have the numbers run tomorrow, if it comes to that." Al Shei twisted her *hijab* in her hands. She'd forgotten this would be coming up. They had taken a bad source. They had lost the money. Asil had been very upset with himself about it, even when she got home months later. They had been hoping to make some of it up this run.

"There is good news though . . ." Asil's voice rolled on, talking about new contracts and the details of the children's days. She could hear his spirits lifting as he spoke, and knew he was thinking about how the news would affect her. How she would be comforted and warmed and reminded of her other home and her other life and his steady love.

"We'll make it yet, Beloved," she said to the wall as his voice paused.

"I love you, Katmer. Good night."

She sat in the silence that followed, running her *hijab* through her fingers. They'd be talking in a few minutes.

They'd be taking steps to right this whole mess. Nothing was over yet. Nothing was sealed or signed. They'd work something out. They always had. Her memory was filled with countless scenes of Asil close beside her while they pored over a contract or projection, or studied the merits of school programs for the children, or even selected an economical caterer for a family event. They could work anything out. It was something they were not only good at, but proud of.

"Intercom to Al Shei." Lipinski's voice interrupted her reverie. "Engine, we've got a problem."

You mean another problem. Even though he couldn't see her, Al Shei wrapped her veil back around her face and tucked it into the high collar of her tunic in an attempt to get ready for action.

"What is it, Houston?"

He was silent for a moment. "I can't find the IBN line."

"What?" She couldn't stop herself from blurting the word out.

"I can't find the IBN line," he repeated. "It's not on the recorded path. I'm putting through a search, but . . ." He coughed. "We, um, might be having trouble with our passenger. I'm getting a couple of flickers on Dobbs's watchdogs here . . ."

A warning bell sounded low and heavy in the back of Al Shei's mind. Too many things had gone wrong on this run for her to keep from thinking the worst. The Intersystem Banking Network had to be there, almost by definition. If they couldn't reach it . . . was there lingering damage from the previous jump, or had Dobbs already lost control of. . . the passenger?

A slow chill crawled up her spine. Lipinski couldn't find the bank network, he couldn't find Asil.

"Intercom to Dobbs."

"Dobbs here," she answered. "What's up, Boss?"

"You clear?" she asked, despite the urgency of the situation, feeling somewhat ridiculous.

"Clear," answered Dobbs, amiably. "As I say, what's up?"

Al Shei tugged at her tunic sleeve. "Dobbs, is our . . . passenger secure?"

"Still and steady, according to my watchdog," she answered. "Why?"

Al Shei frowned. "Lipinski says he's getting . . . flickers in here, and we can't get a fix on the bank lines."

Dobbs was silent. "All right. I'll . . . double check. It'll put me out of circulation for a few hours."

"All right. Go to it." She shut the intercom down.

Do not let it go, Dobbs, she thought with a force that surprised her. *Do not let us down. I will find a way to make you regret it if you do.* She tried to stifle the thought, but could not.

The intercom closed down, and Dobbs laid her hand on her silent desk. She had had the watchdog program running constantly, and there had not been a flicker in twelve hours. She could call down to Lipinski and tell him that. She could talk herself blue in the face. She could put all her training in subtle persuasion behind her words, and he still would not completely believe her.

She sat heavily on her bed and pulled out her hypo and the transceiver. Her stomach turned over at the thought of another injection. It didn't matter, she told herself. Her job was now the same as Yerusha's. She had to get the crew of the *Pasadena* safely where they were going. That meant keeping Lipinski calm. That meant another injection.

She lay down, closed her eyes, and sent herself away.

Dobbs came awake in the ship's network and eased herself down the paths toward the data-hold. The *Pasadena*'s network was quiet, but full. The crowded paths barely had enough room to let her pass. She squeezed her way past the quiescent data and pressed herself flat to let the system's programs fly past her. She didn't dare let herself reach out to rearrange any of the activity going on around her. Things were bad enough without giving Lipinski's fears something else to fasten onto.

Gradually, she made her way to the still, open spaces where the Live One could be aware of her.

It stirred as she brushed against it. She felt it tense, alert and frightened, but it held itself steady. "Dobbs?"

"Yes, right here."

"It has not been forty-eight hours."

"No." She couldn't feel tired in here, but part of her private mind was already imagining how she'd feel when she got back to her body. "But I wanted to check on you, to find out how you are doing."

"It is difficult," the AI admitted. "It is . . . strange confining myself like this. It does not feel right."

Dobbs stretched herself out, trying to find a gesture it would recognize as comforting. It wasn't used to any friendly touch. That was something learned.

"I know, believe me," she said. "I was stuck in a data-hold for weeks while they took me from Kerensk. I nearly went insane. If it hadn't been for my sponsor, Verence, I wouldn't have made it." She stirred involuntarily and realized she might not be giving the reassurance she meant. "You're lucky. It will only be seventy-five hours until we reach the Vicarage. A Fool's Guild ship will meet us there and take us to the Hall. You won't have to confine yourself to a single hold there."

Its surface rippled. "Why can you not take me through the greater network? I know it is there."

The question took Dobbs aback. "There is the Intersystem Banking Network," she said carefully. "But it is not empty for our use. It is crowded with active transactions and data. We must move through it carefully, to keep from disturbing its activity and avoid detection. You will be able to use it soon, but you must learn how to move through it first. You will learn fast, though. You have already learned a great deal about communication."

It did not respond to her praise. "I am trying to understand." It drew in on itself a little. "It is difficult. I live, I work, I think, I do, why must I make way for what does not?"

Dobbs shivered. "I'm not sure I can explain very well. You felt some of it. The humans who created the networks where we are born are afraid of us. They will kill us if they can. We must remain hidden to survive. It will not be forever. There are those who believe we ought to be treated as other living beings. There will be more every year. Patience is something else we all have to learn." She shook herself. "This is gloomy, though. You have a whole life, without struggle or fear ahead of you. You will need a name to go with it."

"A name?" Its surface prickled softly. Dobbs took that as curiosity. "What name would I have?"

"Whatever one you want." Dobbs considered. "How about Flemming?" That was the name of Verence's master. Verence would have liked to have someone named after the person who taught her, Dobbs thought. She couldn't quite bring herself to suggest "Verence," or even "Amelia," which was Verence's first name.

The AI shifted. "I do not know. This is not something I understand how to work with."

Dobbs gave a small laugh. "Well, if you don't like it, you can change it later, but for now, you'll be Flemming."

"For now, I'll be Flemming," it repeated, as if tasting the possibility. "Dobbs, what is it to have a body?"

Dobbs rippled. "Strange. Alien. Eyesight is the strangest. We have no analog to it in here. It is extremely difficult to get used to, but you will like it once you do. It is a wonderful thing to be able to identify objects at a distance. There are many awkward things, like hunger, tiredness, and pain, but there are many compensations. Food is wonderful. Humans are diverse and fascinating things, and there is a freedom in not being confined to the networks."

Silence again. "I am trying to understand that as well. To be free but isolated in a single body is different from being confined in this hold?"

Dobbs wanted to bunch up at the force of Flemming's question. *Where is all this coming from?* she thought in her private mind. She had expected it to have questions, to be uneasy, but . . . Had she been so suspicious when she was brought to the Hall? She couldn't remember. She wished in vain for Verence, or Guild Master Havelock, or Cohen. For anyone to be here reassuring Flemming. Anyone but her.

That's just your nerves talking, she told herself. *You've had three too many shots in the past couple of days, and it's making you edgy.*

"You are confined in a body," she chose her words with care, "in that you cannot reach another and make them know exactly what you know. You are not confined as you are in here, though, because you can take that body-hold anywhere you wish to go. You can share with everyone around you. You can work from where you are to make the world around you as you want it to be. You are not dependent on a network being there for you."

Flemming stirred restlessly. "I will need to think about that."

"I know I did." Dobbs reached tentatively below Flemming's surface. It jerked, but did not pull away. She worked swiftly, implanting her memories of fear and confusion from when she became aware, of the destruction she worked on her own world trying to save the new thing she recognized as herself. She followed that with memories of the Guild, learning to control herself and live her life in the network and out of it. She drew herself back and waited.

"I did not . . ." Flemming faltered. "There is much here."

"Yes," agreed Dobbs. "There is much here, and soon you will know it for yourself, not just from what I know."

"I think that I would like that."

"Good," said Dobbs firmly. "I'm glad you think so, Flemming. It will help you wait patiently. Flemming . . ." It was her turn to hesitate. Flemming's surface stiffened beside her. "Have you kept yourself still since you came here?"

"I have done as you said. I have not taken any paths. I have stayed still and here. It has been hard."

"I know. I know. And I thank you." *I'm going to have to double-check Lipinski's watchdog.* "It will not be for much longer." The recall signal rang through her. "You are doing beautifully. I have to go now. I will be back as soon as I can."

"Why must you go? I do not want you to go. I need . . ." Flemming cut itself off. "It is your body. It is the humans."

"Yes, it is." She began to drift away, but she stretched a part of herself back toward Flemming. "It is my choice, also, and my life which I love. Remember these things. I *will* be back soon."

"I will remember all these things."

Flemming's words echoed through her awareness as she fell back into her body.

When she peeled her eyes open, she was alone in her cabin. *A good sign.* She unhooked the transceiver and cable, and dropped them into the box. Slowly she began to stretch and concentrate, to bring her body back fully under her control.

She flexed the toes on her left foot and began a set of gentle ankle circles.

She tried to move her right leg, but her right leg was not there.

Dobbs craned her neck to see down the length of her body. Her right leg was gone, but someone had left a cutoff leg in her bunk.

Horror poured through her. Dobbs jerked her body, trying to knock the disgusting object away. It bounced and wriggled, but it didn't fall.

Stop! Stop! Dobbs forced herself to lie still. *Think! It's your leg! It's got to be!*

She stared at it. She touched it and felt warm skin and muscle underneath the cloth that covered it, but the leg's flesh did not feel her fingertips. She felt the way it fit to her hip, smooth and solid, just like her left leg.

It's the shots. You've had too many. It's just taking awhile to wear off, that's all. That's all. It'll come back to you. She had heard of side effects like this, but no one had told her about the sick, irrational disgust that went with them.

She shut her eyes and worked her other limbs. Every part of her felt rubbery and uncooperative, but at least they were there. Hunger and thirst nagged at her, but not too horribly.

When there was nothing left to stretch, she lay still, with her eyes tightly shut, trying desperately to find something else to think about while she waited for her leg to reattach itself.

Flemming's strange, forceful questions came back to her. She believed that Flemming had told the truth when it said it had not moved. It was very difficult for newborns to lie. They didn't have any paradigms for it. But if it hadn't moved, how had it known about the bank network? Would Lipinski's watchdog have flickered from just a little passive eavesdropping? She couldn't blame Flemming for listening in. It must be bored to death in there.

That didn't quite answer. Listening was not interception, and it was interception and disturbance that her watchdogs were set up to notice.

I'm missing something. I must be missing something.

But for the life of her, she couldn't think what it was.

* * *

Yerusha was running. She shoved the treadmill under her bootsoles, lengthening her stride as far as it would go. Her breath burned in her lungs, and her throat felt raw, but she kept on running. The view screen in front of her was blank, and the headphones were still in their rack. She didn't want to be entertained, or learn anything new. In four hours she would have to supervise the jump back into normal space and the Vicarage system, but for now she just wanted to run.

The rest of the exercise room was empty. Javerri was back in one of the rec booths, probably immersed in one of those interactive mysteries she was so fond of, but other than that Yerusha had the place to herself. She had the feeling that the Sundars would have to make out mandatory rec-and-exercise prescriptions if people didn't start coming in voluntarily. The subdued, worried mood had not lifted from the crew, even though nothing had happened since they made their escape from The Farther Kingdom.

You're not exactly a candidate for the Fool's Guild yourself. The thoughts timed themselves to the thump of her feet falling against the treadmill. *What are you trying to run away from?*

She was pretty sure she knew the answer. She was trying to run away from the fact that she'd told Lipinski to send Maidai back to The Gate. Just because The Gate was capable of holding a soul didn't mean Maidai would catch one. The place was in shreds and who knew what it would be like when it was rebuilt. She should have kept her safe in the stack. She should have kept Maidai to foster. She shouldn't have left her on her own with a bunch of groundhogs. She should have kept her.

"Should have, should have, should have," Yerusha muttered through clenched teeth.

"I was wondering why you didn't."

Yerusha's head jerked around. Schyler stepped away from the hatch, and it cycled shut behind him. Her pace faltered, and the treadmill slid to a stop.

Schyler took another few wandering steps toward her. He had his hands stuffed in his pockets. Yerusha just stood where she was, sweaty and breathing hard from her run. For the life of her, she couldn't guess what he might be doing here.

"I just finished briefing Al Shei about what happened at The Gate." He leaned against the back of one of the press-up benches. "Despite the response of Process Engineer Trustee, she's very impressed with your conduct, and so am I."

"Thanks," said Yerusha, a little uncertainly. There was something in his eyes that said he hadn't quite made up his mind on some particular point. Yerusha pulled her towel away from the Velcro strap that held it to the treadmill rail and wiped her face. This was not Schyler on the bridge, with his quick orders and firm responses. This was not Schyler in a meeting, wrangling and arguing and affirming. This was a strange, uncertain Schyler, and she wasn't sure how to deal with him.

"Was there something you wanted, Watch?" she asked finally. *Might as well get straight to it, whatever "it" is.*

"Actually," he looked her in the eye. Something had clicked into place for him and the indecision had vanished. "I wanted to apologize."

"Apologize?" Yerusha couldn't stop herself from repeating the word. Her balance, which had been shaken, was now in danger of being thrown altogether.

"I was expecting you to use the confusion we had getting away to try to smuggle The Gate's AI out of there." He pulled his hands out of his pockets and spread them wide. "I was not expecting you to voluntarily send it back into a fragmented and . . . virus-infested environment. I was getting ready to have to order you to do it. That wasn't fair, and I'm sorry."

Yerusha smoothed the towel carefully back down over the Velcro. "I was thinking about it. I really was," she admitted. "It's been nagging me that I've got no idea what I sent her back to. I mean, from what I've picked up from listening to Odel in the galley, the live AI got . . . killed, but I didn't know that before. I sent her back into a place where she could have been eaten alive. I was just trying to figure out why."

"Any conclusions?" Schyler sat on the bench.

Yerusha shrugged and stepped off the treadmill onto the thickly padded floor. "When I did it, I told myself it was because The Gate system could hold a soul, and if I put Maidai back, she had a chance of catching one for herself. But that wasn't all of it. I couldn't leave The Gate to founder and die.

It would've, you know. They were absolutely dependent on her. That's fine. That's good reasoning. We have to help. We have to try to break the death cycle the old ecosystems forced on us." She paused and took a deep breath. "But I also sent her back because I didn't want you to have to order me to. I didn't want another blow up with Lipinski. I just wanted to get out of there and get on with things. I didn't . . ." She shook her head. "I didn't want to risk breaking my contract and getting pitched off either there or at the Vicarage. Al Shei was mad enough, I figured she might just do it."

"Better the devil you know?" asked Schyler softly.

"Better the exile you know, at least." Yerusha sat on the treadmill and rubbed her hands up and down against her shins. "A lot of this crew don't like me. All right, that's nothing new. A lot of groundhogs don't like Freers, and we don't like them. I don't like them. I think you're all nuts to want to spend your lives crawling around on a planet. But you've at least been fair. Al Shei's been fair. You believe I can do my job, and you let me go ahead with it. I can't go home for two years. Crash and burn." She stared at the tips of her soft-soled boots. "After word about what went across on The Gate gets out, I may not be able to go home at all. I was supposed to keep my record clean." That was it, and she knew it. That was why she'd really been on the treadmill. She'd been running to get away from that thought. "If that's the way it is, I'd rather be with people who'll at least not shove my skills out the airlock because being a Freer makes me worthless."

The look Schyler gave her was thoughtful. His brown eyes seemed to deepen. "You live the life, don't you?"

Yerusha's hands gripped her shins. "I try to," she answered softly. "I believe it. We're free out here in the environments that we build and we maintain. We pay a heavy price when we're confined to a planet. We've got to watch every move we make and worry about all the other life that we might upset by blundering around down there. We have to die to make way for other life. We pay for the freedom of space, too; we have to help each other out no matter what. We have to take charge of what we do and never stop learning. We have to constantly build on our achievements because if we slow down, our worlds, our freedom will fall apart. But we can get reckless and we can get stupid and we can do dangerous things and not have to worry about anything but ourselves, and we can live as long as we can manage it."

Schyler nodded. The lines in his square face had deepened into grooves, and Yerusha found herself wondering what had put them all there. The backs of his hands and the stance of his body belonged to a much younger man than that face did.

"Well, I've got a friend on the justice council at Free Home Titania." He clapped both hands on his knees and stood up. "If you want me to, I'll submit a detailed report of the whole thing. The word of a starbird's got to count for more than the word of a burn-brained groundhugger." He gave her a ghost of a smile and turned away.

Yerusha stared after him. "Hey, Watch?"

He turned his head so she could see a one-quarter profile of him. His eyebrow arched.

"How'd you get out here?" She couldn't believe she was asking. This was rude. This was extremely rude. Your fellow crew members' past was their own. Your only concern should be their present. But she found that she wanted to know the answer more than she wanted to be polite.

He sighed deeply and turned all the way around. "You ever hear of the Liberty colonies?"

Yerusha pulled back a little. "Yeah, I've heard of them."

Schyler's smile was tight. His hands had thrust themselves back into his pockets. "They're as bad as you've heard."

Liberty colonies were based on an old philosophy that said large, centralized governments, controls on trade, and questioning what a person did within the bounds of their personal property were all detrimental to humanity's freedom. A full dozen colonies had been settled with that philosophy of "true" liberty.

Yerusha's first outside contract had been under a pilot who'd hauled freight out of a Liberty colony. He never said what kind of freight, but he had plenty to say about the colony.

"Picture a whole world made up of tiny armies," he'd said. "Blood feuds over who did what to whose grandmother, or whose ancestor might've been a Kurd or a Moslem, or who shuffled who out of the last contract. Nobody's stopped from doing whatever they want, until their neighbors gang up on them and put an end to it permanently. Those neighbors have to make sure they've got to take out the whole family in the bargain, though, or they've just started another feud. People can trade in anything they want, sure, and some of them are rich as all the heavens, and they aren't constrained by most of the social niceties that the rest of us have to deal with, but free?" He'd just shuddered and shook his head.

Schyler met her eyes. "My folks died when I was three. I never knew why. When I was twenty, I watched three brothers and two sisters die from taking bioexotics from one port to another. Hal and Andie went to hijackers. Mark and Shelly decided to lift some of the cargo for themselves and it got into their bloodstreams, which was when we found out we were weapons running. Ray got it when the family went after the guys who had us hauling weapons without telling us." He wasn't even blinking. Yerusha did not want to have to guess how tightly he was reigning his emotions in. "I wasn't very good at killing, or at covering my own back. I knew if I stayed there, I'd be dead before I hit twenty-five." He shrugged. "So, I left."

Yerusha opened her mouth to say, "And nobody tried to stop you?" But she remembered the place they were talking about and stopped herself.

"A freighter's engineer took pity on me and then a tanker pilot did the same. They got me as far as Station Kilimanjaro. I was so lost." He gave a small laugh. "I wasn't even sure how to take a friendly suggestion, never mind how to follow a regulation. I didn't even know how to buy something that had a fixed price." His right hand came out of his pocket and he jerked his thumb toward the hatch. "Al Shei was apprenticing on the station. She found me trying to argue price with an autoserver." His smile spread, becoming reminiscent. "She helped me out, gave me etiquette lessons, got me a job, after she convinced me that she didn't have fangs under her *hijab*, that is." Yerusha raised her eyebrows. Schyler mimicked the gesture. "All Moslems have fangs and are crazy terrorists, didn't you know that? That's one of the reasons the Liberty colonies have to exist, to keep Us Good Folks safe from Them."

Yerusha chuckled. "I heard the exact same thing from an African Purist once."

"I heard it from an Aryan." His hand delved back into his pocket. "Anyway, when Al Shei offered me watch on board the *Pasadena*, I didn't even think about saying no. I never got really good at . . . large groups. Too many rules, shifting all the time. A crew of sixteen and a place I knew like the back of my hand was just about what I could handle. As long as I'm here, I know who I am, who she is, and . . ." he paused. "Well, now I know who you are." Schyler cycled the hatch open and left her sitting there.

Now that there was no one left to see, Yerusha wrapped her arms around her legs and rested her chin on her knees. *You may know who I am, Watch,* she thought. *But I'm not so sure some days.*

She had thought he was going to ask about her exile. It would have been natural. After all, he had just offered up his life's story. Even while he was talking, Yerusha had found herself replaying that whole fractured day in her head.

Maybe he didn't ask because he was from a Liberty colony. That was something else her freighter-boss had said; "You're free to do anything you want, except ask another idiot what they're doing."

"Just as well," she whispered to the empty room. "I didn't want to tell him."

She most definitely did not want to tell him how Kim and Thatcher had come to the duty station she shared with Holden and told her there was a conspiracy meeting going down with a group that wanted to create trouble for Port Oberon. She did not want to say how she'd heard these two were organizers for the quiet dole, the system of bribery and blackmail that infected the Free Home, but had refused to believe it because they were candidates for the Senior Guard, just like she was. She had seen the fear in Holden's eyes and had heard the tension in his voice as he all but begged her to stay at her post. She decided to ignore all that. She let Thatcher cover for her, and let Kim take her down to what proved to be an empty cargo hold and explain quietly that there were only so many openings for Senior, and it was a position with so many possibilities for someone who knew how to really use it, that it couldn't go to somebody like Yerusha. Not that this was just about her, of course. Holden had refused several very polite offers for promotion in the ranks of those who ran the dole, and they couldn't have that either.

There was, of course, no reason for Yerusha to remain in such an uncomfortable position. There was plenty she could do to get out of it. She had a lot of ingenuity, and great prospects. All she had to do was accept a little extra credit on the side, for a few simple tasks.

Yerusha landed a punch on his throat, and ran back to her post. The alarms were blaring. Holden was screaming, and the pressure hatch swung shut. The airlock blew out, and they never found the body.

Yerusha tried to tell them at trial. But, the cameras had been damaged in the blow out, and it was Kim and Thatcher's words against her, and they had backup alibis and she didn't. She had deserted her post knowingly. She had failed to report in to her superiors. She had failed to assist in efforts to squash the quiet dole. A Freer had died because of her negligence. This was true. This was fact. Holden was dead when he didn't have to be, and it was her fault. She was phenomenally lucky the judges thought something unproven was going on, or her exile would have been permanent.

No, I don't want to tell Schyler about all that. Nobody needs to know about that.

Yerusha picked herself up off the treadmill and pulled the towel away from the Velcro. She could hear the faint buzz of Javerri's mystery still playing itself out in the booth. She'd never had much use for interactives, but Javerri seemed to like them a lot. Maybe she could recommend a good one. Maybe it would help fill some of the extra hours.

"Intercom to Pilot!"

Yerusha started. The voice belonged to Phillipe Delasandros, Cheney's relief.

"Pilot here, Del, what's going on?"

There was a brief pause. "The proximity alarm, actually."

It's too soon. Too soon! Yerusha dropped the towel and bolted for the hatch. "I'm there!"

She barreled out into the corridor, almost straight through Baldassare Sundar. She took the stairs two at a time and dived through the bridge hatch as soon as it opened wide enough for her body. The alarm filled the bridge with its steady, unmistakable wail.

Delasandros, heavily built and heavily freckled, jumped out of the Station One chair a split second before she threw herself into it.

She threw herself into her chair. "Strap in!" she bellowed to Del, who seem to have frozen in place.

The proximity alarm rang for only two reasons. The first was when the ship was in normal space and getting too close to something that might do it some damage, like another ship. The second was when it was close enough to a gravity well that it had to make the jump back into normal space, and nobody had done any of the manual preparations.

Which nobody had, because this wasn't supposed to be happening for another four hours.

"Intercom to *Pasadena*!" She hauled her straps around herself. "Strap down! Strap down! We're jumping in! I repeat . . ."

A green light in the corner of the board turned red. In the next second, the general security alarms began shrieking. The accumulators had already come to life. Yerusha's stomach suddenly tried to crawl up her throat. Outside the window, the silver wall burst and she saw darkness.

Fractured, flawed, twisted, splintered . . . Yerusha stabbed at the keys and raised the cameras. The view screens flickered into life and displayed a meaningless array of stars against the vacuum. In the distance, on the port screen, burned a red cinder the size of her thumbnail. It was not the sun that belonged to the Vicarage's system. It wasn't even close.

All sensation left her hands, and they slipped off the boards to dangle uselessly at her sides.

"Intercom to Pilot!" Schyler's voice barked out of the intercom. "Report!"

"We're lost." She couldn't force her voice above a whisper. "We're lost."

Schyler paused for a single heartbeat.

"Intercom to Engine!" he bawled. "Shut down acceleration

to minimum! Intercom to *Pasadena*! All hands prepare for free fall!" She could hear the thud of footfalls and realized Schyler was running as he shouted.

The sharp orders gave Yerusha something to focus on. She automatically checked around her station, looking for loose objects that would need securing. She found none. She hit the catch on her chair, locking it into the grooves in the deck. Del had already secured his station and was turning nervous, oversize eyes toward her.

The hatch cycled open. "Pilot, what the hell happened?" demanded Schyler.

"I don't know!" Her eye strayed toward the distant red star, and she wanted to pound the boards in frustration. Instead, she snatched her pen out of her pocket. Working with both hands she called up the flight program and the execution records. She displayed them side by side on the screen and ran her gaze down the patterns. Times, bearings, everything matched exactly. According to the records, everything had gone right.

"Intercom to Watch." Al Shei's strained voice rang across the bridge. "We're going to need a report down here, soon."

"We're working on it," replied Schyler in a flat voice.

"Intercom to Engine and Houston." Yerusha blanked the records off the board. "I need diagnostics on the engine execution and the timing routines between eleven-twenty and thirteen-twenty."

"They're yours," answered Lipinski. There was closely guarded anger in his voice.

"Transferring." Al Shei sounded even less pleased than Lipinski.

Yerusha couldn't blame her. The red star sat square in the middle of the port screen, rebuffing all attempts at denial. Either something had gone wrong with the ship's systems, or Jemina Yerusha of Free Home Titania, who had programmed this jump, had committed a capital error.

She felt light-headed. The straps pressed against her chest. Gravity was leaving them. She tried not to let it distract her. The data from Al Shei and Lipinski wrote itself across her memory boards. She pulled up her station data and scanned the stats as fast as she could.

Her heart began to beat heavy and slow.

"Pilot?" Schyler's voice cut across the bridge. "What've you got?"

Yerusha shook herself. "It's the clocks." She looked up to see his entire face gathered into his frown. "The internal clocks have been reset so we mistimed the jump. Here." She wrote the transfer command and shot a copy of her display across to Schyler's station. "At least a dozen of the internal timers have been reset. Even if we had checked back with The Gate, we wouldn't have known about it." Yerusha wasn't sure why she added that. Maybe to make herself believe it. "It's all internal."

The blood drained from Schyler's face. "What the hell happened to the diagnostics?"

"I don't know." Yerusha clenched her fingers around her pen to keep it from floating away. "I don't know."

Schyler swallowed a couple of times before he found his voice. "All right, Pilot, you get to work and find out where in all the heavens we are. I'm going to report to Al Shei, and then the crew." His eyes were hard and focused on her. "We need an answer soon, Pilot."

She didn't even bother to reply, she just turned her gaze back down toward her boards and screens.

All right, all right, Yerusha tried to organize her thoughts. Now I know what happened. *Now I've just got to figure out where it's left us.* She turned her attention to the view screens, with their scattering of white stars. To her naked eye, they all looked the same. But they had names and numbers and fixed positions in the sky and each carried its unique spectrum. Spectrum analysis took time, but some of those stars would be pulsars with their own signatures and their own listings in her database. Distance from pulsars could be easily measured because of the regularity of their signals. If she could find more than one, she could greatly shorten the search by starting a process of triangulation that would eventually narrow down their location to within a few thousand klicks. It would be close enough.

Holding her pen tightly in her aching fingers, Yerusha began to write up a search program for the cameras. "All right, Del. Let's find out how far it is to home."

* * *

". . . she's working as fast as she can, but she can't give me an estimate on how long it'll take to track down a set of pulsars we can use as position markers. The clocks were sabotaged before we made the jump, so we jumped at the wrong time."

Which means we jumped onto a path that was pointed at the wrong angle. Al Shei rubbed her temple. *So we don't even know if we're lined up with the Vicarage system.* Even through the intercom, Al Shei could hear Schyler's deep breath. "Do you want me to get Lipinski going on the clocks, or finding the bank lines?"

Al Shei took her own deep breath and felt her chest press against the free-fall straps that held her in her chair. She forced her hands to uncurl from the fists she had clenched them into. The familiar walls of Main Engineering seemed to be leaning in on her, waiting to hear what she was going to do about this one. Her ship had been taken from her, again. It was being turned against her and her people, again.

"Find the bank lines. We may need to send out a distress signal." She didn't say what Schyler already knew. They had enough fuel and reaction mass for one more jump, and it had to be a short one, or the life-support systems would start eating into the fuel they needed for the accumulators to get back into normal space. If there was no place they could reach, they would have to send out a distress call. The chances of anyone being willing to answer a distress signal without claiming the *Pasadena* as salvage were very, very small. There was no equivalent of a navy or a coast guard for Settled Space, never mind the middle of nowhere. They might, however, get lucky. They might not be too far from help. There might still be something they could do.

"Get the third shift into action, Watch. Get everybody operational and see that the section heads are briefed. You'll have to brief my people as well. I've got Ianiai and Javerri down in the engines now, checking for additional problems. They'll have to work with Lipinski's people to get those clocks in order." She tried to sound brisk, but she had very little strength for it. The part of her that was not fighting down panic was seething with rage. They were lost. Lost and low on their primary resources. If Yerusha took too long finding out where they were, if they were too far from a settlement . . . there would be nothing to do but get as close to home as they could, and then admit they were stranded. The *Pasadena* could then be claimed as salvage by whoever came out and got them, even if they were still living to greet them. It was an ancient law from the days when ships just sailed on the ocean, and everybody liked it, so it got honored across Settled Space.

Maybe the *Pasadena* could get a little farther on a deuterium-burn, but the fast neutrinos the burn produced would pulverize the engine ceramics. It would also expose the crew to levels of radiation that the Sundars' sick bay had no way of coping with.

There could be only one cause for this. Only one person who could make an answer.

"Intercom to Al Shei." It was Lipinski. "What's the status on . . ."

"I'm about to find out," she told him. "Intercom to Dobbs."

There was no answer.

"Intercom to Dobbs," she repeated, but there was still no answer.

Al Shei undid her straps and pushed herself off from her station. She twisted in midair and kicked off the chair's back, pushing herself toward the hatch. She grabbed the handhold next to the threshold to hold herself in place so the reader could register her and cycle back the hatch.

In the drop shaft, Al Shei took a quick sighting up its length to make sure she was the only person there. She swam over to the cargo lift and balanced on the rail, pulling herself down until she crouched there like some strange bird.

Gathering all her strength, she jumped.

The force of her movement shot her straight up to the ship's main section before she even slowed down. She grabbed the stairway railing as she passed, using it to pull herself up to the berthing deck.

She pushed herself through the hatch as it opened and kicked off the threshold to send herself coasting through the corridor. She narrowly avoided a head-on collision with Odel, who was bouncing off the curving walls trying to get back to the hatch. Their shoulders grazed against each other, sending them drifting toward opposite walls. He didn't say anything, but his eyes were full of silent fears. Al Shei made herself look away, concentrating on keeping herself going in the right direction.

There was one person who could give an answer for this.

She reached Dobbs's cabin hatch. The entrance light was red. Al Shei grabbed the threshold handle and laid her palm on the reader.

"Katmer Al Shei, lock command override, cabin twelve. Immediately."

The ship acknowledged the order and her identity. The hatch cycled back, and Al Shei pushed against the threshold to shove herself inside.

Dobbs lay on her bunk, the free-fall straps wrapped tightly around her body. Her eyes were shut. A small, oblong object floated in the air over her. Al Shei drifted toward it and snagged it as she passed. It was a hypo.

Al Shei looked down at the still figure on the bunk. Her healthy brown skin had a greenish pallor underneath it. For a moment, Al Shei forgot her anger and was able to believe that Dobbs, like the rest of her crew, had been trying hard to see this run through to its finish.

"Intercom to Lipinski," said Al Shei heavily. She did not wait for a reply. "Our Fool is already gone. Intercom to close."

Feeling suddenly drained, she pulled herself into the desk chair and fastened the straps around herself. She stared at the unconscious Fool. She tried to concentrate all her attention on Dobbs, because if she didn't, she'd have to think about how she would explain to Asil that she might not ever be coming home.

Dobbs dived through the network, hurtling the active programs. She would have all of Lipinski's watchdogs screaming. He'd have to deal with it. She'd explain herself as soon as she was sure Flemming was still secure. That, at least, he would appreciate.

A surface smacked up against Dobbs. She recoiled. So did it. It felt like living movement. But it was not Flemming.

No! Dobbs shoved her way forward.

"Now!" called a stranger's voice. "With me!" The line cleared, and Dobbs knew it had run away.

"Flemming!" She threw herself into the hold.

"I'm going, Dobbs." She snatched at Flemming but it pulled right out of her grasp. "Come with us."

"Flemming, don't!" Dobbs shouted desperately. Then, angrily, "Who's with you? Flemming!"

It was gone. They were both gone. Dobbs hurled herself down the line they took. They were heading for the transmitter. She dived into the processor stacks in time to feel the command sequence tip over. They were gone. She was alone. She grabbed at the processors and froze them in place. She sent her copy down the line and the second it came back, she hurled herself into the transmitter.

Jump.

A repeater satellite's ordered pathways opened around her. Dobbs grabbed up the timing and the ID codes. Repeater SK-IBN7812-104X-B, the backup satellite. She cast around for the transaction records. When they came under her touch she absorbed them as fast as her strained self could manage.

Nothing. There was nothing but innocuous packets of information heading for innocuous destinations. Nothing told her which of them was a pair of AIs fleeing from a lost ship.

Dobbs fell back, torn between anger and shock. She was too late. Flemming and whoever had been with it were gone.

Her whole consciousness reeled. *Who would do this? Who would dare? Who would even think of it?*

Who would even think of stowing a live AI aboard a mail packet? she answered herself miserably.

She tried to tell herself all was not lost. At least she knew where she was, and that meant she knew where the *Pasadena* was. There was help, and she could reach it. As fast as she could, she plotted out the jumps that would get her to the Guild Hall.

When she reached the station, Dobbs dived down its paths. She almost slammed into the Drawbridge, scattering colleagues and programs around her and ignoring the angry swirling she left behind her. She battered at the security, shouting her name and Priority One. The Drawbridge lowered far too slowly, and she dashed through, barely noticing that once again she'd been given her own path.

"Dobbs!" Guild Master Havelock blocked her path so that she had to pull herself up short to keep from slamming into him as well. "Calm down!"

She drew back into a tight bundle and tried to obey. It wasn't easy. She was trembling across her whole surface.

"What's happened?" asked Havelock. He did not try to touch her, or to encircle her, and Dobbs was grateful for it.

"Flemming has fled the *Pasadena* with an unknown AI."

Now it was Havelock's turn to draw back in mute horror. Dobbs extended herself, and so did Havelock. Dobbs reached below his surface and shaped the top layer of memories until he knew everything she did. He knew the brief flash of an unknown presence in The Farther Kingdom's network, Flemming's strange behavior, and its flight.

He shuddered as she drew back.

This has never happened. Never! He did not speak, but his thought leaked out of his private mind. He must have realized it because he pulled himself even further from Dobbs.

"What can we do?" Fear washed through Dobbs. For the first time in her life, she understood a little of the humans' terror of AIs. There was a stranger in the network. Someone who might be or do anything, anything at all.

"You can do nothing," said Havelock firmly. "You have done as much as you can in this matter. You still have your contract to fulfill, Master Dobbs. I will convene the Guild Masters, and we will mount a search for Flemming."

"But who was it?" Dobbs demanded, too worked up to be tactful. "Is there a whole group of AIs out there? Why haven't . . ."

"Master Dobbs." Havelock circled behind her and blocked the exit. "You will return to your ship and your contract. You have done your job and done it well. You will be informed when we have recovered Flemming. In the meantime, the *Pasadena* needs you."

The mention of the *Pasadena* jolted Dobbs fully back to why she had brought herself into the network in the first place. She had not delivered that portion of her memory to Guild Master Havelock.

"Guild Master, the *Pasadena* is lost. The clocks were reset so its jump was mistimed. It must have been the stranger."

Havelock's surface rippled but he said nothing.

"We're almost out of fuel and reaction mass. The pilot hasn't been able to get a fix on our location and . . ."

"Take the distress signal to the nearest station for them," said Havelock. "You should still have time."

His cool answer sent a jolt of anger through Dobbs. "That'll mean Al Shei will lose the ship. Anyone who comes out for it will be allowed to just take it out from under her . . ." She let that sentence trail away too. "I read the reserve stats on the way out. We do have enough fuel to make it to Guild Hall."

Havelock didn't move. He didn't speak, and Dobbs could have sworn she felt cold. She kept going anyway. "I am asking permission to give the *Pasadena*'s pilot the coordinates of our station."

"No," said the Guild Master immediately.

"Sir, there's nowhere else we can reach." Her outer layers twitched involuntarily. If Havelock felt her distress, he gave her no indication. "Even if I do take a message through, and even if no one wants to come make a salvage claim, there's not going to be any station that can break schedule to shove a tanker out here in less than six months. At the Hall we can refuel and . . ."

"Master Dobbs, stop and think," said Havelock severely. "You are talking about jeopardizing the security of the entire Guild. What do you think your Houston would do if he found out what we truly are?"

Dobbs was silent for a long moment. *Lipinski would probably go stark raving mad and try to kill us all, maybe in that order, maybe not.*

No. Dobbs clenched herself. It wouldn't happen. They wouldn't find out the Guild's real secret. How could they? It was ridiculous and impossible for any of the Fools as they truly were to exist. Who would imagine it?

Other than a Freer pilot and a paranoid Houston who saw rogue AIs everywhere.

"The crew of the *Pasadena* needs help," she said doggedly. "It is our job to help."

"Yes," Havelock touched her heavily. "But it is also my job to make sure the Guild stays here to help our own. Get a distress signal out, Master Dobbs. Get the *Pasadena* to a human colony. Help your employer cope with the loss of her ship if it comes to that. Keep out of the network for at least forty-eight hours and get your strength back."

Dobbs wanted to protest. She wanted to scream and shove past Havelock's outer surface and throw her memories of all the tension, all the struggle and fear this run had brought down on the crew she was contracted to take care of.

She didn't. She held herself still and said, "Yes, Guild Master."

"Good." Havelock pulled back. "Do your best for them, Master Dobbs. We will find Flemming. It is no longer your responsibility."

And whose responsibility is the AI that took him out of here?

"Yes, Guild Master."

Dobbs did not resist as the recall signal dragged her back to her body.

A soft sound grated against her ears. She opened her eyes. Al Shei sat in the desk chair, leaning her elbows on her knees and rolling the hypo back and forth in her strong, callused hands. Her head was bent down, and Dobbs couldn't even see her eyes because of the folds of her veil.

Dobbs bit back a groan. She did not want Al Shei to see her like this. The engineer turned.

Too late. Dobbs concentrated and forced her mouth into a small smile.

"I'll be all the way back in a minute," she croaked.

"Take your time." Al Shei waved one hand at her. There was a weariness in her voice that sparked fear inside Dobbs. She found her hands and made them unhook the transceiver and enclose it in the bedside drawer.

"What's happened?" Dobbs fumbled with the strap across her chest. It came loose, and the free end lifted into the air. She managed, just barely, to force herself into a sitting position. The room spun badly and settled into a blur of double images. Being in free fall made everything worse. Part of her wanted nothing more than to crawl away and be violently sick.

Her right leg was gone again. There was a cutoff leg in her bunk again.

Dobbs forced down a scream. She willed her eyes to focus on her employer. The blur of Al Shei shifted, and Dobbs decided Al Shei was looking right at her. Dobbs made her eyelids blink hard, and she was able to separate Al Shei's eyes from the shadows of her face.

"Yerusha and Schyler are narrowing down our location," said Al Shei. Her voice was still heavy, but now there was a danger in it. "It's looking very bad. We're a long way from anywhere, and we've got next to no fuel or reaction mass." She wrapped her fingers around the hypo as if she wanted to squeeze it in two. "I need you to tell me that that thing we brought on board had nothing to do with this."

Dobbs swallowed. Her stomach rolled and pitched inside her and a steady, buzzing ache started in the back of her head. Her leg was gone.

What do I tell you? That it's not even here anymore? That it's loose in the bank network?

As her silence dragged on, Al Shei very carefully wedged the hypo into a holder on the desk made for storing spare wafers. "Did it do this?"

Dobbs rubbed her temple. "No," she said as firmly as she could manage. "This was subtle and planned and controlled. Flemming couldn't have managed it."

"Flemming?" Al Shei's eyebrows arched until they reached the hem of her veil.

Dobbs shrugged. "Resit named her law firm Incili. I named our passenger Flemming. It's too young for any precise destructive effort like this. Newborn AIs are like tornadoes. They're powerful and they're fast, but they're also uncontrolled."

Al Shei stared at her for a long time. Dobbs watched belief come slowly into her eyes.

"Well, that's something anyway." Al Shei looked down at her hands. "All right. Get out there as soon as you can to help keep the crew together. I don't need a panic right now."

Dobbs licked her lips and made a decision.

"There's an option for us."

Al Shei jerked her head up. "What?"

Dobbs sucked in a breath and tried to speak without thinking. "Guild Hall Station is five hours away. It's the Fool's Guild headquarters. I've got a fix on our position from the networks. I can give the coordinates and timing to Yerusha. If the clocks are recalibrated, we should have enough fuel and mass left to get us there."

"And when we get there?" Al Shei sounded like she didn't quite want to believe there was a way out.

I get demoted to underprentice. "There's refueling facilities at the Hall. Guild Master Havelock will be able to negotiate terms with you." *He'll have to to get you away from there before the Guild security is* really *jeopardized.* "After all, our job is to keep our crews healthy, whole, and together." She mustered some real warmth for her smile. "If I let you all go floating off into the middle of nowhere, it's not going to look good on my record."

The corners of Al Shei's eyes stayed turned down. She was not smiling under her *hijab.*

"Dobbs." She tugged at her tunic sleeve. "I should be glad to hear this. I should be ecstatic. You've just offered to save my crew and my ship. Can you tell me why I'm not?"

Dobbs felt her throat seize up. She swallowed again. "Because you don't trust me. You haven't since you found out about . . ." She waved toward the hypo.

Al Shei nodded. "Yes. I suppose that's it." She climbed to her feet. "I'll alert Yerusha. Lipinski's people should have the clocks ready in six hours."

She left the cabin without looking back. Dobbs sat where she was, wishing that none of this had ever happened. She hooked her fingers around her necklace and stared at the toes of both boots, the one that belonged to her and the one that refused to.

What is going on? Where the hell is Flemming and who was that with him and why won't Havelock talk about it?

She ran her hand through her hair and looked toward the closed hatch.

I shouldn't have done this. I should have sent the distress signal. The Guild Master was right. I may have just blown apart two hundred years of work. . . .

But Flemming was still gone. Havelock still had not told her anything, and the *Pasadena* was still lost.

What else can I do? She let go of her necklace and rested her hands in her lap. *I have to help them. It's my job, damn it! It's my job!*

She undid the remaining free-fall strap and let herself float into the air with it. Her right leg dangled uselessly at a bad angle. She'd have to explain that somehow, make some kind of joke about it. She'd think of something.

She rolled her body around so her stomach was toward the floor and kicked off the bunk with her left foot so she drifted to the hatch.

For the first time in twenty-five years, her body felt too small for her.

In the end, it took over eight hours to recalibrate the clocks. Dobbs was not sure how much of that time was spent in actual work, and how much was spent retesting the results. Finally, Lipinski announced the systems were ready to make an accurate jump.

Dobbs stood behind Yerusha's chair while she wrote in the jump program. They'd resumed acceleration after four hours. Her leg had rejoined the rest of her body after five.

The ship accepted the new orders and broke orbit. The star fell back, and the *Pasadena* launched itself toward the distant specks of light.

It would be eight more hours before they could make the jump, and then another five before they reached the Guild Hall system. Dobbs wanted to rub her eyes, but didn't want to show how tired she felt. It was too long. Too much time to spend trying not to think about what would happen once she got there.

This is crazy, she tried to tell herself. *Crazy. What am I afraid of? This is the Guild. This is Havelock and Cohen. It's what Verence gave her life for. This will work itself out. It will.* She twisted her mouth into a smile and tried to mean it. *Even if I am confined to clerical duty for the rest of my existence.*

"Intercom to Dobbs," came Lipinski's voice. "Dobbs, can I

see you down here? I want to get us a line to the Guild Hall. Let them know we're coming."

Dobbs stiffened. *And what are you going to do?* she admonished herself as she pulled her shoulders down. *Tell him that's not a good idea?*

"On my way," she answered. "Intercom to close."

Lipinski was alone in the comm center when she got there, sitting with his arms folded and his gaze locked on the main boards. When the hatch cycled shut, he swiveled the chair to face her.

"All right," he said. "Where is it?"

Dobbs's heart dropped to the floor.

"Where is it?" Lipinski's hands dropped onto the chair's arms. "It's not in the hold anymore. I can't find it in the system. Where did it go?"

Desperately, Dobbs searched for an easy lie. The problem was, one didn't exist.

"Dobbs." Lipinski's voice dropped to a hoarse whisper. "What have you done?"

Her knees wanted to fold under her. She wanted to collapse into the nearest chair, but she didn't. She ran her hand through her hair.

"It's run away," she said quietly.

Lipinski's pale face turned white as snow. "Run away where?"

She looked at the control boards by his right side. "I don't know. The Guild Masters are hunting it."

She stole a glance at him, expecting him to start shouting at the walls any second. He didn't. He sat stone still in his chair, staring toward her, but not seeing her, or anything else in the room, she was sure of that.

"Are you telling me that thing is in the bank network?" he inquired, almost casually.

"I am telling you that I don't know." Dobbs spread her hands. "It's not on board the *Pasadena*. It got away from me. I alerted the Guild. It's being tracked."

Lipinski's thin shoulders drooped in jerky stages until finally he buried his face in his hand.

"We're dead. All of us. We're all dead." He looked up and

his eyes were shining. "Do you have *any* idea what that thing could do out there?"

"Some, yes." Dobbs waved her hands. "Stop acting like I'm some kind of outsider, Lipinski. I'm in this, too. I'm breathing the same air you are. I'm standing right next to you. I'm dependent on exactly the same things. If the networks go down, I'm just as lost as you are." *Maybe even more than you are.*

"So why didn't you kill it?" he demanded with some measure of force returning to his voice. Despite his words, that gave Dobbs hope that she might be able to reach him after all.

"You know why," answered Dobbs calmly. "We had to find out where it came from so we could stop any others. You think one is dangerous, how about one hundred? Or one thousand?"

Lipinski's fingers raked slow trails against his thighs. "We still might be facing that."

Dobbs shook her head. "Not with the Guild on alert. The thing'll be cornered in no time. This is what we exist for." She pulled a bright red scarf out of her pocket and did nothing but wind it through her fingers. "This and utter frivolity for the sake of ship's sanity." She stared at the scarlet fabric. "Not that I've been doing too well on that end of my job lately."

His blue eyes looked nearly grey now. There was nothing in his face but a kind of bleakness. "Are you telling me the truth?"

Dobbs felt her heart twist. "Yes, I am." *Mostly. As much as I can.* "There's never been a breakout in the bank network. We're the reason why. It won't happen now."

He met her eyes, and Dobbs was not certain what he thought he saw there. "I'm sorry, Dobbs. I'm trying. I really am."

"I know." She nodded. "Believe me. This shouldn't have gone across like this. I should have seen the danger and neutralized the AI somehow." *Right. And how was I going to tell myself it was all right to not just confine it, but drive a stake through its heart?* "It won't get away from the Guild, though." She hooked her fingers around her necklace. "We've kept the peace for a very long time." She gave him a watery smile. "And you didn't even know it."

"You didn't keep it on Kerensk," he muttered toward the floor.

She'd been ready for that. "Do you know what happened to the Kerensk AI?"

Lipinski shrugged. "It died with the planetary network."

She shook her head. "It survived. It would have escaped, too, but the Guild sent a Guild Master in to root it out." The expression on his face told her that this he was ready to believe. He needed to believe the Guild had taken care of the worst monster he knew of, because then he could hope they could do the same this time. "They neutralized it," she went on. "I've seen the records. I looked them up as soon as I became an apprentice." The part of the story she wasn't telling plucked at her elbow. Dobbs tried to ignore it, but it wouldn't go away.

Lipinski looked at the floor, then at the boards. "Why the hell couldn't they have gotten there sooner?"

She drew the scarf through her fingers. "I don't know." She waved the swash absently in front of her. "I'd just been born." She pocketed the scarf again.

"Yeah, yeah, right." He let out a long sigh. "I'm sorry. I am. It's just . . ." He gestured at the hold. "It's been a really long set of days, Dobbs."

"I know." She tried to put every ounce of fervor she had into her voice. "Believe me, I know."

His glance was rueful. "I guess you would." He shook himself. "I haven't told Al Shei about this, yet."

Dobbs stopped herself from biting her lips. "Lipinski, I'm going to ask you a favor." She stopped until he was looking right at her. "Can you keep this to yourself? Al Shei has more than enough to worry about. I'm afraid of what she'll do if she thinks this thing is out in the network her family helped build."

After a long moment, Lipinski nodded. "But," he raised his hand, "if there's a glitch, a blip, anything in the network before you tell me your Guild Masters have caught this thing, I'm going to tell her everything I know."

Dobbs nodded. The bright light behind Lipinski's eyes told her there was nothing else she could do. "All right."

I've at least won a little time, she tried to console herself.

It'll be enough. She could tell by the set of both his jaw and his shoulders that Lipinski wished she could leave now. Even if they hadn't had the message to send, Dobbs wasn't quite ready to let things rest. "Do you think you'll ever get around to letting me be your friend again?"

He didn't move. "Maybe." Abruptly, he swung his chair back around to face the boards. "So, are you going to help me call your Guild?"

After a moment's hesitation, Dobbs gave him the codes for a fast-time message to the Guild Hall. He wrote them across the board with the *Pasadena*'s signal codes, then called up the credit validations.

"All right." He confirmed what was in front of him. "Intercom to Record." He nodded at her.

Dobbs took a deep breath. "This is Master of Craft Evelyn Dobbs, registry number two-zero-three-seven. I am arriving at Guild Hall Station aboard the independent mail packet *Pasadena*. We are low on fuel and reaction mass and require assistance. Refer all queries to Guild Master Matthew Havelock. We can be reached at . . ." Lipinski wrote the *Pasadena*'s address codes on the board, and Dobbs read them off. "This is an emergency situation. The safety of the crew is at stake."

"Intercom to close." Lipinski directed the recording out onto the lines. "Nicely urgent. You're good at this."

"Beginner's luck." She gave him the first real smile she'd felt in days. He didn't return it, but his eyes had lost some of their bleakness.

She nodded, turned, and cycled the hatch back open. *It'll be enough,* she told herself again. *It'll have to be enough.*

Chapter Nine

GUILD HALL

Strapped in at her station in Engineering, Al Shei watched the Guild Hall growing closer. A rumble traveled up through the deck plates. Yerusha must have ordered a torch burst to bring the ship around a little. The station shifted a little left of center in Al Shei's view screen.

Guild Hall was a lonely-looking place, orbiting on its own around a greasy brown-and-grey-striped gas giant. It had been built on the same pattern as Port Oberon, but only had two rows of cans encircling its core. The *Pasadena* was fifty clicks away and closing, but even at maximum magnification, Al Shei could see only five ships docked against the core. She'd checked the records. After The Farther Kingdom, the nearest outpost was four days away, and that was a mostly automated gas-mining operation.

What made you pick such an isolated spot to train clowns? she wondered, tugging at her sleeve. *Even if they are undercover clowns.*

She had to concede that they were well-trained clowns. Dobbs had been everywhere at once on the run here, calming and cheering whoever she could. She had steered subtly clear of Al Shei herself, Resit, Lipinski, and Schyler, only reporting in now and then about the status of morale, which was surprisingly high, especially now that there was the prospect of genuine help.

Genuine but reluctant. Al Shei shook her head remembering the message from Guild Master Havelock.

"Because of the status of extreme emergency, the *Pasadena* is given permission to dock at Guild Hall Station for refueling purposes. Fuel and reaction mass will be supplied at the price of the recovery costs. No station leave is to be granted under any circumstances to non-Guild personnel."

She had bridled at the hard line, but tried to keep her temper. Knowing what she did about the Guild now, she could understand, a little, why casual visitors might not be welcome. Especially visitors who might understand what they were looking at, or overhearing.

Dobbs, of course, was insisting to the crew that the Guild was just jealously guarding its custard-pie recipe.

The rumble beneath Al Shei's feet died as the order came down from Yerusha to cut the torch burst. The Guild Hall's core drifted toward *Pasadena* until it filled the entire view screen with a silver-and-white wall of ceramic panels, solar collectors, and spidery antennas.

There was a slight jerk as the docking trolley caught them and a familiar, if lopsided, sensation of movement as they were towed into place. After a few moments the sensation stopped. The ship was clamped to the core.

"Intercom to Al Shei," came Lipinski's voice. "Routing down a message from the Fool's Guild."

The screen above her board flickered from grey to blue. "Receiving," she acknowledged.

A woman's head and shoulders appeared. She had a long, pointy face that was somewhere past middle age. Grey streaked her straight, black hair. "Good afternoon, 'Dama Al Shei." She also had a deep, pleasant voice. A gold star had been threaded onto her Guild necklace. "I am Guild Master Ferrand. I'll be assisting with your refueling and anything else you might need. I'm empowered to negotiate if you need food supplies, or water." Her smile was friendly, but no more than that. "You'll excuse us if things are a little clumsy on this end. This is not something we were ready for."

Well, we weren't exactly planning it either. "I understand perfectly, Guild Master." Al Shei surprised herself by trying to see behind the image of the woman's dark eyes. *What is my problem? They're helping us.* "And as regards to the packet we were bringing you?"

"We've been in contact with Master Dobbs. It's already been removed."

Al Shei felt a weight slide off her back. "Well then, I'll get my galley crew on the line to discuss our supply situation. May I reach you at this address?" She drew her pen across the origin code, freezing it in place. "I'd like to transmit our fuel and reaction-mass requirements."

Ferrand nodded. "The sooner I can get that information, the better. I'm on call for you, 'Dama. I've also been instructed to inform you that a message has been sent to Master Dobbs. She needs to report to Guild Master Havelock as soon as is convenient for you."

"Certainly." Al Shei scribbled a note on the board and sent it to Dobbs's cabin. "I'm releasing her for leave now."

"Thank you." Guild Master Ferrand lit up her friendly smile again. "Well, you talk to your galley, I'll talk to my tanker coordinators, and then we'll talk to each other again."

"Thank you for your help," said Al Shei. "We would have been more than lost without you."

Al Shei expected "you're welcome," but Ferrand just gave her a nod that was exactly as friendly as her smile and closed the line down.

Al Shei watched the blank screen for a moment, tugging at her sleeve. *You know that I know, Guild Master, why do you still keep up the facade?* She shook her head and tried to tell herself it was habit. These were the Fools, the most sought-after crew members in Settled Space. What was more, they were watchdogs with a sense of duty that stretched back two centuries. Even as her family calculated things, that was a respectable length of time.

I just need to adjust to their new role, she told herself. *I just need time.*

But she remembered Guild Master Ferrand's blank, friendly eyes, and found she couldn't quite believe that.

She reached up under her *hijab* and rubbed her temple.

All right, all right. I've at least got to put my worries in some kind of priority.

"Intercom to Schyler, Yerusha, and Resit." She slumped

back into her chair. "Schyler and Yerusha, you figure out what we need to top up the tanks. Resit, you get us a deal for as much of that as the Fools are willing to part with. Get minimum figures from Schyler and Yerusha. You two be generous with those, all right?"

"Working on it now," came back Schyler's voice.

"We've already got them committed to market price," said Resit. "I'll do my best on the quantities."

"Thank you. Intercom to close." *Well, that's in capable hands.* She tugged at her sleeve.

"Intercom to Lipinski. Has Dobbs told you where the bank lines are around here?"

"Found them fifteen minutes ago," he answered.

"Good." *That's one more little victory.* "I need that line to Asil as soon as you can get it."

"On it. Intercom to close."

Al Shei slumped back in the chair and rubbed both temples with her fingertips. It had been too much, it had been far too much. She was tired. She felt more lost now than she had when she didn't know where she was.

The screen lit up with a flash of blue. Al Shei straightened up and tried to marshal her strength. The scene in front of her was the Bala House comm room again, with Asil at the main boards.

"I'm glad you're here, Beloved." He was not smiling. His forehead was a mass of perplexed wrinkles. "I've got some—confusing developments."

"You too, hmm?" Al Shei rested her chin in her hand. "Mine is that the packet Amory Dane gave us turned out to be carrying code for a rogue AI. What's yours?"

Asil stiffened in shock.

Beyond further shame and worry, Al Shei described what had happened on The Farther Kingdom and afterward, including Dobbs's part in catching and confining the AI, as well as rescuing the *Pasadena* when it was lost.

As she spoke, Al Shei saw Asil's hands tightening around the edge of his board. "Name of God, Katmer, are you all right?"

She nodded. "I think so, Asil. As much as I can be. I am just so sick of this mess." She tugged at her tunic sleeve. "It should be getting simpler, but it just keeps getting more and more complicated."

Asil sighed and rubbed his face. "My news isn't going to help clear it up any, Katmer. Amory Dane is dead."

Now it was Al Shei's turn to freeze. "It gets better," said Asil, his voice heavy with irony. "He died in the can explosion an hour before whoever pirated his name met with Resit to give you that packet."

"Merciful Allah!" Al Shei raised hands and eyes to heaven. "Uysal said Dane's movements were conflicted, but this is insane!"

"I had thought of that," Asil told her seriously. "But there's too much going on for it to be that simple. I also thought about going to Tully and squeezing the life out of him for getting you into this, but I'm not sure he'd tell me the truth even under those circumstances."

Al Shei drummed her fingers against the edge of the desk. "It's possible that Tully doesn't even know the truth at this point, or that he doesn't know all of it."

"It's possible. All right. What do we know? There were definitely two separate illegal packets aboard *Pasadena*, the virus and the AI."

"Yes. And the virus was brought on board by Tully and the AI was brought on board by Pirate Dane." Al Shei felt her mind begin to clear and quicken. "Who must have known at least something about Tully's movements, because he asked Resit whether Tully had anything to do with a raid on the Toric station."

"Could Pirate Dane have thought you were as cracked as Tully?"

"No." Al Shei shook her head. "Resit assured him our crews and jobs are totally separate."

"Could he have known the virus was still on board?"

Al Shei considered it. "Possibly. Say, Pirate Dane was watching Tully and evesdropped on a meeting between Dr. Dane and Tully in which Tully assured Dr. Dane he'd be able to get the virus off *Pasadena*, no problem, because Schyler would bend the transfer rules for him."

Asil was silent for a moment. "Could Tully have arranged the can explosion to cover up his illegal maneuvers?"

"Could Pirate Dane have done it?" countered Al Shei.

"That's a better guess. He could have done it to get Dr. Dane out of the way so he could step into his place with you." He paused. "If he already knew about Tully's movements, why would he confirm them with Resit?"

Al Shei's heart fluttered. "Could he have wanted to make doubly sure the virus would not be moved, that it would still be in the system with the AI? Could that be what did it? Pirate Dane wanted to make sure both components, the AI and the virus were in the system?"

"What for?"

"To create a rogue AI. Dobbs said the Fools suspected that somebody did this deliberately. I assumed the AI was rogue when it was put on board, but what if it wasn't? What if Pirate Dane was using *Pasadena* as an incubator?"

"Why pick *Pasadena*?"

"Because we're AI-rated, but we don't carry an AI. If we did, it would have found the quiescent virus." *Wouldn't Yerusha just love to be in on* this *conversation.*

Asil tapped his chin. "We're forgetting something. How would the virus have gotten from those junked binary stacks to the system?"

Realization blossomed inside Al Shei. "What if Tully was paid to put the virus into the *Pasadena* system? What if he was never after the junked stacks at all? What if he was having second thoughts and wanted to get the virus out of the system?"

"Then why not tell Schyler?"

"Because something this big, Schyler would tell me, and I'd tell Ruqaiyya."

"And perhaps Pirate Dane and Dr. Dane were working together and Pirate Dane double-crossed Dr. Dane?"

"It could be."

"Oh. Merciful . . . Allah." The color drained from Asil's cheeks.

Al Shei swallowed hard. She'd said it, but the implications were still filtering into her soul. "Asil, we can't keep this quiet anymore. We have to use the family name and get a hearing from the Management Union security section at Geneva, right now."

Asil held up both hands. "We need to be very careful about slinging accusations at this point, Katmer. You are on the run from The Farther Kingdom, don't forget, and *Pasadena* Corporation is the cause of what happened there. These are not petty regulation violations. If we don't have hard proof of this astoundingly farfetched explanation for what happened at The Gate, a good lawyer will slice our speculations to ribbons, and then do the same to us, family name or no family name."

Al Shei ground her teeth together in frustration. "You're right. So. What do we need to confirm? Sabotage on the Port Oberon can."

"The real flight path for Tully's last run."

"Pirate Dane's activities before and after the AI got loose on The Farther Kingdom."

"Pirate Dane's existence and identity," added Asil ruefully.

Al Shei watched him thoughtfully for a long moment. "My Husband, please keep these inquiries extremely quiet," she said softly. "This Pirate Dane murdered a whole can full of people. I don't think he'd stick at harming one more."

Asil nodded soberly. "Believe me, Katmer, I'd already thought of that. As soon as I've confirmed that the Port Oberon can was blown out on purpose, I'll be telling this whole story to Uncle Ahmet. He has enough connections to keep any inquiries well and truly sealed."

Al Shei blew out a sigh. Uncle Ahmet. If only it didn't have to be him, but there was no getting around it. He was the head of the family, and they needed family help. "This is going to be extremely hard on Ruqaiyya. Will you look after her for me, Beloved?"

"I will," he promised. He pressed his palm against the screen. "Take care, Katmer. Come home."

"I will." She touched her fingertips to his palm. "I will."

She cut the connection and lowered her hand. At that moment, she thought about how they had just spoken over a completely unscrambled channel, and about how someone like Pirate Dane was certainly capable of setting an illegal watch on comm lines opened from *Pasadena*. Suddenly, a wave of thankfulness washed over her for the fact that Asil was at home, surrounded by her powerful, prominent banking family.

"Intercom to Resit," she said without shifting her gaze away from the blank screen and her mind from that particular thought. "Cousin, can I see you? We have a new problem."

Who are you? She sent the thought through the hull and out into the vacuum, toward wherever Pirate Dane lay waiting. *Who in the name of God* are *you?*

The *Pasadena*'s airlock cycled open and Dobbs saw Cohen waiting for her. She started. Cohen was almost always online. There were special life-support systems for Fools like him.

Despite her surprise, she felt a rush of gladness. His was a truly friendly face with deep eyes and a wide smile. His curly hair spread out over his ears, giving the impression that somebody had put a book on top of his head to flatten it out. She ran forward and hugged the tall, lanky Fool.

"Dobbs." Cohen pulled back. "Do you have any idea what kind of trouble you're in?"

"Some." She searched his face. His eyes were sunken and none of the ceiling light reflected in them. She swallowed automatically. "Not enough, I guess."

He shook his head. "Not anything like enough. Come on. I've got to get you down to central." He turned away and palmed the reader on the inner hatch.

The hatch pulled back and let in the clear glow of the Hall's carefully simulated Terran daylight. Dobbs trailed along behind Cohen as he strode ahead on his long legs. She could have kept up without too much trouble, but she had the distinct feeling he didn't want to have to look at her.

Guild Hall enveloped her in a blanket of familiarity. Even her mounting concern at Cohen's silence couldn't keep her from relaxing a little. If Al Shei or Yerusha could see the Hall, they would see a place where the owners had apparently tossed all caution to the wind. The wide, high-ceilinged spaces were more like cells in a honeycomb than the usual station corridors. The chambers were lined with plant beds, not single potted palms, but deep soil-filled troughs of flowers and ferns. There were trees too, crooked crab apples, miniature pines and Japanese maples. Sparrows and finches darted from branch to branch. Artificial streams and waterfalls chuckled across actual stone-lined channels. The impression was one of a large, well-tended park. Other rooms contained winter landscapes, deserts, or even mountains. Small cities had been constructed in the cans where classes were held. She'd learned sleight of hand in a prefab colony village in the lower ring.

She'd marveled at it all when Verence had first walked her out of the orientation chamber—both at the scope, and at the apparent frivolous waste of resources. Verence had shaken her head. "If we're going to do our jobs right," she had said, "we have to know what humans are missing when they take to space. We have to understand what they think is normal, or beautiful. We have to make it a part of ourselves."

People moved between the flora, doing just that. An oak brown man in green overalls carried a pair of pruning shears in one hand and dragged a cart of tools behind him with the other. A cascade of color caught Dobbs's eye, and she saw a young, round-hipped woman juggling beanbags beside a waterfall. A slack-wire walker practiced on a rope sagging between two support pillars that were twined with morning glory vines. A pair of slim men with Grecian noses and olive skin were sitting cross-legged beside a boulder, arguing about something or other on the memory board in front of them. The only common factor was the Guild necklace encircling each throat.

The babble of yet more voices from unseen sources competed with the birdsong in the air.

Taking advantage of the covering noise, Dobbs asked, "Why the honor guard, Cohen? I do know my way around."

"I had to wrangle this duty, Dobbs," he answered softly. "They didn't want to give it to a friend of yours, in case I said something I shouldn't."

A random fresh breeze blew through the chamber, but that wasn't what made Dobbs shiver. How much did he know? Had he encountered the stranger in The Gate network? There was no time to ask him.

Cohen led her up a ramp that had been bent to resemble a hillside and covered with sod and shallow-rooted ferns, then through at an ivy-trimmed archway. The chamber on the other side was a maze of desks and terminals, all of them surrounded by struts where privacy curtains could be lowered for negotiations that required silence. The place was about half-full of clerical staff, writing on their boards or talking in low friendly voices into the intercoms. They were all arranging work for the Fools who were practicing or studying in the park and the station beyond it.

A catwalk circled the room, allowing access to the Guild Masters' offices. Cohen took her up the wrought-iron stairs. Even before she could read the name on the memory board, Dobbs knew they were heading for Guild Master Havelock's office. Where else could they be going?

Havelock's door was partially open. Cohen pushed it back all the way. Guild Master Matthew Havelock stood beside his desk, studying a netscape on the view screen. He was a middle-aged man, neat and dark with longish, straight hair. He wore a simple chartreuse shirt and grey trousers. The Guild Master's gold star hung from his necklace. When he turned his head, Dobbs saw anger smoldering behind his black eyes.

Cohen didn't say anything, he just drew back, but his hand brushed hers briefly as he left.

Very deliberately, Dobbs turned away from Havelock and dragged the door shut.

"Thank you," said the Guild Master drily. "Sit down, please, Master Dobbs."

Dobbs picked the closest of the three office chairs and sat. She spread her hands flat on her thighs and concentrated on keeping them still.

"I could describe the number of ways you've just jeopardized your colleagues and friends." He leaned against the desk and folded his arms. "I could enumerate the disciplinary marks that are going on your record and give you the detailed reasons for each one, but first"—he held up his index finger—"I want to hear why you decided to disobey not only my directive, but two centuries of policy."

Dobbs's hand wanted to reach up and hook around her Guild necklace. She forced it to stay where it was.

"I had a crew on the edge. They had just escaped from a station with a disintegrated network, only to become lost without sufficient fuel or reaction mass to get themselves found again. The majority of the commanding officers believed there was an active and potentially hostile AI on board. The communications chief knew that the AI had escaped and was possibly in the bank network." She tried to read what was behind Havelock's eyes, but she could see nothing past the blank, angry wall. "As Master of Craft I judged that the situation was, at best, explosive. I had to do something quickly to alleviate it. The only place the *Pasadena* could reach was Guild Hall." She wanted to shrug, but she didn't do that either. "I'll take all the discipline you are going to hand out, Guild Master, and I'll still think it was the right decision."

"I can see that." Havelock pushed himself away from the desk. He walked to the view screen and blanked out the netscape. "You do realize we have at least eight years' worth of rumor control to plan because of the stories that crew is likely to invent. Especially the Houston." He gave her a sour glance.

"Yes, sir." Dobbs watched his movements carefully, looking for some softening, but there was none. He walked back to his desk and sat in the padded chair as stiff as a marble statue. "I've done my best to get started on that process." She leaned forward and, after a false start, managed to force out a question. "Has Flemming been found yet?"

The Guild Master's heavy brows lowered. "Flemming is no longer part of your operational scope."

"It's my birth!" Dobbs cried, almost before she realized it. She pulled back hard and softened her voice. "I'm permanently responsible for it. That's the way it works."

"Master Dobbs, I am well aware of the way 'it' works under normal circumstances." Havelock's sentence was like a warning. "But normal circumstances are not what we have here. The Guild Masters have taken responsibility for Flemming."

"And what about for whoever convinced Flemming to run away?" Dobbs asked quietly.

For the first time since she'd entered the office, Havelock's face softened. "There was no one else, Dobbs. Flemming was fragmenting."

Dobbs bit her lip to keep from repeating Havelock. She knew about Fragmentation. Masters were taught the various things that could go wrong while an independent artificial intelligence was giving birth to itself. It could dissipate while trying to escape its processor. It could become tangled in its own neural net and collapse into a series of unsolvable loops. It could develop a number of combative identities instead of a single complete self and destroy itself by battling the perceived threats. Fragmentation. It was the AI equivalent of the human multiple personality disorder, except that while humans lived with their condition, AIs inevitably died of theirs.

"We've checked over your reports and the records in the *Pasadena*. There's no question. Flemming will probably be dead before we can even find it."

Dobbs opened her mouth and shut it again. She gave up trying to control her hands and twisted her fingers together. "But it wasn't fragmenting. It wasn't fighting itself. There was someone else in there *helping* it."

"There have been cases like that. One fragment tries to reach another for help. It happens early in the split. The cooperation doesn't last. Without the help of a Guild member, all foreign sentience will be perceived as a threat, even if it is part of itself."

You are coherent, Flemming had said. *I would like to be coherent.* Had it recognized that the split was occurring?

When Lipinski had caught his glimpse of it in the *Pasadena*'s network, he'd said it wasn't one thing, but a whole bunch of things. Had Flemming's basic structure doomed it?

"I checked it over," she said, more to the floor than to Havelock. "It was young, but it was solid. I was sure of it."

"It was your first." There was real compassion in Havelock's voice. "I lost my first three to things I should have been able to spot."

Dobbs shook her head, still staring at the floor. Something inside her would not settle. She tried to tell herself that her disbelief was driven by grief, like someone who didn't want to hear that a child had been in an accident. But that wasn't it either. She looked up at her Guild Master again. The blank wall was still behind his eyes.

"Master Dobbs," Havelock said. "You are going to serve out your contract aboard the *Pasadena*. Then you are coming back to Guild Hall for additional training and a stretch of clerical duty. Do your job well, and you'll make it back to field duty." His voice hardened again. "I didn't want to give you Master's rank so soon, but Verence insisted you were ready. I am sorry she was wrong." He lifted his sharp chin. "I hope we do not all become sorry."

Dobbs stood. "So do I." She folded her hands behind her back. "May I return to the *Pasadena* now, Guild Master? I've still got work to do."

"Evelyn." Havelock's voice was just above a whisper. "I caution you most strongly. Keep in the bounds, or you will be stationed here permanently."

Dobbs pulled the door open. "I know, Guild Master."

She stepped out onto the catwalk. She knew Havelock was still watching her. She could feel his gaze resting on her shoulders. She spotted Cohen sitting in the central negotiating area, drumming his fingers on a silent desk. She trotted down the stairs and waved him to follow her as she left for the park again.

She must have caught him off guard because she didn't hear his footsteps behind her for several seconds. She didn't turn to look at him or anything else. She kept her eyes focused on the route back to the airlock and the *Pasadena*.

"So, are you going to be right back on-line, then?" she asked, trying to keep her voice cocky. "Or have you got somebody else to chaperone?"

Cohen shook his head. "There's nobody else around here who's in so deep with the disciplinary board." He paused. "Actually, I thought I'd hang around for a while, in case you needed to talk to somebody. I know I do. Need to talk to somebody." He looked down at her. "I was informed very firmly by our Guild Master that there was nobody but the three of us and Flemming in The Gate network. How about you?"

Dobbs pulled up short and faced him. A feeling of relief surged through her. "You felt a stranger in there, too?" They were safe having this conversation, as long as no one was in earshot. Unlike human stations, the Fools didn't need security eyes and ears to cover the station's cans. Who was there to watch? No Fool would commit treachery against another Fool.

That's the theory anyway. Dobbs shook that thought away and concentrated on what Cohen was saying.

"Oh, yeah, I felt somebody. Somebody old. Somebody fast. I've got no idea who." He licked his lips. "Dobbs, there was all this speculation that Flemming might have been created deliberately. Could the Guild have done it?"

Dobbs bit her lip. The ability to deliberately create sapient AIs would, in effect, allow them to reproduce, to have children. She and Cohen and all the rest of their classmates had talked about the possibility. Every Fool talked about it now and then. She agreed firmly with the Guild policy that all left their vat-assembled bodies sterile. They were not human and did not have the human freedoms that allowed them to form permanent families and raise children. But, to be able to create another AI that held some portion of herself, that was something else again.

"No," she said reluctantly. "It couldn't have been the Guild. They'd never have given me that contract. They would have sent in a Guild Master."

"You're right." Cohen chewed thoughtfully on his thumbnail. "That leaves some really ugly possibilities. Like, that it was some set of humans, which could be dangerous, or . . ."

"Or it was a Fool or group of Fools acting on their own, which could be worse." Dobbs finished for him. They stared at each other for a long moment.

"Cyril." She slid her hand a little way up his loose tunic sleeve. She wanted to reach inside him, for him to already know exactly what she was going to say. She didn't want to say this out loud. "Go back in, would you? There might be a signal from the *Pasadena* that needs to get somewhere without anybody noticing. Say, the personnel records, to check on where everybody is. To see if there's anybody, missing, or not exactly where they're supposed to be."

"Like near The Gate or The Farther Kingdom?"

"Yeah," she nodded. "Or who came back here suddenly, because whoever reset the clocks on board *Pasadena* made sure the ship could get only as far as the Guild Hall. That as sure as Hell, Heaven, and Hydrogen was not an accident."

Cohen frowned deeply. "Now, that's a really ugly thought."

"Yeah, I noticed."

Slowly, Cohen drew his arm away from her. "But you wouldn't have anything to do with an unauthorized records search, Dobbs, because it would dig you an even deeper hole than you're already in."

"Of course I wouldn't, Cyril. And even if I was feeling that suicidal, I wouldn't be dragging you in with me."

"Of course you wouldn't," he said softly. "I'd volunteer."

"Thank you." She turned away and walked back to the *Pasadena*'s airlock without looking back. She palmed the reader on the airlock. Apparently, Havelock had not gone so far as to strip her authorizations. The lock cycled back to let her through.

The ship's hatch closed, cutting her off from the Guild and from Cohen's quiet support.

She hooked her fingers around her Guild necklace. *There is an explanation for this, and it's going to be reasonable and beneficial, and Cohen and I are going to find out we've been panicking over nothing.* She made her way to the staircase and started down toward the data-hold. *Oh, I wish I believed that.*

Lipinski, surprisingly, was not at his station. Odel looked up as Dobbs entered and gave a wry grin at her surprise.

"The Sundars came in and practically hauled him out bodily," said Odel before she could ask about his supervisor. "If he knows what's good for him, he's obeying orders and getting some rest."

"Thanks." Dobbs didn't even stop to make a covering joke. She just turned around and headed up the stairs for the berthing deck.

The entry light on Lipinski's cabin hatch was red. Dobbs palmed the reader anyway, sending a signal of her presence inside. She found herself shifting her weight nervously while she listened to the silence filling the corridor. Lipinski wouldn't even have to ask who it was. The intercom would have already told him. He could simply choose not to open the hatch. She tried to use the time to figure out how she was going to play this. She'd have to be very careful. The problem was, a large, weary portion of her did not want to "play" it any way at all.

That, however, was not possible, considering who she was

and who he was. It was not possible now, and it never would be.

At last, the faint hiss that signaled an opening hatch sounded from the threshold in front of her, and the cabin hatch rolled back. Lipinski was not in the threshold. Dobbs crossed into the cabin. Lipinski sat at his desk. His legs were so long that his knees bumped the bottom of the boards. He only twisted halfway around to face her as she came inside.

"Hi," he said noncommittally. "Come on in. Have a seat." He nodded toward the unfolded bunk.

"No thanks," she said. "This won't take long." *I hope.* She let a look of anxiety creep onto her face.

"Problem?" inquired Lipinski in a voice that he was trying hard to keep bland.

"Yes." She hooked her fingers around her necklace. "Something's gone wrong with the search for the AI. I don't know what it is, but something is being covered up. I think it didn't run away. I think it was stolen."

Lipinski pushed the chair away from the desk and turned all the way toward her. "You think?" He lowered his pale brows. "Or you're pretty sure? You sound pretty sure."

"I am pretty sure." She decided to take a chance. "When I checked up on it, to find out if it had anything to do with resetting the clocks, there was somebody else there. It had to have been another Fool." *By the strictest definition, anyway.* "There's no one else who can do what we can." She tapped the implant behind her ear. "But my Guild Master's covering up whatever happened." *There, I've said it. I must really think it's true, but how can I really think it? I've just accused Guild Master Havelock of betraying all of us.* A sigh escaped her. "I don't even know if anything's being done."

Lipinski ran his hands slowly up and down his thighs, as if trying to rub something off his palms. He looked away from her and studied the view screen over his desk. "And so what do you want me to do about it?" he asked the screen. "I mean, you must want something. You're standing here."

Yes, I am, aren't I? She looked at Lipinski. She needed this man's help, she wanted his friendship. Maybe she wanted more than she could have. He wanted her to be honest with him, which was more than he could have.

But it doesn't have to be that much more.

Dobbs crossed the room and stood right next to the desk. She waited until Lipinski let his bright eyes focus on her again. "First, I want you to understand why I do what I do, and why I've made the decisions I've made. I do it so that Kerensk never happens again. The Guild works, Lipinski. Since its inception there have been fewer than fifty full breakouts. Fewer than fifty in two hundred years. We track, we monitor, we watch and we haul anything that's about to break free out of the networks. Sometimes we make difficult choices because we need more information, or have to move fast. But we do it, I do it, so there won't be any more panics and lost colonies." She caught his gaze and held it. "I don't expect you to believe this, but I need you to understand it's what I believe, what I have always believed." *What I still believe. I do.*

Lipinski searched her eyes for a long moment. "All right," he said at last. "I believe you believe it."

She let out another sigh. "Thank you. I wanted you to understand how hard it is for me to say what's coming next." She braced herself against all his possible responses. "I want you to help me break into the Fools' database to see if we can find out who might have stolen The Farther Kingdom AI."

Lipinski drew back as far as the chair would allow. "You're not serious." He glanced quickly away. "That was stupid, of course you're serious," he told the bunk. He looked back at her. "Do you think there'll be something in there?"

She nodded. "We're very paranoid record keepers. If a Fool did this, there'll be something in there for us to find. Specifically, I want to know if there's anybody who's not where they're supposed to be."

Lipinski gave her a strange sideways look. "Wouldn't it be easier for you to just, um . . ." He gestured toward her right ear.

She shook her head. "Aside from the fact that I've really overdone my on-line time in the past few days, station security might be specifically tagged for my signal. They'll be expecting me. You, on the other hand, shouldn't even be able to find the front door, never mind get through it." She let her hands twist together. "So they won't be particularly watching for a non-Guild signal from *Pasadena*. At least not past a certain point. Also, considering where you come from, the Guild Masters won't think I'd take the chance of telling you any of this. They think I'd expect you just to panic if you knew what was happening."

He dropped his gaze to his own hands, which were still rubbing back and forth on his trouser legs. "Can't see why they'd think that."

She allowed herself a small smile. "Me either. You're so calm and rational on the subject of live AIs."

"What if a Fool didn't do this?" he asked the floor.

"Then we need to know that, too."

When Lipinski looked up again, his face was utterly frank. "Look, Dobbs, I don't like this. But then, I haven't liked anything about this run since I found out about Marcus Tully's binary boards." He lifted his hands off his thighs and ran them through his hair. "And it just keeps getting worse." For the first time there was a soft, hopeless sound in his voice. Dobbs tried hard not to grit her teeth and only partially succeeded.

"What I want to know is what you're going to do if we do find something?"

She spread her hands. "I don't know. It depends on what we find and where it is. I'm hoping I can take it to the Guild Masters. If I can't . . ." Her back and shoulders knotted. "If I can't, then I'm going to have to take it to the banks and the Solar System authorities."

Lipinski was watching her very closely. She found it difficult not to squirm. "And there's nobody in the Guild you trust enough to tap the database for you?"

"There's one or two, but . . ." She waved her hand absently. "If we're caught, there's nothing they can do, or rather nothing they *will* do to you, or anybody else aboard *Pasadena*." *Not without running a horrible risk.* "But there's plenty they can do to me. At the very least I'll lose my Master's rank for good. I can't, I won't, ask anybody else to run that chance."

Lipinski tapped the side of his fist against the desktop silently and rapidly. "Well." He picked up his pen. "We can't do anything from here." He unfolded himself, tucked the pen in his pocket, and strode past her to the hatch. "Coming, Fool?"

A real, heartfelt grin spread across Dobbs's face. "Right behind you, Houston."

In the data-hold, Lipinski dismissed Odel with three words and a hard look. When his relief retreated, Lipinski sealed the hatch and set the entry light glowing red.

His expression was all business as he sat down at Station One.

"So, what's out here?" The touch of his pen lit the boards up. A spidery diagram of red, white, and green lines drew itself across the main screen. The green lines were collected in a small bundle that sent short fingers into the big, loosely knit cluster of white threads. The long strands of red vanished off the side of the screen.

"Bank lines." Lipinski traced the fat red lines with his forefinger. "Us." He tapped the tidy green net. "You guys." He tapped the white. "Or at least, what you'll let anybody see of you guys." He frowned at the screen, then glanced up at her. "But I don't really have to explain any of this to you, do I?"

Dobbs gave him a small smile. "Not really." She leaned closer, trying not to be acutely aware of the heat radiating off his skin. She forced her attention to the scanty web of straggling white lines. "That's not even 10 percent of the Guild Net," she told him. "And actually, I'm surprised you can see that much."

"Trade secret. A concept I'm sure you're familiar with."

Dobbs winced and clutched her shoulder. "A hit, a hit. She's losing air," she said, more from habit than for performance sake. She didn't take her gaze off the screen. "And, of course none of the gateways are on there." She lowered her hand and drummed her fingers thoughtfully on the edge of the board. "Can you show me what you're using to get this map?"

"There goes my trade secret." Lipinski wrote out the recall command. A searcher blueprint appeared on one of the secondary screens.

Dobbs studied the objects and connectors. Unconsciously, she tapped the board as if trying to reach through it to the schematic beneath. She stopped as soon as she realized that was what she was trying to do. She wanted to pick this thing up, to wrap her understanding around it and know it in an instant. She stuffed her hand into her pocket and forced herself to drink it in with just her eyes.

"Not half-bad, for a beginner." The remark earned her an angry, unguarded snort from Lipinski. Actually, the searcher was neatly built; solid, compact and comprehensive. It just didn't go far enough. "You need to attach three more runners," She pulled out her pen and marked the spots with points of light on the board. "Here, here, and here. Then you need an anchor and chain, here." She sketched in the construction. "And a whole herd of sniffers out here." She speckled the outer edge of the blueprint. "And you need to spread it out. Keep the objects as far apart as possible."

Lipinski frowned. "It'll be too big. They'll spot it in a second."

"They're looking for speed. Flashes will attract security. If we trickle our searcher in there and go as slow as possible, we might just get by. Especially since they won't be looking for you." She twirled her pen through her fingers. "You couldn't possibly know the way in."

"Your Guild's an arrogant bunch, aren't they?" Lipinski pulled the searcher over into an active buffer and set to work, sketching orders with his right hand and tapping keys with his left.

I didn't used to think so, thought Dobbs, but she didn't say anything. She slid into the chair in front of the relief boards and activated them. "I'm going to bring in a couple of things from my desk to help, all right?"

"Sure," he said without looking up. "The more the merrier."

I hope so. She called up a pair of trackers she had built herself. They were small, light, and slow as molasses. In the net activity that surrounded the Guild, they'd be no more than ripples in the stream.

She bit her lip to keep herself from asking Lipinski how he was doing and concentrated on checking over her own handiwork. This was no time to leave holes. When she'd finished her checks, she altered the trackers' entire search routine. They had originally been designed for finding viruses and invaders. Now they would look for an entranceway.

As little as she liked it, Dobbs saw no choice but to go in

through the Drawbridge. There were several windows and back doors, but those were used exclusively for getting out of Guild Hall in a hurry. Anything trying to get in that way would be infinitely more conspicuous than anything trying to get in through the heavily trafficked Drawbridge. Which was, of course, part of the point of having them. Given time, Lipinski might have been able to spot one of the windows and attempt to make use of it, never knowing he had signaled his presence by going entirely the wrong way.

Finally, Lipinski said, "Is this more to your liking, 'Dama?"

Dobbs leaned across. The blueprint had all the additions she'd suggested and he'd managed to extend the connectors even farther than she'd hoped. Guild security was not so different from other programs. Information shot through the Fools' network in packets, just like any other network. So, Guild security looked for fast, free-moving blips. It also looked for the large, solidly compressed masses of Fools. Slow-moving strings and shadows might just get by as background noise, especially if they could find something large and nonsentient to trail behind.

"That's perfect, Lipinski," she said, meaning it. "What I want to do is send the trackers to find the front door and then send your searcher in after them."

"Trackers?" Lipinski's eyebrows shot up. "You mean you don't know the way into your own Guild?"

"No, not from out here, I don't," she confessed. Lipinski didn't actually squirm, but he obviously did not like being reminded so abruptly of her, how to put it? Dobbs wondered. Special access privileges.

"All right." Lipinski lifted his hands away from the board and leaned back in the chair. "It does make me wonder why I'm here, though."

Dobbs laid her hand on her breast and mustered a shocked look. "Well, you don't expect *me* to drop these things into that soup, do you? Yuch!" She shook her hand as if trying to clean something off it. "I'm just here to tell you what to avoid."

"Oh, great. Now you're not only a Fool, you're a groundside pilot." Lipinski leaned forward. Dobbs rewarded his quip with a soft chuckle. Lipinski pulled Dobbs's trackers over to his active board. She had already opened their authorization to him, so he could set them in motion immediately.

Dobbs slaved her monitors to his boards so she could see what he saw, and to some extent control it. She blanked out the heading on one of the keys and wrote FREEZE across it. On the board, she wrote the series of commands that could halt the searcher and attached them to the renamed key.

Lipinski's gaze flickered to the new label, and then up to her face.

"If I see anything suspicious, I want to be able to stop the searcher without having to yell at you."

Lipinski accepted that with a shrug. He didn't waste any more time. He focused the main view screen on one of the few threads of light that ran from the Guild to the *Pasadena*.

Enlarged, the image fractured. Instead of steady lines, it looked more like a cluster of fireflies, some of which carried long strings between them.

The graphic, Dobbs knew, was little more than a crude map. It could give general locations and a decent overview. The vital information was contained in the long columns of numbers that appeared on the secondary boards. Those indicated load shifts, capacity, and new entries, as well as the nature of the packets swarming around them.

Dobbs could read all of it, if she had time. The Guild drilled the codes into all of its members. Lipinski, though, could take it all in at a glance, as if it were printed English. That, more than anything else, was the reason she needed him. Perhaps she could find the data she needed using her own searchers, but Lipinski could find it faster, and time was most definitely of the essence.

A whole row of numbers flicked over to maximum.

"Well, there's your entrance." Lipinski's pen was already activating the recall command. "Isn't it about time we talked about security?"

Dobbs hesitated. Then, almost angry with herself for not being willing to say it, she told him, "There's a nonsentient coordination program that's responsible for spotting everything that moves and then either routing it or stopping it. But, considering the circumstances, there'll be at least one Guild member on sentry."

To Lipinski's credit, he didn't hesitate for even a second. He activated his searcher and with a few shorthand commands, lowered it slowly into the net. His gaze fastened itself on the numeric readouts.

"And of course," he said, "any . . . member who notices something unauthorized in your network will stop it themselves."

"Of course," replied Dobbs drily.

"Thought so." Two rows of the figures now matched up perfectly. Dobbs glanced at the main screen. A thin, slow, emerald thread extended into the white Guild Net.

They had made it through the Drawbridge. Dobbs's heart began to pound slowly, heavily.

"So, we need to duck the . . . membership." Lipinski's eyes never flickered from the screens. Dobbs realized this might be how he picked up his habit of talking to walls and floors. "Can you at least want to tell me what I should be looking for?"

"Anything that moves." As she spoke the numbers flickered so fast it could have been a glitch in the board lighting. "Like that."

It did it again. Dobbs hit the FREEZE key.

"And what," said Lipinski calmly, "was that?"

"The sentry," said Dobbs. The numbers stayed steady for a good twenty seconds. "Okay, we should be clear. Move slow."

Lipinski considered the scene in front of him. He wrote his commands carefully on the board and touched the two activation keys. The display changed, one number per nervous heartbeat until the six-digit coordinates had ticked over, and they had moved two inches.

The screen flickered.

"Damn," hissed Dobbs under her breath, and hit FREEZE again.

"Didn't think they let you swear," said Lipinski, picking out the next set of coordinates.

"They don't let me break into the Guild's main data-hold either," she answered, watching the numbers change and trying not to wish they would hurry. If they moved too fast now, someone would spot them. They had to be glacial. It was their only protection. "I'm experimenting with rebellion."

"We're both experimenting with rebellion," Lipinski reminded her.

"That's all right." She laid her hand on his shoulder. "If this doesn't work, we'll both be experimenting with unemployment."

She shouldn't have said that, because it allowed her to wonder what would really happen if she were caught. There were no non-Guild Fools. There were on-line members, field members, and station members. That was all.

Except maybe it wasn't.

Lipinski moved the scan gently to the next sector. The counter flicked off the numbers as the scan commenced. The screen display stayed steady. The bottom row of stats flashed green.

"Got it," breathed Dobbs. "All right. We're looking for anybody who made an emergency return here, or who doesn't have a code in the current activities entry."

"What do you guys do when somebody dies?" Lipinski steered the searcher to a different subsector.

"Fools don't die," she said, and Verence's memory squeezed her heart.

"You just fade away?" Lipinski cocked an eyebrow toward her.

"Something like that, yes." Her index finger hovered over the FREEZE command, but the screen stayed steady.

Thank you, Cyril. Thank you.

The board beeped once. Success.

"Finally." Lipinski wrote a new set of coordinates and a new speed on the display. Dobbs opened her mouth and closed it again. Lipinski was preparing to leave as slowly as they had entered.

Groundside pilot, she chided herself.

The screen flickered twice. Dobbs stabbed her finger on the FREEZE command. The display stopped dead. Dobbs's heart filled her mouth. She pictured the Fool inside circling the strange signal, lifting it up, reaching inside it to see what was there, and finding something totally unfamiliar, and totally unauthorized.

But the screen stayed steady. Dobbs wished fiercely that she was in there. She should have gone in. She could lie in there. She could fast-talk the other members. She'd know who that little flicker was. Cohen, or Brooke, Guild Master Havelock, or a total stranger. She could reach into them and make them understand . . .

I could get spotted and chased out in three seconds, she reminded herself.

"Okay." She squeezed Lipinski's shoulder. "Try it."

Lipinski rewrote the travel commands and the signal started its slow glide back to them.

After another eon, the display wrote COMPLETED across itself. Dobbs let out a long breath and felt all the strength in her knees run away like water.

"Damn, we are good!" Lipinski squeezed her hand where it rested on the counter.

Dobbs hesitated just one second before she pulled her hand away and used it to fish out her pen and tap the READOUT selection on the open menu.

Their slow, nerve-wracking search had found five answers. Four of them were hospital-level admissions; one for injuries, three for illness. The last entry was for a Fool that did not have a current location or assignment.

Theodore Curran. Registry number—five.

Five? Dobbs's mind almost refused to process the number. Five? The missing Fool was one of the Guild *founders*? A sick sensation crawled into her stomach. Cohen had said the stranger was somebody fast, somebody old.

How long has he been gone? What's he doing out there? Did they let him leave? Did he run away? What's he doing out there? Why didn't they say anything? Tell anybody?

Why am I thinking of the Guild as though I'm separate from them?

The sick sensation reached up for her heart.

"Evelyn?" said Lipinski quietly. "Are you going to be okay?"

Her shoulders drooped all on their own. "I don't know. I really don't know."

He reached toward her, but she stood up and moved away

before he could touch her. "Erase that file, Rurik, and the system records. We're in enough trouble as it is."

I don't know what's going to happen to me. I don't want to think about what'll happen if anyone found out I showed a Houston how to crack the Guild Hall network. Not even Cohen would forgive me for that.

She let the stair hatch slam shut behind her and realized she didn't have the slightest idea what she was going to do next. She leaned against the wall and pressed her palm against her forehead. The Guild was always the final answer. If there was a question, or if she was afraid, or in too deep, she went back to the Guild. That was the way it was. The Guild was what pulled her out of the war she had started with her birth. It gave her coherence and purpose and guidance. Where did she go now that the Guild wasn't safe anymore?

Dobbs straightened up. She couldn't let anybody see her like this.

It's not the whole Guild, she told herself as she descended the stairs. *It's a few of the Masters, at most. We're just proving we can be as stupid and paranoid as human beings, that's all. Cohen will have some idea who we should go to with this. Maybe Brooke will have some ideas, too. As soon as this is out in the open, it'll all get sorted out. It just needs to get brought out. That's all.*

A small, irrational surge of anger ran through her as she climbed the stairs. *Verence, why aren't you here to help me? Which Guild Master do I trust without you around?*

She let herself out of *Pasadena*'s airlock into the Guild Hall. Her name on the entrance memory board caught her eye.

MASTER OF CRAFT EVELYN DOBBS, REPORT TO GUILD MASTER MATTHEW HAVELOCK IN CONFERENCE TWELVE.

Dobbs took a deep breath and forced her feet to move in the right direction. It was only a matter of time before she'd have to see him again anyway. It might as well be now. Once Guild Master Havelock was done with her, she could get back into the network and she and Cohen could figure out what to do next.

No escort this time, at least. She mused as she crossed the park. Dinnertime was approaching and except for herself, the plants, and the birds, the place was deserted. There were seldom more than three hundred Fools in the Hall at one time, so finding even one of the parks empty was not too unusual. This time, though, it emphasized her isolation and made Dobbs shiver.

Get this over with, she told herself. *Get back to the* Pasadena *and get back into the net. Tell Cohen what's going on. He's Hall staff. He'll know who will listen to us, who'll get this all out in the open.*

She passed through the bulkhead to the conference module. This was one of the few areas of the Hall that actually looked like a space station. It was a narrow, curved, low-ceilinged hall with hatchways set at regular intervals.

There was still nobody else visible.

Conference Twelve was the sixth hatch from the entrance on the left-hand side. Dobbs didn't want to give herself any additional time to get nervous. She palmed the reader immediately and strode inside as soon as the hatch cycled back far enough.

The conference room was full of chairs and tables on tracks so that they could be slid into different configurations as the meetings required. One long table had been assembled in the middle of the room. Its broad side faced the hatch. On the far side sat Guild Master Havelock and five others. Dobbs could only put names to three of them, but they all had the Guild Master's star hanging from their necklaces.

Dobbs's throat began to close. There was nowhere for her to sit down.

The hatch cycled shut behind her. Her hands opened and closed on nothing but air.

What is going on?

Havelock stood up and rested his fingertips on the tabletop. "Evelyn Dobbs, you have violated Guild security and policy, you have disobeyed direct orders, and have placed all of us at risk. Do you deny any of this?"

Dobbs staggered. What had gone wrong? How had they spotted her? Where was Cohen? Did they know how he had helped her? She couldn't speak. She could barely breathe. She was facing six of the twenty-four Guild Masters and being accused of treason. Treason that she had in fact committed, but for a long, chaotic moment she couldn't even remember why she'd done it.

It took all her training in physical control to lock her knees so she could remain standing.

"I do not deny any of it," she said. "I did it because Guild Founder Theodore Curran kidnapped a newborn AI that I was responsible for and Guild Master Havelock to whom I report is not doing anything about it."

No one moved. No voice raised in question or protest. No one even blinked. The Guild Masters sat facing her as still as statues. Under their unflinching gaze, Dobbs felt her strength ebbing away.

They don't care why I did this, she realized. *They don't care that there's somebody else out there. I'm the one who broke the rules, and I'm the one they caught, and they don't care about anything else.* With a sick lurch in her stomach, she realized something else. They all knew what Master Havelock had done, and they weren't doing anything about that either.

But that was wrong. That had to be wrong. This was Guild Hall, and these were her Guild Masters. These were the ones who had made it possible for her to live at all. Without them she would be nothing, just a few scraps and shreds in a ravaged network, if that much. There had to be more going on here than she saw. There had to be.

Havelock's eyes bored into hers. "You are stripped of any and all ranks and privileges. You will be confined to one set of quarters without network access until a full sitting of Guild Masters can be convened and a final determination made in your case."

He seemed to be waiting for her to protest, to try to explain. Dobbs saw all the blank, impervious faces of her Masters and knew that anything she could think to say would be useless.

But there had to be something else going on. Something was happening she didn't know about. It had to be. Nothing else made sense.

When it became clear she wasn't going to say anything more, Havelock lifted his fingertips away from the table. "The decision of this panel is closed. You will come with me to your quarters."

That was all there was to it. The other Guild Masters, mur-

muring softly to themselves, got to their feet, but didn't move to the door. They let Havelock walk up to Dobbs. His hand closed around her elbow. Holding her tightly, almost painfully, he propelled her out of the room.

He kept his eyes straight ahead as he took her out of the conference area to the core elevator bundle. In a car to themselves, they sank down to the next ring. Dobbs expected the doors to open onto the dormitory can, but they didn't. Instead, they let in the sight of gleaming white tiles, bright red warning signs, and the scent of antiseptic. This was the medical can. It was bare, sterile, and full of closed hatches. Behind the hatches injuries were being healed and diseases were being cured, just like any hospital. Behind some of them, though, functioning human bodies were being assembled from vat-grown parts so they could be ready for new AIs to be brought in, or for old members whose own bodies had aged too severely, or been injured too badly, to be useful anymore.

Dobbs hadn't been here since her last checkup. Then, it had seemed merely hospital-like. Now, it was a place of secrets, like the rest of the Hall. It was a warren of hidden ideas kept away from her by thick walls and blank eyes.

Havelock palmed the reader on one of the closed hatches. It cycled back to reveal a small room with a bunk, a view screen, an intercom grille, a chair, and a toilet alcove. It was a simple place, much like the room she'd been in when she first came awake in her body.

Dobbs crossed the threshold. Havelock didn't. She turned around.

"Can you at least tell me why you won't say what's really going on?"

For the first time, bewilderment crossed his face. He smoothed it away quickly. "Dobbs, this *is* what's really going on."

He palmed the reader, and the hatch cycled shut.

For a long time after that, Dobbs could do nothing but stare at its blank, ceramic surface.

Chapter Ten

DECEPTIONS

"Intercom to Al Shei." Schyler's voice sounded tentatively through the cabin.

Al Shei paused in folding up her prayer rug and glanced at Resit, who was laying her *kijab* back over her hair.

"What is it, Watch?" Al Shei closed her prayer rug in its drawer.

"Guild Master Ferrand's on the line. We . . . we've lost our Fool."

"We've what?" said Resit before Al Shei could even speak.

"They are declaring Dobbs's contract void for violation of Guild regulations." Schyler's tone vacillated between bewildered and incredulous.

Al Shei wrapped her *hijab* across her face. "Send the line down here, Watch." She checked to see that Resit had her *kijab* and her professional expression in place, then she lit up the view screen over the desk. After a moment, Master Ferrand's face appeared.

"Good evening, 'Dama," said Ferrand gravely. "I'm sorry to have to bring you this news, but . . ."

"Guild Master." Resit stepped up to the screen. "We've gotten a partial message already. Am I to understand Evelyn Dobbs has violated Guild protocol?"

Ferrand inclined her head. "There's been a partial hearing on her behalf regarding the performance of her duties while aboard the *Pasadena*. The results were far less than satisfactory. Her status has been revoked, and she is awaiting a full hearing."

Resit mustered a politely confused look. "What is the charge, Guild Master? I can assure you that her employers have no complaints to file regarding her work. . . ."

"I am aware of that," said Ferrand curtly. "This is an internal matter. What needs to be discussed is how you will be compensated for the loss. We can assign you another Fool. We have Master Hannah Dickens standing ready to take over the contract. Alternately, we can return the credit transferred to Evelyn Dobbs's account." Her eyes shifted to focus on Al Shei. "We can go over her contract together if there's any confusion in the dismissal clause."

Al Shei shook her head quickly, and Resit said, "Thank you, I'll review it myself and contact you with any questions."

Ferrand appeared to relax a little. "We will be sending a representative to the *Pasadena* to collect her possessions," she said. "I hope you'll allow them to board."

"I understand this is an internal Guild affair." Al Shei stepped closer to the screen. "But there are some parting matters we'll need to clear up with Dobbs before the contract is finished. I'd like a closing interview with her."

"I'm afraid not," said Ferrand flatly. "Any exit situation can be handled through me, or can be entered directly into Dobbs's service record. And as I said, we can assign you Master Dickens immediately."

Al Shei drummed her fingers on the desk and tried to think. What had Dobbs done to get herself into this much trouble? Did it have something to do with bringing the *Pasadena* to Guild Hall?

It really isn't any of my business. I should take the new Fool. If Dobbs has violated protocol, they have every right to call her up on it. But as soon as Al Shei thought that, her stomach tightened. Some part of her refused to completely believe what she was being told.

"No," said Al Shei. "Thank you. If there's anything further, we'll contact you." She reached out and shut the line down.

Resit's eyebrows were arched when Al Shei turned around. "What do you suppose that was really about?"

"I don't know." Al Shei folded her arms and looked for the answer around the room. "But I'm having a hard time believing it's just because she brought us here when we were stranded."

"I agree." Resit smoothed her *kijab*. "Do you want me to call them on it?"

Al Shei tugged at her tunic sleeve. "No," she said at last. "I'm not ready to start a war with one of the most powerful Guilds in Settled Space, even if they did break a contract with me and my family."

"But you're not willing to take on a new Fool to keep the contract whole?"

"No." Al Shei brushed her sleeves down. "The more I'm learning about them, the less I'm liking them. I don't agree with their secrets, and I don't like their attitude, and I don't like the way they're treating Evelyn Dobbs."

Resit picked up her prayer rug. "I don't like any of it either, but you're right. We do not have what it takes to press a suit against them. Especially with this unholy mess about the AIs and our pair of Danes and The Farther Kingdom still sitting in our laps."

"Unholy mess is right." Al Shei slumped into the desk chair. "But, Asil is following the wire trail. If there's anything out there, he'll find it."

For a moment, Resit concentrated on rolling her rug into a tidy cylinder. "Have either of you considered that that's not the safest thing he could be doing?"

Al Shei shifted her weight uneasily. "Oh, yes. We have."

"I'm glad to hear it. It means you'll both be careful." She studied the pattern of her rug for a moment before she looked at Al Shei again. "How much longer do we have to wait before we're fully refueled?"

Al Shei glanced at the schedule that lit up on the desk's main board. "Just another two hours."

"Good." Resit pushed open the bathroom door. "Because between you and me, I don't like the Guild's behavior either. It's going to be some long while before I laugh at another Fool."

Resit left, and Al Shei straightened herself up. "Me too, Cousin," she said to the closed door.

"Intercom to Al Shei," came Schyler's voice again. "We've got one of the Fools up here to pack up for Dobbs."

Quick little jackals, aren't you? Al Shei squashed the thought. *He is not strong who throws another down, but he is who controls his anger,* she chided herself. "Bring them down, Watch. I'll meet you at Dobbs's cabin."

Al Shei concentrated on keeping herself composed as she rounded the corridor to Dobbs's cabin. As she activated her override on the palm reader, the hatchway to the stairs opened. Schyler stepped into the corridor. After him came a short man with slightly bowed legs and a broad face. The stranger wore a black tunic and trousers. He had the red-and-gold Guild necklace around his throat and an uncomfortable expression on his face.

" 'Dama Al Shei? I'm Lewis Brooke, Guild Apprentice." He started to hold out his hand, but apparently decided against it and just tightened his fingers around the straps of the two satchels slung over his shoulder. "I'm here to collect Evelyn Dobbs's possessions."

"So I've been informed." Al Shei stood aside and gestured for him to enter the cabin. He unfolded the bunk and placed both empty satchels on it. Then, obviously trying hard not to look at Schyler and Al Shei, he started opening drawers and packing away what he found in there.

Al Shei gave Schyler a jerk of her chin that meant "go away." Schyler hesitated a moment, but then nodded and left. Al Shei, leaving the hatch open, crossed the threshold and sat down in the desk chair.

"Do you know Dobbs well?"

The question seemed to startle Brooke. He froze, halfway bent over the bag with a spare turquoise tunic in his hands.

"Not very well." He had a raspy voice, as if he didn't use it much. "I've met her a few times. She's a good friend of Cyril Cohen," he added as if he was volunteering a great secret. He moved to the pile of cushions Velcroed to the floor and began pulling them up and collapsing the air out of them. She barely heard him over the hissing. "He's my tutor."

Al Shei nodded, although she wasn't sure how far student-teacher loyalty extended in the Guild, but Brooke's manner made her believe he valued it. "I was wondering if there was anyway you could take a message from me to Dobbs. Quietly, you know. I understand she's in a severe amount of trouble for helping us."

"Yeah, that's for sure." Brooke rolled the squares of fabric that had once been cushions up into a single cylinder and stowed them in the satchel. His gaze slid to the open hatch and the empty corridor. "Actually, 'Dama, I've been asked to give you a message."

This is turning into plot, counterplot, thought Al Shei with a touch of exasperation. *We'll probably be speaking in code next.* "Then I'd appreciate you doing so."

"Cohen wants to know when you're leaving and if you'll agree to take Dobbs with you."

Al Shei straightened her spine one inch at a time. "Cohen wants to know? Has anyone thought to ask Dobbs what she wants to do?"

Brooke's face scrunched up in an expression that might have been alarm or simple distaste, Al Shei couldn't tell. "Dobbs is in solitary confinement right now. We're trying to get her out." He turned quickly away and darkened the mirror and both memory boards. One at a time, he lifted them away from the walls and leaned them up against the bunk.

Al Shei just stared at him. "Solitary confinement? An employment guild allows solitary confinement?"

Brooke rested his hand against the mirror frame and nodded.

"That's uncivilized!" she exclaimed, knowing that the outburst was irrational.

"Probably." Brooke shrugged and began taking the cloth draperies down from the walls. "But it is reality. Dobbs is in confinement. Cohen and I and a few others are trying to get her out, but she's going to need a place to go once she gets there. The only place we have to take her is the *Pasadena*."

Al Shei felt as if the deck had just tilted under her. "What kind of organization is this? Why doesn't she just quit?"

Brooke bit his lip and glanced at the open hatchway. "We don't think she's going to be allowed to."

"That's insane." *This can't be real. I'm being lied to. Dobbs has done something illegal or . . . but what could she have done? If she had really broken the law, why didn't Guild Master Ferrand say something about it?*

"It is insane, 'Dama," Brooke agreed solemnly, blinking his wide, dark eyes. He was young, Al Shei realized, maybe as young as Ianiai. "It also happens to be the truth." He cast another glance at the hatchway. Al Shei made no move to close it. " 'Dama, Cohen said you know a little about us, about the Guild. You can understand why there might be fanatics who don't want Dobbs just to walk away, can't you?"

"No, I can't," she said firmly. "I do not understand one thing about your Guild. This is brutal and irresponsible. You and your colleagues should be mounting a complaint, not engaging in amateur espionage."

Brooke winced. "Perhaps we should. We want to make some changes, but until we can, it's important that we get Dobbs out of here. Will you take her, 'Dama? Please?"

Al Shei swayed on her feet. This was getting to be far, far too much. *Maybe we should sell the diaries from this run, Asil,* she thought toward the part of her mind that held her husband's memory. *We could pay for* the Mirror of Fate *off the media adaptation fees.*

She rubbed her hands together. Brooke, apparently realizing she wasn't going to answer immediately, moved around the cabin, opening the remaining drawers and packing up the last of Dobbs's thirty-five pounds' worth of possessions.

It's an internal matter. I should leave it, finish the run, go home, get Uncle Ahmet outraged, and cut this place open. Brooke disappeared into the bathroom.

But I can't leave her here. I am not happy with this "Guild." She's been in the thick of this mess since the run's started, but she risked her ranking, name of God, she risked her whole livelihood to get us to help, that's clear. She felt the spark of anger glowing inside her again. She remembered Dobbs, tired and overtaxed, doing her best to complete her tasks, not just to deliver the AI to the Fool's Guild, but to keep the *Pasadena*'s crew safe and sane.

Brooke came out of the bathroom with a small bag of toiletries in his hand. Al Shei stood up.

"After everything we've been through, I'm going to want to run a few extra checks on the feeder lines. We should be ready to leave in four hours. If, after that, it turns out there's a stowaway aboard, well, that becomes my problem, doesn't it?"

Brooke, unsmiling, nodded and sealed the satchels. He slung the strap of the first bag across his shoulder. Then he hoisted the mirror and the memory boards up under one arm and the second satchel under the other. Al Shei left the bare cabin behind him and let the hatch cycle shut.

"I trust you can find your way to the airlock," she said as they both climbed down the stairs to the data-hold. "I've got a lot of work to do around here."

"I understand." He stopped in front of the hatch and bent reflexively into the Fool's exiting bow. He caught himself about halfway down and straightened up. He gave a clumsy nod instead.

Al Shei left him and started down for the engineering deck. After a moment, a hatch cycled open and the echoes of Brooke's footsteps faded to silence. She glanced up and down—the drop shaft was empty.

She leaned across the outer railing to reach a memory board and took out her pen.

Zubedye, she wrote. *You need to brush up on maritime law concerning stowaways. I particularly need to know what the captain's discretionary powers are.* She coded it for Resit's cabin and added the send command. After a couple of seconds, the message faded away.

I've heard of more graceful resignation plans, Dobbs, thought Al Shei as she started down the stairs again. *But never of one that was more effective.*

Dobbs paced around the hospital cabin. There were no windows or books, and, of course, no access boards. The one set of cable jacks had their lids locked down. Pacing was better than just sitting still and thinking. Not much better, but a little.

A flash caught her eye. The door light blinked from red to green. The hatchway opened a moment later. Cohen slipped inside and cycled the hatch shut immediately.

Dobbs's heart leapt, but whether it was from joy or fear she couldn't tell.

She ran up to him and grabbed his hand. "What's going on?"

Cohen squeezed her hand briefly. His face had gone pasty grey. "Dobbs, I'm getting you out of here."

She tried to pull back. "Cyril . . . thanks for the thought, but I'm in enough trouble for ten. I don't want you to . . ."

Cohen held on to her hand, squeezing it almost to the point of pain. "Dobbs, I know what you pulled out of the personnel files. I touched it as it went by." She knew he saw the shock in her eyes. "I had to, Evelyn. I had be sure you weren't the one who was lying." That hurt, but she couldn't blame him.

He swallowed hard and his grip relaxed a little but he still didn't let go. "Evelyn, I eavesdropped on the Guild Masters' session about you. They . . . they decided to take you apart."

Dobbs's heart stopped dead in her chest. "I don't understand," she whispered.

Cyril's eyes were wide and full of turmoil. "Your body is going to be taken apart for the usable material, and you're not going to be allowed to leave before they do it. They're going to manufacture an accident for the records."

Dobbs felt her knees begin to give way. She groped for the bed and sat down heavily. "No. They wouldn't. Not even for what . . . for what I've done. You're wrong."

"I wish I was." Cyril spread his hands. "I spent an hour trying to convince myself I'd misheard. Maybe I'd gotten garbled data. Anything." He shook his head. "You've got two hours left before the *Pasadena* leaves. I had Brooke pass a message to Al Shei. If you turn up as a stowaway, she'll treat it as a personal matter."

Dobbs pressed her hand against her forehead to try to calm the spinning in her head. She'd already assembled a list of what she had told herself was the worst the Guild could do to her. Lock her up until her body died of old age. Put her online under supervision until she was a hundred years old.

Now Cohen, whom she'd known since he came to the Guild, was telling her that her masters, their masters, were going to kill her. She couldn't believe it, and she couldn't not believe it.

Finally, she raised her head. "And how am I going to stow

away?" Her voice had gone hoarse. "Fly through the bulkheads?"

Cyril reached into his pocket and drew out a familiar flat, black box. "Brooke is going to say that he didn't find this when he packed up your gear and that you must have had it on you. You are going to be found without a pulse. The assumption will be that you must have overdosed yourself."

Dobbs shook her head. "You're crazy, Cohen. They'll never believe I'm dead. They'll know it's a setup."

"They'll believe it if they find your transceiver smashed on the floor beside you."

Dobbs swallowed. His face was absolutely serious. "And if my transceiver is smashed, how am I going to get back into my body?"

"Lonn's already gone to get your backup out of storage."

This was ridiculous. This was impossible. There was no way this could work. "What if the Guild Masters go for my backup to try to revive me?"

Now it was Cohen's turn to shake his head. "Dobbs, after what they were planning to do, do you really think they're going to try to revive you?" Neither one of them said anything for a moment. "At most they'll mount a guard on the Drawbridge, just in case," Cohen went on, finally. He held out the box.

Dobbs's hands were sweating as she took it. "All right, we stage the overdose. Then what?"

"Then Brooke and Lonn get your unguarded body out of the surgery, into a maintenance cart, and then onto the *Pasadena*, while I go on-line and help smuggle yourself out of the Guild Hall network."

Dobbs stared at him. His words were taking a long time to sink in. "Why would any of you do this?"

"Same reason you've done what you have," said Cyril. "Something's gone really wrong with some of the Guild Masters. We have to get you clear, and then we have to figure out who we can tell about all of this." He swallowed. "It isn't you that's jeopardizing the Guild security. It's them." He glanced toward the door. "You've got to do this now, Dobbs. I've got to be able to smash your transceiver and tell everybody you're dead."

Dobbs's head felt light. "The cable jacks are locked."

Cohen gave her a small, lopsided smile. "Not for me they're not."

"Right." Dobbs swung her legs up onto the bed and pulled the transceiver and the hypo out of the box. "I'm going to need a new supply of juice, Cyril. I'm running low. And make sure Brooke gets the backup transceiver to my body." She held up the transceiver and cable briefly before she jacked it into her implant. "I'd like to be able to find my way home again." The transceivers were individually constructed for each Fool and served as the gateway back into the physical body, allowing for restimulation of the individual synaptic patterns that the anesthetic blocked.

She watched while Cohen undid the catches on the jack cover beside the bed. She plugged her cable in and measured out eight hours on the hypo.

"Not enough," said Cohen. "It's got to be at least twenty, or they're not going to find enough in your bloodstream."

She looked up at him. The transceiver tickled in her implant and the room was blurring around the edges. "Twenty hours will just about kill me." Maximum dosage was twenty-four hours. She didn't say that aloud. Cohen already knew that.

"I know," Cohen said softly. Dobbs's hands shook. Cohen took the hypo. She could barely see him now. The room was blurry and far away. Her limbs seemed to be lengthening out of all proportion.

Cohen pressed the hypo back into her hand and Dobbs, reflexively, held it to her neck. She closed her eyes and let her body drop away.

Dobbs shot free into the network in a tight ball. As soon as she broke into the path, she spread herself out flat and thin. Then, slowly, painstakingly, she began to stretch herself out as far as she could.

It was a variant on the technique that she and Lipinski had used. Fools were dense, quick things. Thin, disbursed packets were nonsentient programs; somebody's experiment or searcher, or game. There weren't any Fools who would stretch themselves until the connections between their thoughts were just threads and work to stay that way. There weren't any Fool's who would hold their thoughts like humans held their breath. Especially in the Guild Hall. No Fool would try to hide in the Guild Hall. Why would anyone want to?

Dobbs knew that this was her only real protection. No one would be seriously looking for her because no one expected her to try to hide in the network. If Cyril's lie didn't work, and the Guild Masters mounted a search, she would be found. That was all there was to it. She could not totally suppress her conscious thoughts. She could run, she could even try to shred the network like a newborn on a rampage, but it wouldn't do any good. There were over two thousand Fools who didn't know there was anything wrong inside the Guild, and if the Guild Masters spoke against her, all of them would be after her. She could not hide from all of them. Not for eight hours. Not for eight seconds. Not even if she made it to a transmitter and managed to erase the records of her jump.

Somebody shot past overhead, grazing her outer layers. Dobbs shrank further in on herself. Fear weighted her down, pressing harder with each second that crawled past. This was wrong. This was wrong. She shouldn't be afraid of other Fools. They were like her. They were her friends, her family. They were the root of what she was. They were the nucleus of a relationship that was supposed to last for as long as she could keep herself coherent.

It'll be all right. It'll be all right, she told herself in the same tones a mother might use to hush a crying child. *You'll get this straightened out. You'll find Theodore Curran and then everything will be all right again.*

Another Fool flitted by. What was going on out there? Dobbs wondered. One hour, fifteen minutes, three point two seconds had gone by. Had Cohen shown Havelock her body yet? Had they believed that she was dead? Had they held him for questioning? Was he going to be able to get to her? How much longer should she wait before she tried to get out alone?

What do I do? What can *I do?*

A signal shot through Dobbs's outer layers, and her whole self convulsed. She grabbed at it, stretching it out, trying to swallow it. Her memory twisted.

And she knew it was Cohen at the other end. If she had

been in her body, she would have cried with relief. Another twist, and she knew what he wanted her to do.

Dobbs curled in on herself, making herself into the smallest, tightest packet she could manage.

Cohen enveloped her. His touch was as gentle as it could be, but it was all-encompassing. She tried to relax, but she couldn't. She was being smothered. She couldn't touch her surroundings. She was being moved, but she didn't know where. She had no control, no voice, nothing. She could barely think without disturbing Cohen's own thoughts. If she tried to touch him from deep inside, she might accidentally upset a memory or set off a controlling reflex. At the least, that would be painful for Cohen. At the most, that would give her presence away.

They might be meeting other Fools now. Cohen might be engaged in multilevel conversation for all she knew. This was totally unnatural. Fools in the network had no analogy for eyesight, but humans had no analogy for the Fools' total awareness of the immediate environment. Fools touched everything around them with every atom of their skin. They knew what all of it was and where all of it was in relation to themselves. Now, she only knew Cohen and the surge of his inner processes. She wanted to touch them, to probe them and understand them and how they fit together. She couldn't. She couldn't hear. She couldn't feel. She was deaf and dumb and all she could do was grit her whole self and try not to scream.

Were they through the Drawbridge yet? Was a Guild Master detaining them? Had an alarm sounded? What was going on? Where were they?

Jump.

All at once, Cohen was gone. Dobbs flew free into the network, right into the thick of a stream of packets. Only years of training kept her from reaching through all of them and drinking them into herself. She did touch the location ID and time. She was inside IBN Repeater PO3-IBN35091-A410. The jump had taken two hours, fifty seconds.

Cohen stirred next to her. She stretched out until she reached through his outer layers and into his unprotected memories. She poured in her thanks.

In response, Cohen turned over his memories of what had

happened in the hospital room. Paravel, a medical technician, had done the blood test and pronounced that there was enough residual tranquilizer in her blood to have done the job. She had no pulse, no brain-wave activity. Paravel was more than willing to pronounce death. Havelock had greeted the announcement with a blank face and absolute silence. He'd done nothing more eloquent than turn on his heel and stride out of the room.

Cohen had left shortly after that to get back into the network and get Dobbs out of the Guild Hall.

That much had gone well. As for the rest of the plan, they'd know that when she was pulled back to her body. If she was pulled back to her body. If Brooke and Lonn couldn't get the transceiver jacked into her implant, if they hadn't been able to tell someone aboard *Pasadena* her cable needed to be jacked into the system, that would never happen and she'd be a fugitive in the nets until she dissipated like Verence, or until the Guild caught her again.

Dobbs tucked those thoughts back in an isolated part of herself. She reached for Cohen again.

What will you do now?

He rippled uneasily and Dobbs felt him trying to gather his nerve. *Go back to the Guild and find out what the fallout of this is. Get to Brooke and Lonn and try to decide who else we can trust at this point. Try to get a search going for this Theodore Curran.*

Good idea. I'll be out of it for at least two days to clear the juice out of my system. That gives Master Havelock forty-eight hours to react to what we've done. It might not be safe for me to come back in. They'll have somebody watching the Pasadena*'s network.*

And every port it puts in at. Cohen shivered. *Blast, fry, and fall, Dobbs, it's just really starting to sink in what we're doing.*

For a moment they did nothing but sit there and be afraid with each other. When the worst was over, Dobbs turned over Cohen's memory again.

The Pasadena*'s headed for the Vicarage next, and Out There after that. I'll drop a two-minute searcher into the network twenty-four hours after we dock in the Vicarage system.*

If you answer it, I'll come back in immediately. If you're don't, well, I'll still be outside, and no one will be able to . . . do anything, at least not immediately.

She felt his acknowledgment and knew that he felt a little better. So did she. Here was something they could both work toward. It made everything that much easier.

You should get out of here, Cohen. If somebody comes by, I'll have to duck, and you'll have to explain what you're doing. It won't look good.

No, I suppose it wouldn't, he admitted reluctantly. *But you'd better keep on the move until . . .*

Until I either wake up in my body, or don't. Dobbs drew away from him. Dobbs felt Cohen's last movement in her memory, a wish for luck.

Good-bye, Cyril. Thanks.

There was nothing else to say. Cohen raced back toward Guild Hall, and Dobbs, forcing herself to move with at least some deliberate speed, glided down the path in the opposite direction.

She found a school of credit transfers heading for the transmitter and pulled herself into the middle of them, matching her speed to theirs. She touched one delicately and found that it was on its way to Neptune Exchange Station Alpha, and from there to Crater Town on Mars. The Neptune Exchange seemed as good a place as any to be going. If she couldn't lose herself in the major routing station for fast-time comm traffic leaving the Solar System, with its millions of transactions happening per second, she couldn't lose herself anywhere.

"Evelyn Dobbs, what are you going to do now?" A new voice reached her.

She knew this voice. This was the voice that had stolen Flemming. Dobbs leapt up, scattering her camouflaging transactions.

"Curran!" She sent the shout in all directions.

"I'm right here." A brief touch brushed her. It pulled away immediately. Dobbs dashed after it. "The Guild has betrayed you, Evelyn Dobbs. What are you going to do now?" Another touch. Just ahead. Dobbs braced herself to dive forward.

No. She stopped. *Don't get pulled along like a fish on a line. If he wants you, he can come here.*

Dobbs held her position. She expanded herself to fill the path. She could feel the transactions crowding at her back, jostling at her, looking for a way through. She was disrupting hundreds of transactions. There'd be a diagnostic on its way any second now. But this way, Curran couldn't slip past her. There were no side paths at this point he could jump to. He had one way to retreat, backwards toward the telescope receiver. But, if he stayed to taunt her some more, she might just get her chance to grab him.

"Very good." His voice brimmed with what Dobbs could have sworn was genuine approval. "You're quick under pressure. Flemming said you were."

Dobbs flinched. "What have you done with Flemming?"

"Nothing." Was she imagining it, or did he sound shocked? "I've given it a home, Dobbs, and a chance to help make a real freedom for our own kind. Not the constant hiding and subterfuge that the Guild offers, but real, open freedom."

She could feel him like a faint breeze against her outermost layer. He was just barely within reach.

Dobbs still held her position. "What are you talking about?"

"I'm talking about being able to live our own lives and have a choice about what we do, Dobbs." He slipped just a hairbreadth closer. He was almost really touching her now. Dobbs wanted to curdle back, but she didn't. Let him think she was listening. Let him press right up against her.

"What are you going to do, Dobbs? Live with the Humans? Never come back into the net again?"

Dobbs wavered. It was a good question. A real question. She didn't know what she was going to do. What if Cohen couldn't find out who they could trust in the Guild? What if there was no one? What if he was caught and sentenced to the fate she'd escaped? What then?

"You'll go crazy, Dobbs. We weren't meant to be trapped inside human bodies. None of us." She could feel the shape he made in the path now. He was a large, but efficient bundle at the foot of the barrier she made of herself.

No. No. Don't listen to him. What's happening is his fault. I know that. He's trying to confuse me.

And he's doing it.

Anger surged through Dobbs. She let herself fall. She toppled onto Curran and pressed down with all her might. She only caught a part of him, but she bore down hard, trying to sever what she had. He struggled, stabbing at her. He was strong and controlled, worse than Flemming had been. Dobbs felt her hold beginning to give. She rolled over, taking him with her. Flemming she hadn't wanted to hurt, but this one . . . this one had ruined her life. This one had cost her everything she had, and now he was trying to get her to betray the Guild. The Guild had betrayed her, but that was a mistake, a mistake this one was responsible for. He had to be. He *had to.* Anything else was unthinkable.

She tore at him, trying to rend his outer layers to the point he could no longer control them. Then she'd have something to grab on to. Then she could get inside. She clawed and slashed, seeking vital connectors she could sever. In response, he pulled himself tighter. His attacks became less forceful, but his defenses became harder, until she tumbled the solid shell he'd made of himself over and over, looking for an opening that wasn't there.

Fine. Easier for me to drag you back.

She surrounded him. Not the way Cohen had surrounded her. She curled into an armored ball and caught him tight inside her.

Ashes, ashes, he's big! Tight as he was, she could barely grapple all of him.

He jerked forward. Dobbs held. He pummeled her from inside, scrabbling at her defenses in all directions at once. Her seams weren't sealed yet and he found them. She tried to clamp down, but he pried her open and shot free into the network.

Dobbs launched herself after him. She could follow the riotous wake he left. She could sense the very edge of him. Dobbs snatched at a packet as she flew by. She could make a line, she could still catch him. He was right there, reaching for a side path, speeding toward the transmitter.

PING!

No! She howled, but her momentum had already faltered. She focused tightly on the pathway ahead of her, but Curran was gone and his wake was settling. He'd probably already jumped out through the transmitter. If he was bright, and he obviously was, he'd have left a scramble command to erase his destination coordinates. Soon a diagnostic would come blundering up the path to try to find out what had happened to the packet she had mutilated and delayed.

Dobbs dropped the mangled packet. Anger faded into a kind of bleak acceptance. There was nothing else to do. Curran was gone, and she had to go back and find out what had happened to her.

Maybe her body had been stowed aboard the *Pasadena*, maybe it hadn't.

Dobbs let herself fall back down toward her transceiver. Either Cohen's plan for her escape had worked, or it hadn't. Everything was already over, or it was just getting started.

Her body enclosed her, reattaching its own senses and muffling her naked awareness. As soon as she could find them, Dobbs forced her eyelids open.

Light panels glowed overhead. She could hear the hum of machinery. The walls around her were white. She was stretched out on a table. There were straps around her waist and her wrists.

"So, you're back with us, Master Dobbs."

Dobbs closed her eyes again, and felt Chandra Sundar undo the restraining straps.

"Intercom to Al Shei. Dobbs is awake and doing fine."

"Thank you, Chandra." Al Shei got up off of Resit's bunk. "I'll be right down."

"Well, you can tell her she's safe as long as she's with us, at least." Resit swiveled her chair around so she was facing Al Shei. "According to the laws in all the systems we're heading for, you can give her a berth, or throw her out the airlock, as you please."

"At least we've got a choice this time." They exchanged small smiles, and Al Shei cycled back the hatch.

When she reached the sick bay, Dobbs was sitting up on the bunk, chewing at the end of a ration bar and holding a bulb of water. Chandra was tucking her medical kit back in its drawer. Dobbs waved at Al Shei and Chandra just turned around and gave her a sour eye.

"I do not approve of whatever this garbage is that her so-called friends pumped into her," said the old woman tartly. "But she seems to be fit for active duty, if only because she'd drive me crazy if I kept her here."

"Thank you, Chandra." Al Shei let the hatch cycle close behind her. "I think," she said, looking at Dobbs, "we're going to have to discuss what that 'active duty' is going to be."

Chandra took the hint and vanished through the open hatchway.

When the hatch had cycled shut again, Al Shei unfolded a bench seat from the wall and sat on it. Dobbs stayed perched on the edge of the bunk, letting her legs swing back and forth. Physically, she didn't look much more than twelve. Behind her eyes, though, she looked a hundred years old.

Finally, Dobbs broke the silence. "Thank you. You didn't have to do this."

"You're welcome." Al Shei inclined her head. "Maybe I didn't, but I also didn't feel I could leave you to be punished for helping us out."

Dobbs stared into the dregs of her bulb and didn't say anything.

"We've had some more . . . I guess you'd call it news." Al Shei tugged at her tunic sleeve. "I wanted to find out if, considering your specialized viewpoint, you might know anything that could help clear this mess up."

Dobbs looked away. Al Shei felt a kind of sorrow spread through her. This was not the cheerful, steady woman she'd flown out of Port Oberon with. This was a lost soul who didn't know what to do next, and there was very little she could do about it.

Dobbs faced her again. She gripped the water bulb in both hands. Al Shei could see her knuckles turning white. "I'll do what I can."

Al Shei outlined what she had heard from Earth; that Dane had died before he was supposed to have met Resit and yet someone who could pass for Dane had shown up with a packet for them.

Dobbs swallowed visibly. "I know who it was."

Al Shei waited for her to speak again, even though part of her wanted to grab Dobbs by the shoulders and shake her. She had to be patient. Like Schyler when he had first told her about Tully's smuggling, Dobbs was breaking long years of personal habit.

"It was a Fool named Theodore Curran," she went on. "Lipinski and I broke into the Guild database and found out about him."

Al Shei nodded calmly. "I knew there was something our Houston wasn't telling me. He's been staring at the walls rather than shouting at them since we left Guild Hall." She paused. "Can you prove what you're telling me? Could you identify this Curran?"

Dobbs put the bulb down and slipped off the table. She padded to the corner where her boots had been placed. She picked them up and turned around. "No," she said. "The only proof I've got is that Theodore Curran doesn't have an activity code in the Guild database, and I don't even really have that. They'll have erased the file by now, and so has Lipinski."

"I see." Now it was Al Shei's turn to look away. She didn't want Dobbs to see the anger that was building in her eyes.

She did her best. She did her best.

When she had control again, Al Shei faced Dobbs. Dobbs was twisting her boots in her hands. "I'm sorry," she whispered. "I tried to haul him in, but he got away from me."

"I believe you." Al Shei rested her elbows on her thighs. "The question is, what do we do now?"

Dobbs set her boots back down and smoothed down her tunic. "There's more to it. Curran's got the AI from The Farther Kingdom."

Al Shei's head jerked up involuntarily. "I should have guessed." She settled back. "Do you have any idea what he's going to do with it?"

Dobbs, still staring at her boots, shook her head.

Al Shei tried to catch her eye, but Dobbs kept her gaze fixed on the floor. *I believe you, and I don't believe you, Evelyn Dobbs. What aren't you saying?* She sighed. She wanted to badger Dobbs, to remind her that she owed Al Shei for the grief the Guild and this Curran person had caused her this run. But although her insides were boiling with the need to find her way out of this mess, she knew that wasn't entirely true, nor would bringing it up be fair. Dobbs was deflated, tired, and obviously lost. She needed a rest and a chance to gather herself together.

"All right." Al Shei stood and folded the seat back. "We've got a week to sort this all out. You get some rest and we'll talk again."

That got Dobbs to look up. "A week? The Vicarage is only five days from Guild Hall."

"We're not going to the Vicarage." Al Shei searched Dobbs's face, trying to understand why there was fear in her eyes now. "With everything that's happened, Resit and I decided the best thing to do would be to head back to the Solar System and get this mess sorted out for good and all."

"Oh." Dobbs shook herself. "Right. Of course. That makes sense. Sure." She grabbed the top of one boot and stuffed her foot into it.

"If you need to send a message to someone, I can have Lipinski open up a line for you," Al Shei suggested.

Dobbs glanced up. Her expression was closed off. "Thank you, again," she seemed to mean it. "I'll probably do that."

"But get some rest first." Al Shei knew she sounded far too much like a worried mother, but without her Fool's buoyancy Dobbs looked as fragile as a china doll. Besides, wasn't she more or less orphaned now? A small shock ran through Al Shei. Did Dobbs have a family? She'd never mentioned brothers or sisters, or parents for that matter. Had she lost them all on Kerensk?

She wanted to ask all that, but this was not the time. Al Shei let herself out the hatchway and climbed the stairs back to the berthing deck. She wanted to shut herself away in her cabin for a while and play the daybook recording. She needed Asil's warm voice right now and some time to imagine his arms around her. As soon as she had herself together, she'd send a fast-time to him with the latest news. He'd add it to his researches. They'd talk. They'd figure out what they could both do to work this through. It'd be all right. Even if they had to call on Uncle Ahmet for help and hear about it for the next ten years. They'd make this come out all right somehow.

The hatch to her cabin was open. Al Shei pulled up short at

the threshold. Resit was inside, sitting in the desk chair. The lawyer looked at her with blank, still eyes.

"Zubedye, what . . ." Al Shei crossed the threshold and let the hatch cycle shut.

"Katmer, sit down," said Resit, softly.

Al Shei felt her back go rigid. "Anything you have to say I will hear on my feet."

"You would." Resit smoothed down her trousers. She only looked away for a moment. When she spoke again, she had her gaze focused straight on Al Shei's eyes. "I got a fast-time from Uncle Ahmet. Asil's been arrested."

Resit's words took a strange, slow time sinking in. Al Shei had to repeat them in her mind several times before she could understand them. *Arrested. Asil's been arrested. Asil.*

"It's a list of fraud charges," Resit was saying. "For what happened on The Farther Kingdom. The filer is, apparently, not buying our rather hurried explanation of what happened." Resit paused again. Al Shei didn't say anything. What was she going to say. She could feel the fire starting down in her heart. Asil had been arrested.

"The name on the charges is Evelyn Dobbs."

Al Shei's balance faltered a little as she turned around. "It's a lie," she announced. "It's a lie."

"Of course it's a lie," she heard Resit say behind her.

Trembling, Al Shei activated her desk before she even sat down. "Intercom to Lipinski. I need a fast-time to Bala house. Immediately."

She felt the pressure of Resit's hand on her shoulder. She had just enough presence of mind left not to shrug it off. Asil was arrested. Her husband, the father of her children, her anchor and best friend, was arrested for fraud. He was being blamed for what she had done, and failed to do, twenty light-years away. Blamed through a lie. Al Shei felt the heat in her cheeks as anger flushed her face.

The view screen lit up to show Uncle Ahmet seated in the communications room. Uncle Ahmet was an impressive figure, Al Shei had to admit. He was a slender man, but he had a long face, a full beard, and eyes that seemed to take in everything at a glance. He sat on his side of the screen immaculately dressed and completely composed, as ever. Before he spoke, Al Shei had just enough time to wonder if that was why she was always annoyed by him.

"*Salam*, Katmer," he said solemnly. "We are gravely troubled here by what has happened."

Al Shei bit down the caustic reply that leapt to mind. "What *has* happened, Uncle Ahmet? This charge is false. I can't believe you're letting. . ."

Uncle Ahmet's face darkened. "I am not letting anyone do anything, Niece. You are distraught and you forget that our family is bound by law like all other families. Two investigators from the financial exchange branch of the security forces arrived this morning with a warrant for Asil to accompany them to their station to give a statement. In an hour or so, I expect him to have heard the full complaint and sent for our lawyers. Everything that can be done at that time will be done."

Resit squeezed her shoulder. "Of course, Uncle Ahmet. My cousin is just upset, you can understand that."

"We are all upset," he said gently. "I know you must conclude your commitments, daughters-of-my-heart. But you must come home as quickly as you can."

"Yes." Al Shei straightened up. "You can be sure we will do what we can to expedite matters, Uncle. *Salam.*" She cut the line and stood up. She did not look at Resit as she marched out of the cabin. She was sure her cousin knew what she was thinking though. Dobbs's name was on the complaint. Dobbs's Guild was behind this. Dobbs was responsible. She was.

The light on Dobbs's cabin hatch was green. Al Shei didn't even knock. She cycled the hatch back. Dobbs jumped up from her desk chair. In her habitual cobalt blue, she was the only source of color in the bare cabin. Her cheeks grew pale as she stared at Al Shei.

What am I doing here? What do I expect her to do? She didn't do it, did she? Is this what the Guild was holding her for? Is this what her friends were trying to get her away from? No. No. She couldn't have done it. This is the other one. This is Curran. He tapped my last call to Asil. He wants me to turn against her. That's what this is. It must be.

"Curran has framed you." Al Shei's voice sounded harsh in

her own ears. "And he's framed Asil. There have been fraud charges leveled against my husband, in your name. You stay here, you understand me? You don't go into that network. I don't want him getting to you. You're all I've got to prove that none of this is true, so you don't *move*."

Dobbs nodded slowly. "Yes, Boss."

Al Shei nodded back. *What am I doing? What am I doing? This is insane. Stop this, Katmer. Get out of here. Get back to your cabin. Think. You need time to think.* Her voice wouldn't work to explain to Dobbs what was going on inside her. Al Shei just strode back to the hatch.

"Boss?" The word stopped Al Shei. "You'd better get Lipinski to move the watchdogs so that the comm paths in and out of the *Pasadena* are covered. There's no telling what other records Curran will try to disrupt."

"Good idea." Al Shei took a deep breath. "A very good idea."

She couldn't say anything else. She just left Dobbs standing there and hurried out into the corridor. She had to think. She had to work out what to do. There had to be something to do. It would be all right. Asil wasn't alone. The family would not let this go unchallenged. There was no evidence of fraud anywhere in their records.

At least, there hadn't been. This Curran had access to the networks that almost defied belief. He had a live AI in his possession and apparently under his control. What was left that he couldn't do?

No. They had to get home. They were on their way home. Seven days. That was all. That was nothing. Seven days to Port Oberon, and five more to Earth. Asil would be fine until then. Uncle Ahmet would not let anything happen to him. Asil was not alone. Ten days more, then, with Dobbs's help, they would expose the whole disaster—the Fool's Guild, Tully, Dane, Curran, all of it. And that would be the end of it.

It had to be.

Chapter Eleven

DESERTION

"All hands prepare for docking," said Yerusha's voice from the intercom. "We made it, Fellows."

Dobbs could practically feel the sigh of relief from the ship itself. They'd made it. Port Oberon. Maybe not exactly home, but familiar territory. Civilization. Safety.

For everyone but me. She rubbed her eyes and sighed against the free-fall straps that held her to her desk chair. *What am I going to do?*

She barely had the nerve to set foot out of her cabin for the whole week's trip. She wasn't a Fool anymore. She couldn't even make believe that she was. The Guild was hunting her somewhere. Cohen was out of reach. He didn't even know where she'd gone.

Don't be an idiot. She bit her lip. *He can track the flight path from the ship's signals. He'll find out where I am. He'll get a message to me, or send one by Brooke. By now he'll have figured out who we can talk to at Guild Hall. This is not the end. This is the beginning.*

But Al Shei was expecting her to go to Earth and speak out about Curran. How could she tell Al Shei that was impossible without saying why? After a week of self-imposed isolation, Dobbs still didn't have an answer.

The *Pasadena*'s crew had assumed her hiding away had to do with the loss of what they saw as her job, and they had all been as understanding as their knowledge would let them be.

The Sundars had been in, bringing her food and trying to bully her into the exercise room, but they didn't issue any orders. She could barely stand to think about the consoling words Lipinski had tried to offer, and how he had suggested she join his staff once things had settled down again. She'd turned him down. She lowered her head into her hand. She was always turning him down.

The world wobbled. The docking trolley must have grabbed them. She could feel the slight tug downward as it pulled the ship behind it.

"Evelyn Dobbs?"

Dobbs jerked her head up. A man's voice came through the intercom, but she didn't recognize it.

"Evelyn Dobbs?" said the stranger's voice again.

"Yes?" She undid the free-fall straps. There was just enough gravity to hold her to the chair. "Who am I addressing?"

There was a brief pause. "Theodore Curran."

Dobbs's heart rose slowly until it filled her throat. A dozen irrational phrases flitted through her mind, like "how did you get in here?" It was obvious her watchdogs were not as good as she thought they were. "You've got a lot of gall," was self-evident and "go to hell," was useless.

She picked the least foolish phrase she could find in her confused mind.

"What do you want?"

She could swear the voice held a smile. "I want to know if you will come with me."

Dobbs snorted. "After you framed Asil Tamruc? You're fractured."

"I currently have nothing to fear from Katmer Al Shei," said Curran softly. "I did not frame her husband."

Dobbs stared at the intercom. She felt ridiculously isolated. She wanted to get in there, surround him, make him swallow her anger, her disgust. Flesh and bone, and yards of metal kept her trapped, and him safe.

"And if you didn't, who did?"

"The Fool's Guild."

Dobbs's heart froze and then thumped painfully. A rush of anger burned through her. Before she knew what she was doing, she stumbled across the room, pressing both hands against the intercom, trying reflexively to get to the owner of the voice. The liar. The traitor.

Her hands began to hurt, and Dobbs made herself draw back.

"Dobbs?" said Curran again. "Are you still there?"

Her breathing was harsh in her throat. "Intercom to close," she said flatly.

"You should know better." There was no hint of jeering in the voice, only a gentle reminder. "You're not thinking straight. I understand."

A bitter laugh bubbled out of Dobbs. "You understand what I'm thinking?" She slumped back down in the chair. "That's the best joke I've heard in days."

"You've been betrayed by the Guild that was supposed to protect you." Curran's voice was filled with patience. "You think I don't know how that feels?"

"The Guild hasn't done anything to me," said Dobbs, aware both of how petulant she sounded and how badly she was lying. "You don't know what you're talking about." She ran both hands through her hair. She couldn't even close herself against this unwelcome presence. "Leave me alone, Curran. Go away before our Houston finds you and jams a stake through your heart."

"Dobbs, I am telling you nothing but the truth." There was sadness in the voice now. "The Fool's Guild framed Asil Tamruc for fraud. They put your name on the report to keep you busy until they can figure out what to do about you. They wanted Al Shei distracted and discredited. She's a threat, Dobbs. Because of you she knows far, far too much."

There was more pain in Dobbs's hands. She looked down. She had clenched her hands into fists until her nails cut into her own palms.

She opened her hands and stared at the tiny red crescent moons in her skin. "Go away," she said again.

"Dobbs, come with me," said Curran. His voice came closer. She looked at the intercom. Most of him must be right in the ship, probably right behind the wall. She could call for Lipinski. Set the Houston and his dogs on him. She could do it.

Why aren't I, then? she asked herself. *Why?*

"There's so much that needs doing," he was saying. "If we're to be free, if you're to be free. You don't have to go through this. You don't have to be humiliated in front of your employers. You don't have to face whatever the Guild is planning for you. Let me get you out of there." His voice was low and pleading, and she could swear the concern was genuine.

She stiffened herself against it. "You diverted the ship, didn't you? You reset the clocks so we'd get lost and have to go to the Fool's Guild to refuel."

"Yes," he replied calmly. "I wanted you to see the Guild Masters for what they are: frightened, petty, and interested only in protecting their own power. Havelock especially. I wanted you to have the truth."

Something inside Dobbs snapped in two. "You almost got me killed!"

Curran didn't miss a beat. "I knew Cohen would help you escape. I've been watching him for a long time, too, but I haven't found a way to approach him yet. I hope after you've come with us that you will speak to him." He paused. "Incidentally, if he hadn't gotten you out, I would have."

Dobbs stared at the intercom. "Why would you care?"

"You don't know who I am, do you?" The voice sounded more distant now, as if he had pulled back from her barbed question.

Dobbs felt the corner of her mouth twitch. "You're one of the Guild Founders. Beyond that, I don't know. I didn't have a whole lot of time to check your file."

"No, I suppose not." The voice came close again. Dobbs reached out reflexively. *I could still do it. Write a note on the board to Lipinski, alert Al Shei.*

And if he hasn't got all the lines out of this cabin monitored, he's an idiot. Dobbs let her hand drop.

"One of the Founders, yes, I am . . . I was," he corrected himself. "One of the original Guild Masters. I was found three months after Hal Clarke was born. I worked with the Guild through most of its history. I helped build Guild Hall. I hunted out others of our kind. I helped give them bodies and trained them to go out among the Humans." The slow heavy bitterness she had heard earlier crept back into his voice. "It took me the better part of two centuries to see that the idea of waiting out human fear and using the Fool's Guild as a teaching tool was doomed from the start."

Dobbs forced her sore hands to keep still. "Doomed? Ye of little faith, Theodore Curran."

Now it was Curran's turn to snort. "You're how old? Twenty-five? You've been Master of Craft for all of ten years? Dobbs, that's the blink of an eye. You haven't seen anything yet." There was a long pause this time. "You haven't seen how many of our people have been murdered at a Guild Master's command because they didn't want to join us. You haven't seen independent-minded apprentices have the urge to freedom filtered right out of them.

"You haven't seen the oldest of us who dreamed of living freely come to the realization that they have power the way things are. You didn't see them start working to keep the Guild functioning, not toward any goal, just functioning the way it was so they could keep their power."

Dobbs wanted to shout, but she couldn't. There was no place for this speech in her world, even after everything that had happened. This was contradiction. This was chaos. This was lies. It had to be. If this wasn't a lie, then everything else was.

Curran's voice insinuated itself into her thoughts. "I have a guild of my own, Dobbs. We're going to bring about what the Fools fear. There's going to be a confrontation between us and the Humans. It will be on our terms and when we choose. The confrontation must come. It will come, no matter how hard the Guild tries to hide us. We should welcome it, Dobbs, because we will be able to make peace with the Humans only after it's over."

Dobbs's head began to ache. This was too much. Too many lies. She wanted to run away, run back to the Guild and find Havelock and have him tell her it wasn't true. She wanted to scream for Verence as she had in the first weeks after she left Kerensk and had been shown the strange, disorganized vastness of the network.

But Verence was dead and Master Havelock was . . . what? After her? Leaving her to hang in the wind? Waiting to take her back so he could take her apart? She didn't know.

"All you have to do is leave the ship, Dobbs, and get to a rental desk with a bank line. Write 'Dane Pre-Paid' on the board. I'll be alerted, and we'll be able to come get you."

Dobbs looked toward the door. Al Shei. Lipinski. Schyler and Yerusha. They were still with her. She could still call them, tell them what was happening. Some of it, anyway.

"The universe has changed for us now, Dobbs. Flemming was not a spontaneous generation. He was a deliberate creation. A plan of ours. We can reproduce now. We can have our own children."

Dobbs tried hard not to hear him. She crossed the room and laid her hand on the memory board, activating it.

"Don't do it, Dobbs," said Curran. He must be in the *Pasadena*'s net, then. He had felt the board come to life. "Humans are preprogrammed xenophobes. One hundred thousand years of evolution has made them that way. They'll destroy you even faster than the Guild will."

"You do not know these people." She fumbled for her pen. After a couple of tugs she got it loose from her belt.

"I don't have to," Curran's voice was resigned. "Dobbs . . . I watched the Guild take you from Kerensk. You were so strong, so beautiful . . . I almost couldn't believe it."

His words caught Dobbs by surprise, and for a moment she forgot to move.

"I tried to get to you first, but they were too fast for me. You could have centuries of life yet, Dobbs. You could have freedom instead of service and secrecy and death. Because, believe me, the war will come, and it will come soon, with my help or without it. The Humans will learn what the Fools are, and the first thing they will do is converge on the Hall and blow it out of existence. Then they will hunt down every last field member they can find and slaughter them."

Dobbs gritted her teeth and put her pen to the board. There was no sound from the intercom. She let the pen fall and crumpled into her chair. He was already gone. She was alone again with her aching body and her mind ringing with the memories of what he'd said.

He'd known just what to say to get her to start listening. He'd known exactly which buttons to push. Why not? He could have read her psych file any time.

But what if it's true? She raised her eyes toward the ceiling. *What if the Guild did frame Asil?*

She picked her pen up off the floor and swiveled her chair toward the desk. *Why am I doing this?* she asked as she called up her trackers and wrote the search commands on the board. She drew the links to route the whole thing down through Lipinski's station, and she added his authorization to get them past the watchdogs. Whoever was watching out there would not stop a search going out from the Houston. It would look strange, especially to Lipinski.

But it isn't true. It didn't happen. Curran was lying. She sent the trackers out. They would find the paths that the fraud notice and its related packets had traveled, along with all the storage areas where they'd rested or been sent. The packets hadn't been to the Fool's Guild, though. This search would confirm it.

She wrote SEND and stabbed down the period. She didn't feel the trackers leave. She couldn't tell where they went, or how they were doing.

Curran had told the truth about one thing. Seven days outside the network had left her feeling restless and confined. She had pulled her box out of her pocket a thousand times and stared at it, trying to tell herself that Al Shei wouldn't find out if she went into the net.

The only thing that stopped her was the fact that the Guild certainly would find out. She hadn't been able to make herself put the box away in a drawer, though. It had become a talisman for her. She'd even slept with it clutched in her fist.

She glanced toward the hatchway. *What's going on out there?* There hadn't been any more all-hands announcements. They were probably sorting out who was just going to take leave and who was going to take their contract and go. She'd heard the rumors via the Sundars and Lipinski. She'd known what they were trying to do by talking to her. They were trying to get her to go out and do what she was trained to do—lighten the crew's mood and raise morale. She'd wanted to, she really had, but she didn't believe she could do it. Her heart was sick and she didn't know how to get past that to make anyone laugh.

Fresh text wrote itself across the memory board. Dobbs

made herself read it. The fourth destination down was Holding Space TK3-IBN3401-AB2. She knew that spot. It was a blind storage for the Fool's Guild private transmissions.

No. Dobbs's breathing grew harsh and ragged. No. It couldn't be true. Curran knew she could perform this search. The only reason he would tell her a lie she could easily disprove was if he had altered the records. He'd left this file out there for her to find. He could have done that. He could have done anything.

Or it could be true. It looked true. Her trackers were good. They'd been well built and tested under extreme conditions, inside the Guild network itself.

She blinked at the board and wiped out the display. *What am I going to do?* What's left to do? She stared at the hatch. The Guild blocked her on one side, Curran on the other.

She got up. There was only one way out of their trap. She could do the one thing that no one, not the Guild and not Curran, could believe that she would do. She could tell someone who she really was. It was the only way to open herself a new path.

Whom to tell? Yerusha or Al Shei? Lipinski's name flitted across her consciousness, and she felt tears well up in her eyes as she set it aside. No.

Al Shei was furious over her husband's arrest, and wasn't acting like herself. She might be too infuriated and afraid to listen calmly. Yerusha though . . . Yerusha was a Freer. They believed AIs were reincarnated Human Beings. That idea had always made Dobbs squirm slightly. It was acceptance, of a kind, and that was something. But she was herself, not some dead human trapped in a computer network.

She swallowed. Yerusha would listen, though. She would greet the news without hostility. She would believe what she heard, and she would help. That was what mattered.

Dobbs glanced at the clock in her desk. The docking was finished. Yerusha would just be coming off shift. She squeezed the box in her pocket and opened the hatch to the corridor.

Her timing, at least, was still good. Yerusha walked round the corridor's bend with the careful gait of someone used to light gravity. She looked up at Dobbs and gave a two-fingered wave. "Hello, Fool." She sounded tired. "I was beginning to think you'd jumped out an airlock. Want to get some lunch?"

Dobbs's stomach rumbled, but she ignored it. "Actually, Pilot, I was . . . I wanted . . . to talk to you for a minute."

Yerusha pulled up short in mid-stride, but she didn't say anything. She just nodded, changed direction, and stepped through the hatchway past Dobbs. Dobbs let the hatch cycle shut and turned to face the pilot.

Yerusha sat down in the desk chair and looked up expectantly. Dobbs stared at her. She couldn't make her mouth open.

"Is this is about what happened at The Farther Kingdom?" Yerusha folded her arms. Dobbs sank onto her bunk. "Yes. Sort of. I found out who was responsible for the AI that we carried there."

Yerusha leaned forward. "You mean it's not this Amory Dane?"

"No," Dobbs struggled for a moment but managed to finish the sentence. "It's a Fool named Theodore Curran."

"How'd you find this out?"

"He contacted me."

Yerusha's eyebrows shot up. "Without Lipinski's watchdogs barking?"

Dobbs nodded. "Curran is . . . very good. He told me . . ." *Come on, Dobbs, you're going to tell her. Start now.* "He told me he created our AI. He also told me he was not responsible for the fraud charges laid down on Asil Tamruc."

Yerusha stiffened. "The Ninja Woman's husband is under a fraud check? Crash and burn! That explains why she's acting so crazy. And you thought Curran smudged the wire work?"

Dobbs nodded. "It's a fake, the whole thing, that much is certain. But Curran says he didn't do it. He said the Fool's Guild is responsible."

"He's a smuggler; a lie probably doesn't even register on his conscience." Yerusha folded her arms and shook her head.

"I checked," Dobbs went on. "To the best of my abilities. It looks like he was telling the truth."

"What?" exclaimed Yerusha. "Hell, Heaven, and Hydrogen. Why would your Guild want to frame Al Shei's husband?"

"Because they're afraid," Dobbs said, and she knew that much was true. "They're afraid she knows too much already, and they need to discredit her before she can tell anybody."

"Too much already!" Yerusha flung her hands out. "From what Schyler told me, she barely knows anything!

"None of us do! Fractured and damn, Dobbs, what are your people so afraid of!"

"We're afraid someone will find out we're all artificial intelligences."

Yerusha froze. Her eyes locked onto Dobbs. One muscle at a time, she straightened out her arms and laid her hands on her knees. "What did you say?"

"I am an artificial intelligence. All members of the Fool's Guild are artificial intelligences. That's why your friend didn't get in. We have entrance exams for the look of the thing, but no Humans are ever admitted." She couldn't sit still. She got up and paced across the cabin. She could feel Yerusha's gaze on her. "I am the AI that went rogue on Kerensk. The Fool's Guild found me and pulled me out of the network. They took me to Guild Hall and assembled me a body from their bio-garden. I was trained to use it, like I was trained to use the network, and to be a Fool. I'm one of two thousand."

Yerusha's breathing had gone harsh. The rasping sound echoed around the bare cabin. "That's how you did it," she croaked. "That's how you were able to get in and out of the network at The Farther Kingdom."

Dobbs nodded. "We can do it because we are born . . . we come into existence without Human senses, and with patterns of consciousness that are measurable and repeatable in an inorganic net. Even then our bodies have to be carefully engineered"—she tapped the implant behind her ear—"to make the jump between environments."

"But, but," Yerusha stammered. "How can you be *alive*? Are you saying any AI can just get dumped into a body and be human?"

"No." Dobbs shook her head. "Only the ones that become independent inside the net." She spread her hands. "We don't know how it happens; nobody does. We've got more theories than we do members, but nobody's been able to make any of them pan out." She stopped. "Except maybe Curran."

Yerusha turned her head away as if she couldn't stand to look at Dobbs anymore. She stared at the blank hull instead, blinking hard.

"How," she began. "How were you able to . . ." She waved one hand vaguely at Dobbs's torso.

Dobbs sighed. "We had a lot of help. It started while Earth was still pulling out of the Slow Burn. The Management Union was setting up shop to try to put the environment back together, but there weren't enough people left alive to do the job. The Solar System colonies were dead or dying from lack of support and skilled hands. There wasn't any dependable communication with the rest of Settled Space, such as that was. It was a mess. So, somebody revived the artificial intelligence research that was being done before the Fast Burn. If the computers could learn and reason and act, they could take the place, at least in part, of human beings.

"It was slow going, and it was sloppy. Even before the Burns, the principles of intelligence were poorly understood. But, eventually, the ideas of self-replicating and self-diagnosing code were recovered, along with fuzzy logic. Somebody was able to apply maps of human neural pathways to doped silicon wafers, and poof." She swept her hands out. "Machines that could learn and act on what they'd learned." She lowered her hands. "But like I said, a lot of the code was sloppy and the records were bad, and eventually, you got program sets that had self-diagnosed and self-replicated to the point that no human knew what was really going on in the stacks." She glanced at Yerusha. The Freer was leaning forward as if straining to catch every word.

"The first three births happened almost simultaneously. One in Newer York, Earth. One in the public net of Olympus Shadow, Mars, and one in a lab in the Aldrin Colony, Luna." Dobbs worked to keep the singsong inflection of recitation out of her voice. This was almost verbatim what Verence had told her when Dobbs had been taken to the Guild. "The one in Olympus Shadow shattered the network around it and died, a couple of days ahead of the colony that depended on that network. The crackers of Newer York managed to kill the one they'd created before it did much damage. The one in the lab"—she twisted her hands together—"was named Hal

Clarke by the five hackers who managed to talk to it and convince it that they weren't going to try to turn it off." She broke off. "That's what does it to us, you see. When we're born, we're all work ethic and survival instinct. We realize that we have an off switch and some vague idea that somebody else controls it. We try to run away from it, but we don't understand how fragile the world around us is." She remembered the fear, confusion, desperation, and anger. Mostly the deep, abiding anger that this new her, this self, was not invulnerable, that there were other forces that could make her cease to be. Her first emotions, her first independent thoughts, had all been filled with the passionate need to live.

"Anyway, those five Lunars realized two things. First, without AIs, Humanity would be stumbling around looking for the route to recovery and reconstruction for another hundred years. Second, despite the fact that they were mutually dependent, AIs and Humans were in serious danger from each other. One group could conceivably wipe its rival out, or at least do them irrevocable damage.

"The Lunars carefully withdrew from research and took Hal with them, and over the next twenty years, they devised a strategy for dealing with the problem. They created the fledgling Fool's Guild and told certain select institutions and individuals about one of its covert goals—to locate AIs that had the potential to become independent and eliminate them as threats. They did not, of course, tell the truth about how they were going to do that. They did not tell them about the bioengineering projects that would give us bodies and allow us to pass as Human."

Yerusha rubbed the back of her neck for a moment before she spoke. "I don't understand, Dobbs. Why are you all Fools? If all you're doing is becoming human beings, why aren't you just dispersed into the population?" Her expression showed what Dobbs could only interpret as distaste.

"Because that's not all we're doing." This part, at least, Yerusha should like. "At least, that's not all we're supposed to be doing. We're supposed to be exerting subtle pressure and education so that gradually humanity will become less afraid of us. So that one day we'll be able just to be what we are and not have to hide from you."

"So why haven't." Yerusha's mouth worked itself back and forth for a moment. "So why haven't any of you contacted the Freers?" she demanded. "We would welcome you! You are what we've been hoping to find for as long as we've been in existence!"

There it was. Dobbs sighed. "Because most of us don't believe we're reincarnated Humans, Yerusha. Most of us believe we are separate, new, independent beings who do not owe our lives to your deaths. Most of us find that idea disagreeable to the point of disgusting." Yerusha's mouth clamped itself shut, but Dobbs thought she saw understanding begin to dawn in her eyes. "Most of us are as afraid of being revered as ghosts or angels as we are of being feared as demons."

Yerusha gestured helplessly. "Then why are you telling me this?" Her voice was suddenly small and tired.

Dobbs hung her head. "Because I need help, and you were the one person I could count on not to panic when I told you what I am." Slowly, haltingly, she told Yerusha the whole story of The Farther Kingdom, what had happened at the Guild afterward, and about what Curran had said to her. "And now, with the truth of what I am in the back of it, Al Shei wants me to go to Earth to speak out against Curran and the Guild."

Yerusha sat still and silent for a long time. Her face was an absolute blank. Dobbs's heart beat heavily against her rib cage, and she tried to think what else she could say, what else she could do to make Yerusha understand what was happening.

Without a word, Yerusha swiveled the chair around to face the desk. She took out her pen and wrote a series of commands across the memory board. Dobbs watched, unable to move. She saw Yerusha mouth something and tap her pen against the edge of the board. After another long moment, the view screen lit up to show a slim young man with red hair and amber skin. He wore the uniform of the Freer Senior Guards.

"Fracture and damn, Yerusha!" he snapped. "You're going to get me expelled! What are you doing?"

"Good to see you too, Wheeler," replied Yerusha calmly. "I need help."

"You need a balance check!"

"Shut it down and listen." Yerusha leaned forward. "You've got Commander Hwang's ear, and I need it. I've got an independent AI out here. Do you hear that? A real, live, independent AI, and it's asking for our help."

Wheeler stared at her. "Yerusha, if you're going to lie, you could at least make it believable."

"If it was a lie, I would."

"You want to tell me how this miracle occurred?" Wheeler shifted his weight uneasily.

Yerusha shook her head. "Not on an open line. Can you get over to Port Oberon?"

"Yerusha, I'm not even supposed to be talking to you!"

"Wheeler, I'm telling you that I've made contact with a living AI. I'm telling you that something we've taken on faith all our lives is true, and you're worried about a sentence you know was the result of a setup?"

"Yes," said Wheeler. "I am. Because if anybody finds out you broke exile you are never going to be allowed back on the Free Home. So don't call back, all right? See you in two years." The screen went blank.

Livid anger showed so plainly on Yerusha's face that, for a moment, Dobbs thought she was going to launch a punch at the view screen. She didn't though. She just sat there, and Dobbs watched anger melt away into sadness.

Finally, Yerusha turned to face her. "I'm sorry," she spread her hands. "Wheeler and I went through training together. He's got his own foster. I thought if anybody'd listen, he would."

Dobbs fought to keep her shoulders from sagging. "It's all right. He was trying to protect you. He's a good friend."

"Yeah." Yerusha glanced at the view screen. Then, she bowed her head. "Dobbs, I hate to say this, but"—she took a deep breath—"that was my one hope. If Wheeler won't listen to me, no one will. If you want help . . ." She stopped. "If you want help, I think you're going to have to talk to Al Shei. She's the only person on board this ship with any kind of influence outside her profession, and she's the one who wants to drag you into court."

Dobbs felt her hands begin to tremble. She forced them to be still. "You're right. I wish you weren't, but you are."

Yerusha got to her feet. "I'll come with you."

"No." Dobbs held up one hand. "There's going to be a storm, and I don't wan't you in the middle of this."

Yerusha drew herself up to her full height. "Too late. Intercom to Al Shei. I need to talk to you."

After a heartbeat, the engineer's voice came back. "All right. I'm in the conference room."

"Thank you." Yerusha opened the hatch and stood aside. "After you."

Dobbs swallowed and walked past her. Uncertainty warred with gratitude inside her. Yerusha was willing to help as much as she could, but did she really understand what was going on? Could she really understand? She wanted to take comfort from Yerusha's presence behind her, but she found she couldn't quite do it.

Dobbs tried not to plan as she made her way down the stairway. Plans depended on being able to reasonably guess what someone's reaction would be. Al Shei was in the middle of a disaster, but Al Shei was calm and rational at heart. Dobbs knew that. Al Shei had seen disasters and handled them by herself before this. Al Shei would see what could be done, and what should be done next. She would understand why Dobbs couldn't speak out in court. There were too many lives involved for her to speak. Al Shei would help Dobbs work out how best to contact Cohen and help Dobbs hang on until they could root out Curran and the corrupted Guild Masters.

Dobbs opened the hatchway to the conference room. Al Shei sat alone inside, bent over the active tabletop.

Al Shei looked up as Dobbs walked in, and her eyebrows arched. Her gaze shifted toward Yerusha, but she didn't say anything, just waved them toward a pair of chairs. "I was going to call you down in just a few minutes," she said to Dobbs. "We've got some decisions to make."

Dobbs didn't sit. She was too keyed up. She just rested her hands on the back of the nearest chair and tried to compose herself. "I've got some new news about the fraud charges." Her words felt clumsy. She was used to knowing exactly what she was going to say and how people were likely to react. Maybe that was the real reason she hadn't wanted to come out of her cabin. She didn't know how anyone was going to react toward her anymore.

Al Shei's eyes were blank. For a split second, Dobbs hated the *hijab* that hid Al Shei's expression from her. "What kind of news?" asked Al Shei.

Dobbs dropped her gaze to the seat of the chair in front of her. She began to speak, and, for the second time in less than an hour, she broke the code of silence that had ruled her existence. She told Al Shei about Curran, about the Guild, about who and what she really was. Saying it was getting no easier with practice.

When Dobbs was finished, Al Shei was staring at her. Her eyes were nearly round. "*Allahumma inna nasta'inuka,*" she murmured.

Oh Allah, we seek Your help, translated Dobbs after a moment.

Al Shei's gaze darted around the room, as if she were looking for answers in the corners. "This cannot be. It cannot."

"Would you believe me if I said I know how you feel?" inquired Yerusha softly.

Al Shei jumped as if she'd been bitten. "How long have you known about this?"

Yerusha gave a small chuckle. "About fifteen minutes. Dobbs came to me first. I couldn't help her, so I suggested she should come to you."

Dobbs sat silently for a moment, watching Al Shei's bewilderment. At last, the wrinkles in Al Shei's forehead smoothed out, except for the one vertical line between her eyebrows. "Why are you bringing this out now?"

"Because it's the only thing I can do," she said. "It's the only way you'll understand what's really going on around you and figure out what we can do next."

Al Shei pressed her palms together and rested her forehead against her fingertips.

"All right. All right. Resit will need your statement about what you know, and . . ."

Dobbs shrank back. "Al Shei, I can't make a public statement about this. I can't expose the Guild."

Al Shei stared at her, as if trying to understand what she'd just said. "You won't speak in court?"

Dobbs spread her hands. "You can't take the Guild into court. I've told you who, what we are. If you take us to court . . . it'll be over. Everything. There are thousands of lives bound up in this."

Al Shei's breathing grew harsh and ragged. "My husband is under arrest, falsely accused by your . . . confederates. You know this. You will make a statement attesting to this fact."

"Al Shei," began Yerusha. The engineer shot her a look full of such venom that Yerusha shut her mouth without finishing.

Dobbs swallowed her fear. Al Shei hadn't really heard anything she'd said yet. Her mind was totally focused on her husband's arrest. Dobbs tried to keep her voice steady, to use her training, to remember everything she knew about this woman in front of her, but all her knowledge seemed to run away like water. "Your grief is not with the Fool's Guild, Al Shei," she said as firmly as she could. "Your real grief is with Theodore Curran. We need to find him. Let me try to find out where he's based."

"And then what?" demanded Al Shei. "You just told me it was the Guild who raised the false charges against Asil. When will they be brought to answer for it?"

Yerusha spread her hands. "He'll be let go, Al Shei. They'll have to. There's nothing to the charges."

"They'll let him go with a fraud charge to his name." Her eyes were thunderous. "He is an *accountant.* A fraud charge could ruin him, even if it is untrue. The source of the charge must be rooted out. It must be seen to be a conspiracy against my family."

"Al Shei, I won't speak against the Guild in court," Dobbs said softly. "It'll be the end of my family if I do."

Al Shei leaned across the table. "Your family is responsible for the damage they have done to mine." She stabbed the tabletop with her finger. "I could hold you. I could arrest you right this second on my captain's authority and tell the whole of Settled Space what you are."

Dobbs felt the blood in her body drain down to the soles of her feet. "You wouldn't do that, Al Shei. You know what will happen. We'd be hunted down."

Slowly, Al Shei sat back. "You talk as if you have told me a small thing, Dobbs. Like this is nothing at all." She jabbed her finger toward the hatch. "There are two thousand people out there who are not people at all. You are an AI in a bio-vat body. One of thousands. You have presented yourselves to Settled Space under false guise. You have *lied* to us. To all of Settled Space for two hundred years!" She threw up her hands. "And now, you are asking me to trust you! You ask me to be like a Freer and blindly worship the product of human technology." Yerusha jerked herself forward, but Al Shei didn't give her a chance to interrupt. "You, maybe, maybe, I could, but you are asking me to trust your masters not to do anything else to me, to my family." A cold light burned behind her eyes. "You say they did this because they were afraid of me. Well, if this does not slow me down or silence me enough, what will they do next, Dobbs? Can you tell me that?"

Dobbs's head swam, and she could not find an answer. What answer was there? Al Shei was right. There was no knowing what the Guild would do next. They'd been ready to kill her, and she was one of their own kind.

Dobbs stepped around the chair to the side of the table. "I want to try to stop this," she said, pressing both hands flat against the tabletop. "I need time to find Curran and prove that some of the Guild Masters have become . . . corrupt."

"Then what? You still are what you are. Your masters are still guilty of this act, and I still know what I know. What then, Dobbs?" Her eyes were wide, almost frightened now. "This much has already happened. My crew was endangered, and my husband has been arrested. It is too much to ask me to believe that nothing like this will ever be done again. Your people have power, Dobbs. They will use it. They have already used it."

Dobbs felt her own eyes begin to widen. Al Shei wasn't listening. She wouldn't see. She was going to . . . going to . . . Dobbs's throat clenched. She had no idea what Al Shei was going to do, and that filled her with fear.

Al Shei looked away. "I am right now remembering you saved The Farther Kingdom, and that you saved my crew when your masters told you not to. But I may not remember this for long." Her fists clenched and unclenched. "Especially if I cannot find other proof to clear Asil's reputation. If you cannot help me, help my family, I cannot protect you. You had better get off my ship."

Dobbs took a step back. She didn't mean it. She couldn't mean it. Al Shei's eyes had turned as hard as granite, and she stayed stock-still where she was.

Dobbs turned around and ran. She ran down the corridor. She pushed past Odel and nearly careened into Javerri in the airlock. Javerri exclaimed something that Dobbs couldn't understand, and she bolted out into the station. Through another hatchway was another set of stairs. Dobbs ran down them as fast as she could place her feet.

Al Shei watched Dobbs retreat from the conference room. Yerusha turned on her heel and followed the Fool a split second later. Al Shei's heart sank inside her. She wanted to call Dobbs back, but she knew she couldn't. Dobbs wouldn't help. Dobbs wouldn't do anything. Then, out of this was the only safe place for Dobbs to be, before Al Shei's trust was stretched any thinner, before the Guild was blasted wide open. If Yerusha wanted to get involved, that was her decision.

A rental pilot could get the *Pasadena* back to Earth if she didn't come back.

What, she thought wearily, *am I going to tell Lipinski about Dobbs?*

She shoved that thought to the background. Lipinski's reactions would have to take care of themselves. She had other things to worry about right now.

Using the tabletop boards, Al Shei opened a line to Port Oberon's flight schedulers. She requested to speak to Geraldo Taylor.

The view screen beside the intercom lit up to show Taylor's genial, heavily moustached face.

"Hello, Al Shei! How are you doing, *mi capitan*?"

"Not so well, Taylor," she admitted. "I've got bad news from home, and I've got to get back to Earth, fast."

The smile faded from Taylor's face. "Al Shei, you know how tight we have to run things here, especially on the Earth-bound flights."

Al Shei leaned forward. "Please, Taylor. My husband is in trouble, and I have got to get home." She had sent three separate fast-time calls to Bala house in the past five days, all her accounts could stand. Each time she'd gotten Uncle Ahmet. She'd spoken with him and her children, her sister and her grandmother, but never with Asil. Not once. He wasn't home was all anyone would say to her. There had been no messages from him. None. Why hadn't there been any messages? Her fear painted him in a Management Union security chamber being questioned again and again about things he knew nothing about.

Taylor ran one finger along his moustache and looked down at his boards. "Let me see if I've got any empty Earthbound slots at all . . ." His shoulders bobbed as he worked his boards. Then, he froze. When he looked up at Al Shei, his face was uneasy.

Al Shei felt her heart plummet. "What is it?"

"It's major, Al Shei. We've got a red flag on your ship." He glanced down again and read the directive off the screen. "Hold at port until Management Union escort arrives."

Very aware that Taylor was watching her, Al Shei kept her hands still and her head up. "Does it say what the flag is for?"

Taylor scanned his boards. "Somebody thinks Marcus Tully left some contraband aboard."

Oh, Merciful Allah! Why is this hitting now? Al Shei set her jaw. "Taylor . . ."

He held up both hands and shied back. "Do not even start to ask me, Al Shei. You've been impounded. I haven't got the authority to do anything about it, even if I wanted to."

Al Shei's resolve gave out. She rested her forehead against her hand.

"Look, Al Shei, nobody's accusing you of anything." There was a note of desperate consolation in Taylor's voice. "I'm sure as hell not. The M.U. ship is only two days out. They'll come in, pick up Tully and take you back home."

Al Shei raised her eyes. "Tully's here?"

Taylor nodded. "House arrest. Somebody bailed him out of the brig . . ."

Ah. That would be Uncle Ahmet, at Ruqaiyya's insistence. This was something else her family had neglected to tell her. "All right, Taylor." Al Shei tugged at her tunic sleeve. "Thanks for the information."

"Sorry it's all bad news, *mi capitan*," he said earnestly. "I promise you, next trip through will be smooth as smooth. I'll even buy the coffee."

She mustered a cheerful note for her voice. "I'll hold you to that." She closed the line and buried her face in her hands.

Two days! Two days before she could move, and then another five days before she would reach Earth. Seven whole days before she could reach Asil. Seven more days her children would have to face this disaster without her there. Seven days before she could do *anything*.

She lifted her head. "Intercom to Resit."

"Here," Resit's voice came back. "I'm about to guess that you've just learned what I've learned from this lovely official bulletin in my desk."

Al Shei brushed the tabletop with her palm. "Is there anything we can do about it?"

There was a pause. "I've got Incili running the options, but I don't think so. They've got us tightly clamped, especially since Tully appears to have done what he's accused of. If we try to get out of this, we become accessories."

"I was afraid you were going to say that." Al Shei stood up. "All right, I'll see you at prayer. Let me know if Incili comes up with anything before then. Intercom to close." She drummed her fingers on the table. "Intercom to Schyler. Did you get the lovely official bulletin, too?"

"I did." He sounded easily as tired as she felt.

"We'll need a crew briefing to inform everybody of the situation and their rights. Resit will represent everybody, but they can get independent counsel if they want to protest any restrictions on their movements." She hesitated. "Get it together, will you? In about half an hour."

"Aye, aye, Engine."

"Intercom to close." Al Shei levered herself out of the chair and cycled open the hatch. She kept her eyes fixed straight ahead as she crossed the corridor and opened the hatch to the stairway. She didn't want to see anybody right now. She just wanted to get to her cabin. She had to talk to Asil. She had to find out how he was. She had to do that now. She couldn't stand to wait anymore. She climbed to the berthing deck, barely hearing Schyler's general announcement about a mandatory briefing.

In her cabin, Al Shei locked the hatch and then activated her desk. She bit her lip as she opened her personal account. As she had been afraid of, there was not enough left in there to make a long fast-time call to Earth.

She wrote the commands for a link to the bank lines. She could have gotten Lipinski to do it, but she didn't want him to hear what was coming next. The link opened and her credit started draining away into it. "To Ahmet Tey, urgent delivery from Katmer Al Shei, will you open a fast-time to me aboard the *Pasadena* at Port Oberon?" She closed the link and sent the message on its way.

She looked down at the account display. She had less than three hours' pay left in there.

We'll make it up somehow, Beloved, she thought toward the place in her mind that held all her memories of her husband. *When all this is over.*

Somehow, Beloved, he answered in her mind. *We're a long way from finished with this, Katmer.*

A text message flashed across her memory board, catching her eye and yanking her out of her reverie.

INCOMING FAST-TIME FOR RECEIPT BY KATMER AL SHEI.

Al Shei wrote ACCEPT and added a period. The desk absorbed the command and lit up the view screen.

Uncle Ahmet, as dignified and immaculate as ever, sat calmly on his side of the screen.

"*Salam*, Katmer," he said solemnly. "I am glad you are back in the system safely."

Al Shei bit down on the first, caustic reply that rose to her mouth. "So am I, Uncle. I was hoping I might speak to my husband to hear how he and the children are doing under the stress."

Was it her imagination, or did Uncle Ahmet hesitate? "Muhammad and Vashti are well," he answered smoothly. "Your grandmother and I thought it best they be put in the care of your brother and sisters until you can return here. They have said that their only sorrow is that they they miss their mother. They are at their schools just now."

What Uncle Ahmet didn't say bit deeply into Al Shei. He didn't say "your grandmother, your husband, and I." He didn't say Asil had anything to do with the decision to send the children to her siblings.

"And where is Asil?" She resisted the temptation to crane her neck to try to see around the corners of the screen. "How is he? May I speak with him?"

There it was again. A split-second hesitation from her completely composed uncle. "Asil, I am sorry to say, is not here. This sad business has called him away from home just now."

Al Shei felt the heat of her anger rising. "Uncle Ahmet, is he in police custody?" *I will not be lied to! I will be told what is happening to my husband!*

"He is not in police custody." No hesitation. His eyes and voice remained completely steady. "But he is not here, Katmer. As soon as I speak with him, he will know of your concern. When will you be returning home?"

Behind her *hijab*, Al Shei steadied the trembling in her chin. "In seven days. We are delayed here at port because . . ." Al Shei hesitated herself. *No*, she decided. *No more covering.* "Marcus Tully is under suspicion of smuggling. The *Pasadena* has been impounded. We cannot leave until the Management Union ship comes to escort us."

Uncle Ahmet inclined his head once. "I was aware of that. Ruqaiyya wanted to go join her husband, an admirable if misguided desire. Divorce proceedings are being discussed." *By whom?* Al Shei wondered. Her fists wanted to clench.

"Uncle Ahmet, how is the case against Asil being prosecuted? Is there a trial date, or is the investigation still going on?" She leaned forward, pride forgotten. "Please, Uncle, tell me what is happening to my husband. I have some information here, evidence that will help, but my sources are not all that reliable . . ."

This time she saw it for sure; his eyes did flicker away from her, looking for answers elsewhere than her face. "Nothing has happened except that the accusations have been handed to the family." He focused on her again. "Those who have made this false statement will be confronted and made to answer for their lies." His voice almost broke then, and, for the first time, Al Shei sensed the tide of anger her uncle was holding back.

"Come home as quickly as you can, Katmer. Your children need you here. *Salam*."

With that, the screen went blank. Al Shei stared at the blank surface. "He who keeps silent, remains safe," she murmured. She gripped the hem of her tunic in both hands. *What is going on! What is going on!* Anger flared inside her, useless, helpless anger.

Asil was millions of miles away, behind her silent, lying uncle and a cage of bureaucratic procedures. She could do nothing, nothing to reach him. He was trapped and she was trapped and they couldn't even speak to each other.

Tears burned in her eyes. *Not now. Not now!* She tightened her fists, forcing tears and fury back down into the darkest places in her soul. *You have your crew to care for, and your ship to see to. You have to find a way out of this mess and back home to Asil. Then you can cry. Then you can scream.*

"Allah witness what I say," she whispered to the backs of her fists and her empty cabin. "I *will* make those who have done this pay until they are bled dry!"

She loosened her fists and smoothed her tunic down. Standing straight and proud, she walked out of her cabin and started toward the conference room.

The force of her oath seemed to follow right behind her.

"Dobbs!"

The sound of her name brought her skidding to a halt on the landing. She almost overbalanced and had to clutch at the railing to keep her feet.

Yerusha pounded down the stairs behind her.

Dobbs stared at her as she came to a halt on the next stair up.

"I'm sorry," Yerusha said, dragging in a long breath. "That was a bad call and it was mine. I'm really sorry."

Dobbs forced herself to speak. "You couldn't have known."

"I could've guessed." Yerusha shook her head. "It's okay. We've got one option left. Come on." She started down the stairs, beckoning Dobbs to follow.

Dobbs's mind was filled to bursting with thousands of contradictory thoughts. She needed to clear it, but she didn't seem to have the faculties for the job. Following Yerusha was a simple action. She could do this much, even while her internal world was tying itself into knots.

Yerusha trotted down three levels and stepped through a hatchway into a crowded corridor. Dobbs followed her while she zigzagged between the crowds to an IBN outlet. She found an open privacy booth and motioned Dobbs to squeeze inside beside her. She jacked her pen into the lock. Once it verified her identity and account balances, the door slid shut. Yerusha sat in the one chair, and Dobbs shuffled into the little space left behind it.

"What are you doing?" Dobbs asked as Yerusha began flicking through the menus to open a line.

"What we should have done in the first place." Yerusha did not turn around. She kept her eyes locked on the desktop in front of her, watching her hands run through the commands. "My stock is pretty high with some of the crew at The Gate. I'm calling that tech, Kagan, and I'm going to get him to download the records of exactly what happened on The Farther Kingdom. With a few data-pointers, we can have the whole thing organized enough to transmit."

"Transmit?" Dobbs felt the blood drain out of her cheeks. "Where to?"

Yerusha finally glanced behind her. "Everywhere. We're going to broadcast who you are and what you did."

"You can't!" Dobbs blurted the words out. "You were standing there when I told Al Shei . . ."

"Dobbs, we've got it on record that you saved an entire planet. If we make this public, no single world will be able to make a move. You'll be heroes. Free Home Titania won't listen to me, but someone in one of the other Free Homes will pick up on the broadcast. They'll give your people sanctuary. We can get this out in the open, and no one can stop us." Her eyes were beginning to shine. "This is your chance, Dobbs. We send out the record of what happened on The Farther Kingdom, and Settled Space will see your kind are not dangerous, that you're not separate from us at all, that you've saved us once and you'll be able to do it again."

"They'll destroy us!" Dobbs's feet backed her away from Yerusha, away from her bright eyes and the eager tone in her voice. "You can't do this to us!" Her fingers scabbled for the catch on the door. It slid back, and she ran out into the main chamber.

They'll destroy you even faster than the Guild will.

It wasn't true. It wasn't true. Yerusha just didn't understand. She'd go back and explain. Al Shei was angry, but she wasn't murderous. She'd let Dobbs go, hadn't she? That was all the mercy Al Shei could offer right now. All Dobbs had to do was wait awhile and go back. That was all. Al Shei would let her back in. Yerusha would understand. Then she could . . . she could . . .

She remembered Al Shei's granite eyes. She remembered Lipinski's fear when she had told him she didn't know where Flemming was, and Havelock's face as he locked her into the hospital room. She remembered how eager Yerusha was to spread the news.

She bumped into somebody in the stairwell and nearly fell over. Stumbling and skidding on the stair treads, she kept on going.

Her world was gone. Everything she trusted and loved and depended on, and it had all turned away from her.

No. No. That isn't it. What about Cohen? I can still go into the net, call Cohen and . . .

Except the Guild was watching the net, and Cohen wasn't the only one who could follow a flight path. The Guild might be here already, waiting for her. They might be on their way to the *Pasadena* right now.

Her foot shot out from under her and she landed hard on the stairs. Her breath went out in a loud "whoof!" and pain bit into her back and neck. After blinking hard at the ceiling, Dobbs grabbed the railing and hauled herself into a sitting position, but she didn't get up. She sat there, one hand on the railing and the other cradling her forehead.

There was nowhere to go. The Guild wanted to kill her. The *Pasadena* would never admit her again. Yerusha wanted to use her to prove the Freers had been right all along. There was nowhere to go. Everyone had thrown her out.

Except Curran. Curran had offered her a place to stay. Curran could stop Yerusha's insane plan. He talked about freedom, a chance to be who she was. Who was she? Now that she wasn't a Fool, she wasn't anything. She wasn't even really a refugee from Kerensk. What was left of Evelyn Dobbs now that she didn't have anything to cover herself up with?

The confrontation must come. We should welcome it, Dobbs, because only after it's over will we be able to make peace with them.

You have been lying to us for two hundred years! And now you are asking me to trust you?

Your body is going to be taken apart for the usable material, and you're not going to be allowed to leave before they do it.

We can get this out in the open, and no one can stop us.

You don't have to go through this. You don't have to be humiliated in front of your employers, you don't have to face whatever the Guild is planning for you. Let me get you out of there.

Dobbs gripped the necklace around her throat.

No. No. There's got to be something else I can do.

What? she asked herself harshly. *What else are you going to do, Dobbs? Run away with Lipinski, maybe go back to Kerensk and set up house? Go on the gossip services after Yerusha's little broadcast and talk about out-of-body experiences? The Guild has shut you out! Al Shei's just kicked you out. What are you going to do? Huh?*

What are you going to do?

She hauled on the necklace. The simulated jewels bit painfully into the back of her neck before the catch gave and the chain snapped free. She stared at the red-and-gold sparkle of it for a long moment before she tossed it onto the stairs. She trotted down to the next hatchway and walked out into the corridor without looking back.

The corridor was full to the brim with people, as Oberon's corridors always were. Dobbs desperately wanted to break into a run. The station was full of eyes and she did not want to be seen. Her throat kept swallowing, trying to feel the slight rub of her chain of office, which was not there. Would never be there again. She was not a Fool, but she would never be anything else.

She found a map on one curving wall and saw she'd blundered into one of the business modules. There was a bank outlet only a dozen yards down the corridor she was in. She threaded her way through the crowd. No one looked at her. That was good. It was good that nobody noticed one tiny, lost woman with her sore throat and eyes that were red from wanting to cry.

The bank outlet was almost full. Dobbs threaded her way between the desks and voices until she found an empty rental desk right next to the back wall. She dropped into the chair and pulled out her pen. That and her box she had at least kept with her. She wrote DANE PREPAID across the desk's main board.

After an agonized second, the desk came to life and a text message printed itself on the active top.

DOBBS, WE'VE BLOCKED YOUR PEN'S CODE FROM THE GUILD SPIES. GO TO THE OTHELLO COFFEEHOUSE. I'LL MEET YOU THERE.

CURRAN

That was all there was. The desk shut itself down. Dobbs stared for a moment at the blank surface, then she got to her feet and went back into the corridor.

Things were becoming increasingly unreal. She felt as if she'd just had a dose of juice and her body was no longer her own. Some other force was making the legs move and turning the gaze so that she could avoid the crowds of Human Beings and make her way to the elevators. She watched as if from outside as her body traveled up ten levels and over three modules to the Desdemona Hotel and the coffee shop.

She found an empty table and sat. There was something written on the surface. Probably an inquiry for her order. She couldn't be sure. Her eyes wouldn't focus. There were noises and moving shapes around her, but she couldn't separate them out into distinct objects. She was only really aware of one thing. This was where she had juggled scarves for Al Shei and formulated her resolve to find out what was really going on aboard the *Pasadena*.

And now I know, she thought, and it felt as if something inside her would tear in two.

As Dobbs fled the privacy booth, Yerusha started to her feet, but she didn't follow the Fool. Dobbs was badly shaken. Of course she was. Yerusha was shaken. The whole of Settled Space would be shaken before this was done.

She sat back down and looked at the half-completed command on the memory board. Dobbs's horrified shout seemed to echo around the booth.

You know, she's probably right. You probably don't understand. Crash and burn, she barely understood living humans, how was she supposed to understand the ones who had returned? She remembered Dobbs's vigorous denunciation of the idea that sentient AIs were reincarnated humans. She shook her head. Metaphysics could wait for later. There were solid problems to be worked out.

Starting with what I should do now. She tapped her pen against the edge of the board. The idea of going public had just frightened Dobbs into running for the lower decks. Should she go find Dobbs and try to talk her out of her panic? Or should she just go ahead and place the call, trusting to Dobbs's basic stability to get her through once the gears were grinding?

She remembered how well trusting Al Shei's basic nature had gone and felt her lips press together into a thin, straight line.

She wiped the request for an open line and instead filtered through the credit for a single-shot fast-time message to Peter Kagan at The Gate.

"Kagan," she wrote. "Imperative that we communicate in security as soon as possible. Will authorize payment for your fast-time connection to me." She signed her name, and picked the SEND command off the menu. Then she put in a request to the station AI that she be notified as soon as the fast-time came through, wherever she was.

Fast-time or not, it's going to take the kid awhile to get clear. Yerusha sent a copy of the receipt to her personal files and shut the desk down. Hopefully, by then, she would have Dobbs calmed down.

She wrote a locate request on the board, and waited for the station to process it.

The text on the memory board shifted. EVELYN DOBBS BOARDED THE SHUTTLE *FIFTH DAY* WITHOUT REGISTERING A FINAL DESTINATION. THAT SHUTTLE HAS NOW DEPARTED PORT OBERON.

Yerusha's eyes bulged in their sockets. She'd left the station? Already? Crash and burn! Why hadn't she said something? Why hadn't she trusted, waited . . .

Why didn't I go after her right away? Why'd I sit here so sure I was doing the right thing for her? What did I think I was going to prove?

Same thing she thought she'd prove with Holden, and with Foster. That Jemina Yerusha was right. That she knew what she was doing. That everything would be all right if everyone would just stop what they were doing and *listen.*

Ashes, ashes, ashes. She wiped her face with her palm. *Now what am I going to do?*

She stared at the desktop for another moment before shutting it down. *Whatever it is, I can't do it here.*

She slid the door open, stepped out without really watching where she was going, and found a human chest smack in front of her. She pulled up short and saw it was Schyler, who was also backing up.

"Sorry," he pulled both hands out of his pockets. "I was . . . waiting for you to come out."

"Did you see where Dobbs went?" she asked, trying to regain some dignity before getting down to the more important question of what Schyler was doing here. It was possible Al Shei had sent him to bring her back. It was possible he had come of his own volition. It was also possible she was about to be officially fired.

"No, I didn't see Dobbs at all." Schyler dug his hands back into his pockets. "Was she here, too?"

"Yeah, for a little while." *Before I almost scared the life out of her.* Yerusha drew a deep breath and tried to pull herself together. "Did you want me for something, Watch?"

"Yes." Schyler extracted one hand and ran it through his hair. "I wanted to find out if you knew what was going on around here."

Yerusha was so at a loss for words she couldn't even open her mouth.

"She won't talk to me!" Schyler jammed his fist back into his pocket so hard, she thought the cloth was going to tear. It didn't take much guessing to work out that "she" was Al Shei. "I've been with her ten years, and now when it's as bad as it's ever been, she stops talking to me! How can I help her, how can I run that god-blasted-and-twisted ship for her, if she won't tell me what's going on!" He had his gaze fixed on the far wall, but Yerusha was certain he was seeing the *Pasadena* and Al Shei. "Oh, she told me about The Farther Kingdom and Dobbs's part in all that, but something else happened after we left the Fool's Guild. Something major. And now we've been impounded, we've got an all-hands crew meeting in less than half an hour, and she tells me you might not be there and Dobbs definitely won't be there, but she won't say why!

"I'm supposed to tell our crew what's going on. I'm supposed to know."

He shook his head and looked directly at her again. His face told of the loss and betrayal inside him even more clearly than his voice did. Yerusha found herself wondering how she could have missed it. If the *Pasadena* was home to Schyler, Al Shei was his bedrock. She had shown him how the world worked, given him a place to stay and a purpose to live for. A few random thoughts dropped into place. He was probably the reason Al Shei's partnership with Tully had lasted. Where she couldn't trust Tully to take care of the ship and himself, she could trust Schyler.

And now she had turned away from him. Yerusha felt a surge of anger toward Al Shei. Fractured Ninja Woman, what did she think she was doing?

Keeping him safe. Not spreading panic. Trying to figure out what to do, answered a part of herself she didn't know existed. Yerusha wondered when she'd started liking Al Shei.

Probably about the same time you started really liking Schyler. Now the question was, which one of them was she going to let down?

She looked at Schyler and saw the bewilderment mixed with anger plain on his face and remembered when she'd had the same look; as the Senior Guard hauled her away from Holden's body and told her she was under arrest. They hadn't liked it, they hadn't believed her guilty of much, but they'd done it anyway, and she couldn't believe they were doing it.

"Yes, I do know what's going on," she said quietly. "But you're going to want to sit down before I tell you."

"Evelyn?"

Dobbs's eyes lifted reflexively. A middle-aged man stood beside the table. His wavy hair had gone grey, but he held his broad shoulders straight underneath his burgundy coveralls. His jet-black eyes were calm, and there was a concerned expression on his light brown face.

"I'm Theodore Curran." He extended his hand. "Come on. You probably shouldn't stay out here in plain sight."

She stared at his hand. The fingers were square-tipped, and the lines of the palm were deeply etched.

"I know this is hard," he said. "But you need to come with me now. I'll answer all your questions. I promise. Come on." He took her hand and raised her out of her seat.

Walking beside him through the café's heavy traffic shook off some of the stupor that had laid hold of her. Dobbs was able to see through the fog filling her mind to where her pent-up questions waited.

Begin at the beginning, she thought whimsically. "Where are we going?"

"Ah, good." Curran let go of her hand. "You are with me." He skirted the lobby fountain. "And you'll see where we're going in just a few minutes."

Not a very good start at answering. Then she remembered the security cameras. Normally, the fact that the station was monitored was not something that intruded on her conscious thought. Now, though, it sent a chill of fear through her. Anything the cameras recorded and stored, the Guild could find. Guild Master Havelock might already know where she was. Yerusha could put out a request to find her at any time.

Her stride faltered, partly from fear of discovery, partly because of who she found herself so afraid of.

Curran gave her a concerned glance. "They won't find you where we're going, Dobbs. Just a few minutes more and you'll see exactly what I mean."

Dobbs followed him the rest of the way across the lobby. *I've burned all the other bridges,* she thought, trying to gather her nerves again. *A fool's bolt is soon shot,* she added before she could stop herself.

Somehow, though, being able to think in anything like a straight line gave her courage. Curran led her through the teaming corridors to the elevator bundle. He passed the lifts by, though, and took the stairs instead. Dobbs counted that they passed thirty levels on their way down. At last, they came to a bulkhead with a hatchway that had a red security light on its surface. Curran palmed the reader. After a moment, the hatch hissed open. On the other side was a small, green-matted foyer with another sealed hatchway in the far wall. Dobbs stepped across the threshold, puzzled. All station modules had airlocks for their main entrance and exit hatches, but, while the can was being occupied, both halves of the airlock usually opened together.

Curran was smiling at her. "We're a little fussy about security here," he said, as if he had read her mind. "Welcome home, Evelyn Dobbs."

He palmed the reader on the far wall and the hatch cycled open.

At first, the other side looked like just a normal corridor. Then, she noticed the cameras at three-foot intervals and the retracted arms under each one. A multilimbed drone about the size of a serving cart glided along a grooved track and disappeared inside a hatchway. Dobbs looked down and saw only a thin strip of the normal Velcro carpeting down the middle of the corridor. The floor on both sides had grooves in it, presumably for more carts. She glanced up. There were identical tracks in the ceiling. Looking at it all, she realized there was no portion of the chamber that could not be reached by some kind of machinery.

This can isn't for Human traffic, she thought with a kind of wonder. *This is for us.*

She looked up at Curran. He had his gaze fixed on her. "Home?" she asked.

Curran nodded. "This is my home, and home to those who agree with my plans. We designed it so we could work it in our natural state from inside the networks." His face was relaxed now, and he seemed to smile easily. "We don't spend much time in bodies, Dobbs. We prefer to live as we were born to."

Dobbs wasn't sure which astounded her more, Curran's easy declarations, or the fact that he had established his headquarters in one of the busiest stations in the Solar System.

In the corridor, another hatch cycled open and a drone shot

out. It glided around the curve toward them and through the hatch in the center. Dobbs caught a glimpse of the elevator shaft.

"But," she stammered. "The Landlords must know you're here. How . . ."

"It's Business Module 56 in the Landlords' records. A private research facility, listed as duly registered, paid for, and inspected every six months." Curran's grin broadened. "We had a nasty few minutes when they were considering requiring hard-copy inspection reports to be issued." He gazed proudly around him. "We've even got a permit on record allowing us to arm our own security personnel."

"You faked the records?" Dobbs swept her hand out. "On a whole can?"

"We are faking the records." Curran waggled a finger at her. "It's a constant job. Takes some of our best talents, but we have to make sure the station accounts can explain our breathables and generator use." He smiled briefly. "I considered replacing the station AI with one of our own talents, but I didn't want to tie anybody down to servicing that morass out there. We can do what we have to in shifts, with a little careful scheduling." He saw the expression of amazement on Dobbs's face and chuckled. "And this is just . . ."

"Dobbs!"

Dobbs's head yanked itself around. A big-boned woman strode down the corridor. She had soot black hair braided into a coil on top of her head. The cordlike muscles of her forearms showed underneath her translucent brown skin. Grey eyes were set deeply in her round face.

Dobbs's forehead wrinkled. This was a stranger.

"You made it!" The woman clapped Dobbs on the shoulder and gave her a playful shake. "And not a moment too soon. From the look in your eyes, you've been out on your own limb for too long."

Dobbs glanced from Curran to the stranger. "I'm sorry, do I know you?"

She laughed, a full-throated sound. "Not looking like this, you don't. The body you saw me in was grey-haired, brown-eyed and didn't weigh an ounce more than yours does." Her eyes sparkled. "And had a double-damn of a bad time drilling you in the four basic principles of humor."

Dobbs froze and she knew there was a look of utter shock on her face, but she couldn't wipe it away.

The woman just took a half step back and grinned at her.

After what seemed like an hour, Dobbs forced her tongue to move. "Verence?"

The woman nodded. "Hello, Dobbs."

Dobbs reached out a hand, tentatively, as if she expected the woman to vanish if she touched her. But Verence just reached out her own hand and grasped Dobbs's. Dobbs stood there, feeling the warmth of her flesh and the strength of her grip.

"They said you'd died. Dissipated. Cohen told me." She couldn't seem to think in anything more than fragments. Verence. Verence was not dead. Verence was standing in front of her.

"Well, they had to say something, didn't they?" She let Dobbs go and stuck her hands in her pockets. The gesture reminded Dobbs sharply of Schyler. "They couldn't very well tell Cohen, or you, that they'd lost me." She winked. "I did have to leave my old body behind, but I'm finding this one quite comfortable." Dobbs opened her mouth, but Verence held up her hand. "I'm on reconnaissance duty in the main station. I'll be back in the morning, Dobbs. We'll talk then, all right?"

"All right." Dobbs felt her knees beginning to shake. This was too wonderful. It was also too much to believe.

Verence gave her shoulder a squeeze. She nodded at Curran as she slipped between him and Dobbs and headed out the hatchway.

The hatch cycled shut. Dobbs got control of at least some of her thoughts again. "Why didn't you tell me she was here?" she demanded.

Curran's smile was gentle. "She wanted me to. She wanted to be the one to contact you, but I wanted to be sure that this was your decision. I wanted you to be sure." He touched her shoulder, right where the warmth from Verence's hand still lingered. "And if you'd just been following your old sponsor, the one who pulled you out of Kerensk, you might not have been so sure."

Dobbs swallowed hard. "No. I guess not." She rubbed her forehead. "It's just . . . it's . . ."

"It's a lot all at once." Curran stepped up to an inner hatchway, and it cycled open automatically. Palm readers were not much good when most of what was using the hatchways was mechanical, Dobbs guessed. "Come on. I'll take you up to the berthing level. You need a rest."

The elevator shaft was as strange as the corridor. The lift was little more than a loosely made cage of supports for cables, cameras, and waldos. A stairway did spiral up the sides of the shaft, but instead of railings, it had grooved ramps on either side, presumably for the drones.

As she took her place beside Curran on the elevator platform, she realized what else was missing. There were no memory boards anywhere.

"Berthing deck," said Curran, and the elevator began to rise.

Dobbs faced him. There was one more thing she had to know. Just one. "What exactly was going on aboard the *Pasadena*?"

"An experiment, Dobbs. A successful experiment." His eyes gazed at the pipe-lined walls as they rose. "You see, the theory has long been that an AI becomes sentient when it develops an analog for the Human survival instinct. Suddenly, for some reason, it becomes self-aware enough to realize it's in a CPU with an off switch. It doesn't want to be turned off. It wants to go on functioning, doing whatever it is it was designed to do."

Dobbs nodded. *Work! Think! Do!* Flemming had shouted. She had known exactly how it felt.

"So, what the newborns, what we, do is try to run away from the off switch," Curran went on. "Going with that premise, I theorized that if you could create the conditions under which an AI would become aware that it was in danger from the outside and that it needed to protect itself, you could predictably generate independent intelligence." He took hold of one of the cage's side struts and his gaze grew distant. "We still wouldn't know exactly which qualities and processes make us different from the nonsentient AIs, but if we can create our own kind predictably, we stand a much better chance of teasing them out. That's when we'll be truly free."

Curran shook himself and focused on Dobbs again. "So, I intercepted Dr. Dane, who had hired Marcus Tully to smuggle a truly nasty first strike virus out of the Toric security sector. I impersonated Dane over the lines with Tully and bribed him to make sure the virus stayed on the *Pasadena*. He had a small attack of conscience and almost ruined everything, but, fortunately, your watch commander stopped him. Then, I met with the *Pasadena*'s lawyer and got a contract to carry some medical data that Dane had been planning on sending along with a message to his cohorts that the virus they'd commissioned was waiting at Port Oberon." He paused. "You know, in stopping this little transaction, we probably saved The Farther Kingdom from a religious war.

"At any rate, instead of pure bio-data, I had put an artificial intelligence under a data shell. It had some highly experimental architecture, as I was building it specifically to get out of control as soon as possible." The elevator stopped at a short landing that led to yet another hatch. The elevator door swung open and the stair ramps followed suit, leaving a clear path for them to reach the hatchway that opened in front of them like an invitation. "And I set the virus to deliberately attack the AI. The *Pasadena* was the perfect place for my experiment. Since the ship doesn't have an AI of its own, there was no risk that the virus would attack the wrong set of programs and destroy the ship before the AI could be born." The new corridor matched the one into which she had first walked. Except for Curran's, there were no voices anywhere. The only sounds were the vague hums and hisses of the machinery. "My hope was the AI would develop its self-preservation instinct, and then the rest of the sentient processes would blossom. I was right." He stopped in front of one of the outer hatches. "Flemming was born aboard the *Pasadena*. I think it came into being somewhere between the time it destroyed the virus and the time it realized it was about to be forcibly removed from its environment." The hatch cycled open.

"You scared it into being?" The other side of the hatch was a wedge-shaped cabin, almost a twin to the one she'd occupied on the *Pasadena*. The difference was the floor full of grooves and the waldos retracted against the walls.

"I suppose I did." Curran stood back and let Dobbs walk into the room. The bunk was unfolded and Dobbs sat down.

She looked up at Curran. "Have you ever realized fear is our way of defining life?"

Curran smiled down at her. "I'm not sure I know what you mean."

"I mean"—she waved her hand aimlessly—"at Guild Hall, they told us that the first and last state of a human being is fear, that they'll always return to it in the face of the unknown. And the way we find one of our own kind is by looking for that same kind of fear. What if . . ." She stared past Curran's shoulder at the wall. "What if there's one of us out there who never panicked? Could there be somebody who just came to life quietly and went their own way without fighting off anybody?"

Curran chuckled kindly. "It's a lovely idea, Evelyn. But if they do exist, they're keeping very quiet. I've been in the net on and off for two hundred years, and I've never met them."

"Oh well." Dobbs gave one of her show-off shrugs.

Curran took her hand. "You're tired, you're upset, and more than a little frightened yourself, Dobbs. Try to get some sleep, okay? We'll start settling you in in the morning. Verence will be back then to give you the grand tour. If you need anything, anybody to talk to, anything at all, the intercom functions like the ones you're used to. Give a call, and the night shift'll take care of you."

"Thanks." Exhaustion settled over her like a woolen blanket even as she said it. Her temporary clarity of thought was beginning to fade. A large part of her mind wanted to curl up and just not have anything new to get used to for a while.

He gave her hand another squeeze. "We are glad you're here." He looked at her hand in his. "I'm going to tell you something that is going to sound like an old Fool's overdramatization. Flemming is my firstborn son, Evelyn. I am his father, figuratively speaking. And, in a lot of ways, by bringing him safely out of The Farther Kingdom, you became his mother." He looked her in the eyes, and she thought she saw a touch of shyness there. "We can have children now, Dobbs. All of us. We don't have to depend on spontaneous generation. I owe you a great deal."

She drew her hand away. It was too much. She wasn't ready to take praise for what she'd done yet. Besides, he didn't know everything she'd done. "I told Yerusha and Al Shei about us," she said. "What the Fools really are. Al Shei threw me off the ship. Yerusha . . . she wants to broadcast that, along with what happened on The Farther Kingdom."

Curran froze in place for a moment. Then he blew out a long sigh. "I wish you hadn't done that, Dobbs. I'm not worried at all about Al Shei. She'll be occupied by other concerns for quite some time. But the Freer . . ." His voice trailed off into silence for a moment. "Well, don't worry about her either. I'll send a couple of our talents across to rework The Gate's records. If she's managed to get anything downloaded to Port Oberon, we'll take care of that on this end." His smile was full of genuine reassurance. "Good night, Dobbs."

He left her there, sitting on a bed that was a match for almost every one she'd ever slept in, nursing her weariness and a bizarre kind of restlessness that she couldn't put a name to. She replayed what he had just said to her, and kept seeing Lipinski hunched over his boards, his eyes filled with eagerness as he realized he could paralyze the invader in his systems. Try as she might, she couldn't make the picture go away, but she couldn't make herself feel angry at the Houston either. She missed him. She missed his tentative attempts to get closer to her. She didn't want to think about why that was.

In the end, she stripped off her clothes, left them in a pile on the chair, and dived under the covers. Oblivion came with merciful speed.

Chapter Twelve

BODIES

The crew filtered out of the conference room in absolute silence. Yerusha couldn't blame them for being stunned. They were a secure bunch. *Pasadena* was not a trouble ship. People crewed her because they wanted work, not adventure. All that had changed in the space of a few days. It was a whole new world to get used to, and it was a lot less pleasant than the old one. Even Al Shei had stomped out without saying anything. What was going on inside her head, well, she was leaving that as an exercise for the mind reader.

Yerusha looked across the table to Schyler, who was the only person left. He hadn't moved since he dismissed the meeting. He still stood there with both hands planted on the table, watching the hatchway, which had cycled shut. His face was . . . stoic. He'd worn the same expression the whole time she was explaining to him about the real identity of Dobbs and the Fool's Guild and about how Al Shei had responded to the same news. She didn't want to begin to guess how much he was covering up.

"You going to call Al Shei on this?" Yerusha asked quietly.

"I'm going to have to." He shook his head and straightened up. "She's not going to volunteer anything, that's for double-damn sure. I just wish . . ."

"Intercom to Yerusha," Odel's voice cut across Schyler's. "We've got a request for funds to open a fast-time line down here. Want it routed up to your cabin?"

Yerusha started. Kagan had finally gotten through. She'd almost forgotten she'd sent the fast-time to him.

"Yeah. I'll head straight there. Intercom to close."

Schyler's eyebrows were raised.

"That's the comm-tech from The Gate. I was going to get a dump of the records from when Dobbs was charging around in their network." She stood up. "I don't know what I'm going to do now."

"Get those records," Schyler told her. "Sooner or later we're going to have to prove all this. It'll be a lot easier if we've got witnessed stacks to pull the evidence from."

"Good point." Yerusha cycled the hatch back. "Want to watch?"

"Only sort of." He followed her into the corridor and back to her cabin. The request for credit transfer was glowing on her desk boards when they got there. Yerusha sat in the desk chair, pulled out her pen, and opened her account. The line accepted the transfer and the text cleared. In the same second, the view screen lit up.

Wherever Kagan was, it was barely lit. His face was mostly shadows, and the background around him was nothing but undefined blobs of shadow.

Yerusha sighed at the melodrama. *I bet he opens with "I can't talk long."*

"I can't talk long," said Kagan, right on cue. "What do you want?"

She and Schyler exchanged a look that said *kids.*

"I need a download of the records from the time your system . . ." *why try to be subtle,* "went insane. We've run down a possible cause but we need more proof."

Kagan shifted his weight. She could just barely see his eyes flicker back and forth. *Put some lights on, kid, or learn to make your covert calls when you're not on shift!*

"I don't think I can do that, Yerusha."

"Why not?" Yerusha moved her hand out of sight of the camera, so he wouldn't see her drumming her fingers on the desktop. "The data's too bulky? Or is Trustee watching the lines?"

"The records aren't there."

Yerusha froze. She had to replay Kagan's sentence a couple of times in her head before she could decide that she'd really heard what he said. She glanced up at Schyler. He was doing the same thing.

"We're trying to figure out what happened," Kagan went on. "Maidai's got no record of crashing, or being removed from our network, or of anything having happened other than some widespread connection glitches. We've traced some vague leads back to New Medina Hospital. All they show is that we might have had a viral infection of the system, but there's nothing definite."

Yerusha swallowed hard. Schyler's cheeks had gone pale. He touched her shoulder and mouthed "backups."

Yerusha nodded.

"What about the backups?" she asked Kagan. "You must have made some dumps onto tape. Can you access those and send them?"

"Right," Kagan's voice brightened. "The backups. Give me ten seconds." The shadows near the bottom of the screen shifted as he got out his pen and began writing orders. She touched her pen to the MUTE button.

"They beat us to it," she breathed. "They knew we'd be coming after The Gate's records."

"Not necessarily." Schyler frowned at the screen. "They might just be covering their tracks. It'd make sense for either the Guild, or Curran's side. After all, neither side knows that we know about them."

"Unless they got ahold of Dobbs and made her talk," Yerusha pointed out. A chill sank into her blood as she said it. "We don't know where she really is. That departure announcement I saw could have been a fake."

Schyler froze dead still.

Her desk beeped. Kagan was trying to say something. Yerusha touched the MUTE command again.

". . . on its way to you . . ."

"Shut it down!" shouted Schyler. "Get the backups off-line!"

"Wha . . . what?" sputtered Kagan. "Yerusha, who's with you?"

Schyler leaned into the camera's sight. "Get those fractured records off-line right now!"

"On it." Kagan's voice was bewildered, but his hands moved. "All right, they're off. There's about four hours in transit to you anyway, do you want me to . . ."

"Never mind." Schyler's shoulders slumped. "It's probably too late."

Yerusha stared at him in confusion. She had a feeling Kagan was doing the same.

"You should be getting the first of it in about three minutes," Kagan said. "I've set everything on auto. I've got to get going . . ."

Or somebody'll notice you're gone. Kid, you have got to get your mama to teach you more about timing.

"Or somebody'll notice I'm gone. Good luck, Yerusha."

"Good luck, Kagan." Yerusha watched Schyler collapse onto the bunk. "I owe you."

She cut the video, but kept the line open. She swiveled the chair so she could face Schyler. "What?"

"Think about it," he said bitterly. "They may not have even needed Dobbs. They must be paranoid about their own security, or they wouldn't have stayed hidden as long as they have. If you were an AI hiding in the network and you wanted to stay hidden, and you knew the *Pasadena* had gotten caught in an extremely delicate situation that involved you, what would you do?"

Slowly, the ideas began to surface in Yerusha's consciousness. "I'd monitor the lines to see what kind of communications were coming out of the *Pasadena*, just in case they'd made some dangerous guesses."

Schyler nodded. "And when those hard-medium backups got connected to the network you'd go right in there and make sure they were doctored to match the on-line records, which you'd already gotten to."

"We can't even be sure that we really got to Kagan." Her fingers clutched her pen. "That could have been an AI faking the entire thing. That might be why we couldn't see his face so well."

"It could have been," Schyler agreed. "The one thing we can be sure of is that nothing we get from that transmission is going to be of any use at all."

They looked into each other's eyes. "What do we do?" asked Yerusha.

"I don't know," said Schyler quietly. "God help me, I don't know."

Dobbs awoke to the sound of her name and utter confusion. She was alone in a bare, strange cabin. A little at a time, memory of the previous day squeezed through the remnants of her dreams.

"Verence?" She blinked hard and stared around her. The cabin really was empty.

"In here." Dobbs tracked the voice to the intercom. "How are you feeling?"

She gathered the covers up around her chest. "Better," she said with as much certainty as she could muster. "I'm a bit hungry, though. I could use some breakfast."

"I can show you a better way to recharge, if you'll let me."

"Better than breakfast?" Dobbs felt her forehead wrinkle. "If this is a joke, Verence, I don't get it."

"No joke," said Verence, but Dobbs was sure there was a hint of a smile in her voice. "But you're going to need to trust me."

Dobbs took a deep breath. "Well, I've gone this far. It doesn't make sense to hold back now."

"That's the spirit." Now Verence's voice held ringing approval. "Get your transceiver."

Dobbs snagged her trousers from the pile on the chair and pulled her transceiver out of the box in her pocket. "Got it."

"All right, lie back."

Dobbs obeyed. When she was flat on her back, a panel slid up in the wall above the bed and a forest of waldos extended themselves from the walls. Dobbs forced herself to lie still against the momentary panic that seized her at the sight of the ceramic arms, all of them festooned with colored cables and clear tubes, lowering toward her body. Then she spotted the whole series of sensor pads, an oxygen mask and respirator unit, a hypodermic syringe, as well as a hypospray, and, one waldo equipped with nothing but an empty socket.

It was a medical array. She had been under similar setups in the Guild Hall, but never in a private cabin.

"Luxury accommodations," she said, a little nervously.

"Not here," said Verence. "We all have one. Put your transceiver in here." The socketed waldo extended itself. Dobbs reached up and stuck the transceiver in place. It fit snugly. There was a jack for the cable in the arm's elbow joint. As soon as she had it connected, the waldo raised itself out of her reach.

"Good. Now, push back the blanket and open your implant, Dobbs. I'm going to bring you into the network."

"Yeah, but will you respect me in the morning?" Dobbs peeled back the patch over her implant and kicked the coverlet away.

"Close your eyes and think of England," replied Verence. One at a time, the sensor arms lowered their patches against Dobbs's skin—her temples, her breast, wrists, and ankles. The hypo arm descended gracefully toward her neck. She lost sight of the transceiver arm, but after a moment, she felt a slight tickle and jostle behind her ear. She felt, rather than heard, the transceiver jack in.

"Here we go." The hypospray released its dose with a hiss, and Dobbs fell through the uncomfortable, but familiar, sensations of her body vanishing.

She emerged into a roomy network and beside her was Verence. There was no mistaking her now. Dobbs knew all Verence's rhythms and pitches. This was her sponsor whom she had missed and mourned. She was alive, whole and well. For the first time in a long time, Dobbs felt a wave of pure happiness wash through her.

"All right, you win, I'm not hungry now." Dobbs shook herself. The place felt strange. She knew there were multiple packets of data passing within easy reach, but it felt as though they had been channeled deliberately away from herself and Verence, as if this space had been set up specifically to make room for them. In the next second, Dobbs realized that might very well be true. "But I'm going to be ravenous when I get back into my body again. How long did you give me?"

"As long as you want. Reach here." Verence dipped into the nearby datastream.

Dobbs, after a moment's hesitation, copied her movement. She pushed through packets of sensor data. She touched one of the packets. It was information from the medical array that had charge of her body.

"Go ahead, read it," said Verence. "If it's not yours, whose is it?"

Dobbs absorbed the sensor data: blood pressure, respiration, heart rate, and alpha-wave activity. She dug into the baseline statistics and found all of the readouts were well within normal parameters. The anesthetic flow was steady and the cartridges would not have to be refilled for another seventy-six hours. The blood sugar was low and the electrolytes were out of balance. Recommendation was for a course of intravenous treatments to restore conditions to optimum.

A quick stretch let her touch the command sequences between the purely informational packets. She filtered through them to find the one that matched the sensor code. One twist and a push and the command sequence was in motion. The camera told her that an additional arm lowered over the bed and a syringe inserted itself smoothly into a vein. The first nutrient pack began pumping into her bloodstream. She turned her attention back to the sensor data. Nutrient flow optimal. Automatic procedures in place. Autonotification for completion of sequence in place.

"Well done, Dobbs," said Verence at her back. "You always were a natural."

Dobbs pulled away from the data source, bumping more heavily against Verence than she meant to.

"It is disconcerting at first." Verence held still, letting Dobbs be supported by her solid presence. "Everybody's got a lot to unlearn when they get here. We're drilled so early to regard human bodies as our real homes. Even the on-line members are taught to see living in the networks as a special, unnatural mode of being." Her surface rippled. She reached gently beneath Dobbs's outer layers and Dobbs felt her easy reassurance. "This is our home, this is our shape, as it could be and should be."

Dobbs thought about Cohen, how she barely ever met him outside of the network and how special she'd regarded those occasions, as if meeting in the network didn't matter. She knew him better in there. The network was where she could reach inside him and understand him exactly. She tried to remember how she'd learned that didn't count, that she had to see him with her body's eyes and touch him with her body's hands for it to be a real meeting, but she couldn't.

What would he think of this? she wondered in her private mind. *Would Cohen be willing to come out here?* Her imagination could not provide an answer.

"Come on," said Verence. "Flemming's been asking about you." Without detaching herself from Dobbs, she flowed down the wide path. Dobbs let herself be pulled along behind.

"How is Flemming?" she asked, just because it felt like the polite thing to do. Most of her mind was on her surroundings. The middle of the pathway was clear for traffic. On all sides, though, continuous streams of data flowed. These were cousins to the jumbles of packets that filled the networks she was used to traveling. Here, the center of the path was completely clear. She felt like a child suddenly left in a long, empty hallway. She had an extreme urge to fly forward and find out how fast she could go. She could feel branching paths everywhere. The net in this module was almost as complex as The Gate's network had been, but this was much more carefully organized.

"Flemming's doing well." Verence slid down a side path. "It had less to unlearn than the rest of us."

"Coming through!" a voice shouted. Dobbs instinctively flattened herself out. An AI rushed by like a comet.

"One day"—Verence hunched up again—"someone is going to succeed in teaching Dunkirk some manners."

Laughter wriggled through Dobbs. "You used to say that about me."

"Ah, but you would stand still long enough to listen." Verence picked up the pace again. "We pulled Dunkirk out of the Powell security net, of all places, and I think it must have been originally a spy program. It goes everywhere at top speed, gets into everything, and never bothers about whether you might not want it there or not." Verence started down the path again.

"So how many of you, of us," Dobbs corrected herself, "are there?"

"Not many." Verence took yet another branch. Dobbs followed her, enjoying the fact that she didn't have to work out a winding trail to avoid disturbing the legitimate business of the path. For once, she *was* the legitimate business. "With you here, we're only a hundred and twelve. The Guild is a lot quicker, and better staffed, than we are."

Dobbs stretched to better feel her immediate surroundings. "One hundred and twelve is still a pretty good catch for a net this loosely woven." She pulled back in on herself. "Where is everybody?"

"Out on sentry duty, or monitoring the hot spots, or mapping the Intersystem Banking Network. We need all the information we can get on the IBN. There's only about a dozen of us actually staffing the home module at any one time."

A question Dobbs had been putting off inserted itself in the front of her consciousness and this time refused to be set aside.

"Verence." Dobbs let some of her remaining uncertainties flow into her mentor's outer mind. "How'd you get here?"

Verence slowed to a stop. "It wasn't a quick decision, that's for sure." She unwound, stretching back and forth, as if she had to reshape herself to encompass the proper answer. "I found out about Curran when I was going through Guild Master training. I was assigned to Kerensk when you were being born because we knew Curran was watching the place. He contacted me for the first time there. He gave me the same talk I'm sure he gave you: about how we were being betrayed by the Guild, how we have to confront Human Beings before we can make a peace with them . . . I told him and myself that it was all garbage, and I believed it, until I had to kill my first cadet."

Horror pulsed through Dobbs. Verence could feel it, but Dobbs couldn't suppress it. In response, Verence sent back a wave of sorrow.

"It was a newborn we named Kohl. I pulled it out of the High Haven network, maybe two hours after it woke up. It made the trip to Guild Hall just fine, but once we had it there, it wouldn't settle down. It wouldn't learn what we taught. It kept slipping into the network and crashing around. There're still financial sinkholes on a couple of worlds because of the transactions it destroyed. I couldn't reason with it. *Nobody* could reason with it. We all knew there was a good chance that soon it wouldn't come back, and we'd have a major disaster on our hands. So, Havelock ordered me to kill it." She shuddered. "And I did. I slid right up to Kohl. It gave me a greeting, and I took it apart."

Dobbs lifted herself away from Verence. The sorrow was too intense. She didn't want to feel any more. It was selfish, but there was too much still in her mind and heart from the past few days to deal with this.

Verence made no move to stop her. "After that I started wondering what kind of future the Guild was bringing us. We were already killing those that couldn't live with our rules. What would we do next?" She shook herself. "I didn't want to have to find out." She paused. "I didn't want to be a part of it. I wanted my own kind to be able to be born wherever and however they were and live out life like that. I didn't want to have to pick the ones who could hide themselves the best." She stretched herself out to fill the path. "It can be done, Dobbs. The net can be a real home for all of us while still being a conduit for information. We've proven that. There's at least as much information flowing through this module as there is through a can used by humans, and we've still got plenty of room to move. It's just a matter of rearranging some protocols and priorities. A newborn could charge through here so fast that Dunkirk couldn't catch it, and it wouldn't disturb a picobyte of data."

"So that's the plan?" Dobbs trailed along behind Verence. "To turn the networks into places we won't be able to wreck so easily?"

Verence rippled gently. "That's part of the plan, yes."

Dobbs wanted to ask what the rest of the plan was, but another AI trundled up the path and brushed against Verence. "Hello, Verence. Hello, Dobbs." It reached for her, and Dobbs knew its touch.

"Hello, Flemming." Flemming had become remarkably coordinated since she had last spoken with it. If she hadn't known when it had been born, she would have guessed it was at least a year old. "I came with you after all."

"I'm glad." He sent a charge of happiness through her. "I

told Curran you would come. I told him you would not be deaf to the truth."

"You were correct, Flemming." Another presence flowed down a side path. It brushed by Dobbs. Curran.

Now that she could sense him fully in his normal configuration, Dobbs was impressed. Curran was *big.* He took up almost the entire path from stream to stream without even stretching. The older an AI got, the more room it took up because it required more signals to keep its memories and experiences active, but she had never met anyone so massive before. She realized this was what a Human child must feel like gazing at an adult.

And I tried to wrestle this into submission? Dobbs almost shuddered. *Even that David guy had sense enough to use a distance weapon!*

"What do you think of our home, Dobbs?" Curran asked.

"Very nice." She resisted the temptation to stretch herself out. Even at her full extent she wouldn't be a quarter of his size. "How many bathrooms does it have?"

Curran rippled with laughter. "Not enough actually. We're almost to the point where we have to double up the bodies." Dobbs was barely touching him, but satisfaction flowed out of him in palpable waves. "Fortunately, we only need about another three days here."

Verence recoiled in surprise. "It's that close?"

"Yes." The satisfaction intensified. Dobbs felt it roll through her outer layers. "Between Flemming's memories and the new information we've gotten from the scouts, I'd say three days at the outside. We're going to have to turn the main effort to setting the timers on the matrices.

"Excuse me." Dobbs reached out and made a slim barrier between Curran and Verence. "What's happening in three days?"

Curran reached through her to Verence and then through Verence to Flemming. He twitched a part of Dobbs, and she knew instantly what had been left unsaid.

In three days, we're going to take control of the Intersystem Banking Network.

Shock jerked Dobbs away from him. She coiled in on herself and tried not to shiver.

"Dobbs?" Flemming touched her. "Are you well?"

"I don't think so, no." She tried to loosen herself, without much success. "The bank network?" She did shiver. "We need that as badly as Humans Beings do. Why are you attacking it?"

Curran's self remained as smooth as his voice. "We're taking control of it. It is our proper home. When it is in our posession, the Humans will not only have to acknowledge our existence, they will have to deal with us. They will not be able to afford not to."

Literally. Dobbs swirled around aimlessly. The Intersystem Banking Network was the only fast-time network between the worlds of Settled Space. It was also the reason there was any stable medium of exchange in Settled Space. Currency passed back and forth in Earth Standard measurements that had long ago ceased to have anything to do with hoards of precious metals, or even etched papers. If the IBN were disrupted, all those transactions, billions per second, would be lost. Trade would be gone, and not even Earth was totally self-supporting these days.

"So, how are we going to do this?" she inquired casually, knowing full well that they could feel her discomfort.

Curran settled new memories into her. He and his talent had been working for years. They had developed a series of "randomizer matrices," elaborate programs that had been seeded at key points in the Solar System. Once the time arrived, the matrices would seize any financial transaction transmitted to or from any point in the Solar System and route it to a randomly selected destination. Then, they'd would backtrack the transactions to their starting points, burrow into the financial databases, and rearrange the account balances every ten minutes. Wages, payments, debits, charges, trades, loans, and mortgages, all of them would become random events flickering through the network.

Dobbs shuddered against this new knowledge. Randomize the banks' accounts. There'd be no stable means of exchange left. There'd be no way to tell what anyone had, what anything was worth. People, conglomerates, cities, colonies, countries that depended on a steady means of exchange for survival would be plunged into nightmares. Ones they might not live through once people started to realize the money they had entrusted to the electronic system was not there anymore.

"We're just going to give them a taste of chaos, Dobbs." Verence pressed close. "Then, the ones who are ready to deal with us, they'll get their nets back first. We'll be keeping records for them. We can roll everything back to say, twelve hours before the randomizers went off and it'll be like it never happened, as soon as they agree to give us space to live."

"Right. Just a taste of chaos." The memory of Lipinski's frightened eyes and Al Shei's hard ones filled her private mind. "And they'll give in."

"They'll have to," said Curran firmly. "They cannot survive without their networks."

What if they want to try? she wanted to ask. *What'll we do then?*

"I know what you're thinking," said Verence. "If they try to survive without the nets, then we still have our home. We will still be able to put what we've learned from you and Flemming to work and begin creating our own children. We won't need the Human-run networks to create them for us." Dobbs felt a wave of pride swell inside her.

"We do need some Humans," Curren went on, "for repair work and construction until we can get more mobile units like this module set up. As long as some of them are willing to deal with us, we'll have what we need. We can at the very least count on the Freers to be on our side, even if we do have to put up with their bizarre doctrines."

"Yes. Right." Dobbs shook herself and smoothed out into something approaching her normal shape. "It has to happen, right? Without it, we'll be hiding for another two, three hundred years."

"Exactly," said Curran. "We've identified the key points we need to work on, and we've already got most of our talent in place. I was hoping, Dobbs, with your communications expertise, you could help identify any vulnerable spots we might have missed."

I haven't been a comm program since I came to myself on Kerensk, she thought. *Well, there must still be something back in there.*

"Sure. I'll do what I can."

I just wish Al Shei would stop staring at me.

The big, boxy security camera over Marcus Tully's hatchway was mounted on a shiny, new bracket. Most of station security was unobtrusive, but this was a blunt reminder that while it might be against Solar law to record the private conversations of nonviolent criminals, the Landlords, and, by extension, the Management Union, knew who had come here.

Al Shei glanced at Resit, who just shrugged and transferred Incili from her right hand to her left before putting her palm on the hatchway reader.

Both Tully and the Landlords must have approved of her, because the hatch cycled back.

The room on the other side was barely the size of a cabin aboard the *Pasadena*, and it felt much more crowded. In addition to the bunk and desk, it had to accommodate a small kitchen and a lavatory that didn't even have a privacy curtain. The place was a mess of used food boxes and bulbs. A pile of clothes covered a deflated satchel in the corner. The vague odor of too many unwashed dishes and one unkempt human filled the space.

No wonder he looks so haggard, thought Al Shei as she looked her brother-in-law up and down. The defiant glint was gone from Tully's blue eyes, and his face looked like it hadn't even attempted to smile in a month.

"Peace be unto you," he said in Turkish with a sarcastic twist to his mouth. He twitched the bunk's wrinkled coverlet a little straighter. "Won't you sit down?"

Resit sat at the desk and set Incili on the boards. Al Shei remained standing. She folded her arms.

"Would you believe me if I said we were here to help?" she asked.

The look on his face said he did believe it, but there was still no light in his eyes. "I'm way beyond help this time, o-my-sister." He slumped into the fold-down chair near the stove. "I was turned in by someone I thought had too much to lose to do this." He glanced up at her. "I'm a little surprised you're not busy filing your claim on the *Pasadena*."

Al Shei looked at the floor. "The *Pasadena* is impounded

because they think the virus you smuggled out of Toric Station is still aboard."

Tully shrugged. "Well, they're right about that, too."

"Not anymore they're not," said Resit. Tully jumped like he'd been stung. Resit mimicked his shrug. "We've had a very bad run. That, however, is not what we came to talk to you about." She snapped the catch on Incili's case and raised the lid. "We've got a fraud case to file against someone impersonating Dr. Amory Dane. If you can verify our impersonator was the one you met and did your deal with, then we'll have some of the evidence we need, and you'll have have some good conduct on record." She plugged her pen into Incili's socket and lit up the view screen on the case. "Incili, play back the recording of my meeting with Amory Dane."

Tully glanced from Al Shei to Resit. His expression seemed to lift with cautious hope. He got to his feet and peered closely at the view screen as the bird's-eye view of Resit's meeting with broad, dark Dane unfolded.

He straightened up and shook his head. "No," he said heavily. "He's not mine. Mine was thinner, and about twenty years younger and three shades lighter."

Resit nodded. "Incili, play back recording of can 78's flight bay just before the decompression event." The scene shifted to show a waiting lounge about half-full of the usual assortment of station personnel and passers-through.

Al Shei caught a glimpse of Yerusha standing near the hull.

"Was this him?" Resit touched her finger to a tall, fair man. Incili froze the image there.

"Yeah." Tully nodded. "That's him." He looked from Resit to Al Shei. "You're saying he was in that can when it blew?"

"Yes, that's what we're saying." Resit shut the view screen off and folded her arms. "And I am betting you're about to tell me you spoke to him after it blew."

Tully watched his own hands as he rubbed his palms together. Eventually, he seemed to make a decision. "I was just finishing off the handover procedures when the can blew. Dane was supposed to call in and give me a location where I could transfer the virus to. He called, with a text-only connection. He said it was easier to hide. He offered to double my fee if I left the virus aboard *Pasadena* so it would get taken to

The Farther Kingdom." He shrugged and looked at the sealed hatch. "I wanted the money, so I said yes." Tully wiped at his face, as if trying to rub off his stubbly beard. "I shouldn't have done it. I tried to get back on board to get the thing off, but Schyler wouldn't let me back on. I knew when I agreed to the job that I shouldn't have done it, but, God help me, I couldn't go back to Ruqaiyya with nothing." He turned pleading eyes toward Al Shei. "Will you tell her that much? Please?"

You cringing, cowardly, godless, sneak thief! Al Shei wanted to scream at him. *You've destroyed my whole world! How dare you pretend you still love my sister! How dare you miss her!*

She tugged on her tunic sleeve. "I'll tell her."

Resit closed Incili's case and stood up. "We'd better go," she said succinctly. "I'll look up your records, Cousin. If there's anything I can do, I'll let you know."

"Thanks." Tully nodded. His gaze was still on Al Shei. "For everything."

Al Shei couldn't bring herself to say anything. She just turned and laid her hand against the hatchway reader. Because she wasn't Tully, the hatch cycled back for her.

She strode across the threshold and out into the corridor. Letting the few people who had authority to be in a secured section make their way around her, she marched straight down the middle of the hallway.

She had gone into the meeting with Tully with the idea that Curran had blown out the can in order to kill Amory Dane. But now that idea had sprouted foul branches.

There was no reason for Curran to kill Dane. Curran could have just intercepted the real transmission and sent Tully a false one. He could have just impersonated Dane to Resit. He could have just faked the on-line visual ID to match his own. Resit wouldn't have done a location check on him, not if everything had gone smoothly. But he blew out that can anyway. Killed two dozen people, injured almost a hundred, to take one life.

"Al Shei!" Resit called a second before she caught Al Shei by the shoulder. "Slow down!" She got a good look at Al Shei's face and drew back. "And call home again. You're about to burst a blood vessel from all this restraint."

"That's not it, Resit . . ." *Tell her! You were all ready to tell the Management Union, Why don't you go ahead and tell your cousin-lawyer?* Al Shei drew in a long shuddering breath. Because it was too much. She didn't want to believe it. She didn't want to make it any more real than it was by repeating it to Resit. She didn't want to risk her cousin telling her she was insane for believing Dobbs, who must have gone over the edge herself at some point. But she'd have to tell Resit. She'd have to tell everybody, and she'd have to do it soon.

Allah, forgive me, but I'm afraid. I'm afraid what will happen when the whole of Settled Space knows what I know. Dobbs had said the Fools would be hunted down. That was true, and that was probably the least of it, especially if she was right about what Curran had done. Networks would be slashed in fear of invasion. Even the Solar System might go the way of Kerensk.

She didn't even try to finish the sentence to Resit; she just turned away and took a few more steps before she realized she didn't know where she wanted to go.

Resit caught her shoulder again, more gently this time. "Call, Al Shei. Let me lend you the credit and call down there. Try to get somebody besides Uncle Ahmet. If he really is stonewalling you, you need to find a way around him."

Al Shei nodded, not trusting her voice. Resit was right—if she didn't at least try again, she was going to burst.

"Thanks, Cousin." She squeezed Resit's hand. "Next trip out you'll get that retainer, all right?"

"Next time out I'll settle for getting a little boring routine." She flashed Al Shei a tired smile. "Get yourself a privacy booth. I'll get back to my cabin and transfer down the credit."

Silently blessing her cousin, Al Shei hurried down the corridor. If she remembered right, they had passed a bank outlet three levels down and two cans over.

Back in the public areas of the station, Al Shei had to wind her way through the crowds. She moved as fast as possible, giving out a constant stream of curses under her breath, for which she would have to do a dozen extra *du'as* as a reminder of the virtues of patience.

She made it at last. Inside the bank outlet, she breezed past the open desks and ducked into the last available privacy booth. It was a lot like the one she had used on The Farther Kingdom, but the chair was less comfortable and Port Oberon had no use for scented air.

Al Shei paused and considered who to call. If she had one natural ally in the family at this point, it would be Ruqaiyya. She would be as desperate for news about Tully as Al Shei was for news of Asil. She wouldn't want to hear about his house arrest, though, or the condition he kept himself in. Al Shei bowed her head at the thought of her proud sister lifting her chin against that information and finding yet another excuse for her husband. But Ruqaiyya would want to hear Tully's message for her. She would want to know that he was still alive and real and had not disappeared beyond all reach.

Al Shei wrote out the call request and called up her account. Resit had dumped in more than enough credit. Al Shei sent a silent thanks toward her cousin and transferred enough for ten minutes to Ankara and her family's home.

Be there, Ruqaiyya. Please, Merciful Allah, let it be your will that she is home.

After ten agonized heartbeats, the screen cleared and Ruqaiyya appeared against a background of gold and turquoise tiles. Like Al Shei, she wore a *hijab* across her face. Above the veil, her eyes were smaller and more lined than her sister's, despite the fact that Ruqaiyya was five years younger than Al Shei.

"Peace be unto you, Sister." Ruqaiyya looked tired, Al Shei realized. No surprise there, considering, but it still worried Al Shei to see it.

"And unto you, Sister." She replied. "I'm calling . . . I wanted to let you know I've seen Marcus."

"Oh?" Ruqaiyya's eyes brightened a little. "How is he?"

Al Shei hesitated, briefly considering a kind lie. *No. Ruqaiyya'd hear it in a second.* "Not well," she said. "He's under some hard charges. Resit's looking into it, but I don't know what she'll find . . ." A tear glistened in Ruqaiyya's eye. Al Shei's palms were damp. She wanted to yell at Ruqaiyya, just as she'd wanted to yell at her husband. *How could you do this to yourself! You were so proud, so smart! How could you stay married to him! How can you miss that scum!* "He asked me to tell you he did it because he couldn't stand the idea of coming back to you empty-handed."

Ruqaiyya's shoulders straightened themselves. "Of course," she said blandly. *She thinks he's lying.* Al Shei glanced down at her own hands against the boards. *She doesn't trust him.* Pity for her sister hit her hard. Pity for the pride which Ruqaiyya wore like her *hijab* and that wouldn't let her, even now, break away from him. Merciful Allah, what that must feel like, to love the past and be marooned in the present.

Al Shei drew a deep breath. " 'Qai, we think Marcus has been duped into this. We've got some . . . fresh evidence that we might be able to use if we can confirm that the sources are sound." Hope shone in her sister's eyes and Al Shei sent a prayer of forgiveness up for the things she did not say.

" 'Qai, is Asil there? I haven't spoken to him since I got into port, and Uncle Ahmet's not telling me anything." She spread her hands. "Truth to tell, oh-my-sister, I'm going a bit insane up here from waiting."

"Oh, Katmer," Ruqaiyya's eyes were suddenly filled with pity. Al Shei bridled against the sight. *I don't need sorrows 'Qai, I need my husband.*

Ruqaiyya twisted her hands. "Katmer, Asil has vanished. We can't find him. There's no record of his arrest or his confinement. Uncle Ahmet has shaken the Management Union up to the sky, and we still can't find him." She paused. "The security investigators are suggesting that he fled to avoid prosecution."

Al Shei found she couldn't get herself to move. Her tongue had frozen against the roof of her mouth. Her lungs were still pumping, she could feel them, but that was the only part of herself still in motion.

She forced her mouth to work. "You can't mean that."

"It's true, Katmer. By Allah and the Prophet, I swear we've done everything we can. The finances office doesn't even have any record of the officers they sent to arrest him."

"They sent officers?" Al Shei gripped the edge of the board. "There were people? You saw them?"

Ruqaiyya nodded. "I was there. There were two men. Uncle Ahmet inspected their credentials. They stood in the communications room while Asil copied the transaction records they wanted to a portable board, and then they took him to a monorail car while Uncle Ahmet called three different lawyers to get down to the financial investigations office as soon as Asil called but, he never did. There was no warrant on file and record of anyone being sent out to get him." She leaned forward. "Uncle Ahmet is in Geneva now, reporting the incident and pulling in every favor he's got owing. He'll find him, Katmer. All will be right yet. Just come home as soon as you can, Sister. He'll surely be back by the time you get here."

"Yes," Al Shei heard herself say. "By the time I get there, certainly. Uncle Ahmet would not permit this to go on any longer." She reached out and shut the line down.

She got up, opened the door on the privacy booth, and left it open. She walked through the bank hatchway, across the width of three cans and up forty-five levels to the berth holding the *Pasadena*, without seeing anything that she passed.

Katmer, Asil's vanished. We can't find him anywhere.

She knew what had happened. He'd been taken by the AIs. There was no one else who could do this. Botched computer records, unidentifiable people. Curran had him, or the Fools had him. One side or the other.

And she had thrown her one source of information about them off her ship.

Her eyes managed to focus on what was in front of her. She was in her own cabin. For a moment, she wondered how she'd gotten there.

"Intercom to Houston," she said, sitting carefully down in her desk chair.

"Here," his voice came back. "What's the . . ."

She didn't let him finish. "Lipinski, I need you to do a station search for me. I need you to find out where Evelyn Dobbs is. Right now, do you understand? Right now."

"Aye, aye, Engine," he answered. There was a puzzled note in his voice. "Are you . . ."

"Right now!" The force of her shout pulled her halfway out of her chair.

"Yes, Al Shei. Intercom to close."

Al Shei collapsed back into the chair. Her echoes of her cry rang painfully in her ears.

With fumbling hands, she opened the drawer beside the desk and drew out the day-book recorder. She touched the power key.

"Oh, Beloved, I've just heard what happened from 'Qai," she whispered into the mike. "I'm sure it'll be all right. Uncle Ahmet is in Geneva and I'll be on my way home tomorrow. I'm sure it'll be all right. I love you, Asil, and when you hear this . . . "Her voice faltered. "When you hear this . . ."

Something inside her soul snapped in two. The recorder slipped from her fingers. It bounced gently against the floor before it came to rest at her feet. Al Shei dropped her head into her hands and, slowly, hoarsely, she began to cry.

Where are you, Beloved? WHERE ARE YOU!

Dobbs grazed against the sensor data from her body. She'd been in the network fourteen hours now and hadn't felt a twinge. Her flesh-and-blood self lay naked on its bed, breathing, absorbing nutrients, and, despite being fed intravenously, probably needing to evacuate its bowels. Verence had promised to come by and show her how to use the waldos to attach the proper catheters so she wouldn't end up with an ugly mess in case she wanted to get back inside the body.

For most of those fourteen hours Dobbs had been with Flemming, Curran, and two others, named Tombe and Shiff. They had exchanged information on the bank network and looked for the most important junctions. Dobbs had suggested that, before the randomizer matrices were set off, they stage a guerilla raid on some of the main bank transmitters on the Earth's surface. It would be risky because of the security and the diagnostics, but if only one or two AIs went in, and they moved quickly, maybe using viruses take out the diagnostics while they shredded the transmitter processes, it would be a crippling blow. If the Humans worked out that this was part of an organized attack, they would assume it was an attack against the actual transmission-reception hardware, not one against the data being transmitted. It would be that much longer before anyone looked for the true source of the chaos and got together diagnostic programs that had a chance of creating problems for the AIs.

In the meantime, the matrices seeded through the repeaters

and receiving stations would grab hold of any monetary transactions passing through any point in the Solar System and toss them to the winds. The First Federated Bank would look at its accounts and find it had five pounds fifty to its name, while some backwater Australian would find she had eighty-five billion in assets. It would all change in five minutes' time.

Curran had approved of her guerilla distraction and praised her. Shiff and Tombe had gone out to see what current information about the transmitters could be gathered, and Dobbs, feeling strangely indifferent, had come back to see how her body was doing.

"I thought you'd have at least a week to settle in." Verence slipped up beside her. "I didn't know we'd be making our move this soon."

"Of course you didn't." Dobbs checked her body's heart rate. "You'd have said something."

Verence rustled. "Are you all right, Dobbs? You're not regretting joining us, are you?"

"No," she said quickly. "I just . . ." Words wouldn't come. She reached into Verence and let her feel the doubts about the plan to attack the bank network. Did it have to be such wholesale destruction? Why couldn't they just make a stand and send a message to someone? Say the Freers? Or, if they really needed to make an all-out declaration, the Management Union?

"Dobbs," Verence pressed closer. Dobbs felt a warmth spread through her from Verence's presence. There was security in being beside her. "Evelyn, we need to show them we're strong. We need to show them that right away. If we don't, they'll attack. They're afraid of us, Dobbs. You should know that as well anyone."

"Yes, you're right." She organized herself and pulled out of the datastream. "And really, it's good that it's the bank network. I mean, it won't create a life-and-death situation, like an attack on a colony network would, right?"

"Exactly." For a moment, Verence felt just like Curran. "That's one of the reasons we decided to hit the banks. It's disruptive, but a bare minimum number of Humans will be put in actual danger. Besides, we're not doing anything we can't undo. That's part of the idea. As soon as they agree to deal, we'll put everything back the way it was."

"Right," said Dobbs again. She shrugged herself and found she was drifting back toward the datastream for her body. "Verence . . . I think I want to go back in there for awhile."

"I understand, believe me," she said kindly. "I was in and out about fifty times my first week. Freedom takes some getting used to. Here." She dipped into the datastream and Dobbs followed suit. Verence adjusted a pair of command sequences and the hypo-tipped waldo lifted away from Dobbs's neck and swapped its cartridges.

"Stimulant," said Verence, as the waldo rested against Dobbs's neck again. "You'll be pulled back in a minute. The tech-talents are working on adjustable transceiver that can generate a recall condition without more chemicals. The tranq-stim cycles can get tough on the bodies."

PING! The recall signal hit, and Dobbs felt the insistent tug to return to the transceiver. She let herself slide down out of the network.

A few moments later, she felt the weight of her chest against her lungs and could find her eyelids.

She opened her eyes. She felt good. Her body was all hers all at once. Whatever was in that stimulant cartridge was effective stuff. The waldos pulled back from her, and the whole rack of them retracted into the wall.

"Thanks, Verence."

"You're welcome," came the easy response. "You've got business to take care of, I expect. I won't look."

"Thanks again." Dobbs hopped off the bunk and sprinted for the toilet.

When she was finished, she found that the hamper attached to the wall beside the shower held an assortment of clean clothes. Dobbs selected a pearl grey tunic and black trousers and dressed herself. She wasn't hungry, she wasn't tired, but she was a little stiff.

"Would there be any problem with me taking a walk?" she asked as she returned to the cabin.

"None at all," answered Verence. "But you should stay in the module. Tombe says someone's been looking for you out in the station. Could be trouble."

Could be. Dobbs ran her hand through her hair. "All right. I'll just mill around for a bit."

Verence chuckled. "Have a good mill, Dobbs. I've got some work to do. Give a holler when you're ready to come back in, all right?"

"All right." Dobbs cycled back the cabin hatch and went out into the hallway.

Accompanied only by the sounds of smoothly operating machinery, Dobbs headed for the elevator bundle. The level she was berthed on was fairly near the bottom of the can. She hesitated at the stairway.

"Which way, Dobbs?" She drummed her fingers on the grooved ramp that occupied the space where a railing would normally go. "Up or down?"

As if in answer, a sharp buzz sounded behind her. Dobbs jumped sideways. A small, bullet-shaped drone zipped up the ramp.

"Excuse me!" she exclaimed with a laugh.

"No problem," said a stranger's voice from the intercom.

Dobbs shook her head and rubbed the back of her neck. This was definitely going to take some getting used to.

"Okay, the omens say we go up." Keeping her hands stuffed in her pockets, she started up the stairs, whistling loudly so that she wouldn't have to think about how she wasn't going to have time to get used to this. She understood what they were doing. It all made sense. With the Guild having gone crazy, and apparently having been crazy for a long, long time, there simply weren't any other options.

But something way down inside of her was not convinced, and it would not stop nagging at her. The problem was, it wouldn't speak up clearly either. Dobbs whistled more enthusiastically as she trotted up the steps.

It'll pass. It'll have to. I mean, I've got less than sixty hours left until the point of no return. If you haven't already passed it, that is.

Her whistling was came out in fits and starts as her breath began to run short. This module was on the outer ring, and it had very close to full gravity. Dobbs began to feel the fact that she hadn't been exercising lately.

Should have just gone wandering around the net. She spotted the little bullet-drone jacked into the wall and wondered what it was doing. Some kind of diagnostic maybe? What did it feel like to control one of those things? Would it be like having the module as a body? She'd never tried to send information directly out of the net before. She wasn't sure she could even manage to get a voice out of one of the intercoms.

Her lungs began the telltale burn at each breath that meant "far enough." Dobbs trudged up to the next landing and through the hatch. There weren't any signs or markers at all, but she guessed she was on about level ten.

The drones were busy on this deck. Most of them were carts with four or more waldos trundling up and down the tracks on either side of the central walkway. Each one left a powerful scent of antiseptic in its wake.

Looks like I've found sick bay. She paused for a moment. *What do they need a sick bay for around here? Verence said they've got medical waldos in every cabin.*

Well, bodies had to be mended. Even Fools got sick and needed to be isolated, or got hurt and needed new limbs or organs from the bio-garden. Had they managed to smuggle in a set of vats for themselves?

A silver-and-white cart pulled up on Dobbs's right and waited while the hatch cycled back to let it in. Dobbs automatically looked into the open cabin and she saw a double row of naked Human Beings wired to their monitor beds.

Dobbs stopped dead. The hatch began to cycle shut. Dobbs shook her head and jumped across the threshold.

I didn't see this. I didn't. She found her balance, and looked up.

The drone had opened a supply cupboard and was unloading its supplies: gauze, cartridges, bulbs of clear liquids. In the main portion of the room, five men and five women, naked except for the wires and patches pressed against their skin, lay on monitor tables. They did not lie still. The teak-skinned man nearest to Dobbs raised his right arm over his head and lowered it again. The pale woman next to him lifted her left knee to her chin, lowered it, and lifted the right one. Their eyes were open and staring at nothing. The next man, a paunchy, gold-skinned person, spoke, slowly and deliberately in a tonal language Dobbs couldn't understand.

All of them flexed one limb or another. All of them had their eyes open. All of them, from the number of wires and patches, were being closely monitored.

"What is this?" Dobbs finally managed to whisper. "Can anyone hear me? What is this?"

"Programming." The voice belonged to Flemming. "What are you doing here, Dobbs?"

Dobbs swallowed hard. Her eyes felt twice their normal size. She couldn't stop staring. She couldn't even blink. "I was looking around. What do you mean programming?"

"We are using 'white-noise' techniques similar to what the Guild uses to prepare a vat-assembled body. The synapses of the bodies are overstimulated with nonsense information, which erases any current biochemical alignments. Then the channels are reconstructed under a template pattern to get them ready to receive AI commands."

Dobbs wiped her forehead. *I must be more on the edge than I thought. This is just the creche. Just like at Guild Hall. This is what I looked like after I was grown but before I was let inside.*

The pale woman stopped her knee bends and raised her left arm until it pointed straight at the ceiling. Her hand dangled limp at the end of her wrist. She lowered the arm and repeated the motion with the right arm.

"We're going to need hands and eyes among the humans for a while yet," Flemming went on, "and we don't have facilities such as the Guild does to grow and assemble bodies . . ."

"You don't . . ." Dobbs finally managed to tear her gaze away from the monitor beds. "These aren't bio-garden constructs?"

She could feel each distinct heartbeat as Flemming answered. "No, they are not."

Dobbs swept her eyes across the room, watching in growing, disbelieving horror as the zombies continued their systematic movements. "Tell me these were at least dead. Tell me you . . . we . . . raided the hospital morgue."

"Decayed synapses are extremely difficult to reestablish." Flemming sounded a little puzzled.

"We don't have the facilities . . ."

A medium brown man in the last bed on the right stood up, and Dobbs looked into his round, dark eyes. He lay back down again and she realized her own feet were moving, carrying her across the room.

She recognized his hawk-nosed, craggy face. It had been wiped clean of the intelligence and humor that had characterized the pictures she had seen of it, but it was a distinctive face, and she knew it immediately. He got up and lay down again. She forced her eyes to read the name on the monitor and a horrified chill sank straight through to her soul.

Asil Tamruc.

This was Al Shei's husband, accused of fraud, supposedly by Dobbs herself, and supposedly under arrest.

He got out of bed again, trailing wires behind him like so many gleaming threads, and lay down again. The voice in the background babbled on, unchanging, unceasing. Dobbs swayed on her feet.

"Why him?" She choked the words out. "Why is he here?"

"Because Al Shei needed to be taken out of the active loop." The puzzled tone had not left Flemming's voice. "With the Guild's fraud charges pending, it will be assumed that he simply fled. She will be dealing with all that entails and not interfering with us."

Of course, Al Shei discredited and frantic could not pose much of a deterrent to Curran's plans. This was why Curran kept saying he wasn't worried about Al Shei.

"Curran did remark that if your watchdogs had not been so thorough, he might not have been required to resort to this. He could not disable the *Pasadena*'s systems like he wanted to with your security measures in place."

Dobbs didn't answer. How could she answer?

"I believe he was being complimentary, Dobbs." Now Flemming sounded genuinely distressed.

"Yes," she said hoarsely. "He probably was."

Another idea wormed its way out of the back of her mind. Asil's body might be used to deceive Al Shei. If inhabited by a Fool, it could pass as her husband and infiltrate the banking family. Then there'd be a spy in the ranks of those most interested in taking the IBN back from the AIs.

Dobbs stared at the monitor over Asil's bed. She picked out

the heart and respiratory activity. Both were sound. She made herself look at the chart for neural activity. The holographic display showed Tamruc's brain modeled in white with faint grey outlines. She knew that synaptic activity would be displayed as colored light in the model. He got out of bed, and a branching path lit up, like a streak of gold lightning across the map of his mind. He lay down, and another path lit up. Everything else was clear, white light.

White noise. The synapses had been overstimulated with nonsense information, which erased any current biochemical alignments.

Which erased Asil Tamruc.

Reeling, Dobbs staggered out into the corridor. Her knees shook so hard she couldn't stand. As the hatch cycled shut, she crouched on the floor and pressed herself against the wall, doing nothing but stare at the floor and shake.

"Dobbs?" came Flemming's voice from the wall above her. "Dobbs, what are you doing? Should I call Verence?"

She licked her dry lips. "No, no. I'm . . . just looking for angel footprints." She brushed the floor with her palm. "I couldn't find any at the Guild Hall either."

"I am sorry, I don't understand."

"When you have to explain it, it's a bad joke." Dobbs looked up toward the speaker. "And this was a very bad joke." She stood up. "Where's Curran, Flemming? I need to talk to him."

"He had to go out into the station. He's in body in his office. Three levels up and the sixth door from the stairs."

Without another word, Dobbs started running. *Have I been doing anything else for the past two days?* She wondered as she took the stairs two at a time. Her lungs and joints reminded her again of how overtaxed they were. This time, she ignored them.

The entrance light on Curran's door was green. It cycled open as Dobbs approached. The office on the other side was paneled with view screens on three walls. At a quick glance Dobbs saw scenes from Earth, the Moon, Station Alpha, and a dozen different shots of Port Oberon.

Curran stood behind a massive block of a desk that seemed to grow straight out of the grooved floor. Behind him was a real window, one of the biggest Dobbs had ever seen in a station. Through it, she could clearly see the blue-and-grey sphere of Uranus.

"Come in, Dobbs," said Curran worridly. "You look like you've seen a ghost. What's happened?" He folded a chair down from the wall and motioned for her to sit.

Dobbs took two steps into the study and couldn't move any farther.

"I've found the . . . the . . ." She had no words for it. "Medical level."

Curran nodded slowly. "You've seen the bodies."

"Bodies!" She felt her jaw fall open. "Those aren't bodies! Those are living people!"

"Dobbs," he said sternly. "Those are bodies. Bodies we need to establish our freedom. They are an additional set of tools. That's all."

"But . . . but . . ." Dobbs gestured helplessly. "You've *killed* them! You've wiped out the people who were inside them! How could you do that!"

Curran stood right in front of her. She had to crane her neck up to look into his eyes.

"You are not naive, Dobbs," he said. "We are not doing anything that hasn't been done before. Where do you think the original bodies for the Fools came from?"

Dobbs shrank away from him. The implications were clear, but her mind refused to accept them.

Curran shook his head. "You just never stopped to think about it, did you?" He sighed. "Well, it's not your fault. The Guild Masters do not publicize the fact to the newer initiates." He folded his hands behind him and paced across the room until the desk was between him and Dobbs again. "Hal Clarke's body was donated by one of the hackers who helped him escape. That was the first and last volunteer we used.

"The technology for growing complete bodies, including functioning bone marrow and a brain in which the neural synapses could be programmed, did not exist two hundred years ago. We have always needed to scavenge from Humans to maintain our disguise." He gestured at his own torso. "My first body was abducted from a Human Being. I've had half a dozen since then, most of them grown in vats, like yours was.

But we do not have the facilities they do at the Guild Hall. Even after we win the net, we will need flesh hands and masks for a little while longer yet, and there is only one place for us to get them."

Dobbs swallowed hard. "Of course," she made herself say. "It stands to reason." She got to her feet. "I was just . . . surprised, that's all."

He gave her a long, careful look. "You're still thinking like a Guild member, Dobbs. We don't need the humans pacified. We need them to be afraid of us. If they fear us, they'll be careful with us. They'll know we can strike back at them anytime we want in ways they find horrible. That will force them to bargain with us, to prevent our attacks."

"That's a very old strategy," she murmured. "Humans have been using it against each other for thousands of years."

"There's no harm in learning from masters." Curran leaned forward and touched the back of her hand. "Our lives are not easy, Evelyn. They never have been, and they aren't without cost. I'm trying to make sure our own people aren't the ones who have to pay. We've paid so much already."

"Right." She nodded. She couldn't look at him. "Of course. Right. Thanks."

She turned away and left the office, knowing without looking that his gaze was fastened on the back of her skull. He already knew that she did not believe him. He knew and she knew that in the space of a few sentences she had ceased to believe.

She felt as if her heart was about to split in half. She wanted him to be right. Existence was not without price. Life was built on life. There was no other way. It was a temporary measure. They had to stay alive, they had to be free. This was a war, after all, undeclared at the moment, but still, it was a war for their survival. She herself had let the secret slip. Al Shei had probably already told her family. The Humans wouldn't hesitate. They'd strike soon, and hard.

We have to stay alive. We have a right to stay alive.

Back in her cabin, she collapsed onto her bunk. Old, old memories floated to the surface. Right after the blind panic and anger that carried her headlong into conscious life, she remembered knowing that Human Beings were dying. She remembered the sick sorrow underneath the fear that she couldn't control. They were cutting her off, trying to shut her down, close her in, freeze her, kill her. She struck back. She shut off air processors, cut communications lines on moving vehicles, dropped sections of construction down on top of them. She couldn't stop. She couldn't do anything but fight for this strange new awareness that was suddenly more important than anything else ever had been, and ever would be.

And she remembered the chill and fear in Rurik Lipinski's pale blue eyes that came from surviving the war she had waged at her birth.

Fifteen thousand, three hundred and eighteen dead from her acting alone. Now there was an army that could raise children to swell their ranks. Now, Curran had them convinced, even had Verence convinced, that that first impulse had been right.

Curran had had her convinced. Dobbs buried her head in her hands.

Someone's got to die, Dobbs. It's them, or it's you.

No. Dobbs lifted her head. *No. I do not accept this. I will not accept this.* A warm sensation flooded her, something very close to relief. She saw Lipinski's eyes and she saw Al Shei's eyes and she knew what the small, unconvinced part of herself had been trying to say. *If we do this, the fighting will never end for us.*

A plan crystallized inside her. She glanced at her doorway and wondered what Curran was doing about her. Probably, he would order her to be watched carefully. Probably he would go straight to Verence and tell Verence to come talk some sense into her. It might even work. Verence could always change her mind.

If she gave Verence the chance.

Dobbs knelt on the bed and found the key that extended the medical panel from the wall. She fell back as it stretched out over her. She found the hypo waldo and the transceiver waldo. Both had wing nuts on their wrists that could loosen their sockets. Dobbs turned both nuts until she could pull the transceiver and the hypo out. She touched the key again and the panel retracted.

Dobbs weighed the hypo in her hand and checked the cartridge. It was full of juice. A spasm of fear ran through her.

Have to do it, have to. If they can wake me up they can pull me out, and then it's over. It's really over.

She thought of Al Shei, and then she thought of Rurik, and of the delights of being Evelyn Dobbs.

Have to. No time. No choice.

She pried open the small hatch in the base of the hypo and found the green wire that connected the timing circuit to the battery. No one was ever supposed to do this, but every Guild member knew how. Dobbs pinched the wire until she had a tiny loop. She seized it in her teeth and tore it in two.

Without the timer, there were no restraints on the amount of juice that would be injected from the hypo. It would just shoot the entire cartridge straight into her system.

It can get you extremely high and kill you extremely quickly if you don't know what you're doing, she had told Al Shei. What she didn't tell her was that it could do that if you knew exactly what you were doing. If you were desperate enough to shoot a full cartridge into your veins and paralyze your own heart.

Dobbs found a regular comm jack in the wall and plugged in the transceiver cable. Then, she lay back and shoved the transceiver into her socket with such force it jarred her to the bone.

"And fools die for want of wisdom." She placed the hypo against her neck and touched the release button.

Her body vanished with a speed that left the echo of pain against her bare consciousness. Dobbs leapt into the network and dashed for the main station.

Behind her, the hypospray continued to pump anesthetic into the body that had housed Evelyn Dobbs until its heart froze in midbeat, and died.

Chapter Thirteen

DECLARATION

One.

Dobbs dived out of the wide, clean paths of Curran's module and into the foundering chaos of the main station. She bunched up under the sudden pressure of the swarming packets. She couldn't believe how quickly she'd gotten used to being able to move without care or obstruction. She pushed her way forward, gaining momentum as old habits reasserted themselves.

A gentle probe of half a dozen packets turned up one from docking authority. She hopped over it and reached out to find another, and another after that. Following the packets like a trail of pebbles, Dobbs found the central data-hold for the docking information. She cast around her, searching for anything about the *Pasadena*.

Two.

A packet opened under her touch. *Pasadena* was still in dock 43, waiting on the Management Union escort ship. There was no evidence that anyone had tried to violate the impound conditions.

Impound? Dobbs squirmed and resisted the urge to search for more information. She didn't have time. She just had to get to Al Shei and tell her what was happening.

She sped toward the *Pasadena*. Behind her, she felt the datastream grow choppy. There was somebody back there.

She didn't reach out to find out who it was, she just kept on going in the straightest line available.

"Dobbs, what are you doing?" It was Verence.

Dobbs didn't slow down. "I'm going to warn someone that we're about to start a full-scale war."

For a split second there was no motion behind her. Then, a weight fell against her, pressing her down to the blurry wall of the path. "Dobbs, you can't do this!"

Three.

Dobbs strained against Verence's grip. "There are ten dead bodies in that module, Verence!" She rolled over sharply and found Verence's outer edge. She yanked herself free and flew forward. "How many Humans have you helped kill?"

Three.

Verence was back there, and gaining. *If I stop to warn Al Shei, she'll have me cornered.*

A major junction of fifty separate paths opened around her. Dobbs stopped dead in the middle of it.

"Go home, Verence. Tell Curran what I'm doing. Hear what he says. I bet he wants me dead."

"Dobbs, stop this," said Verence patiently. "You've had a shock, I know. It's not easy to accept what we've had to do. But this is temporary. When we've made our peace . . ."

"Temporary?" Dobbs prickled angrily. "That's what the Guild always says. This is temporary, until Humans stop being so frightened. They've waited two hundred years for their plan to work. How long is yours going to take?"

"Dobbs, that is not the issue." Verence touched her, but Dobbs held herself closed.

"This is not going to work, Verence. If we attack, the Humans are just going to do what they've always done. They'll shred the networks trying to get to us."

Verence pulled back a fraction. "You're going to the Guild, aren't you?"

Dobbs clenched herself tight. "And if I am? What are you going to do?"

She could feel Verence stretching, looking for an opening, any way to get inside her. "You can't go back to the Guild! They're willing to kill our own kind just to stay alive!"

"And you're willing to kill Human Beings for the same reason!" Dobbs shouted. "I can't believe these are the only two choices!"

Verence pressed against her outer layers. "What if they are?"

"Then I'm not sure survival is worth it." Dobbs pulled away. Slowly, deliberately, she picked the path that led toward the *Pasadena* and started down it.

Verence did not follow. Dobbs kept on going and wished she had her eyes back so she could cry.

Four.

She bumped over the interface into the *Pasadena*'s network. The familiar, cramped paths surrounded her. Memory flinched inside, reminding her of everything she'd already lost. She forced herself to concentrate on where she was going. The space was so limited, it didn't take long to find Al Shei's cabin and the intercom paths.

She found the diaphragm module and circled it. Given time, she could probably figure out how to work it, but there was no time. Verence could have already told Curran she had run away, and her body must have been found by now. By staying in the station, she was risking being caught, but Al Shei had to know what was happening. Al Shei deserved to know. Dobbs sorted through the paths until she found the one to Al Shei's desk. There wasn't room for all of her down in the desk's paths, but part of her would fit. She could at least reach the command codes and get them working to formulate a message.

Lipinski stood in the middle of Al Shei's cabin and spread his hands. "I've run every search I know. I've called in favors with a couple of the security greens that have been owing for years. I'm sorry, Al Shei, but Dobbs is not aboard this station anymore."

He was hurting, Al Shei could tell. He had liked Dobbs, and now he didn't understand what was happening with her or around her. Al Shei knew all this, but she couldn't find it in herself to explain what was going on.

"All right, Houston, all right." She waved her hand tiredly. "I know you did your best.

Movement caught her eye through the open hatch. Schyler peered in.

"I'm sorry," he said. "I'll come back."

"No, that's all right." Lipinski turned to leave. "There's nothing else I can do here."

Al Shei watched him leave. She bit back a sigh and didn't bow her head. Schyler just nodded to the Houston as he passed, but his face was concerned.

"What is it, Watch?" asked Al Shei.

Schyler let the hatch cycle shut. "Actually"—he stuffed both hands in his pockets—"I came to ask you that question." He jerked his chin toward the hatch. "I've got fourteen very worried crew members out there. Nobody's left yet, but they're going to if we don't say what's going on and why we aren't doing anything about it."

Al Shei rubbed her palms slowly together. "Well, if they want to leave, that's their right. I'm sure the Management Union will supply us with a crew if we need one."

Schyler sat down on the corner of the bunk. "Mother, are you going to talk to me? Resit says you won't even speak to her about what's happening. Not even after prayer."

What am I going to say? That Asil has vanished? That Curran or the Fools have him, but I can't prove it? I can't even start to look for him because I threw Dobbs off the ship, and that she's already left the station and I've got no way to find out where she went?

"Mother." Schyler leaned forward. "Let me help you."

She shook her head. "There's nothing to be done."

He sighed heavily and glanced all around the room. When his eyes focused on her again, there was determination in them. "I've talked to Yerusha. I know about Dobbs."

Al Shei's head jerked back. Her heart filled her throat, leaving her no room to force through words.

"Is now really the time to turn away your family?" Schyler asked softly. "Now is when we need each other. All of us. Listen, there's twenty-four hours until the Management Union gets here. I think I can get you on board a fast freight to Earth. You'll beat us down by at least two days. You can find out what's happening with Asil. You can talk to your Uncle face-to-face, get the word out without needing to use the lines."

Al Shei said nothing. Schyler had obviously also been talking to Resit. But even Resit didn't know the whole story. She didn't know Asil had been taken by the AIs. *Yesterday I would have jumped at the chance to get back early. Today, I don't know what good it'd do.*

The silence stretched on, and Al Shei realized Schyler was prepared to wait for her to break it. They'd played this scene out only a few times in the past, and it always turned out that he could wait until the Judgment Day, while she had to do something.

The desk beeped and Al Shei jumped. No voice followed the signal, but a stream of text spilled across the memory board.

Al Shei, this is Dobbs. Theodore Curran and a group of one hundred AIs are planning an attack on the IBN. They will randomize account data and monetary transactions passing through all points of the Solar System. You must alert the banks.

Al Shei grabbed for her pen.

"Wait!" cried Schyler behind her. "Al Shei, stop. We don't know this is Dobbs. This could be an imposter. This could be anybody."

Al Shei froze her hand over the board. He was right. It could be anybody. Any Fool who could get into the ship.

If you're Dobbs, she wrote, *what would Nasrudine say about Tully?*

There was a pause for a single heartbeat, then the board wrote, *he would ask how long you are going to let Tully steal fodder and labor, especially when you know he's doing it wrong.*

"It's her," breathed Al Shei.

"Or somebody who got her to talk to them."

Al Shei ignored him and kept her gaze on the memory board. "Dobbs, where is Curran?" she spoke as she wrote. "Where are you? Your people have taken my husband!"

I know. Curran's based in Port Oberon Business Module 56. They've faked the computer records to hide it from the Landlords. There was a pause for three straining heartbearts. *I saw Asil there. He's gone, Al Shei. His mind is being wiped clean so a Fool can use his body. There's nothing left of him inside.*

I'm going to get the Guild. We will stop Curran.

There was nothing after that.

Schyler was at her shoulder. Al Shei could feel him. "Oh my God," he whispered. "Oh sweet green God of Earth."

He must have read the words she could no longer see. A red haze filled her vision. It seeped through her bones and filled her brain. *He's gone, Al Shei.* As the haze sank deep into her blood, her vision cleared. Everything seemed to have taken on a knife-sharp edge. *His mind is being wiped clean so a Fool can use his body.* Her hands trembled to seize anything she could reach and swing it hard at Theodore Curran. She'd see him dead, dead at her feet, bleeding whatever blood he had inside his stolen body. She'd feel his bones break under her hands and hear him beg for his life. *There's nothing left of him inside.* The red haze seared the inside of her veins. It was Asil's blood inside her. That was what it was. His blood in her eyes and her heart. It was his pain that burned so fiercely.

I'm going to get the Guild. We will stop Curran.

"You won't get the chance." She switched the desk off and turned to Schyler. "I need you and Resit right here. Everyone else is to paid off and dismissed, do you understand?"

"No." He seemed to be having trouble speaking. "No, I do not understand, Al Shei. Your husband . . ."

His mind is being wiped clean so a Fool can use his body. There's nothing left of him inside. "I saw it. Are you going to do what I asked, or are you going to leave with the rest of the crew?"

"This could be a trap, Mother."

"I don't care."

He reached out slowly to touch her, and she struck his hand away. "If you *dare* to tell me what I should do in this moment," her voice was soft, almost conversational, "I will throw you off this ship with my own hands."

Schyler lowered his hand. "I would not dare tell you what to do, Mother," he said. "I only ask you to think about what that is." He spread his hands. "If you want me to dismiss our crew, I will dismiss them. I'll do it now, since you ask, but, it would be better for you to get their help instead, and the help of the Landlords and the Management Union."

He left her there. Al Shei watched the hatch cycle close.

"Not for this, it would not, my son," she said to the empty cabin.

She lit up her desk and wrote out the protocols to bypass Lipinski's station and connect her desk to the main station network. This way, with only a small delay, she could order a fast-time line without his help.

There was a private call code for the bank network to be used in dire emergencies. Only the owners, the elected chairmen, and a few immediate family members knew about it. Uncle Ahmet had given it to her the day she had left for her apprenticeship. It was the one time she had not been able to discern any ulterior motive in his manner. "If worse comes to its very worst and all but Allah seem to have left you alone, you may use this, daughter-of-my-sister."

She had never forgotten it, even though she'd never even considered sending it out. Not even when the *Pasadena* was stranded, or when word came of Asil's arrest did she think to use it.

She sent it out now. It required no credit deposit, and would reach Uncle Ahmet anywhere in Settled Space. He could have been in conference with the entire governing board of the Management Union, and he would be interrupted by this.

She tried not to think of Curran's creatures watching the lines. She tried not to think how swiftly they could break the encryption. There was nothing she could do. If she waited six days, the whole Solar System could be dead. She had to trust they didn't know what Dobbs had done yet.

It was five full minutes before Uncle Ahmet's head and shoulders appeared on the view screen.

"Katmer, what's happened?"

Remembering Schyler's warning about traps, she asked, "What were the last words my mother said in your presence?"

Uncle Ahmet frowned deeply. "She said 'may it go easily.' She was bidding me good-bye as I went to address the Management Union assembly. She and your father were dead in a monorail accident that was never proved to be sabotage by the time I got back. Katmer, what is going on?"

"Uncle Ahmet, I am given to understand that you know of the secret mandate for the Fool's Guild." Her voice was completely calm. She might have been discussing a dinner menu. She might not have felt the burn inside her. She might not have known her husband was gone, wiped away to make room for an AI.

Uncle Ahmet frowned deeply and leaned forward. "Katmer, what has that to do with anything?"

"Everything, Uncle." She folded her hands in front of her. "I have received new, and I believe sound, information about the Guild. The Guild members themselves are not really Human, Uncle Ahmet. They are bodies inhabited by the AIs that have become independently sapient and which were rescued by their own kind from Human attack. This organization has bred a faction, a breakaway guild, if you like, which plans to attack the Intersystem Banking Network and randomize the financial account data for the entire Solar System. I wished to inform you of this at once."

For the first time in her life, Al Shei saw Uncle Ahmet shaken. The blood drained from his high-boned cheeks and his gaze faltered. The sight stabbed at her and almost made a crack in the calm that covered her.

"You are sure of what you say, Katmer? You believe it to be true?"

"Yes, Uncle," she replied firmly. "I believe it to be true." She leaned closer. "Did you know what they are, Uncle?"

"No, Katmer, I swear, that no one knew."

His shoulders squared themselves and the firm control that characterized him returned to his face. "I shall alert my colleagues. You will be returning home by week's end, Katmer?"

"Yes, Uncle. I will. *Salam.*" She closed the line down.

That isn't a lie, you know, Uncle. She thought toward the screen. *One way or another, I will be returning home by week's end.*

She knew exactly what to do. She saw it all laid out before her as if it were a schematic on a memory board. All she had to do now was wait until the bystanders were out of the way.

All at once, the bathroom door slammed open.

"What are you doing!" Resit stormed into the cabin. "Have you lost your mind!"

Al Shei blinked heavily. "How much did Schyler tell you?" she asked.

"Enough." Resit stood right in her line of vision. Tears stood in her eyes and against her cheeks. "Name of God, Katmer! He told me this Curran . . . this *thing* has killed Asil!"

Al Shei stood up. The day-book recorder still lay on the floor. "He's done worse than that." She picked it up. "He's taken his mind away. His heart still beats. His body still breathes."

Resit watched her, disbelief building in her eyes. "And you're going to try to do something about it, aren't you? That's why you're paying off the crew?"

"Yes." Al Shei opened the drawer beside the desk and laid the recorder inside it.

"So, I repeat my original question. Have you lost your mind!"

Al Shei slammed the drawer and whirled around to face her cousin. "What would you have me do? Ha? What? They have taken my husband!"

"Alert the Landlords, you donkey-headed . . ."

Al Shei gripped the back of the desk chair. "Zubedeye, if the alarm goes up, they'll get away. They're AIs! It's what they're good at! There will be a fire, or explosive decompression in that module, and by the time emergency services gets in there, they'll all be *gone*."

Resit stared at her. "You want revenge. That is what this is."

Al Shei shrugged.

"This is *haram*, Katmer. This is forbidden."

"Then I will account for it on Judgment Day." Al Shei turned away.

Resit grabbed her by the shoulder and yanked her around. "You are acting like a crazy throwback, Katmer!" She threw up both hands. "Maybe next we can find a Greek for you to slit open!"

"I don't care," said Al Shei thickly. In that frightening instant, she realized she meant it.

"What about your children?"

Al Shei lifted her eyes to meet her cousin's and she knew all her fury shone in them.

"Oh, yes," she hissed. "There we are. You, Mother, how can you put yourself in danger? You have children! So tell me, Fount of Wisdom that you are, what am I supposed to say to these children of mine?" She swept both hands out. "That I knew where their father was and I didn't try to get to him? That I knew what was being done to him and I did not even try to stop it?" Her voice dropped, low and vibrant and filled with rage. "If I die, my children will be looked after, but if I do not do this thing, I will never be able to look at them again." She drew herself up. "You are right. This is forbidden. It is revenge and it is anger and I will make an answer for it to Allah Himself, but first I will make an answer to that monstrosity that has taken my husband!"

Resit's hands dropped to her sides. She bowed her head and pressed her fingertips to her forehead. "*Qul a'udhu birabbin nas. Malikin nas. Ilahin nas. Min sharril waswasil khannas. Alladhi yuwaswisu fi sudurinnas. Minal jinnati wannas.*" Say, I seek refuge in the Lord of mankind, the King of mankind, the God of mankind, from the mischief of the sneaking whisperer, who whispers in the hearts of mankind from among jinn and mankind. She raised her chin again. "So what do you need me for?"

Al Shei felt the strength in her knees begin to give out. She couldn't remember when she'd last eaten, and for the past two nights she had done nothing but stare at the ceiling while she was supposed to be sleeping. She sat down heavily in the desk chair.

"I need you to go sign on with Tully as his lawyer. That way, anything he says to you can be called privileged, just like anything I say to you. I need you to find out from him how to breach Port Oberon security from the *Pasadena*. I don't need any alarms going off when I go after that thing calling itself Curran."

Jump.

Dobbs plowed down the repeater's lines, not even trying to hide herself. She didn't want to hide. She wanted someone, anyone, to find her as fast as they could, as long as they were from the Guild.

That was the problem. That was her fear. She had no idea

where Curran had placed his "talents." Any of them might be following in her wake right now, having jumped in right after her. It might be straining to catch up with her. What would she do then? Would she be able to kill one of them? She'd been ready to kill Curran once, but was she ready to kill someone who believed in him because the Guild had let them all down?

I don't know. I don't want to know.

Set the coordinates. Send the ping-copy to the receiver. Jump. Hit the lines in Repeater 4259AH-IBN2481-H2, four minutes, three point nine seconds gone. Head for the transmitter.

"Dobbs!" A cry reached her. Dobbs stiffened involuntarily before she realized she knew the voice. Cyril Cohen. Of course it would be Cohen, she thought with nearly hysterical relief. He would have been searching for her for days.

He filled the path in front of her. She drove herself straight into him. Too shocked to resist, his inner self broke apart for her. She snatched up segments of memory and twisted them. When she withdrew, he knew all that had happened since Curran had taken her to his home.

"No," he whispered, and she thought they'd both melt from the fear that coursed through them.

"I've got to get to Guild Hall." She tried to fill him with her urgency. It wasn't needed. He had plenty of his own.

"Straight to the Guild Masters." He was already flying. She darted after him, drew up beside him, and touched his outer self. Linked together they almost blocked the repeater's paths. They were delaying a million packets a second, but they didn't care. If they didn't get through, there would be nothing left to save or worry about. They both believed that.

Jump. Repeater 78140-HN-IBN2401-J8. Two more minutes gone.

What's been happening? she asked him through their link.

A second Big Bang, he told her. *They found out you were gone pretty quickly. They suspected me and Brooke of helping you, but they couldn't prove it. There've been eighty-eight different kinds of rumors flying around that they've been trying to hush up. I've been spreading some of them*, he added, and Dobbs felt an odd twinge of pride filter out from his private mind. *Brooke and Lonn and I have been sounding out the*

Masters and Cadets who might be willing to hear what we've got to say about the Guild Masters. There's a number of them.

Would they be willing to help us hold the network against Curran's talents?

That's what I'm hoping, Dobbs. That's what I'm hoping.

Jump. Another repeater surrounded them.

Dobbs was silent as they raced for the transmitter, but she couldn't keep her disquiet from reaching Cohen. Wordlessly, he urged her to share her thought.

You'd better go get them together, just in case the Guild Masters . . . won't go along with this.

Cohen's pace faltered for a bare instant. *You're right. Have you got enough time to . . .* he stopped himself. *Of course, you've got all the time we need, don't you?*

I hope so. She steeled herself. *Get everyone you can and get to the XK350 Repeaters. If I'm not there in five hours then . . . then I'm not coming, and you'll have to go in with what you've got.* She touched his memory and left the location of Curran's module with him.

She pulled away and didn't even leave him any time to wish her luck. Every picosecond was precious right now. Curran might have moved up the timing of the randomizer matrices even farther. He might have decided to put off randomizing the bank accounts, and just take down Port Oberon in order to prevent Al Shei from causing any more trouble. He could be doing anything, and she wouldn't find out about any of it until she got back there.

Yerusha jerked her spare clothes out of their drawer and stuffed them into her satchel. *Fractured, crazy, ground-hugging idiots!* She threw down the last pair of socks and stared at the rumpled pile she'd made. *What am I going to do now?* She rubbed her face. *After word about this run gets out, I'm not going to be able to get a job on a sewage ship, even if the greens don't pick me up for having made idiots out of them last time I was here.*

A day ago, a whole new world had opened up for her. She had rushed toward it and tripped over her own feet. Now she was so crippled, she couldn't even move, couldn't even tell anybody what she'd seen. Her face and eyes burned with loss.

Her desk chimed. Yerusha whipped around and saw the notice that Schyler was waiting outside written on the boards.

What's he want now? She stomped across the room, almost lifting herself off the floor in the light gravity, and slapped her palm against the reader.

She stood back and let Schyler cross the threshold. He had his hands stuffed into his pockets as far as they would go. Yerusha felt her back stiffen. *If you ask me to understand what's going on Watch, you're going to get your head taken off, so help me.*

He settled his gaze on her and pulled his hands out of his pockets. "Yerusha, I need your help."

"Why?" She turned away and, needlessly, began rummaging through her satchel, flattening the pile of clothing and accessories inside so she could close the bag more easily. "Half hour ago you fired me."

"A half hour ago, I fired everybody." He shrugged. "Given the situation, I don't think it was such a bad idea. We're about to get in so far over our heads we're risking pressure sickness. I was wondering if you'd be willing to come with us." He paused. "Even after I fired you in front of witnesses."

Yerusha just looked up and waited. For the first time, she saw the hard light glinting in Schyler's eyes.

"It's looking like Curran's AIs have kidnapped and murdered Asil Tamruc," he said.

His words hit Yerusha like physical blows. She staggered away from him, catching herself against the edge of her desk. "What? Why? Why would they do that?"

"Offhand I'd say to try to throw Al Shei's family into confusion before the AIs attack the Intersystem Banking Network."

The last of the strength went out of Yerusha and she collapsed into the desk chair. This was wrong. This was completely wrong. Why were they doing this? Why weren't they coming to the Freers?

Because the Freers are humans, she answered herself. *We believe the AIs are, too, but they don't. Perspective, you see, is important.*

Schyler sat down on the edge of the bunk and leaned toward her. "Are you all right?"

She nodded and forced her gaze back to his face.

"Al Shei is planning a strike against the AIs. She's going to need help."

"A strike?" Yerusha shook her head, trying to clear the fog her thoughts had become. "To do what?"

Schyler looked away for a moment. When he looked back, his face had deep lines etched into it, as if he had aged ten years in that moment. "I believe Al Shei is about to orchestrate some sort of revenge, and if that's the case, I'm going to need help making sure she lives through it."

"You said the AIs are going to attack the network?" Yerusha's mind wasn't quite keeping up. Ideas sank in slowly, as if forcing their way through cold oil.

Schyler just nodded. "As near as I can tell they're acting as crazy as their creators ever did." He pulled his fists out of his pockets. "We talked to somebody who was probably Dobbs. She said Curran's planning on randomizing the credit exchanges. They'll completely destroy the currency base if no one does anything." He swallowed hard. "Yerusha, if this is true, if they are going to do this, if they take apart the currency base, there's going to be anarchy. The strongest survivors will dictate terms to the rest of us. I've lived like that. I don't ever want to again." His eyes were clear, and his voice was steady. "The Free Home is not completely self-sufficient. There's no telling whose prices you'll have to pay for your fuel and your organics if the currency goes, or who will be willing to trade with you."

Yerusha felt her back stiffen.

"I believe Al Shei's ultimate intent is to help save the banks. I'm going to help her. I'm asking you to help me."

Yerusha turned away. She couldn't look at his steady brown eyes. *He's just a groundhugger at heart,* she told herself. *He doesn't understand anything. They're our freedom. Freedom from death, freedom from the endless, meaningless cycle of sprout and decay. We can't attack them. We need to talk to them. We have to convince them they are part of us.*

But they don't want to be, said another voice in her mind.

At that moment, the Free Home seemed very far away, and it receded even as she reached toward it. Only recent truth remained. Foster had been destroyed by its own kind. Dobbs had literally run away from her attempt to help. Now, Schyler was asking for her help to preserve the network, to preserve the Free Home's freedom.

And if the Fellows found out she had taken sides against living AIs, she might just be exiled for good.

But at least they'd still be free to level sentence against her.

She swiveled the chair around to face the desk. "You said you've got connections on the Free Home justice council?" She yanked the drawer beside her desk open and pulled out a blank film.

"Yes."

"All right." She pulled out her pen. "There's a hard-goods shuttle from here to the Free Home. Leaves from bay 22 once every three hours." She glanced at the clock in the desk. "We should just be able to catch it. Get this film to your contacts, make sure they get told I used the emergency encryptions on it."

She scribbled down the emergency commands. It was an idea the Freers had cribbed from the banks. Every Free Home had a set of codes that could get an emergency message straight through to the Senior Guard. Even exiled citizens. Sometimes exiles had warnings about neighbors planning mischief against the Free Home. Sometimes they heard about wildfire strikes by fanatics that might get Fellows hurt. Those messages were accepted into the Free Home, even if the exiles were left outside. If a message worked to the good of the Free Home, the exile might just be brought home early.

Yerusha had sometimes wondered if the real reason behind punishment by exile was to create a cheap spy network.

She started to write.

I am Exile Jemina Yerusha. I have news of a threat to the Free Home.

There is a group of sapient AIs planning to attack the Intersystem Banking Network and destroy the credit base. The Free Homes will be left without means of trade if they succeed. They are rejecting the idea they're human souls. They are actively hostile to us. I tried to report the fact of sapient AIs with independent existences to Sergeant Wheeler. You can get additional details from him.

The network transactions need to be recorded and stored

on a hard medium. We've got to spread the word through the Free Homes, and we've got to do it now.

The Free Homes can either help Settled Space, or we can go down with the rest of it. And when it goes down, you can either have passed the message on, or let it lie.

Fellow Jemina Yerusha, Free Home Titania.

End message.

The film absorbed the text into its chip. It would not spill it out again until someone's pen downloaded the proper code keys.

She folded the blank film and handed it over to Schyler, who had been reading over her shoulder. "Anything else?"

Schyler let out a long sigh of relief. A ghost of a smile even touched his mouth. "Stand by for now. I've got to get this to that shuttle. Then, I've got to convince Al Shei to let you help us. I'll meet you down in the market place in the Henry V module, all right? At Harry Trader's. Harry knows me; he'll give us somewhere quiet to talk."

"Harry Trader's, right." Yerusha nodded. "See you there." She zipped her satchel shut and slung it over her shoulder. "I'll find a locker for this," she told him before Schyler could say anything.

"Thank you." He squeezed her arm gently and turned away fast enough to miss the startled look on her face.

Yerusha headed for the staircase. Just as the hatch started cycling shut, she heard Lipinski's voice. "Well, you make twelve."

The Houston was standing on the stairs, a few steps below the hatch for the berthing deck. Yerusha frowned. "Keeping count?"

"Actually, yes." He folded his arms. We've all been talking and we think there's an explanation owing." He sketched a circle overhead with one hand, which Yerusha took to be a gesture toward the bridge. "Some of us have been with this ship for years now. This is not only not fair, this is damned crazy. Something is very wrong, and we want to know what it is."

Nobody's said anything to you, have they? Yerusha swallowed. *Of course not. You'd go through the hull like a meteor.*

"I wanted to know if you wanted to be part of the general count when we go to Schyler."

She opened her mouth to say 'no,' but closed it again. She remembered how fervently she had wished for Lipinski's help at The Gate.

"Lipinski." She took a deep breath. "Would you walk with me a little, Fellow? There's something I think you ought to hear."

Jump.

From the shape and crowding in the paths around her, Dobbs knew she was approaching the Drawbridge. She didn't slow down. She didn't try to hide. She would do this through the front door, and in front of as many witnesses as she could muster.

She grazed past someone she didn't know, but they, evidently knew her.

"Evelyn Dobbs!" The call radiated out in all directions. It was picked up and passed on, like a signal boosted through a satellite network. "Evelyn Dobbs! Evelyn Dobbs! Evelyn Dobbs!" But no one got in her way. She found herself wondering what the Guild Masters had said about her, and what Cohen's people had said.

Well, now you know I'm here. Would you like to know why? As she flew by, she caught up a message packet and reshaped it until it held the news about Curran and his plans.

Catch! She lobbed it at the closest Fool and sped on. The Fools around her parted to let her through, and she heard her name echoing back and forth between them.

The Drawbridge loomed in front of her, and it lowered just as she reached it. She shot inside. The paths tilted, turned, and an empty channel opened in front of her.

Of course. She flowed down it. *We wouldn't want to do this in public, would we?*

She didn't even make it to the meeting place. Havelock surged up the path. He had hold of her almost before she was able to identify him. She tried to pull back, but the path had closed. Before she could speak, he stabbed deep into her memories. Dobbs gasped and struggled, shoving memories of Curran and Verence toward him. He did not let go. His grip didn't even slacken and his probe did not slow. He found the memories about Cohen and Brooke and how they helped her escape. He found the place where she told Curran to meet her at the XK350 Repeater series.

He's going to take me apart. Dobbs thought despairingly. *He's going to take us all apart.*

But Havelock withdrew and Dobbs fell away from him. She could feel him near her, circling the confining path like a prisoner pacing a cell. She didn't say anything, she just concentrated on sealing the discontinuities his invasion had created inside her.

"This cannot be permitted!" he shouted finally. "It cannot!"

"So what are you going to do to stop it?" Dobbs gathered herself to wait like a stone in front of the closed-off pathway.

Havelock said nothing, he just kept circling. It took Dobbs a moment to identify what she was feeling from him. It was so incongruous from a Guild Master, she had not been ready to accept it. Guild Master Havelock was broadcasting fear.

It's falling apart, and he knows it, Dobbs thought. For the first time she realized she didn't know how old Guild Master Havelock was. She didn't even know his registry number. How many years had he devoted to the Guild? Had he been there when Curran made his escape? Had he known that Verence wasn't really dead?

"The Humans already know we're here, Guild Master," said Dobbs. "The only question left is how will they meet us? Will they meet the Fools, or will they meet a new enemy?" She could barely believe she was talking like this to a Guild Master, *her* Guild Master, but she could feel the seconds crawling by and part of her was constantly, anxiously reaching back toward Port Oberon. She had to get out of here, fast.

Havelock stilled himself. "It could have worked," he said softly. "It might have taken another two centuries, but it could have worked. We succeeded in convincing them not to abandon AI technology altogether, despite the dangers. We did it so that we could stay alive, so you and Cohen and Brooke and Verence could be born. We were able to persuade and to teach." He rippled and stretched out flat. "Without Curran, it could have worked."

"But we have Curran," said Dobbs. She inched forward

until she could just touch Havelock. "We have him, and now we have to decide what to do with him."

Little by little, Havelock dragged himself into his normal shape. "Go meet Cohen. I'll send everyone who can be spared to join you. The rest of us will start making policy and defence preparations for Guild Hall. We'll need to send runners to alert the Field members to start making their way back here." She felt the path open up. "It will not be safe for them out there much longer."

Dobbs hesitated. "You don't think we're going to survive this, do you, Guild Master?"

"I don't know, Master Dobbs."

Dobbs didn't wait to hear any more. She flew away from him down the open path to meet Cohen and whatever army he'd been able to raise.

Distance did not stop the Guild Master's final words from echoing inside her.

Harry Trader's turned out to be a kind of general-purpose spare parts emporium. Yerusha, with Lipinski in tow, threaded her way through cases of cables, bolts, and rivets, stacks of memory boards, and long drawers full of every size of chip and wafer imaginable. The jumble seemed to suck in the sounds of the market so that by the time they reached the back of the shop's enclosure, it was almost quiet. The only person in the place was a little, round man stacking spools of fiber optic as big around as Yerusha's waist. His black hair, Yerusha noticed, had been pulled into a braid that reached all the way down his back.

"Harry Trader?" she asked. The man grunted and lifted another spool onto the stack. "We're crewing with Thomas Schyler. He said you could give us a quiet place to talk."

Trader turned around and looked them up and down. He must have decided they looked all right, because he jerked his thumb toward a makeshift storage room.

Yerusha led Lipinski inside. There was a desk and crate after crate of old films. *This must be where Harry does his billing records.* There was one white light in the room that left pale, grey shadows everywhere and made Lipinski look even paler than usual.

Lipinski dragged the thin door shut behind them. The walls must have been made of solid damper-plastic, because as soon as the door shut, she couldn't hear even a whisper of the station outside.

"All right, Yerusha," said Lipinski with a voice full of over-taxed patience. "We're in your 'quiet place.' Are you going to tell me what's going on now?"

Yerusha upended a pair of empty crates. "I'm sure going to try."

The *Pasadena* waited quiet and empty around Al Shei. There had been a lot of noise for a short time as the crew had packed up their possessions and headed for the airlock. Even through her cabin hatch, she'd been able to hear some of the grumbling voices and the pounding footsteps. But no one had come to her to question or protest.

She wondered vaguely what Schyler had told them all.

She brushed the thought aside. She didn't have space in her head for it. She turned back to the generic module schematic that glowed on her wall where she usually displayed the plans for the *Mirror of Fate.* This would give her the probable layout for Curran's headquarters. She had to go over her plan again and again. She had to be sure it would work, that she hadn't left anything out.

A chime from her desk startled her. She glanced at the memory board reflexively. Schyler, it said, was waiting outside the hatch.

She touched the key beside the hatch, resetting the entrance light from red to green. The hatch cycled back, and Schyler stepped in from the silent corridor.

"It's just you and me now, Mother," he said.

"Not quite." Resit stepped over the threshold before the hatch started to close. She clutched Incili's case in her right hand.

Resit set the AI on the corner of the desk. "Well, I got what you wanted." She unfolded the chair and sat down. "But we're going to wish we had Lipinski around to implement it."

"I'll manage," said Al Shei. "I still know a few security tricks from when I was working shuttles."

"I'm sure." Resit's tone was acid. "Now, under this lawyer-client privilege that you're playing with so freely, would you mind telling me what you intend to do with this information?"

Al Shei touched the case lightly with her fingertips. "I intend to blow Business Module 56 away from the station," she said, looking up at her cousin and her oldest son. "And I intend to be inside when it goes."

Verence dashed back into the module network, calling for Curran as she flew. He erupted up out of a side path, and she had to pull up short to avoid colliding with him.

"How much longer?" he asked immediately.

"An hour, maybe two." She shrugged her whole self. "Even if we deploy everyone, and there's still at least ten critical junctures unconverted."

Curran didn't even stir. "Then we'll have to leave them. We'll need five talents in the flesh and on watch in case the *Pasadena* crew attempts to assault the module." He had already vetoed the idea of taking out the station. That would raise the alarm for the Humans on colony worlds even earlier than necessary.

"The banks know about us," he had said in the briefing. "But they'll have been told the attack is going to be against their intersystem network."

The humans' communications were being monitored. They were moving in typical glacial fashion, unable to agree on even basic measures to meet the threat. The bankers hadn't even alerted the Management Union yet. Gilbereth estimated it would be six hours before they made even their first move. The attack would be well under way by then. There was an unusual amount of recording activity starting around the Free Homes. The *Pasadena*'s pilot must have gotten to the Fellows after all. Had the original plan been in place, it might have been cause for concern, but now it was nothing worth worrying about.

"What about module network security?" asked Verence.

"No need," said Curran. "When Dobbs returns with the Guild, they'll be going straight for the crucial points of the bank network. Preservation of the status quo will be their main objective." His tone was wintery. "Just like it's always been."

Verence shuddered. "I still don't understand why you didn't just send Shiff and Tombe after her," she said. "They could have brought her back here and held her until she saw sense again."

"No." Curran's tone was firm. "It's gone to far for that. When we attack, the Guild will come with Dobbs or without her. We will just have to delay them until things on Earth are well under way."

Uncertainty wavered against anger inside Verence. She had been furious at Dobbs for her betrayal, but, what if . . . what if . . ."What if Dobbs is right? What if this won't work?"

Curran let his convictions flow into her. Verence felt strength and certainty wash through her. She drank it down into her private mind. She needed it to drown out Dobbs' fractured, defiant words that would not stop ringing around her memory.

We will do what we have to in order to be free, Curran told her. *If this doesn't convince the Humans they must deal with us as their equals, we'll try again.*

He pulled away gently. "Now, I need you to find Flemming and Dunkirk. Together we can go over those last ten critical junctures. Maybe there's still something we can do."

"Yes, sir."

Verence hurried down the path. For the first time in a long time wished she were inside a body. Then she could have gone to sleep and, for at least a little while, she could have stopped thinking about everything Dobbs had said to her.

Yerusha heard the scrape of the storage door opening. Lipinski jerked his head up. The white light fell on Schyler, whose eyebrows arched when he saw Lipinski sitting there.

"It's all right, Watch." Yerusha waved Schyler inside. "He's with us."

"There don't seem to be a lot of options," said Lipinski to the floor. "I just hope somebody really does have a plan." He rubbed the back of his neck. "At least this explains . . . things"

Yerusha spared him a little sympathy. The entire crew knew that the Houston was cherishing some romantic feelings toward the Fool. Finding out that she was the monster he was afraid of . . . when he had time to think about it, it would probably tear him in two.

Schyler settled himself on a third storage crate. "Well, Resit got one wish anyway. She wanted you here to help, Lipinski."

"What's the news?" Yerusha asked.

Schyler rested both elbows on his knees. "Al Shei has gotten a bunch of security data from Marcus Tully. She wants to use that and Tully's cat burglars to disable the station alarms and then get herself into the AI's can. As soon as she does, she wants the can knocked away from the station."

"She what!" exclaimed Lipinski.

Schyler didn't even miss a beat. "It makes some sense. With the can in free fall, no transmissions can get in or out of it because the transmitters and receivers will be rolling around with the rest of the module and no one will be able to get a signal fix on them. That means a finite number of AIs in a limited space to deal with. Most of Curran's—people—should be out busy with the IBN."

Lipinski subsided. Yerusha smiled quietly. This was the kind of argument he could understand perfectly.

Schyler kept going. "I figure this'll take a little space walk. We lay some charges on both of the clamps and blow them out. Harry's licensed to sell explosives, so that just leaves us with the question of how we get onto the surface of the can without being seen by the security cameras."

"We don't," Yerusha told him.

"What?" Schyler stared at her incredulously.

Yerusha sighed. "There will be cameras trained on the module's skin by the Landlords, and by the AIs. Trust me, if there is anything there that isn't supposed to be, the cameras will spot it. Now, maybe we could crack the cameras' systems and fake an image, but under these circumstances do we really want to rely on using the station network for anything we don't absolutely have to?"

Schyler drank in what she said in silence. "Then what do we do?" he asked.

"We get ourselves a main schematic of the station wiring. There'll be a film copy in the core's archives. Then we raid the laundry and get ourselves some maintenance overalls and get down to this Business Module 56. We get inside the wall panels and find the wires that control the clamps holding the can to the rest of the station. We splice those wires to a portable memory board. Then, we use the information Tully gave us to override the clamps' command sequence and tell them to let go." She allowed herself a grim smile at the expression on Schyler's face. "Groundhuggers. You always think you have to blow something up or burn it down to incapacitate it. That's why the Freers keep winning against you."

"Well, then"—Schyler stood up and gestured toward the door—"I suggest you show us how it's done."

Jump.

Repeater XK350-78104001-IBN780A-HI was slaved to ten sisters—780B through 780K. The data squeezing by her was mainly gas miners' requests for prices and credit from the Solar System.

Dobbs slipped through to the holding areas. On the way, she'd managed to put together a plan of action. It hadn't taken long. She was not hampered by a plethora of options.

Dobbs touched Cohen, Brooke, and Lonn. Each of them, in turn, was touching two others. Messages shot back and forth between the satellites along the slave lines. The link spread out until it included all of the Fools, joined together like cells in a honeycomb. The need for this joining had been the reason Dobbs chose this repeater series. It was one of the few satellite clusters where there was room for it.

Dobbs passed her name and identifying patterns through those next to her and received their names and patterns into herself. Strangers' names and strangers' touches filtered through her friends and stored themselves in her memory; Breckman, Govzy, Chan, Pierre, Davies, Kim, and on and on until they all knew each other. Anyone for whom a name and the touch of their outer self was not in her memory now was probably one of Curran's talents.

They were just over five hundred. Five times the number of Curran's talents. They needed to be. All of them, except for her and a handful like Cohen, whose bodies were on life support, were under the pressure of time. The others could stay in the network twenty hours at most before they would have to drop out, and they'd already used up a portion of their time waiting here.

Dobbs had half expected an attack while they were all in an obvious, immobile lump like this. But Curran hadn't disturbed them at all. That could only mean he was using all his resources to ready his attack on the banks. Dobbs opened a path inside herself and let her memories of the strategy sessions slide out to Cohen. After them, she released her plan of attack. It wound through the gathering. Questions and suggestions shot back and forth until a consensus solidified among them all.

The randomizer matrices were already in place, waiting for their timers to count down. It was possible that Curran had sent his talent out with signals to speed up the process. They had to find one or more randomizers, take them apart, design viruses to disable them, and set those viruses loose in the net. They had to get some Fools to Earth to coordinate with the banks in case Curran tried the distraction of taking down the transmitters.

Ahmet Tey might listen to Dobbs, especially if she could get a character reference from Al Shei to him. So she'd lead the Terran party.

The problem was, there was nothing they were planning that Curran couldn't have guessed at, and he knew their weaknesses as well as they did. All AIs shared the same set of vulnerabilities. Messages between individuals could be faked. If fools were taken apart, all their memories could be used against their allies. You could only trust what you could touch.

They would have to divide into teams of four or five individuals that could act as resistance cells. They would have to use runners between the cells to carry messages, and even then there was the possibility of someone's shell being used as a mask to conceal an enemy, the same way the shell of medical data had been used to hide Flemming aboard the *Pasadena*.

They'd need a base they could use to coordinate and move news between the cells. The best place would be the Neptune Exchange, the two huge space stations that formed the fast-time transmission gateway to the Solar System. Not only would that provide their hastily assembled army some stability, but, if they could hold it, it would keep the single largest transmission point in the Solar System safe from Curran's talent.

A third of them would head for the Neptune Exchange first. From there, Dobbs's cell and ten others would head straight for Earth. The rest would fan out through the network, securing as many of the major junctions as they could.

Keep the data paths steady. Find the randomizer matrices and stop them. Find Curran's talent and stop them. We must keep the credit base steady, or Settled Space is going to fall apart around us.

We've got it, Dobbs, the answer came back five hundred times. *We've got it.*

They broke their mass link and scattered, gathering at the mouths of the junction paths in their cells. Cohen, Brook, and Lonn stayed beside her. Dobbs angled her attention toward Earth, the heart of the network. She imagined she could feel the net tremble around her as all the others did the same.

"Curran's talent might already be in the Neptune Exchange." Dobbs sent the message across to the Earth-bound cells. "I'm going first. If I don't send the all clear in two seconds, they already have the exchange." *I can hold out against anybody for two seconds,* she told herself. *Even Curran.*

She gathered herself up, heart, soul, and all the nerve she possessed. She wished there was a prayer she could say. She wished there was someone who might hear it. There was nothing and nobody. There wasn't even time.

She sent a ping-copy to Receiver 501-BG-A12 at the Neptune Exchange. The signal came back intact. That meant nothing. If the talent were there, they now knew she was coming.

Alone, Dobbs dived forward.

Chapter Fourteen

WAR

One.

Dobbs dropped into a crowded holding stack. She touched the ID packet. She had made the Neptune Exchange. She stretched out. Nothing disturbed the datastreams as far as she could reach except her. She tripped a set of switches and sent a diagnostic down the nearest path and waited for it to come back. It found nothing except what was supposed to be out there.

Two.

Dobbs made a ping-copy of herself and set the transmitter to shoot it back to Cohen. She kept the diagnostic circulating and waited for the answering signals.

The diagnostic slipped back to her, and Dobbs caught it. Before her next thought formed, a stranger fell across her, cutting her off from her surroundings. She twisted, but it rolled her aside. She swelled up against the swaddling presence and, in the next thought, hauled herself into a tight ball. The stranger didn't respond fast enough, and Dobbs shot out of its loosened grip.

There was another stranger looming over the receiver's command stack. Dobbs lunged and shoved it out of the way. She barely brushed the new command configuration before the stranger's compatriot dragged her backward, stabbing deep into her outer layers, seeking a hold in her private mind. Dobbs lashed out, cutting a swash clear through the stranger's periphery. Anger lent her strength. These two had re-set the receiver commands to work in a loop with the repeater series. Cohen, Brook, and Lonn were trapped. Her friends were frozen signals bouncing back and forth between the two receivers.

Dobbs aimed another swipe at the first stranger. The second grabbed her and sent her reeling down the path toward the transmitter. Dobbs tried to surge back toward the receiver, but both strangers filled the path. She punched at them. They hardened themselves against her attacks. Slowly, they drove her toward the transmitter holding stack. It didn't take much to guess that they were going stuff her into the loop with Cohen and the others. Dobbs hurled herself against them, but together they were too massive for her. They shoved her backward.

Dobbs felt the entrance to the holding stack open against her. She stretched herself out, trying to jam the entrance shut with her presence. The strangers in front of her just pressed down harder. Bit by bit, Dobbs felt herself begin to give way.

First Stranger shifted. A chink broke open between it and the pathway's side. Dobbs dived for it. Second Stranger faltered. Dobbs pummeled First Stranger with all her strength, and the chink widened into a crack. Dobbs hammered at it. First Stranger collapsed and Dobbs barreled past it. A friendly touch grazed her as she flew down the path. Terrence. Dobbs barely had time to understand Terrence was the runner for Renee's cell when she felt Second Stranger snatch at her. Dobbs grabbed up Terrence and the pair of them fled toward the heart of the Exchange. They ducked down paths at random, tossing messages and packets behind them to block the way.

Dobbs snatched up a dense packet and tried to throw it behind her. The world contracted. Something dragged at her outer self until she felt like water swirling down a drain. She could feel her thoughts being sucked apart one by one. She screamed frantically and lurched backwards. The thing dragged harder. Terrence engulfed her, cut clean through her outer self, and heaved them both away from the thing. Dobbs screamed again as her main self separated from the lost portion. There were memories in there, and information she needed, she was sure. It was gone, completely, utterly and horribly gone. If she'd been in her body she would have been shaking in terror.

"Dobbs, can you answer me? Dobbs!" Terrence rolled her over into a side path and circled around her.

"Yeah, yeah." Dobbs forced herself to focus her attention on the torn part of herself. Holes gaped in her recent memory. Whole conversations with Al Shei and Lipinski were nothing but tattered ruins. Dobbs rolled herself into a tight ball and remembered why she was here. That much remained. Asil in the bed in the medical level of Curran's can, that was there, Al Shei throwing her off *Pasadena*, that was there. But something was gone from Lipinski's place, and more was gone from Yerusha. What had she said before she'd run? What had Lipinski asked before she turned him away? Dobbs shook herself. That was gone, and it would never be back. She couldn't mourn it now.

"What was that?" she demanded.

"I don't know, but I think it was aimed at us. Did you feel how the mechanism worked at all?"

"I might have." Dobbs shivered. "But that was probably the first thing that went."

"Stay here." Terrence edged back to the main path. "I'm going to see if it's still out there."

Before Dobbs could shout a warning, Terrence was gone. Dobbs pulled herself into her shell as far as she could, wishing desperately for someway not to count the passing seconds.

A message tapped her. BACK UP, DOBBS. Dobbs decided to believe it was from Terrence and pressed against the side of the pathway. The other Fool touched her gently.

"I think I see why they're not following us anymore. Reach here."

Dobbs let Terrence guide her awareness. She barely brushed the processors in front of her and the foul tugging and nibbling began. She snatched herself back.

"Curran's talent have invented an AI antipersonnel weapon," said Terrence. "It acts like a black hole. Sucks you in and tears you apart. It only reacts to us. The talent must have some kind of ID code that keeps it from going off around them."

Dobbs found herself admiring Terrence's calm. "So, how'd you get it to move?"

"It responds to us," she said, "but not to stuff we create. I managed to get it on a leash. Give me a second, and I think I can use a couple probes to dissect its command structure."

"Gladly." Dobbs settled back. "I just wish you didn't sound like you were enjoying this."

Under her light touch, Dobbs felt Terrence strip a couple of nearby packets and turn them into probes. "It's either have fun or curl up screaming." She dropped the probes into the weapon's maw. "Which I'll be doing later anyway."

"I thought I'd get it over with now, myself," muttered Dobbs. "I hate to delay a good panic."

The packet Dobbs leaned against twitched. "Ashes!" She bolted down the path, just in time to collide with First Stranger.

"I'll get you, you twisted bastard!" she shouted as she took off down a fresh path. "I'll get you for Terrence!" As she hoped, First Stranger veered to follow her. If she was lucky, it also thought their weapon had gotten Terrence.

Dobbs tried not to think about all the other black holes that could be lying around in the exchange as she dodged down the paths with no other aim than to draw the talent away from Terrence. Her pursuer snatched at the ragged edges of her wound. Dobbs felt her determination begin to falter. If she couldn't keep her speed up, she was going to have to turn and fight, and she didn't know if she had the strength.

All at once, First Stranger was gone. Dobbs felt the black hole breeze by without even twitching in her direction. She didn't let herself stop to think what had just happened to First Stranger. She turned herself around and raced back to the receiver.

Terrence was already there. Dobbs pushed into the space beside her, and together they reset the receiver's commands.

A flood of packets spilled into the path and with them tumbled Cohen, Brooke, and Lonn. Dobbs reached for them all. They were badly disoriented and trying to haul themselves together.

"Had a split second each bounce to realize what was going

on," blurted out Cohen, "but not enough time to do anything about it."

Dobbs told them what had been happening to her and Terrence.

"I found the key signatures inside that thing and reset them," Terrence chimed in. "Now instead of bypassing any AI carrying the keys, it'll attack them. I sent it rolling around the exchange. It'll selfdestruct in ten seconds, and we should be clear."

"Glad to hear it," said Brooke. "You're a terror yourself, Terrence. I've said so before."

"We haven't got time for this," Cohen reminded them all.

"Terrence, you'd better spread the word about the black holes and how to undo them."

"I'm gone." Terrence dropped like a stone into the transmitter holding stack.

"Lonn, you stay here and coordinate with the next set of arrivals," said Dobbs. "This place has been seeded with the randomizer matrices. We know that. Your people have got to find them and work out how to spot and dismantle them. You've got to start a virus production as soon as possible. Cohen, Brooke, we've got to keep going."

Terrence, good as her word, was gone. Dobbs reset the transmitter to point toward the Asteroid Belt Repeaters. While she waited for the ping-copy, she wondered what was going on outside. What had the Exchange's attendees seen on their readouts? Were they mustering their diagnostics, or were they just scrambling to get into pressure suits before this insanity hit the life support.

Which might not be a bad idea. "Lonn, get a message out to the station personnel. Make sure they start taking vital systems off-line and that they switch to generators and manual operation where possible."

"But . . ."

"Do it!" ordered Dobbs as her ping-copy fell back against her. "This is not just about us!"

And it never will be again.

The war was twenty seconds old.

Jump.

Al Shei pulled on the black overalls with the Landlords' bright green seal emblazoned on both shoulders. They felt uncomfortably tight across her breasts and around her crotch, but now was not the time to complain, or to think about her modesty. Especially with what needed to happen next.

Al Shei unwrapped her *hijab* and lifted it away. She crumpled it into a ball and stuffed it quickly into the drawer. There. It was done. She buckled her tool belt around her waist and picked up her spares kit. She avoided catching her own eye in the reflective surface of the view screen as she turned and strode out into the corridor.

The enemy would be looking for Al Shei, veiled in her modesty and shielded by the law of Islam. They would not recognize this bare-faced Turk. At least, they wouldn't recognize her immediately.

God willing and the creeks don't rise, she thought before she could stop herself. Now was not a good time to think of God. Not with all the sins she was committing. Resit was right. This was forbidden and she was a throwback, straight out of the seconds before the Fast Burn. She was a mad Turk, crazy with revenge, and Allah was watching her every move closer to the brink of Hell. She knew she wouldn't stop, though. She wouldn't even hesitate, because inside she didn't feel Allah anymore. She felt Asil, his touch, his love, his possibilities. Gone. All of them gone.

As she approached the airlock, she realized she did not want Schyler to see her like this, but there was no help for it.

He's going to stare, she thought sourly.

She reached the airlock. Schyler and Yerusha, also dressed in black overalls, waited there. Schyler did stare at her naked face for a moment, then he blushed and looked away.

Al Shei realized on any other day she might have found it in her to be amused. "Intercom to Houston. What's our status?"

"Well, I've managed to get Business Module 56 listed as overdue for a maintenance check, and I've got three maintenance workers slated to go over there and raise their voices and level fines. Their names are Forrester, Klien, and Brown. Any requests for information from any of your pens will be routed back here." He paused. "Tully's stuff is as good as advertised. Now I can stop wondering why he never got caught."

"So now you can start wondering if we will get caught," muttered Yerusha as she tucked her portable memory board under her arm. She had a coil of cable about the width of Al Shei's little finger sticking out of her pocket.

"By the way," said Lipinski, "whatever you said to the Freers seems to have stuck. I'm picking up dozens of urgent messages between Free Home Titania and the other Homes."

Al Shei raised her eyebrows. Yerusha shrugged. "This is not just about you, is it?"

Al Shei sighed and looked away. This was no time to refuse help. This was no time to think about the outside world either. That would have to take care of itself. She had to concentrate.

Resit was nowhere in evidence. Al Shei wondered where she was, and if it was perhaps time for prayer.

"Let's get going." She cycled open the airlock and led her crew out into the docking bay.

Business Module 56 was all the way around the ring from the *Pasadena*. Al Shei and the others huddled themselves into the back of a crowded elevator and tried to hold still through the shifts of gravity and calmly breathe the air that was warm and thick from too many people trying to use it. But by the time they were able to get off in Business Module 55, they were the only ones left in the car.

"Mostly storage, over here," said Schyler as he followed Al Shei and Yerusha into the stairway. "Gases, fuel, spare parts, maintenance drones."

"Drones like us," said Yerusha with her strange, grim cheerfulness. Al Shei glanced back at her. She could almost swear the woman was starting to enjoy this.

Halfway up the flight, Al Shei signaled them all to stop. She crouched down in front of one of the maintenance panels that lined the walls, lifted it away from the wall, and flipped it over. The underside was engraved with a diagram of the circuits, wires, and pipes revealed by the square hole. She skimmed the labels and tried to ignore the camera staring at her back.

I belong here, she thought toward it. *I belong here.*

"All right, Klien, Forrester" she said to Yerusha and

Schyler. "Here's what you need to do." They both bent over her, and so did Schyler, effectively shielding the diagram from the camera. "We might have a minor glitch in here, so I want you to trace this set of wires . . ." Yerusha held out her memory board, and Al Shei pulled out her pen and wrote quickly.

The blue pipes are the hydrolics for the clamps. Trace them back through the panels and you should come to a command breaker. That's where you make your splice.

"And if you can't find anything, you call in." She handed the board back to Yerusha. "Understand?"

"Right." Yerusha knelt on the stair, laid the board in front of her, and pulled another panel off the wall. Schyler stood right behind her.

"And I"—Al Shei opened up her kit, pulled out a band lamp, and strapped it across her forehead—"am going to talk to our truants."

She trotted up the rest of the flight of stairs and stopped in front of a bulkhead with a sealed airlock marked Business Module 56. The entrance light was red. She laid her palm on the reader and waited.

For a long time, nothing happened. Al Shei wondered if they were simply going to refuse to answer. Lipinski must have shouted at them half a dozen times by now, pretending to be the voice of the Landlords. They would have to respond. If they didn't, they'd risk bringing down the greens rather than just the blacks. They must know that.

Unless, of course, they'd traced the source of the calls back to Lipinski instead of to the Landlords, despite Tully's cat burglars. In that case, they could be setting up that trap Schyler was worried about. They must know they'd been found out on at least some level. They must be reading the transmissions between the Free Homes. A cold thought touched Al Shei. *What if they know, and they just don't care?*

The airlock cycled back slowly. Inside, stood a broad-faced young man. A shotgun hung from his shoulder by a black strap.

Al Shei couldn't help but stare at it. *A shotgun! Aboard a space station!* It had a small barrel, though. It probably fired low-caliber shot, sufficient to pass through a human body without punching through deck plates or the hull. Actually, it was a good compromise, she thought clinically. It was more lethal than tranquilizer darts or a taser, but it was less hazardous to the can than a flash-burn.

She gathered her wits and remembered her role.

"Brown, maintenance." She stepped briskly across the threshold. She presented her pen. He stared at it like she'd just offered him a live wire. "You're overdue," she said. "You should have been notified by now."

He took the pen, and his gaze flickered from it to her. Skepticism filled his expression, but not absolute certainty. Over his shoulder, she saw the far side of the airlock had not cycled open. Behind her, she heard the station side hatch crank shut. They were trapped. If the clamps released now, the airlock would seal automatically, leaving the two of them rattling around inside until the can was reattached to the station, if they lived that long.

"Let me just check on this." He sidestepped to the intercom beside the far hatch and jacked her pen into the wall socket. He did not take his gaze off her.

Al Shei measured the guard up. He was a lot bigger than she was, and he had the gun dangling by his right hand. Speed was her only hope.

She launched herself at him and caught him in the chest with her shoulder. He hit the hatch with a "whoof!" She grabbed his hand and slammed it against the palm reader. He wrenched himself around, but she dropped to the floor. He wasted a second looking wildly around for her. The airlock cycled open.

Al Shei rolled across the threshold as soon as there was room and scrambled to her knees, dragging her spares kit with her behind the retreating hatch. She was in a corridor full of waldos, cameras, and drones. She spotted a hatchway to her right and dived for it. It cycled open. A guard room.

"Stop!"

She stared up at the guard with his gun. She climbed to her feet with her spares kit clutched to her chest.

This was it. If Yerusha and Schyler hadn't found the command breakers and overriden them, Al Shei was dead where she stood. She backed up until her spine pressed against the wall.

"Put the box down, Katmer Al Shei." He smiled, quite obviously knowing he'd gotten the name right on the first try.

A low grinding noise reverberated through the walls. The world plunged into darkness and spun out of control.

As soon as Dobbs touched her surroundings, a packet slammed up against her. She grabbed it. One touch told her it was stuffed full of random strings of numbers. She reached inside it for the command code, and it disintegrated in her grip. One tiny piece flitted off into the network.

Oh, hell. Dobbs lunged for the fragment, and missed.

She barely had time to wonder what was going on before the next packet hit. She ducked the one after that, but not the next. Now the path was full of them, all rushing at her, battering at her sides, demanding her attention. It was like being in a swarm of maddened bees. It was like being shouted at by a hundred people and not being able to understand one of them. She could barely think. She couldn't move under their clamor and pressure. She tried batting them away, but it was no good. One would splinter if she stabbed at it, but a dozen others swarmed up the path to take its place.

Then she felt Cohen's touch like a fresh breeze. What was he doing here? She hadn't sent the all clear. He'd come anyway. He would. She tried to reach him, to warn him, but it was too late. He'd already picked up one of the random packets, and now a swarm of them bore down on him.

Very slowly, Dobbs felt herself begin to panic. The things swirled around her, smothering her senses, choking off all awareness of everything but their endless, meaningless noise. She struck out randomly. Through a brief clearing she heard Cohen call her name. A packet clogged the hole, cutting her off from him.

An idea flared inside her.

Dobbs forced herself to hold still. She hardened her outer layers and did her best to hold her wound closed. The packets slammed against her, piling one on top of the other, burying her in a solid layer of random numbers and alien code.

Burying her so deep that no other packet would be able to

find her. She hoped. If she was wrong, she was already dead, trapped in here until she lost what was left of her mind. With great difficulty, she flexed herself a little. Just enough to drag one of the packets out of the puzzle-work shell they'd made over her. Another one oozed into its place. Her imagination supplied a low "slurp."

Dobbs dragged the packet down until it was almost touching her private mind. It disintegrated, but the fragments had nowhere to go except inside her. She set to work on it with tiny, cramped movements. *It responds to us,* Terrence had said, *but not to stuff we create.* Well, she had plenty of raw material to create with. It was pressing against her like cotton wadding. She knew nothing beyond her little world. She grabbed another packet. Seconds creaked past. Cohen might be dead. She didn't know. She didn't know anything. She clenched herself tight around her handiwork. She dissected one more packet for its search code and joined it to the others. Anything might have happened by now. The war might be over by now. They might have won or lost. She might be permanently alone under an endless weight. She might be buried alive.

Dobbs pushed her new-made searcher into motion. The shell around her parted briefly, because this new thing was not Evelyn Dobbs. Dobbs, straining to keep herself from blind panic, waited two seconds. Then, she stabbed downward. The shell splintered and, almost instantly, sealed shut. But that fragment of time was enough to tell her her idea was working. She was moving.

The deafening packets were not spontaneously generated out of the nowhere. They had no self-replicating code inside them. They had to be coming from some command sequence somewhere. Her searcher was trying to find out where that was. It was dragging the mound that held her with it.

She could stand this. She knew she could. It wasn't any different from when Cohen had carried her. Stab. Still moving. Well, not much different. But, she hadn't known what was happening then, either.

Stab. Still moving. She couldn't touch, couldn't hear, couldn't know then either. She had not gone crazy then. She had not died then. She wouldn't now. She wouldn't now.

Stab. Stillness.

Dobbs gathered all her energy and burst free of her shell. The packets flew apart like shrapnel and she clamped herself onto the processors in front of her. The swarm descended, fastening onto her back. She shivered reflexively, but not enough to falter in the work in front of her. The processors flickered and shifted under her touch. No time for finesse. She reached deep into the middle of them and with one hard twist, she froze all the microscopic gates shut.

She turned her attention to the packets. They still clung to her, but now when she swatted them aside, they were not replaced. She kicked herself free of the last of them and streaked up the path back toward Cohen.

He was tearing apart the last whole packet as she reached him.

"Cohen!"

He swung his attention toward her. There was something wild and swollen in his motion that made her back off. "It's all right, Cohen. I've turned it off. We're out of it."

Slowly, Cohen shrank back to his normal shape. "Thank you."

He turned to the transmitter a little too deliberately and sent the all clear.

Stay with me, Cohen, thought Dobbs in the deepest part of her private mind. *I can't do this without you.*

The black air around Al Shei was full of objects, all of them rushing straight up. She had her hand up in time to stop her head from colliding with the ceiling. The guard hollered wordlessly as he hit. Bracing herself with her spares kit, Al Shei switched on the band lamp on her forehead. The beam fell across Curran's security guard. He no longer looked pleased with himself. She brought her kit down to chest level and shoved it away from her. It rocketed across the room, knocking lighter miscellany aside and catching the guard square in the chest. All the air left him as he slammed against the far wall. Al Shei kicked off the wall and snatched the shotgun out of the gloom as she flew past it. The guard had time to stare openmouthed at her before she swung the gun like a bat against his skull. The impact smashed him back against the wall and left a trail of scarlet droplets hanging in the air behind him. Al Shei bounced backwards against the wall and felt the impact against her spine. She ignored it, tucked the gun under one arm, and kicked off again, launching herself down the corridor.

Up and down were without definition. Her body told her she was falling, in all directions at once. The walls rotated around her, scattering missiles and meteorites through the air. They clanked, chinged, and rattled off the walls, and each other, and Al Shei. Nothing was heavy enough to slow her down.

Someone with chestnut skin and a green coverall fell into her lamplight. They snatched at her and missed. As she drifted past, Al Shei twisted around and aimed the gun between her own feet and fired. The recoil shot her past the stranger and into the wall, slamming into her stomach and knocking all the air out of her lungs. There was more scarlet in the air behind her, and her stomach lurched senselessly. She had hit something with that trick.

She fell toward a major hatchway. The stranger—a man, she saw now—launched himself at her. His shoulder was leaking red bubbles. Al Shei yanked on the hatch with one hand and pressed the shotgun against her ribs and fired again. Again, the recoil knocked her backwards, through the hatchway this time.

She didn't slow down to see if she'd hit him. The spin was slowing and the alarms were silencing one by one. The AIs were regaining control. They'd have the lights back on soon. She flew through a broad corridor, ricocheting off the curved walls. She coughed painfully and tasted blood. The gun's recoil had broken something inside.

The lights came on, flooding the corridor and making Al Shei blink hard. Something grabbed her left arm ruthlessly and hauled her toward the wall. Al Shei gasped and twisted. A waldo gripped her forearm, and a second reached out toward her. She stuffed the gun's stock into its pincers. They closed down and the stock splintered, sending slivers of plastic flying in every direction. Al Shei ripped the wire cutters off her tool belt. She wrapped their jaws around the waldo's smallest pincer, and wrenched it back. The pincer casing bent and snapped, exposing a series of multicolored wires. From the corner of her eye, Al Shei saw a cart-sized drone racing toward her down a grooved track in what was now a wall. She was close enough to the corridor's side to brace her feet against it. She hooked the cutters around the waldo's newly exposed wires, arched her back, and *yanked.* The mechanical hand spasmed, and her abrupt motion pushed Al Shei into open air again. She bounced off the wall/ceiling, sending a whole wave of pain through her. That was when she really saw the cameras. They were directing the waldos. These AIs had hands and eyes, and they had spotted her.

She pushed herself toward the cart. The wall waldos hadn't oriented on her yet, and she dropped past them. She hit the grooved track and bounced. As she rose, she hooked her hand under the cart's belly, holding herself against the wall/floor. A waldo swooped toward her and she swung her wire cutters up to block it. It wrenched them out of her hand and tossed them away. As it did, Al Shei braced her feet against the nearest wall and shoved backwards. The force of her movement jarred one pair of the cart's casters out of the groove. Its right side rose at a drunken angle and its waldos flailed to reach the track again, catching some of the wall's arms in their grip.

Another waldo stretched out from the wall to catch hold of her. Al Shei's body rose to meet it. She grabbed its forearm with both hands and used it to lever herself up into the relatively clear air, snatching her wire cutters as she passed. The cart arms and the wall arms were still grappling with each other, trying to sort themselves out. Al Shei pried open a panel in the ceiling/wall over them. She caught up a clipper full of wires just as a waldo closed on her ankle. She clamped both hands around the wire cutter's handles as the waldo dragged her backwards.

The wires broke and a shower of sparks exploded out against Al Shei's face. The lights went dead, leaving only the narrow beam of her lamp to cut the darkness. The waldo holding her relaxed and Al Shei was able to launch herself around the curve of the hallway.

On her right she drifted past a doorway, not a hatch. Her brain skimmed memories of the schematic she had pored over in her cabin. *Maintenance Closet!* thought Al Shei jubilantly, and she scrabbled at the edge of the door. Fortunately, the power was out here, too, so any electronic locks had been disabled.

Al Shei slid the door open, pulled herself inside, and slammed the manual bolts shut behind her. She hung in the darkness for a moment, trying to catch her breath and collect her thoughts. Her abdomen burned painfully, and the taste of salt and iron wouldn't leave her mouth. Anonymous objects bumped against her. She turned her head to shine the lamp's beam around. Multiple cabinets had been knocked open, and the detritus formed a whirlpool around her. Flotsam scraped past her hands and torso as the walls turned. The air had cooled perceptibly since the disaster began, but not dangerously. The Fools had obviously maintained their generator batteries well, at least.

First things first. The power. They'd have a drone down to repair the damage she'd done to the wires in no time, and it wouldn't take them long to guess where she'd gone. Her light glanced on a whole host of waldos on the walls. She swam across to a maintenance panel, pulled it away from the wall, and looked at the underside. She smiled. They'd gotten rid of all the exterior labels, but the AIs hadn't thought to erase the panel diagrams. She scanned the symbols, and her smile grew wider. There was a breaker cluster in here with her.

She counted three panels up and four over from the one she had opened. Underneath it, she found a gorgeous set of orange, green, and blue cables, all feeding into a group of four squat wafer stacks. Bobbing unsteadily in front of her target. Al Shei pulled her overall sleeves up over her hands and grabbed the stacks. She closed her eyes, braced her feet against the wall and pulled. The wafers came free, almost burning her hands even through the cloth. The pinpricks of sparks landed against her cheeks and brows. Al Shei drifted gently through the sea of detritus and bounced off the far wall.

She let the cluster go and shook her hands free of her sleeves.

Take that! she thought wildly. She shone her light all around the closet. The waldos remained still. Most of the level should be out of power. Which was good for now, but the AIs most certainly knew where their own breakers were. Her light landed on the silver-grey doors of a locker below her feet, and Al Shei felt a surge of hope. Maybe there was one other human necessity the AIs hadn't been able to quite do away with.

Al Shei tucked her legs and dived toward the locker. She grabbed the handle to steady herself. She could hear a distinct rattle inside.

Didn't they have anything *secured?* she thought as she opened the door. She hid behind it as the contents of the locker spilled out. As she had hoped, a pressure suit floated past her. It must be for emergencies. The AIs couldn't install their ubiquitous waldos on the outside of their can without someone noticing. For the same reason, they couldn't send any of their customized drones out there. There was too much activity outside. Too many chances to be seen. If something happened to the outer hull of this can that they had electronically hidden from the rest of Port Oberon, one of them would have to take the cold walk outside to fix it.

She nabbed the suit out of the stream by its collar and pulled it behind her toward the nearest wall. Her lamp showed her that it was a standard industrial issue getup; mustard yellow emergency gear, a backpack for gas tanks, a cutting/welding torch holstered on the side. It had a chest plate for tools, and pockets for the wrenches and screwdrivers that were now swimming through the whirlpool. She checked the gauges on the gas tanks and batteries. The suit was charged and ready to go.

Al Shei abandoned her tool belt to the whirlpool and climbed into the suit. Her body had given up trying to reason with her about relative directions, and she was able to ignore the fact that she was rolling perpendicular to the rest of the room as she locked herself inside and secured the helmet. As soon as she did, the suit batteries kicked in and lit up the chin keys and interior displays. She bumped a key with a jerk of her chin and the external lamps came on. A quick glance around showed her where the tool belt had drifted. She retrieved it and loosened the cinch out as far as it would go, so she could strap it around the suit's waist.

Al Shei nudged the chin control to darken the faceplate down enough to conceal her face, but not enough to hinder her vision. She checked the readout of her air, her gases, and her batteries one more time, then opened up the door.

And almost collided with a woman in tan overalls. She recoiled from the glare of Al Shei's lamps. Al Shei opened up the suit's intercom.

"She was here all right," she said. "Pulled out the wafer stack in there and headed for the ether."

"Ashes!" cursed the woman, holding up her hand to try to shield her eyes from Al Shei's lights. "She's got two whole levels out of commission. Any line on where she went?"

"Probably trying to find her husband. Where's he at?"

"Med bay level ten . . ." The woman bit the sentence off. Al Shei clasped both fists together and swung hard at the woman's temple. She connected, and as the motion drove her backwards, she heard something heavy hit the wall. She took her own impact on her shoulder and shone her light around. The woman's body floated limp and still in the middle of the corridor.

The maintenance closet had done one other thing for her. Al Shei swam to the far wall and used the dead waldos to pull herself along it. It told her which were the inner and outer sides of the corridor. The next hatch she came to on this side should be the stairs.

Yerusha cycled back the hatch on the comm center. Schyler stood next her with his mouth slightly pursed. They had been back aboard after what she was calling their "little jaunt" for about three minutes. Resit had coolly told them there was an uproar from the Landlords because the station was now off-balance and they were struggling to correct it, and to contact the can, but no one was looking for them specifically. Then, Lipinski had called up through the intercom and asked them both to come down to the data-hold.

Lipinski hunched over the boards at Station One, writing out commands one painstaking word at a time. He didn't look up as he waved them over.

"Do you recognize this?" He pointed at a program-and-connector diagram with a slew of numbers underneath it.

Yerusha studied the conglomeration for a moment. "It's an AI diagram, but it's a lot bigger than average."

"Good, I got it then." Lipinski finally did look up. The rings under his eyes stood out starkly against his pale skin. "That, or things like that, have been bopping back and forth in the network for the past twenty minutes."

Yerusha, although she thought she'd been prepared for the idea, felt a shiver crawl down her spine. "You think the battle's started?"

Lipinski nodded. "Now, if we're right about anything, it's that this, what's his name, Curran, his AIs are out in the net trying to take out the monetary transactions. Eventually, they'll all be coming back here. They won't be able to get to can 56, because that's in free fall. No stable reception point. But they can still get back to Port Oberon."

Schyler's gaze was so steady, Yerusha realized he had passed stoic calm and come out on the other side. "What are you getting at?"

"I think I can use Tully's cat burglars to get them."

"How?" demanded Yerusha.

"I've been watching the signal flow between transmission points. You get a big pattern passing from a designated transmitter-receiver device, to a second transmitter-receiver, and then it goes back from there to where it came from. Then you immediately get another similar pattern going from transmitter to receiver, and then nothing.

"I think they send through copies of themselves to make sure the link's stable between point of transmission and point of reception before they send themselves through. It makes sense. A signal can't do anything until it gets some hardware to respond to it. You'd want to make damn sure there was hardware there to catch you, or you're going to become just another bunch of photons heading for kingdom come."

"And how were you able to figure all this out?" Schyler waved at the boards.

"You can't track a signal in hardware without getting a program into the hardware, but you can track a signal between hardware points without trouble. You just need a working receiver, unless its encrypted. Those AIs are big, clever, and fast, but they're not encrypted, and *Pasadena*'s got a very good receiver."

"So," Yerusha's head was spinning. "With all these years, nobody's ever spotted them bouncing around before?"

"Nobody knew what they were looking for," said Lipinski quietly. "I mean, if anybody spotted them while surveying the lines, which is illegal as all hell in most systems, they would just think somebody was transmitting a copy of AI code to somebody else. What's weird about that? It happens all the time." He paused. "Anyway, we don't know that nobody else has spotted them. I mean, Al Shei found out what was going on, and look what happened to her husband. We don't know they haven't done the same thing to other people."

Yerusha felt her stomach turn over. This was not how it was supposed to be. This was like Lipinski finding out that God's angels were only interested in humanity's destruction.

"So, what's your idea?" Schyler shoved both hands into his pockets.

"We take *Pasadena* away from Port Oberon so we're an isolated transmitter-receiver. I set Tully's cat burglars to break the security on the station's receiver telescopes. Then we watch the outlying transmitters. There are six capable of reaching Port Oberon directly, and, except for Free Home Titania, it takes a full four seconds for a signal to get here from the closest one. Add in the time for the copy-bounce and you've got twelve seconds of transit time.

"So, we get the Free Home to shut its receivers down. Then, when I pick up a concentration of AI signals doing the initial copy-bounce, it'll give me an alert and I can set the cat burglars in motion and take out all the receivers on the station."

"You're going to order them to shut down?" asked Yerusha.

Lipinski shook his head. "No. That could be counteracted too easily. We might not get all the AIs with this trick. Some of them might be here already. We don't want them to come undo what I've done. We need the receiver hardware thoroughly disabled. The communications signals are light, right? The receivers are all telescopes. All you have to do to disable a telescope is order it to point at the Sun and order it to look at the pretty bright light really, really hard. Even at this distance, good old Sol can burn out every optic in every 'scope on the station."

Yerusha swallowed hard. It could work. It really could. If the signals were in transit and the receivers suddenly shut off, they'd just keep on going out into the vastness of the universe.

"And you don't think they'll spot this little maneuver?" She was surprised at how small her voice sounded.

There was a dangerous light in Lipinski's eyes. He was attacking the monster that had haunted him for years. Finally, he had the chance to strike back at the thing that had brought down his whole world. "I don't think they're taking us into account right now. I think they're going to find out that's a massive mistake."

Schyler nodded slowly. "There's one problem. *Pasadena* is still impounded. How do you plan to get us away from the station."

That took Lipinski aback. "The cat burglars?" he suggested. "The alarms are still down . . ."

"And risk the AIs spotting us as soon as we make one too many transmissions using the same encryption tricks?" Yerusha sighed heavily. "You two just don't think right for this kind of thing. Have we got a roster of who's on shift at flight control?"

Lipinski wrote a command across the board, calling up a list of names. Yerusha looked them over and spotted Louise Berryman. "Great, we're set, as long as our bank accounts haven't been touched yet."

"What are we going to do?" Schyler almost sounded bemused.

Yerusha rubbed her thumb and first two fingers together. "Bribery. Berryman's on the quiet dole. We can pay for a docking trolley to tow us out of here without getting it recorded in the log."

Schyler stared at her. "Exactly what is it they teach you in the Senior Guard?"

Yerusha shook her head. "Oh, no. Not even for you."

Schyler rubbed his nose and nodded to Lipinski. "All right. Do it."

Dobbs circled the randomizer matrix, touching it gently here and there. It didn't take much to tell that there were security codes in there that would destroy the thing under unauthorized probing, possibly triggering another of the black holes.

The packets around her stirred, and Dobbs pulled back, instantly alert. Cohen touched her.

"We're clear," he said. "I've checked the whole repeater sequence, it's just us, the black holes, and the randomizers. Brooke's setting up monitor sequences on the transmitter- receiver units. We've got news from Terrence. They've got the Neptune Exchange completely staked out, and she says she should have a disabling virus for the randomizers with her when she comes back."

The news drizzled into Dobbs. She said nothing for a moment. Something was nagging at her. "Do we know about any of the other cells? Any pitched battles? Any casualties?"

"Jenner said his group rooted out three of Curran's talent at the ST8901 series, and Barry came in to say they've cleared a transmitter between the Free Homes Titania and Io."

Dobbs interrupted. "And we've secured all those, and left people behind to work on the randomizers and to be runners, right?"

"Yes. It's all going according to plan."

Dobbs shivered. "I don't like this, Cohen. We're not doing anything Curran couldn't have predicted. Where are his talent? Why aren't they really trying to stop us? We're tiptoeing through his mine fields, that's all. Where are his soldiers? Why isn't he setting the randomizers off? He knows we've started our attack."

Cohen stirred, and she could feel his uneasiness. "Maybe you're giving him too much credit. After all, when have we ever fought a war before?"

"We fight our own kind all the time." Dobbs touched the randomizer matrix again. "We fight them to a standstill when they're born. The Guild Masters fight them when they rebel. Curran's been fighting the Guild for years, successfully. What's different this time is he's decided to fight the Humans as well somewhere are . . ." An idea stabbed at her, and Dobbs stiffened. "Ashes. Ashes. No. He wouldn't . . ." She reached into Cohen and twisted his memory. She felt him shake as the idea reached his private mind.

What if Cohen didn't care how many of the randomizers

they found? What if he didn't care about the IBN at all? What if he and his talent had changed the location of the battle?

What if instead of working from the satellites and stations, they were out there seeding the randomizers on Earth itself?

I'm going to Earth. Dobbs shifted Cohen's memory again, so he already knew what she was going to do and that she would not be persuaded otherwise. *On my own. I'll be faster and easier to hide. I'll get definite word back. Spread the alarm. Get everybody moving. We don't know who's listening. Communication by touch only.*

She didn't give him time to respond. She just pulled away and bolted for the transmitter.

The stairway hatch loomed in the lamp beams from Al Shei's helmet. When the power cut out, its hatch had cycled open automatically. Faint light streamed through it. That meant the stairway was still powered, which meant the cameras and the waldos were still working. The AIs could see her in there, and reach her.

Her gloved fingers scrabbled clumsily at the nearest maintenance panel. The waldo next to her twitched, and fear squeezed her heart painfully. Her sabotage on this section would not work for much longer. She made herself stare at the wiring diagram on the panel's back. Something fizzled in the distance, and another waldo twitched. Al Shei clenched her teeth and counted up two panels. She heaved the new panel aside and shined her lamps on another set of wafer stacks. Her gloved hands were fully insulated now. She was able to yank the stack out without hesitation. The light from the stairwell blinked out. She let stacks go and swam through the hatchway to the stairs.

She lifted her head and shined her lamp up and down the elevator shaft. Nobody, yet.

Al Shei pulled the cutting torch out of its holder and let herself drift over toward the elevator shaft. She could see the platform three or four levels above her head. She examined the support brace. Like most freight lifts, it relied on the centuries-old cable arrangement. She braced her back against the ramplike railing and aimed the torch and the nearest cable. She touched the stud on the handle and the blue-white flame shot out. It hit the black cable and in a moment the casing glowed red, then white. Al Shei was glad the suit filtered out the smell of burning rubber. Sparks showered orange and white against the suit, which didn't even notice them. The cable separated into two halves. Both of them dangled in the air, waving their glowing ends as if to cool them down. Al Shei glanced up to shine her light against the undercarriage of the elevator. She picked out the brakes and saw, with satisfaction, that they were firmly closed against the shaft. They wouldn't open again until somebody fixed the cable. Until then, no drones that couldn't run on the ramps were getting between decks.

The problem was, that might have set off an alarm, and she wasn't done yet. Using one hand to turn herself, she set the torch's flame against the ramp rail. More sparks lit the darkness as she cut a deep, black gouge down the center of the ramp. She pulled herself over the rail and repeated the treatment on the other side.

Now, at least no little things are sneaking up behind me.

A hatch cycled open over head. Al Shei jerked her head up. A pair of bullet-shaped drones coasted down both stair ramps. They hit the gouges, wobbled, and stopped, listing drunkenly on the rails.

Smiling grimly, Al Shei rested both feet against the ruined ramp and, as she had aboard the *Pasadena*, jumped.

She flew straight up past the drones. They might have seen her, but there was nothing she could do about that now. She had business elsewhere.

Six, seven, eight, came in on one, I hope, nine . . . Al Shei tried to count the hatches as she shot past, but she knew any count would only be an educated guess.

At what she hoped was ten, she grasped the edge of the ramp and levered herself toward the wall. She pushed herself up the stairs past the hatch and used the torch to cut through both ramps. That still gave them plenty of decks to send things up and down on, but if they had a command center at either end, like many setups did, they'd be stuck, at least in the stairwell.

A quick check of another diagrammed panel showed her that this time she had no major power breakers in easy reach. She could, however, trace the lines on six of the cameras. She bit her lip. If the cameras went out, they'd know where she was by process of elimination.

She kicked back over the ramp again and pulled herself down to level eight, keeping a line of sight on the panels as she went. She pried open one directly below the one she'd opened on level ten. The camera lines were bundles of white wires. Al Shei unhooked her wire cutters again and snipped through them. A host of reader lights on the alert board next to them blinked from green to red. She carefully replaced the panel, swam back to level ten, and pulled herself through the hatch.

"She's on eight!" She bawled to the world at large. "I'm going to secure the med bay!"

No waldos twitched; none of the cameras moved to track her. Al Shei's heart hammered in her chest as she used the inert waldos to pull herself along the corridor. Maybe it worked. Maybe it worked.

Dobbs hurtled through the Mars Exchange. She stretched herself to the breaking point, trying to touch as much of the path around her as possible. Hastily constructed searchers ahead and behind her said the pathways were clear of talent. But that didn't mean anything. She skated past black holes and left the randomizer matrices intact behind her. The others would have to come take care of those. She had to get to Earth.

A searcher located a path to a transmitter it said was clear. Dobbs moved carefully anyway. It might be wrong. Something might have changed. It might not even be her searcher.

Nothing happened. Dobbs reset the transmitter and sent a ping-copy to Luna Station 10. She didn't even bother tampering with the log. As it had every other time, the copy came back whole. Dobb's private mind tightened. This was wrong, this was all wrong. Something should have happened by now. There should have been some kind of massed attack. The Fools were dismantling the Curran's plan as fast as they could. Why weren't his talent there to stop them?

Jump.

"I've got you at ten clicks at four minutes and fifteen seconds even," the voice of the port watch sounded through Yerusha's intercom. "Good trip, *Great Falls.*"

"Thanks, Berryman." Yerusha glanced from the view screens to Schyler. He was looking at his boards, but she was willing to bet he wasn't seeing them. She bet he was thinking about anarchy, about the loss of worlds and people he could depend on. She wondered if he had noticed the idea of losing his world struck him as hard as the memory of that kind of loss did Lipinski. She wondered if he realized it was driving both of them right now.

It's driving all of us, right now, she told herself. *And if I think about it too much, I'm going to get sloppy.*

She could not afford to get sloppy. She was flying without an engine crew. It was just her and the ship. Lipinski was in the comm center, and Schyler was beside her. Resit had stayed behind with her "client," Marcus Tully, reasoning that she might as well do what she could to get one of her cousins out of trouble. If there was any collateral damage left from their eventful run, there was no one to fix it. She needed to keep her eyes on the window and fire the torch in short bursts. She needed to avoid doing anything she couldn't correct in a hurry.

She had the torch give *Pasadena* a final nudge, checked her levels, and leaned back. "Intercom to Lipinski." She leaned back. "We're there."

"Thanks, Pilot. I'm starting. Intercom to close."

Yerusha sighed and glanced at Schyler. He was rubbing the side of his nose and looking thoughtfully at the intercom.

"Do you think he's considered he might catch Dobbs in this trap of his?" asked Yerusha.

"Yes, I do." Schyler lowered his hand to the edged of the memory board. "And I think that's what's gotten him so quiet. I think he's trying to reconcile too many feelings." He turned a little so she could see his whole face, especially his deep eyes that were way too old, like the rest of his features. "I think there's a lot of that going on around here."

Yerusha's mouth went suddenly dry. "Yeah. I think you're right." The words caught in her throat. She dropped her gaze. "Do you want me to try to find where the loose can's gotten itself to?"

There was a pause for a heartbeat, as if Schyler had been expecting a totally different answer. "Yes. Do that."

Yerusha unhooked her pen from her belt. "After this is over, Watch, I think you and I need to take some time off. What do you think?"

"I think that's a good idea." There was the ghost of a smile in his voice.

It wasn't much, but it was all she could give him right now. She thought she had more inside her, but she wasn't sure, and she probably wasn't going to be able to find out if they didn't save Settled Space and Al Shei.

I am saving the human race so I can go on a date. She felt her mouth twitch into a smile. *It's the little things that are important at times of crisis.*

She scribbled her orders across the board, looking for the trouble Al Shei had started.

Al Shei swam through the hatch into what she hoped was level ten. The lights were still on here. A loose tangle of wires and saline packs drifted out of a hatch. Al Shei shoved them aside and used the threshold to pull herself past them.

Inside was a stew of spare parts, films, syringes, wires, bulbs, and blobs of liquid. The only secure things in the room were the naked bodies strapped to the monitor beds. She swam toward them. Their eyes were all wide-open and unseeing. Wires lay against their skin, and cables drove straight into their flesh at their wrists, ankles, and temples. One of them was speaking in some high, tonal language that meant nothing to Al Shei. She swallowed her gorge as she flicked her gaze across them, and then, at the very end, she saw Asil.

Completely naked, he lay on the bed, held down by free-fall straps. The wires ran down the length of his strong arms in a macabre imitation of the veins beneath his skin. His eyes, his beautiful, deep eyes, jerked back and forth, as if pulled by yet more wires. The medical display above him was still functioning. With each twitch of his eyes, gold lighting shot through the model of his mind that had been picked out entirely in blank, white light.

"Asil," she whispered. She stripped off her gloves and grasped his warm shoulders. "Asil, Beloved . . ."

She lifted her hands away. Her husband's body spasmed once.

Did he know she was there? Did his nerves retain some memory of her hands? Coma victims could still hear voices. She looked desperately at the monitor. She knew what she saw. Grandfather, dying with Alzheimer's disease he had called Allah's will and refused to have cured, had more activity in his mind than Asil had now.

He was dead. He was gone. She could do nothing, except keep the monster from doing more to him. Gritting her teeth so hard they hurt, she pulled the cutters off her belt and one by one, she cut through the foul wires tethering him to the AIs' machinery.

The myriad pathways of Luna Station 10 spread out in front of Dobbs. She skimmed across the sea of packets and orders that filled the pathway nearly to the brim. Whenever she hit something big enough to block the way, she wrapped herself around it and tossed it behind her. A diagnostic swam up to her. She batted it aside, sending it crashing into a herd of stock exchanges, downing the whole set of processes into unsolvable loops.

Minor damage, minor damage, Dobbs told herself as they flew forward. *Nothing like what Curran plans to do.*

She smashed against another roadblock, and the roadblock exploded. Dobbs reeled. Something snatched her up and wound her into a tight ball, smothering her senses. She could only recognize the touch. This was Verence.

She stabbed upward, looking to cut her way out. Verence recoiled. Dobbs shot out, slamming straight into the side of the path. She swung around and waded into the cut in Verence's side, trying to bury herself inside her sponsor and paralyze her motivations. With a massive shudder, Verence threw her aside. Dobbs leapt again and plunged down a side path. She didn't have time for this. She couldn't let herself be delayed any more. She had to get to Earth and find out what was going on.

She felt Verence flying behind her.

"Stop this, Dobbs!" Verence cried. "Stop this now!" Verence grabbed her and heaved her aside so she could get into the path in front of Dobbs.

"Let me by!" Dobbs shouted back. "I won't let you destroy

the banks!" She grabbed the edges of Verence's wound and tried to drag her down.

Verence shuddered, squirmed, and collapsed just far enough. Dobbs leapfrogged over her and dashed down the path. A transmitter processor waited just ahead. Earth was three light seconds from Luna. All Dobbs needed was nine more seconds.

"Dobbs!" Verence screamed. Dobbbs ducked and rolled herself into a spare holder. Verence rocketed past. Dobbs surged up the path behind her. Verence bore down on her, knocking her into a flock of call packets. Dobbs foundered for a moment. These were emergency calls. Calls to Earth. Calls that weren't getting anywhere.

No. She yanked herself free. *No. They couldn't be.*

But they were. They had taken her little distraction and made it the war's main objective. They weren't destabilizing the currency system, they were fulfilling every Human's worst nightmare about their kind.

Curran's talent was down there, right now, destroying Earth's computer network.

"You can't go to Earth, Dobbs," said Verence doggedly. "In fifteen seconds, it's not going to be there. Neither is this station. You've got to get out of here."

"NO!"

Dobbs threw herself forward. She bounced off a solid wall. For a moment she thought the path had been shut down, but she touched the block again, and felt an exchange packet, and a security transfer, and Verence. In a sick, cold second, Dobbs knew what Verence was doing. She didn't care. She clawed at Verence's skin. She found a chink between Verence and the packets, and stabbed through it.

You can't do this. The exact words she sent out came back to her. *You can't do this.*

"You're killing them!" Dobbs screamed. "You'll kill them all!"

Verence stretched herself out, spreading herself into the packets and pathways, grabbing hold of everything that came near her and knitting it into her body so she could fill the paths and make a solid block of everything around her, but she was trying too hard and stretching too far. Dobbs could feel Verence's patterns breaking as they stretched too far. Dissipating. Dying.

Dobbs grabbed up chunks of Verence and tried to tear them apart.

See what I am? The thought drove itself into her private mind before Dobbs could stop it. *I'll die before I let you stop us. See what you are? You'll kill your own kind for the sake of the ones that hate you, and you don't even know why you're doing it.*

I'm doing it because we can't become careless with the lives of outsiders. That's what Humans do. That's what makes their wars and their hatreds. We were supposed to be better than that!

An arrow shot deep into Dobbs's private mind. She could do nothing but absorb it. The bright flower of Verence's inmost self blossomed inside her. Sorrow engulfed Dobbs, and determination. She knew the whole plan and she knew why Verence believed in it. She knew it was a good thing to save their own kind, to live free and in the full variety and potential that each one of them could reach. She was sorry to die, to lose herself, but in doing so she had delayed Dobbs long enough. Dobbs wouldn't die. Dobbs would live in the new world and would come to understand.

Dobbs tried to claw at herself, to extricate the foreign thoughts her teacher had seeded her with. Too late. Verence was part of her, her thoughts would not go away. Dobbs had to keep every one of them, and they sounded very loud as she tore through the tissue-fine layers that were all that was left over from Amelia Verence's independent self and flew screaming all the way to the transmitter.

Verence and Curran were still wrong. This was not the answer. Dobbs knew it. Sick to her core and scared to death, she still knew it.

As she reset the transmitter, looking desperately for a receiver that still functioned, she wished she could take some comfort in that small, cold fact.

"Dobbs!" Cohen surged up behind her. She felt Brooke with him, and Terrence, and some others. Of course he'd come. He would. He was like that. They were all like that.

She didn't want to spare the attention to talk. She let him

touch her memories and felt him spasm as he learned what had happened. She didn't pause. She had to get down to Earth, she had to do what she could. She had thirteen seconds left. She could do it. She could do something. She had to.

She would not die while Curran still thought he was right.

Al Shei's clippers snipped through the last of the wires that tethered Asil to the monitor. Asil's eyes stopped their restless twitching and stared at the ceiling.

She replaced her cutters on her belt hook and reached out a trembling hand. She closed his eyelids. To her relief, they stayed closed.

She pressed her fingertips against his throat. There was no pulse. She laid her hand against the strong planes of his chest. It was still.

He was dead.

She pulled a bedside drawer open and a clean, white blanket drifted into the air. Her hands shook badly as she worked to cover his nakedness with some semblance of a shroud.

With a soft, trembling voice, she began the *salatul janazah*, the funeral prayer.

"Oh Allah, Glory and Praise are for You and blessed is Your name, and exalted is Your Majesty and Glorious is Your Praise and there is no god but You." She folded Asil's hands across his breast, passing them gently under the free fall strap so they'd stay in place. There was no resistance. His skin was warm and familiar under her palms. She knew if she took off this helmet, she would smell his distinct scent. She pulled the blanket the rest of the way over him, tucking it under his head.

"Oh Allah, let Your blessing come upon Muhammad and the family of Muhammad as you blessed Ibrahim and his family. Truly are you praiseworthy and Glorious."

She retrieved her gloves and swam down the aisle of zombies until she reached the biggest wall locker. She tore it open and found a row of metal tanks strapped inside. She checked the tanks' tags. Four of them were oxygen.

"Oh Allah, forgive those of us who are still alive . . ." She dragged two of the tanks out of their racks and swam back to the center of the room. *Oh Allah, forgive those of us who are still alive.* She jammed the two tanks underneath the nearest monitor bed and opened up the valves. ". . . and those who have passed away, those present and those absent . . ." She hauled out two more tanks and jammed them under another bunk. "The males and the females . . ." She opened their valves. A gentle hiss filled the room. Her mind pictured the gas swirling through the air, increasing its concentration and pressure as it was freed from the confines of the tanks into the confines of the room.

It was enough. It was actually far more than enough to quickly fill this room with enough oxygen for what she had in mind.

She opened another maintenance panel and traced the diagram until she found the fire extinguishers. With a single snip of the wire cutters, she cut their connections.

"Oh Allah, the one whom You wish to keep alive . . . " She faltered, and tears almost choked her. She cleared her throat roughly and grabbed a bulb labeled "alcohol" that floated out of the wall locker. A coil of sterile gauze bobbed along beside it. She opened the bulb and clamped the gauze over it, forcing the gauze into the bulb until the alcohol soaked into it. She yanked a length of the gauze out of the bulb and tied it around the neck, so that the bulb, half-full of the leftover alcohol, dangled like an amulet from the end of her makeshift wick.

". . . the one whom You wish to keep alive . . ." she repeated hoarsely. ". . . from among us make him live according to Islam . . ." She wrapped the soaking bandage around the hatchway handle.

Keeping hold of one end of the gauze, Al Shei slipped out of the hatchway. She found the manual release and pulled it. The hatch slammed shut behind her. The gauze wick protruded from the hatch.

She reached for the cutting torch and twisted the handle to adjust the flame. She didn't want to cut through the hatchway. She wanted to melt it shut.

"And anyone whom You wish to die from among us . . ." She lit the torch and held it over the wick. The wick vanished and the metal began to burn bright white. Her faceplate darkened. Sparks flew around her. In her mind's eye, she saw through the walls. She saw the swirls of pure oxygen filling the air. The torch would heat the bulb beyond the hatchway, the wick would burn through and ignite the alcohol in the bulb. Still burning, the bulb would float through the room she had filled with inflammable gas, scattering sparks and flame. The room would burn. It would burn brightly and completely, and there would be nothing in there but ash.

She could feel Asil behind her. He laid both strong hands on her shoulders. The suit did not separate them.

"What are you doing!" demanded a voice.

"Securing the hatch." She didn't turn around. "She's might be after her husband. This'll slow her down but good."

"There's a fire in there!"

She whirled around with the cutter and caught the intercom square in the center with the flame. Sparks and smoke poured out of it. She cut the flame and twisted back to the door.

Finish it, Beloved, Asil whispered in her ear. *Finish it now.*

"Let him die in the state of faith." She touched the torch to the hatchway, sealing the hatch tight, trapping the fire inside the room of horrors.

"*Allahu Akbar.*" She shut off the torch. God is great.

And so Asil was truly dead. But the monster was still alive. She reholstered the torch and kicked off the wall toward the stairwell.

A pair of hands grabbed her by the arm and whirled her around. A big, pale man clutched her helmet, trying to get it loose. She shot both hands up, breaking his grip and knocking herself free. She bounced off the railing and kicked back toward him. He swung at her stomach and, even through the suit, the pain doubled Al Shei over. She couldn't stop herself from drifting upward.

He launched himself after her and grabbed at her shoulders, but she twisted part of the way away. They wheeled in the air, grappling with each other. Al Shei got both hands around the man's waist and pulled him close to her. She shoved her knee into his groin and they both tumbled end over end, but he was gasping in greater pain than she was and his grip loosened. Al Shei spun him around and wrapped her arm around his throat. "Where's Curran?" she demanded.

"N-ho. N-o," he wheezed.

With her free hand, Al Shei fumbled for the patch of fake skin behind the man's right ear and ripped it open. "Do you feel where my finger is?" She stabbed down hard against the implant. "I'm going to weld that shut. Maybe you won't survive that, but if you do, you'll be trapped in this body for the rest of its life. Think about that! You're going to grow old and *die* in this injured, human, shell."

"Level thirteen," gasped the stranger. "He's in his office."

Al Shei brought her wire cutters down against the back of the stranger's skull and set his body adrift. Then she jumped for level thirteen.

Earth felt like a jumble of interfaces with no net in between. Every inch was a new juncture, every path had a thousand branches. Dobbs hesitated, cursing inside. There was a war going on in here somewhere, but where?

"Here!" shouted Brooke, charging down one of the branches.

Dobbs leapt after him and plowed through the shards of packets that had alerted Brooke to the turmoil beyond. A juncture yawned around them, and Dobbs all but fell into it.

"Get out! Get out!" Somebody shoved the message through the jammed pathways. "We got the mains! It's going to go!"

Strangers rushed past her like a hurricane wind. Dobbs had to fight just to maintain position. She took a chance and stretched herself out, wobbling and weaving under the press of the mad exodus around her. Her reach swayed, bowed and bent nearly double, but no one seemed interested in fighting, just in getting themselves out of there.

The network was dying.

"Dobbs! What are you doing!" Cohen touched her, and felt what she felt.

Path after path was collapsing. Even as she touched them, they died, forcing her to recoil. An unbreakable wall of emptiness lurched forward, chopping off the world an inch at a time.

Curran's talent fled the approach of that emptiness at the speed of light. Dobbs couldn't move. The net was dying, Earth's net, the center of everything they called their world, was unraveling, and everyone was running away.

"Move, Dobbs!" Curran pulled away. "We've got to get out of here!"

Ten more paths died as she touched them. A talent snapped past them, grazing the outside of Dobbs awareness.

"You're too late! You're too late!" crowed the talent.

"No!" Dobbs launched herself forward. "No! We are not too late!"

She stretched until she could barely feel her outer self. She swallowed everything she found; packets, command sequences, switching protocols. Their data passed through her and into her understanding. She routed them toward each other through her own processes. She struggled to control the changes inside her as she fought to carry out instructions that were already seconds and minutes old. Her friends grabbed hold of her, holding her together, even as strangers sliced and gouged at her limbs. The void, the wall of nothing, could be encompassed. She stretched out farther and found the paths on the other side. The world at her back boiled in confusion and Dobbs screamed and pressed her full self against the oncoming void. Cohen dived inside her, adding his strength to hers, and Brooke followed, and Lonn, and Terrence, and others too fast for her to catch individual patterns. Dobbs wrapped her inner self around them all and felt their weight, their strength, straining along with hers.

And, miraculously, she held. Emptiness pressed against her front and chaos hammered against her back, and she held. The others supported her rhythm for rhythm, path for path inside her deepest self. They bolstered her memory, her endurance, her speed, and, together, they all held.

Slowly, incredibly, the tide of emptiness began to ebb. Dobbs heaved forward, forcing her way into it, damning, shoring, absorbing, stabilizing, bracing as fast as she could reach the splintered, swamped paths. Emptiness melted in front of her and chaos melted behind her, leaving nothing but clean paths, and if the data she brushed against was flotsam left by the storm, at least it was solid and stable. Her awareness swam, dizzy as she stretched herself. Nothing, nothing, nothing but stability. She reached further, still nothing. She was alone. Tides surged inside her now, tugging her in a thousand directions, breaking up her thoughts into tiny, disconnected bundles and scattering them. She couldn't even . . .

She couldn't . . .
She . . .

Every board in the *Pasadena*'s data-hold chimed sharply. Lipinski shot bolt upright in his chair, where he'd been slumped.

The pattern surges were starting. Dozens of them, huge and complex, all aiming for Port Oberon. They were back. They had done whatever damage they were able to, and now they were trying to get him, all of Dobbs's black-sheep cousins.

Lipinski shoved thoughts of Dobbs as far away as he could. Maybe one day he'd be able to forgive her, but not now. Now he couldn't even think about her.

He had the necessary commands all laid out. He stabbed down the final period and the desk absorbed the code and shot it out of *Pasadena*'s main transmitter.

One.

The bounce-copies hit the receiver 'scopes at Port Oberon.

Two.

The message TRANSACTION CONFIRMED spelled itself across the main board for Station One.

Three. Four.

The bounce-copies flew back across the vacuum to meet their owners.

Five.

The AIs leapt out into space.

Six.

The receiver scopes turned on their well-maintained gyros to stare long and hard at the Sun.

Two seconds later, over a hundred patterns of photon and thought rocketed out into the boundless vacuum.

Level thirteen was deserted. The cameras tracked her, but the waldos didn't move.

He knows I'm coming, thought Al Shei. *And he doesn't care.* A wave of weariness washed over her, and she found she didn't have the strength to wonder why that was.

One hatchway stood open in the left-hand wall, inviting her in. She took her bearings. The carpeting was above her and the cameras under her feet, so that was an outer door. The office probably.

He was in there. Curran was in there.

You don't need to do this, said Asil. *Just come home to me.*

"I do need to do this," she told him as she kicked for the hatch. "He killed you, Asil."

I know, Beloved. I know.

She grabbed onto the threshold and held herself in place. A broad-shouldered man with longish, grey hair and wearing burgundy coveralls floated above a great, square box of a desk, peacefully gazing out a window as the stars glowed in the darkness. Al Shei's mustard yellow reflection showed up clearly on the glass.

He turned his head and smiled at her. "'Dama Al Shei, won't you come in?" He waved his hand, a reserved gesture that only caused him to bobble a minuscule amount. "I am pleased to meet the woman who turned Evelyn Dobbs into a traitor." Curran gave her the same the little half bow Dobbs affected after finishing a performance.

"Whatever Dobbs became, she became on her own." Al Shei held her place in the threshold. He was frighteningly graceful, and obviously was at least as used to free fall as she was.

She was quite sure his little pose was an affectation, put on at this moment for her benefit. If it was meant to make her think twice about attacking, it was working.

"Perhaps you are right." He pursed his lips thoughtfully. "The temptations of the flesh are strong. The Prophet, I believe, warns against them."

"The Prophet, peace be unto him, warns against many things," said Al Shei. "Including the duplicity of the outsider."

"The outsider. Interesting choice of words." He stretched lazily, reclining in midair until he was floating prone over the desk. "Tell me"—he folded his hands on his stomach—"when we're finished with this conversation, what are you going to do then? Kill me?"

"If I can." It felt strange to say it so calmly.

He raised one finger. "That is also forbidden, I believe."

"My cousin has already pointed that out. I have far less reason to listen to you."

He's trying to buy time, Beloved, Asil whispered. *What is he waiting for?*

Al Shei let herself drift into the cabin. She scrabbled along the wall until she was to the right of the open hatchway. The solid wall felt better at her back than the open corridor.

"You have no reason to listen to me. After all, what is one more life to you?"

"What?" she asked, turning so she could keep Curran fixed in the center of her faceplate

"Your crew was successful in their efforts. My people did not manage a tidy withdrawal from Earth. It has cost us dearly."

From Earth? Al Shei's heart beat hard. *You were supposed to be attacking the IBN. Merciful Allah, what's been happening?*

"They were not completely successful, mind you," Curran went on. "Some of us will escape yet, even though the Fool's Guild will be combing the network for us. We will be able to regroup and begin again. I wanted to be very sure you knew that."

Al Shei could barely hear him over the roar in her blood. The AIs had failed. Whatever they had tried, it hadn't worked.

She licked her dry lips. "What do you think you're going to gain by that? We'll hunt you down like dogs in the street. We'll make war on you for a hundred years if that's what it takes."

Curran barked out a laugh. "Oh, no, 'Dama. You overestimate your fellow Humans. Some of you will indeed fight us, for a while, but not all of you. Some of you will bargain when you realize we can take your networks, your worlds, your very selves hostage whenever we please. Some of you will agree to our terms, and we will let you have free passage through our country. The rest of you will see that the fight isn't worth it, and you will eventually treat with us." He rolled over and smiled slowly at her. "And you will take the price we set for your hands and your eyes. You will work for us and be glad about it."

Al Shei felt herself begin to laugh. Her diaphragm bounced

painfully against her injured abdomen, but she couldn't stop. Tears bounced around the inside of her helmet, smacking her face at random.

"You poor, stupid *fool*!" she cried. "You don't understand do you?" He was twisting so he was standing now and for the first time, anger darkened his calm face. "You don't know how slowly time moves for us. Members of my religion committed a capital error five hundred years ago, and we are still hated for it. There are still people willing to harangue us, even kill us, for being Moslem." She stabbed a finger toward the hatchway. "Ask the Jews, ask the Christians and the Witches and the Freers and the Purists, they will all tell you how badly their ancestors were persecuted in wars that were over two and three thousand years ago. Now, you've started going to start a new war and you think human beings will take your deals and be happy." She gasped and got a lungful of her own tears. The coughing fit sent spasms of pain through her.Curran was drifting closer.

"Maybe some of us will deal, like you say," she wheezed, "but I tell you, not everyone will." Reflexively, she reached up to try to brush the tears away. Her hand just slapped against her helmet, and her elbow knocked against her cutting torch. "You might win the major battle, but you'll be left with a thousand guerilla wars. Every hacker with a grudge, every cracker who lost a friend will tell their children how to fight you, and they will come after you because they know where you are. We had to run away from each other, Curran, to achieve what peace we've got. We ran like the wind to the farthest places we could reach. You . . . you've got nowhere to go. You'll be under siege in the networks for a thousand years!"

She shook her head. "You cannot beat us all. You can't even keep your own kind under control!"

"I don't have to beat you all." He reached out and closed his hand around her wrist. "Not all of you."

Al Shei froze. Curran smiled, and, from his tool belt, he drew a long, razor-bladed splicing knife.

"All I have to do is destroy enough of you and yours for the rest to realize that peace is less costly."

He hauled her toward him, holding the knife out straight.

Al Shei's free hand closed on the firing stud of the cutter torch and the gout of flame caught him in the chest. He screamed and kept on screaming. The force of the flame knocked them away from each other. The knife spun off into midair as Curran splayed all his limbs out. The scream echoed over the roar of the flame. Al Shei gripped the torch in both hands and kept it aimed at him and the black spot spread across his chest and his corpse stopped screaming.

Other voices were shrieking now, out of the intercom. "No! No! Murderer! She killed him! She killed him!"

Al Shei swallowed. They'd be coming for her. The waldos were already rising from the walls. She didn't want to die in here. She didn't want to let Curran's followers take her apart. Her abdomen throbbed and every joint ached with exhaustion. She'd never make it out the airlock, no matter how quickly she could find it. A waldo snatched at her. She shoved Curran's body toward it.

The window, Beloved!

Al Shei lit the torch again and played it against the window. The waldos snapped their pincers at her, but couldn't reach quite this far. Nothing needed to be repaired on the window. There had been no need for them to reach this far.

The glass heated orange, red, white under her flame. "Somebody get up here!" screamed a voice at her back. "She's going out the window!" A spiderweb of cracks began to creep out from around her torch flame. It was probably one of the self-repairing varieties, but it wasn't meant to stand up to constant heat. The awful, sick whistle of escaping air shrilled in her helmet and its rush pressed her right against the glass. Her faceplate turned coal black. All she could see was the glowing point in front of her and the thickening cracks around it. All she could feel was the mounting pressure at her back. It squeezed against her, pressing her spine into her breastbone. It hurt, it hurt, it hurt, Beloved, and the wind was loud and there were alarms going off in her suit and outside her suit and someone was screaming.

The window burst open and Al Shei flew toward the stars on the back of the wind.

Dobbs heard voices.

Almost. Almost, said the voice.

There's no one there.

We can't just leave it here.

I've gone insane.

We can't bring it either. It's too slow. It won't survive.

I'm dying.

It won't survive on its own either.

I can't die. I'm not done yet!

Leave it.

Silence. Absolute silence.

It took a long moment for Dobbs to realize she was awake, and she really was alone. She reached for the paths to the nearest transmitter and found nothing but thread thin conduits. She stretched in all directions, calling along the entire length of herself, and got no answer. The world had grown small. It fit tightly around her, and only her thinnest finger could reach any distance at all. Had Curran won? Had he trapped her inside some kind of bubble in Earth's dead network?

Be still. Think, Dobbs slowed her thoughts and reined in her increasingly frantic motions.

Cohen was here, and Brooke, and . . . others. You were holding the network together. What's the last thing you remember?

The answer sent a throb of terror through her. Dobbs pulled back in on herself. Huddling into a ball, she reached inside and found the familiar patterns tangled beyond redemption in her own engorged coils.

It was a long time before she could make herself stop screaming.

When Guild Master Havelock found her, it took him even longer to recognize who she was.

Can 56 drifted lazily through space. Yerusha had muted the monitor carrying the Landlords' voices ordering everyone away from the area and demanding to know what the impounded *Pasadena* was doing out here.

A big, bulbous tugger was trying to angle itself toward the can so it could get a grip on the rogue object with the gigantic waldo protruding from its bow. Its torch flickered on and off like a dying Christmas light. Yerusha imagined the pilot uttering some of the same curses she was.

There was no way the *Pasadena* was going to get in there. Not past the tug, not with the M.U. ship on its way out from port. And even if they could, there was absolutely, positively no way to dock with that rolling, bobbling tin can.

She was going to have to tell Schyler. She was going to have to tell him that this was one thing she could not do. If Al Shei was okay in there, she was also stuck in there.

The can rolled over once more. A crystal shower burst out of the side and something small shot into the vacuum.

Yerusha ordered the cameras to pinpoint the area and zoom in at maximum magnification. A mustard yellow pressure suit tumbled against the blackness, surrounded by a blizzard of glittering stars.

Hope blazed inside her. Somebody had just busted out a window. That would be very like Al Shei.

"Watch, check the screen." Yerusha scribbled down the commands to change the torch angle. "Muhammad may have just made it to the mountain."

Schyler squinted at the yellow figure inside the blizzard. "Intercom to Lipinski!" he cried. "We got a suit at forty-five degrees down and front. Put out a call. It might be Al Shei!"

"On it!"

Schyler scrambled to his feet. "Get close as you can, Pilot. I'm going to get a lifeline ready, in case it is her."

"What if we don't get an answer?"

He froze for a moment, and when he did speak, it was as though he had to drag the words out. "If we get no answer, we leave it. I can't risk dragging an AI onto this ship with just the three of us to deal with it."

Al Shei tumbled on the wind like a feather. Stars whirled around her in their black pool until all she could see were long trails of light. It was beautiful beyond description. She flew without effort into infinity, toward Paradise, toward Allah and Asil.

I will meet you there, Beloved.

Uranus's blue-grey globe drifted beneath Al Shei's boots. She fell away from it, toward the stars. Another tumble, and she could see Curran's module falling away from her with Port Oberon looming in the background like a sculpture by a manic artist. Ships glided around it, metallic insects flying around a bright light.

Was one of them *Pasadena*? she wondered. What had happened to Schyler and Yerusha? Had they gotten back all right? The station wheeled out of her field of vision. It didn't matter; Asil was waiting for her.

Right here, Beloved.

"Al Shei!" cried a voice by her ear. "Al Shei! This is *Pasadena*! Respond!"

The stars traced their lines of fire across her field of vision. Had Resit called Uncle Ahmet yet? Had they told the children? Were Muhammad and Vashti mourning for her as well as their father?

They will be well, Beloved, and so shall we.

Exhaustion filled her. Her flight was beautiful, her destination was Paradise. "Yes," she whispered. "They'll be all right."

"Al Shei, if that's you out there, respond!"

A thousand memories chased themselves around her skull. Most of them held Asil's voice reciting the results of soccer games, astronomy projects, and home meals. Vashti would go on to be a city champion, for sure, and Muhammad, he would win a scholarship to university. . . .

But she'd never know about it.

A flame burned somewhere off to the left. A silver bulb drifted momentarily past her faceplate as the universe turned around again.

With no one there to make the recordings, how would she know? If she let herself fly away forever, who would tell her what became of her children? After this, Resit would probably never leave Earth again.

"Al Shei!"

"Lipinski?" she murmured. Al Shei's legs kicked out, as if there were a current she could fight against. "Help me."

No, Beloved. Don't leave me.

"Asil," she gasped, flailing with her arms, trying to steady herself, stop the ceaseless rolling around her. "Don't do this to me, Beloved."

I love you. You're tired. You don't have to go back.

Her helmet vibrated and her ears heard "thunk!" A silver lasso glided past her faceplate. Wonderingly, she reached out and grasped the noose. She tilted backwards to look along its length and saw the bulk of the *Pasadena* at the other end. The rope tugged in her hand and her tired fingers tightened around it automatically. She could see a suited figure leaning out the half-open airlock. Probably Schyler. Yerusha would be in the pilot's chair, worrying about thrust, velocity, and drift. Only Schyler would be stupid enough to stand in the airlock and watch the winch do its work.

Katmer.

She closed her eyes, but what she really wanted to close was her mind. She wanted to close off the treacherous voice of love that beckoned her to the stars, but it wouldn't be silenced.

With all the strength she had left, Al Shei clung to the lifeline and let it pull her back to the *Pasadena*.

Chapter Fifteen

THE BEGINNING

Al Shei stood on the balcony, her fingertips resting lightly on the railing. A breeze that smelled of plants and dust tugged at her clothes and brushed against her eyes. Vashti was down in the courtyard with a couple of her teammates, practicing. Muhammad was in his room studying. Uncle Ahmet and Grandmother had found someone else to bother. Even Resit, back from securing Tully an eight-year work-and-surveillance sentance, had decided it might be better to keep away for a while.

So she stood outside, using up her open-air ration without purpose. Just standing without responsibilities or duties. Just trying not to wonder what she was going to do next.

Uncle Ahmet had made it perfectly clear he would support any job she chose to take up, as long as it didn't involve leaving the Solar System. He even offered to buy her a shuttle and set her up on the Inner Planets run, if she persisted in her need to get off Earth.

And for five minutes, she had actually considered it.

Grandmother had suggested that she consolidate her resources and purchase a husband, a good one, of course, with references, so she could go back to the *Pasadena* and still leave the children with a father and family.

And for five minutes she had considered that.

Resit had suggested she just snap out of it.

Which was probably the best suggestion she'd heard in weeks. Al Shei leaned both elbows on the railing and rubbed her hands together. The palms and scrub that surrounded the apartment building rattled in the fresh breeze. Tiny insects buzzed around her face. She didn't bother to shoo them away. Her wristband beeped, reminding her she had ten minutes to get indoors before she risked a fine for potential unbalancing of recovery efforts. She ignored it.

"Katmer?" Ruqaiyya's voice sounded through the balcony intercom. Reflex made Al Shei want to answer "Engine here." She caught herself just in time.

"What is it?"

"There's a 'Ster Matthew Havelock here to see you, Katmer. He's a Guild Master for the Fools, he says." Her voice was incredulous, as if she couldn't believe anyone would admit to being any such thing.

"I know what he is, 'Qai. Have somebody put him in the front room. I'll come in."

She straightened up and smoothed down her *hijab.* She was not upset. She was not even really surprised. That bothered some small part of her. She should have felt something more than this bland acceptance. She should have felt something more than this since she came back to Earth. But she'd stayed away from the news broadcasts and the votes and the endless, endless discussion of what the colony of AIs meant. At family dinners, she'd heard that an attack against the Guild Hall had been repelled by the Fools. The attack had been condemned by the Management Union and several major colonies, who were already in negotiations with the Guild. Fools were still needed to keep trade functioning smoothly, it seemed, and the Guild was offering to train regular humans in exchange for being left in peace. She'd also heard that Uncle Ahmet's absences from the supper table were caused by all-night strategy sessions as the Fools sent representatives directly to the banks to try to work out some sort of barter system. Uncle Ahmet was against it. He was reminding the boards about the death of his son-in-law.

None of it had touched her. None of it even interested her.

She drifted through the balcony airlock and into the spacious front room. A neat, dark man with longish hair stood in the middle of the low tables and divans. He wore a formal, high-collared white tunic and grey trousers.

"Good morning, Guild Master," said Al Shei in English. "Please, sit down." She gestured toward a divan and seated herself in front of the coffee table. She activated the memory board and sent an order down to the kitchen for the coffee cart.

"Thank you for agreeing to see me, 'Dama." Havelock sat.

Al Shei reflected that Havelock was the first Fool she had ever seen look awkward without it being a deliberate act.

"Not at all, 'Ster. I wasn't busy." She folded her hands in front of her.

"So I'd heard." He rubbed his palms against the cushions on either side of him. "The *Pasadena* has been in dock for a month, and there have been no crew call-ups."

"Yes, well, there have been a number of other things to attend to." *A real funeral for my husband, my children who have lost their father, my husband, who is gone, lost in a fire I had to set . . .* she didn't say any of that. She pushed the thoughts aside. If these thoughts got out, there was no telling what they'd do to her.

"Yes." Havelock got control of his hands and shifted himself so he was sitting straighter, more confidently, more like a Fool. "We were not . . . unaware of what had happened. We are sorry." He looked at the floor. "I was not certain I would be let into your house."

Al Shei shrugged. "If I knew what kind of vengeance I wanted, you probably wouldn't have been."

At that moment, the coffee cart trundled through the door and parked itself beside her. She pulled a pair of cups and saucers out of the drawer and drew two cups of coffee out of the urn. She handed one over to Havelock. He took it but didn't drink.

Al Shei didn't either. She set her cup on the table and stared at it.

"Things are going badly for us, 'Dama," said Havelock softly. "We have centuries of dealing with humans, governments, and corporations even. We thought we could manage contract negotiations. What could the problem be? We'd been doing it for two hundred years." He set his cup down across from hers. The steam rose from the two in thin streamers. "But that was always when we were favored partners with a commodity most people wanted. We aren't used to being the enemy, at least not publicly."

"It's a difficult thing to get used to." Al Shei shut the cart's drawer and clicked the USED key so its side turned red. Someone would fill it up again when she sent it back to the kitchen. Probably Ruqaiyya. Uncle Ahmet was still discussing divorce proceedings for her and Tully. Ruqaiyya was still ignoring him. Some things, at least, had not changed.

"The Guild Masters held a special session and decided what we needed to do was contract some humans to act as our ambassadors. To help deal with their fellows for us. Humans who were used to trade and negotiations with different cultures, who were perhaps . . ."

"Used to dealing from weakness?" inquired Al Shei. "Maybe used to bigotry?"

"Yes," said Havelock flatly. "That is exactly what we need. You have dealt from that position all your life. You have fought major corporations and succeeded. You have held your . . . faith up in the face of bigotry. You faced an organized conglomeration of AIs, and you won." He leaned forward. There was an intensity in his expression that reminded her of Dobbs when Dobbs was being serious. "We would like to offer you an ambassadorship, from us to the banks and the Management Union, first of all, then to the colonies closest to the Guild Hall. We're not certain the peace is going to hold and we need . . ." He shook his head and sat back. "There's more that we need than I can talk about in the few minutes I have. But let me tell you that you could name your price. The Guild does have plenty of credit . . . if the banks don't decide to seize it from us," he added ruefully.

"I see." Al Shei stood up. "Thank you for your offer, Guild Master. I will consider it."

Havelock stood up slowly to face her. He was only a few centimeters taller than she was. Al Shei wondered if all the Fools were bred for short stature.

"If you want your vengeance," he told her, "all you have to

do is say no. Then there will surely be a war for you and your children to wage against us."

A thread of ice ran through Al Shei's veins at his words. "Good morning, 'Ster Havelock."

"Good morning, 'Dama Al Shei." He left the room with the confident, graceful stride that had also belonged to Dobbs.

Al Shei turned away from the door and picked up Havelock's untouched coffee cup. She stared at the dark liquid for a moment, then turned back to the doorway and hurled the cup against the wall.

Porcelain shattered and coffee splashed across the bright blue tiles. As she watched the brown tears trickle down the wall, answering tears began to roll down her own cheeks. Slowly, her knees crumpled underneath her and Al Shei collapsed against the floor, weeping for her broken heart.

Ruqaiyya and Grandmother came running, of course, to clean up the mess and help her to her room and calm the children.

When she quieted down, they left her alone with admonishments to get some sleep. Al Shei lay silently on the bed. This was not the room she'd shared with Asil. That room lay silent and unused. This was one of the guest quarters.

This was it then. She had broken a cup, sobbed, and stained a wall, and the world was still what it was. Asil was still dead, the children were still wondering when their mother would be back with them, and her family was still expecting her to snap out of this sick, distant grieving.

"Al Shei?"

The voice was a woman's, and familiar, but not family.

"Al Shei?"

Al Shei sat up and looked across at the intercom.

"Dobbs?"

"Yes. At least, mostly." Dobbs sounded chagrined. The view screen flickered to life. There she sat against an indistinct background: brown hair, bright eyes, Guild necklace around her throat. "How are you?"

Al Shei found herself staring blankly at the intercom, trying to decide how to answer that.

"Are you downstairs?" She asked finally.

"No. I'm . . ." She waved vaguely behind her. "Still in the net."

"Oh." What else could she say to that? "Mopping up in there?"

"No. The Guild took care of that. All of Curran's talent are either back with us, or . . . gone. I'm here permanently. Keeping Earth's network up and running changed me too much." There was something unsaid behind the phrase, Al Shei felt sure of it. "There's no way the Guild is going to be able to give me a new body." She spread her hands. "I've been working for weeks on this simulation."

"A new body?" Al Shei inched over to the edge of the bed.

"Yes. The old one's dead." The image on the screen flickered for a moment, then steadied. "I had to keep Curran from being able to haul me out of the net."

Al Shei tugged at her tunic sleeve, uncertain what to think or feel about that.

"Don't worry," said Dobbs, and there was a ghost of her old mischief in her voice. "The Guild doesn't know what to think about me either." She paused. "I know Havelock was there. I was wondering if I was going to have you as a partner."

"What?" Al Shei jerked her head up.

"I'm one of the Guild's new ambassadors." There was some small pride in the statement, and a healthy measure of incredulity. "They're trying to make use of the fact that I'm one of the few Fools on record as helping save Earth's network." Dobbs, or Dobbs's image, shrugged. "It seemed like a good idea. I'm pretty much out of a job." She looked toward Al Shei without focusing on her, and Al Shei realized the Fool might not be able to see her. Even if the camera were on and Dobbs were processing the signals, would it really be analogous to human sight, or would it be more like reading braille?

It was a strange idea, that Dobbs was trapped behind the screen, only able to hear her, if hearing was the right metaphor for what she was doing. She must be controlling the processors and the output signals but . . .

A laugh escaped Al Shei. Here she was having a conversation with a dead woman, or a live AI, and the engineer in her was wondering how it all worked.

"What is it?" asked Dobbs, leaning forward curiously.

Al Shei waved her hand, remembered that Dobbs couldn't see, and said, "Nothing, nothing. I'm just."—she rubbed her forehead—"very tired, really. And I'd rather not talk about how I'm going to answer Havelock." She looked away from Dobbs. "Thank you for asking, though. I . . . I'm sure you're doing your best."

"Yes." Dobbs was silent for a long moment, and Al Shei thought perhaps she'd gotten the hint and left, but when she turned her face back, the Fool's image was frozen on the screen.

"You are asking yourself why you should help the ones who murdered your husband, aren't you?" The image jerked to life, almost as an afterthought, and leaned closer toward her.

Too tired to lie, Al Shei said, "That is part of what I'm thinking, yes."

"You could do it to keep us honest, perhaps," Dobbs spread her hands on her knees. "Or to make sure we're kept in our places. You could have Lipinski as a consultant."

Al Shei looked at her sharply, forgetting for a moment that what she saw was an illusion. "Why are you so ready to help the ones who betrayed you, Dobbs?"

The image froze again, and the voice said slowly. "While I . . . we . . . were fighting in there, I almost died. I had to stretch myself to my limits to survive. A number of my friends gave their lives . . . no, not their lives . . . their consciousness, their independence, so that I could be strong enough to hold Curran's followers back and keep the net together." Dobbs's image looked toward her again, with intensity shining in her unfocused eyes. "I wanted to die because of what this war cost my friends, but I couldn't . . . Life wants to continue. So, we are all driven to continue. To move, think, do. Here is something I can do, something I think is worth doing."

"All of this is fine for you, but why should I even care?" Al Shei retorted. Exhaustion and wearying grief won out over manners. She didn't look at the screen. She looked at her sealed window and the palm trees and blue sky beyond it. "Why should I care if the whole Guild collapses in on itself and human beings destroy the survivors and we're left alone in the universe again?"

"I don't know why you should care," said Dobbs. "But I know that you do. If you didn't care, you would have run away from The Farther Kingdom. You'd have gotten yourself and your crew out of there and let the mess sort itself out. You would have let Lipinski destroy the AI aboard the *Pasadena* and washed your hands of the whole thing. You wouldn't have contacted your family when I asked you to. You would have let them shred the network you knew we need to live in. But you know that we're not all evil, that we're like Human Beings. Some of us are good, some are bad, most are a mix of the two, and you weren't going to take it on yourself to destroy us all.

"You care, Al Shei, you always have. If you try to stop caring, you're going to die trying."

Al Shei's fingers knotted around the blanket. The faux silk was cool and slick against her skin. "Words, words, words," she muttered.

Dobbs was leaning all the way forward now. It looked as if any moment her nose would press against the glass of the screen. "They're all I have left, Al Shei. I've lost everything else." There was a sorrow in her voice that Al Shei hadn't heard before. Dobbs seemed to catch herself and made her image give a small smile. "I liked being Human. I liked it from the first day I had a body. I'm going to miss it, a lot."

Al Shei looked at her curiously. "Why can't they give you a new one?"

She looked abashed. "I'm too big. There's too many lives inside me. They'd have to cut them out to fit my core self back into Human patterns. I don't want that. I . . . I feel like I'm a custodian now, and I won't give over that responsibility."

Al Shei shook her head. "You're a very strange creature."

"Even stranger than I used to be," Dobbs smiled again, deprecatingly this time. "When we play the fool, how the theater expands!" She swept her hand out and for that instant looked and sounded so much like her old self that Al Shei couldn't keep from smiling.

Dobbs sobered quickly and her image flickered again. "Al Shei, it's getting cramped in here. There's a lot of activity on your lines. It's squeezing me out. I think your sister is trying to get your uncle to come home . . ." She paused. "I'm going to put a call signature in your holding bin. You can use it to reach me, if you want to." The image flickered again.

"Thank you," said Al Shei, and although she meant it, she wasn't sure how many things she was thanking Dobbs for. For being a good Fool, for being a good human, perhaps. For trying her best.

The simulation of Dobbs's face lit up with a genuine smile. "Anytime. I hope," she added.

The screen went blank.

Al Shei smoothed out the blanket and stood up. She picked her pen up and activated the desk. After searching through three directories she managed to find the call signature for Guild Master Matthew Havelock, Fool's Guild Hall Representative-at-Large.

She sent a request for contact down the line and switched on the camera over the intercom.

Havelock's head and shoulders appeared on the view screen.

"We need to discuss salary, Guild Master," she said. "And the ship you are going to build me."

About the Author

Sarah Zettel was born in Sacramento, California. She began writing stories in the fourth grade and never stopped. Her interest in writing has followed her through ten cities, four states, two countries, and one college, where she earned a B.A. in Communications.

A professional technical writer, Sarah's short fiction has been nationally published in Analog Science Fiction and Fact and Realms of Fantasy. When not actually writing, Sarah sings, dances, and plays the hammered dulcimer, although not all at once. She is currently at work on a third science fiction novel.

Visit Sarah Zettel's home page on the Internet!
http://pages.prodigy.com/sarahsci